D1210121

DAUGHTER
DALLOWAY

BOOKS BY
EMILY FRANCE

ADULT FICTION
Daughter Dalloway

YOUNG ADULT FICTION
Zen and Gone
Signs of You

WITH NATALIE BECHER
Krit Dreams of Dragon Fruit

DAUGHTER DALLOWAY

EMILY FRANCE

**BLACK
STONE**
PUBLISHING

Printed in the United States of America

First edition: 2023
ISBN 979-8-200-81337-7
Fiction / Historical / General

Version 1

Blackstone Publishing
31 Mistletoe Rd.
Ashland, OR 97520

www.BlackstonePublishing.com

For my mother,
who struck the match of literature in the caverns of my mind
and lit the way.

DECEMBER 8, 1952

CHAPTER 1

Elizabeth

"I'll pick the flowers myself," Elizabeth Dalloway said.

For every flower shop in London was closed. Even Mulberry's was shuttered. At least Miss Pym wasn't alive to see it, her shop locked for the past three days. What a storm! What a morning to prepare for a party—bleak as if under someone's bootheel.

"I know this is disappointing," Theodore said gently. He put a hand in his pocket, looked out the window at the dense fog. He was in his navy sweater. The one that made him look like a captain in an advert for the Royal Navy. He'd deny it. How dashing he'd always looked in that blue. "But I believe you need to send word to your guests. Your party—"

"No one will come?"

"No one will come." He slipped an arm around her shoulders, pulled her close. "But cheer up, that was Rose who just rang. She's bringing something over for you. Seemed very keen to bring it straightaway. Didn't say what it was. Perhaps it will boost your spirits."

Rose.

Rose Purvis.

Perfectly put-together Rose.

She was the same age as Elizabeth; she'd grown up next door. She'd married and become the dignified Mrs. Alfred Foster, but to Elizabeth, she would always be Rose Purvis. Now she lived with her perfect husband

and perfect sons (three of them!), surely bound for Eton. She of all people knew what disasters Elizabeth's parties typically were. There was that spring affair when Elizabeth had made the salmon herself, desiccated, each filet obstinate, impenetrable. Or that early-summer catastrophe. How was she to know Rose had just returned from an ocean voyage to Lisbon with her children? It was an offhand comment, that Elizabeth wouldn't let a child near one of those dreadful ships. They'd fall overboard! Rose had been so insulted. She didn't have an appointment to get to. Everyone knew that.

But that wasn't the problem today—Elizabeth's record of disastrous attempts at entertaining. Her inability to drum up polite party chatter. Her utter failure at filling her mother's shoes. Mama—

Mrs. Dalloway.

A lioness in London society.

A woman who'd never arrived for a party in the summer of 1923. And hadn't been heard from since.

A woman who had simply and abruptly—disappeared. It had been nearly thirty years since she went missing; to Elizabeth, it felt like one day. One very long, very dark day.

No, it wasn't all that.

It was the fog.

It had paralyzed London for the past three days. Yellowish clouds had descended on the city, a jaundiced pall of smoke and sulfur. It burned lungs, scraped throats, forced medical masks onto faces. It killed the vulnerable; it killed some who had no health problems at all. The death toll was nearing four thousand. Elizabeth had heard bits of explanations. Coal smoke was pinned to the sky over London by odd movements of the atmosphere. And something about England burning the cheap coal and exporting the finer rocks, the cleaner ones, to pay off the debt. On account of the War. Always on account of the War. Elizabeth had lived through two now. Why on earth anyone thought wars ended was beyond her. This fog, this fog was the War itself, back from a grave it was never buried in.

How dark! Really, you must be more positive. You must.

"But Churchill isn't even flummoxed." Elizabeth stood in the doorway, waved an arm at the thick white clouds hovering over the lawn.

"This is an overreaction. I won't cancel! If every flower shop in London is closed, then I'll—"

"Pick the flowers yourself."

"Precisely. I'll pick the flowers myself." Elizabeth rolled up the sleeves of her blouse and put her hands in the pockets of her slacks. She started down the garden path, determined. Surely, she could throw one party. One successful party. Fog be damned.

Theodore followed. "Might I remind you that it's December?"

"There's the heather," Elizabeth protested. She didn't slow her pace. "The Helleborus aren't brave enough to show yet, but there are the holly bushes we just put in. They'd survive a blitz. A few sprigs of those will suit. Especially if their berries are out."

Theodore caught up to her. "If you insist on being out here in this fog, at least put this on." He pulled something from his pocket, a square of fabric and gauze with thick elastic loops for the ears.

"Is that a mask?" She knew it was. What a dear, she thought. So concerned about her well-being. She wondered how often he regretted marrying her. He never said so, but really, she was so complicated. She was certain other women were easier. More rational. More even-keeled. More—what to call it?

Pieced together.

"Go on," he said. "They say these help you breathe. And your lungs—"

"You're such a love." She took it from him, put it on. The elastic pushed her ears down, awkwardly pinned her hair back. She could feel it; she looked like a goblin. The last time she'd worn one of these dreadful things had been in 1918. During the influenza. She had been twelve. A child of twelve had been told to wear a mask to survive; her mother had almost died. She'd never gotten over it. "Will we wear these things every thirty years or so? Cyclical calamities of the lungs?"

Theodore smiled and put on his own mask. "Let's hope this is the last. And may I accompany you to the garden, Mrs. Elizabeth Dalloway?" He gave a little bow, playing the part of a footman.

Elizabeth took his arm and smiled. Of course her surname wasn't Dalloway; it had changed when she married him. And of course they didn't have staff. They'd let them go after the second war; they were worried about their finances. Or rather, she was worried. Her inheritance was dwindling, disappearing by the day, she felt. It was Theodore's that kept them afloat. It was his support that made her life as nice as it was. She had a little job as a history tutor, but it was pathetic, really. It paid next to nothing. No, it was Theodore who had the real inheritance and a respectable position with Export Finance to boot. Elizabeth was . . . beholden. Women didn't have to be that now. Beholden. But there it was. She had failed to grow her own wings. That was how she saw it. She had failed to grow her own wings.

Smart women make good choices when they're young. Take smarter paths than I have. Paths that lead to careers, great passions. Perhaps that's it. Smart women know how to set their feet on the right path.

"Ahem," Theodore said. He was still in his little footman bow. Offering his arm. She must have slipped into one of her ruminating spells. She had them often. She wasn't sure how long she'd been standing there. Thinking.

"You may," Elizabeth said, taking his arm. Theodore did have the power to make her smile. Always, he'd been a bit golden. His way. Seeded with that delicious lightness of irreverence. "But only because I can't see the damned path." It was true; this pea soup was obscuring even her feet. "How are my party guests going to see their way up to the house?" She was being facetious now; she'd relented. If guests looked for ways to turn down her invitations under clear skies, they certainly wouldn't show under dark ones. But still. There were the empty vases, the little glass bowls running the length of the dining table. The ones Mama had always loved. Elizabeth had to fill them. It was a matter of dignity.

There it was.

Elizabeth could just make it out, her little Westminster garden on the other side of the lawn, four feet by six. One of many she'd watched season after season as a child, glorious, perfect, tended by their gardener, Mr. Garrick, fastidious. Ever full of phlox, tiny roses, wolfsbane. All sorts. Elizabeth had inherited it now, the house and the gardens, and—

"They're all dead," Elizabeth sighed. She surveyed the floral carnage in her little plot.

"Again," Theodore said. He was smiling underneath that mask; she could see it in his eyes. It was a kind smile, empathetic. "They're all dead *again*, I'm afraid."

She gently touched the corpse of a heather stalk with the toe of her shoe. She thought heather impervious! Even the new holly bushes had perished. Had she forgotten to water them? They're so vulnerable for the first week or so.

"Don't blame yourself," Theodore said, peering over her shoulder at the flower graveyard. "It's been deathly cold this week. And there's sulfur in the air. They probably burned to death, poor things."

She loved him for blaming the air and not her deficits as a gardener. Elizabeth cast a glance at the house next door, the looming home of the Purvis family, Rose's childhood home.

Old Lady Purvis will love this. More failure in Elizabeth Dalloway's garden!

Lady Purvis and her husband (Scrope!) had lived next door since before Elizabeth was born. Raised Rose to perfection in their grand old house. Lady Purvis had far too many opinions about Elizabeth. She knew too much. Much too much.

"I can practically hear what the old lady is saying," Elizabeth said. "About everything, really."

"I think your attempt at a winter garden is admirable. Repeated failure is evidence of repeated dedication," Theodore said. He put his arm around her shoulders. "Besides, whose voice are you going to listen to? Mine or the old bat's?"

Elizabeth shook her head, still disgusted with herself. "I'll listen to the voice that's loudest. And we all know which one that is. But you're a love for trying."

"Suit yourself," Theodore said. They walked back toward the house.

"Can you imagine what my mother would say?" she asked. "Hosting a party without flowers?"

Theodore gave her arm a gentle squeeze. "No, I can't."

They passed the garden table and chairs. The wrought-iron ones. Just the sight of them took Elizabeth back, blanketed her with a little mist of sadness. "I think I'll sit with her, for just a bit," Elizabeth said. She sat. In her mother's favorite one. It was so uncomfortable, this chair, so unyielding. It rubbed the bones. Why on earth Mama had loved it was beyond her. She'd been sitting in it the last time Elizabeth ever saw her. That summer of '23. Mama had been picking miniature roses from the garden, sitting here admiring the blooms. Elizabeth had assumed they were for her party that night, but Mama had never arrived. Elizabeth had been seventeen.

This very chair. She sat in this very chair.

A sound.

The creak of a hinge.

The gate. Someone was coming through the gate.

"Elizabeth! Yoo-hoo!"

No one could mistake that sugary voice, ever an octave higher than it needed to be, straining to prove its happiness to everyone within earshot.

Rose.

"Elizabeth!" She burst through the fog as if breezing in from the wings of a theater. Center stage now. She was in a blue dress. Delicate pleats jutted out from her tiny waist in sharp creases, perfect as cupcake papers. She clutched a matching purse. "I'm so glad I've found you."

"Hello, Rose," Elizabeth said. She pulled her mask down, kissed Rose's cheeks. Of course, Rose wasn't wearing one, undoubtedly sure her positive attitude would ward off any illness. "Where else would I be? The party is today." Elizabeth feigned a laugh. She became dreadfully aware of herself suddenly. Aware of her blouse and her . . . pants. Yes, her pants. They felt ill-fitting all at once. The wrong color, was that it? They'd felt very modern this morning, a perfect thing to wear to a party, but now they felt so . . . skimpy. Dreadfully inadequate next to Rose's blue dress, those pleats, her blond curls.

"Oh, darling," Rose said gently. "No one's coming to that. Obviously." She motioned at the fog.

"Let's go inside, shall we?" Theodore swiftly rescued the moment. "We shouldn't be out in this." He offered his arm to Rose.

Elizabeth followed them along the stone path she had traversed countless times over the course of her little life—with the feet of a child, the feet of a tipsy seventeen-year-old girl, and now the feet of a woman in her late forties. Even those had started to surrender, her feet. Wider now. Just a bit. She could feel the pressure against the sides of her shoes. Oh, awful. It was awful. This aging.

They went inside.

Chatter, Elizabeth. Light and airy.

"This fog!" Elizabeth said, pushing her voice into one of those higher octaves Rose loved so much. She pointed out the window as if the fog were a party guest who'd overdone it with the tokay, was making a scene, ruining absolutely everything. "Isn't it dreadful?"

"Now, now. You must keep a positive attitude. I've taken the opportunity to do many indoor activities with the boys, to spend a little extra time together," Rose said. It was scolding, her tone. As if anyone who didn't see hardship as a golden opportunity was immature, in desperate need of tutelage. "Such beautiful memories we'll have when it lifts. So many books read by the fire. We've been playing charades! When life hands you lemons! That's what I tell my mother." She sighed and looked back toward her childhood home. A light was on in the sitting room. "That's why I've come, I'm afraid. Mother's not well."

"I'm so sorry," Elizabeth said. Her heart contracted as it did whenever someone's mother was at stake. She knew the pain all too well.

"Don't worry," Rose huffed. She tucked one of her perfect curls behind an ear. How long did that take, anyway? To get curls like that? An hour? Two? Elizabeth kept her hair chopped. Around her fellow teachers, it felt quite sharp. Next to Rose, it felt . . . sad. Her hair felt sad. "Mother isn't dying." Rose looked worn-out with the whole thing— her mother. "She just thinks she is."

"Oh." It was the best Elizabeth could do.

"She thinks this fog will put her in her grave. She's going through things," Rose explained. "And she's found something for you."

"I see," Elizabeth said. "I'm happy to come over and get it, whatever it—"

"It belonged to your mother."

Mama. There it was again, in the center of Elizabeth's chest—a contraction. "Pardon? It belonged to Mama?"

"Your mother gave it to mine in June of that year, about a month before she—" Rose stopped.

No one knew how to speak of it, Mrs. Dalloway's—departure. She'd left her silver-green dress on her bed with a little rip in the bodice, her leather sewing kit on the bedside table. No note, no word. Just a ripped dress she hadn't bothered to finish mending. No one knew what had happened, not really. That didn't stop the rumors, of course. She'd gone off to India with her old lover Peter Walsh. She was dipping her feet in the Ganges. She was in love. Or she was alone. Shopping in Paris. She'd left Bond Street in her wake. Or she—

"Left," Elizabeth said. "Before my mother left?"

"Yes, quite a bit before that." Rose smoothed one of the cupcake-paper creases on her dress and opened the brass clasp on her purse. She pulled out a small box. It appeared to be made of cherry wood with carved blossoms on its top. "Your mother asked mine to find a soldier, his family. She thought it would be easy for Mother, what with all her veterans' charities. She left a little token for a . . . Mr. Smith? A Septimus Warren Smith. For his family. She said they might be Italian. Did your mother mention him?"

"No," Elizabeth said. "I've never heard that name in all my life."

Or she left with a soldier, went to the Milan gardens to run her fingertips along the petals of tall flowers.

"My mother feels terrible. Having it all this time," Rose said. She held out the box for Elizabeth to take. "She says she never could find the Smith family. She asked at the War Commission and everything."

Elizabeth lifted the lid. Pinned to a bit of red velvet was a medal, circular with a piece of blue ribbon hanging from it. Almost like an official military one, but not quite. It appeared to be a token, something veterans received at charitable events.

"Perhaps," Elizabeth ventured, "she gave these out to families she met when she volunteered—"

"But it is quite personal," Rose said.

"Personal?"

Rose leaned in, plucked the medallion from its box. She turned it over in her hands, showed Elizabeth the back. There was an engraving:

For the bravery of
S. W. S.
All my love to you, C. P. 1923

"All my love to you."

Mother didn't say things like that. And she certainly didn't sign things that way.

"C. P."

Clarissa Parry.

Her mother's maiden name. Her name before she was Mrs. Dalloway. Before she was Mrs. Richard Dalloway. Elizabeth wasn't sure she'd ever seen it written out in all her life, save for that letter she'd found to Great-Aunt Helena ages ago. The one about the butterflies. No, Clarissa Parry had always been a specter, some woman unknown who'd haunted Bourton, her childhood home, run about the country, been dissolved. Clarissa Parry was a dream. Clarissa Parry didn't engrave her initials on the backs of medallions.

"I need to speak to your mother," Elizabeth said, taking the medal back from Rose. "I need to ask her about this. I need to know everything Mama said, I—"

Theodore touched Elizabeth's arm. "Darling. Let me pop over and inquire. See if it's worth fussing over. You've been doing so well lately, I don't want to set you back." He was concerned. Of course he was. She wished he wouldn't say things like this in front of Rose, but his worry seemed to make him forget Rose was even standing in the room. She knew what he was thinking—that her mind was a broken thing, prone to falling into trenches that were hard to scramble out of. He was right and he wasn't. No one understood her mind, she felt. She couldn't quite seem to communicate.

"Theodore," she said. She'd worked at acceptance—putting a stop to the wondering, to the questions, to the imagined scenarios. And Theodore knew it, how hard she'd tried to put it all in the past. But he had to know, too, that if this was some relic from 1923, a fossil unearthed from that summer, she wanted to know every single thing there was to know about it. Even if it broke her mind. "Get my coat."

SUMMER 1923

CHAPTER 2

Octavia

STROUD, GLOUCESTERSHIRE

"I've news!" her father said. Shouting. He marched down the path to their little home, waving papers in his hand.

Octavia Smith slipped out the back door before she could be caught by whatever it was. Probably news about her father's brewery on the hill. Some shocking price for hops. Or news that the town pub was finally closing up, sending a fresh new batch of sots their way. Or maybe news of some eligible bachelor coming to town. Octavia should get herself ready, scrub behind her ears, dot lavender down the sides of her neck. She was seventeen. It was time to get on with it.

She escaped.

She took the tin pail from the porch and started up the grassy hill behind their house. All she wanted was to pick flowers. By herself.

Octavia had never bought flowers in a proper shop; the thought had never occurred to her. She didn't even know what something like that would cost—a mess of lilies, a posh bunch of roses. What could it be? The doctor in town charged five pennies to be seen if they had them; Mum had been known to stitch flesh together herself to avoid the charge. What would flowers cost in the village? The same as a doctor's visit? What would they cost in a fancy London shop? She couldn't begin to guess; she'd never even been to the city.

Octavia gently shook her head as if the thought were a sawfly buzzing about. Imagine that, she thought, a girl like her riding the train all the way from Stroud to London. A farm girl from the village with eyes like a mare—clear, true. A girl who would keep her word and do the work. Happy with plain dresses from before the war, collars high, and hair that was always coming undone during her chores. What would it be like to set off the jingle of bells over a London flower-shop door, walk about pots of blooms like some lady, plunk down the cost of five doctor's visits for . . . what really? Flowers she could march into the hills behind her Stroud home and pick herself.

Silly.

The Cotswolds was known for wildflowers this time of year.

She was perfectly happy here.

She stopped and put her pail down, caught her breath. She wasn't sure she'd ever felt heat like this. She cursed her thick stockings, tugged at a few burrs that were stuck to them, the spiky seeds begging for a ride to a different place on the hill, maybe one with better dirt, a place in the shade, a place for new roots. She was too quick about it, and a run sprouted up one stocking. Angrily, she flicked the tiny hitchhikers over the tall grasses, grabbed her pail, and continued her march up the hill.

She would find a special flower for Septimus today; she could feel it. Something that would cheer him. The hills were puffed up, she felt—bluffing, trying to hide their secrets, hidden gems she was determined to find for her brother. Always, always for her brother. Septimus, her mother's seventh child. Out of the six that came before him, only one survived. Mum had lost so many along the way, some after they were born, some before. But she'd named each one, even the ones she never got to meet. It was only right, she said, giving them names. Because she felt she knew them, even if she never saw their faces. She knew them.

The third-born, Tertius, survived. Then Septimus, the seventh, and then Octavia, the eighth. Finally, the ninth, her little brother, Ronald. Mum said she couldn't bear to name a child Nonus, so Ronald it was. Poor child. Seven years old now, sturdy as a pewter tankard. He'd almost died in the space of a few days after he was born. But nobody talked about that now. About what had happened. What Mum had done.

Tertius, Septimus, and Octavia were good Christian birth-order names. A Roman tradition initially, but back in fashion when Victoria was queen. Septimus and Octavia hadn't appreciated the dreams behind their mother's name choices, her secret class-climbing hopes. Octavia was preparing for a life at home, a wife and mother in Stroud, a woman who would bury a few children before she was buried herself in the town cemetery next to those valiant boys who'd enlisted, who'd fallen in battle, the real heroes. Octavia knew her lot in life was to toil and die and rot under a headstone that was engraved with nothing . . . remarkable. And she was perfectly fine with that.

Perfectly fine.

As for Septimus's plans . . . well.

Flowers.

The flowers, Octavia thought. She must concentrate on finding a few special flowers. For Septimus. All for Septimus.

She made her way up the steep limestone hill to her favorite spot—a stand of wych elms and whitebeams. The trees stood like bossy little girls holding green parasols, determined not to let the sun bully the violets and dog's mercury at their feet.

Where are you, Octavia thought as she searched the fields. *Show yourself.*

Ivy vines looped over themselves in a tangle, clearly in a hurry to blanket every spot, caught in the act of trying to make the whole hill its empire. Juniper bushes dotted the limestone, their twisted branches reaching, thinking too highly of themselves. All of them burdened with tight berries cast over their evergreen leaves like the glass glarnies the boys were always trying to sell her, two pennies apiece. She was no genius at the till to be sure, but even she knew that a glarny was worth only a penny, and to her it was worth exactly nothing—what on earth would a girl of seventeen do with marbles?

And then she saw them.

Tucked around the base of a holly bush, brash, red—three

helleborines, a type of orchid found only in the Cotswolds and two other places in Britain. And next to those, a tight bunch of harebells. She hurried over, leaned against the holly as if they were both fighting for the last sack of rationed sugar, the clawed leaves pushing through her cotton blouse, needling her flesh.

She reached for the flowers.

Pluck. Pluck. Pluck.

In the battle between the hill and Octavia, she had won.

Septimus will love them.

Octavia rubbed her arm where the holly needles had dug in. Worth every prick, she thought. Blue harebells and orchids were Septimus's favorites.

> *With fairest flowers,*
> *Whilst summer lasts and I live here, Fidele,*
> *I'll sweeten thy sad grave. Thou shalt not lack*
> *The flower that's like thy face, pale primrose, nor*
> *The azured harebell, like thy veins . . .*

Shakespeare. *Cymbeline.* It was the first she had ever heard. She was seven. She and Septimus had been on a picnic on this very hill. He'd opened the book, its pages parting like waves at the bidding of his hand, offering safe passage through the chop of their lives. He was self-taught, smarter than any Cambridge man, she was sure of that. He'd even lost his Gloucestershire accent even though he hadn't been to a posh school. He'd done that himself. Tamped it down. Forced his tongue to move right. Septimus had told her of Shakespeare's work, how he could be her friend for life, how she could turn to him for jollity or wisdom, whichever was needed.

"Azured harebell," Septimus had said, pointing to the text. "I've seen them up here, you know. They're the poets of the Cotswolds. Look like they're always about to break, but then—they bloom instead." Septimus, with his serious eyes, his poet's gaze, had looked over the town from their perch. The limestone pushed a chill through Octavia's legs, made her shiver in the summer sun.

"The flower? It's a poet?"

"And a good one. Harebell. It's my favorite one, that." He'd looked at his sister with such concern. Octavia was only seven; she wouldn't have known how to say it, but his look, his tone of voice—they scared her. "You be like them," he said. "No matter what happens. All right?"

"Be like what?" Octavia had asked. She'd looked away from his pale face, his dark eyes, tried to study the lines of Shakespeare, too young to understand any of it, really, but old enough to know it was important. Or would be to her one day. Because Septimus said so. Because even though she knew she'd never amount to much, Septimus made her feel that her life mattered, that it glittered a little, like a secret seam of gold twisting through these dull limestone hills. She would always be Septimus Warren Smith's sister.

And that was something.

That was really something.

So she better pay attention.

"Like the harebell," he'd said, kissing the top of her head. "Bloom wherever you are planted. Insist on it."

That was the last time she saw him.

Septimus had disappeared the next day.

He'd left Octavia a fancy note, poetic like he was. One that professed his hatred of their mum for what she'd done to Ronald when he was just a babber, how she'd lied. How he could never forgive her even if he stayed in Stroud another ten lifetimes. And besides all that, he couldn't be a poet in a place like this. Not a real one. Not one whose soul survives. He'd ferment just like the brewery beer, he'd written. Become a cup of rot worth only a few coppers.

But you, sister, have veins like the azured harebell—fine, blue, and sturdy. You will bloom, I know. Take root. Don't hate me for long. I'll write.

Your loving brother,
Septimus

Her family had gotten word that he'd enlisted soon after the war began. But they hadn't heard any news since. He hadn't sent a single letter. The war had been done five years now. The War Office claimed they didn't know of his whereabouts, unsure if he was dead or alive. He might be buried with the other unknowns from the Somme, or he may have come back to England half blown to bits, been creeping about some convalescent home for soldiers, unable to speak, unable to think.

She clutched her flowers and decided to go back home. To put the harebells and helleborines in her flower press, to mash them tight between gray blotting papers until all the moisture was gone and paper-thin petals were all that remained. To put them in her album, in the collection of dried wildflowers she was making for Septimus. To give to him if she ever saw him again. In this life or the next.

"Octavia!"

Her name. Coming up the hillside like a storm romping over pampas grass, bending the air as it pushed past her.

"Octavia!"

She heard it again; it was her father. Reluctantly, she sped up. A begging dog, she thought. A poor old begging dog.

She wasn't going to escape.

She could see the back porch now, the pigs mucking about in their pens, the chickens squawking, trying to look dignified, shocked at having their eggs robbed from underneath them, but determined to make a show over it anyhow. Octavia's father stood on the stoop, his brewery apron on, a slight sheen of sweat on his forehead. His eyes looked strange, Octavia thought. She'd never seen them like that. Burning, almost. Tired.

"I've had news," he said. "I've been calling for you."

"News of people coming to town?" Octavia tried her best to look interested. Who had her father drummed up this time? The son of a banker? The son of a farmer with a hundred acres?

"No," he said. "News of Septimus."

CHAPTER 3

Elizabeth

The stone wall was high and covered with wildflowers; seventeen-year-old Elizabeth Dalloway wasn't sure her horse could make the jump.

Brixby's hooves thundered across the field, his muscles tense and taut underneath her, driving them on and on.

Closer and closer to the wall.

She narrowed her eyes but couldn't gauge the true height or width of the obstacle under all those damned blooms. Wild clematis crept over every aged stone as if it had conspired to hide the whole of the wall, to mask the measure of its risk underneath a duplicitous spray of petals and perky green leaves.

Push a horse over a wall like that and it could be maimed for the rest of its life; the rider's might end entirely.

The hounds were far ahead and well out of sight by now, but Elizabeth could still hear their howls, carried back to her on the wind. The dogs had caught the scent of a fox as soon as they'd been cast into the covert; their feverish barks and wails had started almost immediately—a call, irresistible, daring Elizabeth to follow, faster and faster to whatever was lurking in the English fields.

This way, they seemed to howl. *We've found the path you're looking for.*

Elizabeth dug her heels into Brixby's sides.

Together, they could make it. Couldn't they? After all, she was seventeen now, and Brixby had grown to fifteen hands high. They were a formidable pair, she and her beloved horse, the one she'd gotten just after the war and that awful influenza had ended. Her prize for coming through, a brave child of war and death.

Papa assured her another war like that could *never* happen, another influenza would never roam the earth, but Elizabeth didn't know whom to believe anymore. If all those smart men running things had let an entire generation of boys die on the Western Front, let the survivors come home only to perish with lungs full of fluid, what did they know about the future? About Elizabeth's future, her life? What did they know about anything? She wasn't going to be like her parents, like her mother, like all the fusty generations behind her. Look what it had gotten everyone! Nothing, that's what.

No, Elizabeth was going to follow a different path.

A bright one. That's what people her age were being called. The bright generation.

Now, Elizabeth squeezed Brixby's saddle with her thighs, sturdy, seated—if another influenza began to stalk her, if bombs began to drop, she and Brixby would outrun them all.

After all, she was seventeen now.

On a fifteen-hand horse.

Surely, they could get over this damned flower-covered wall.

She tightened her grip on Brixby's reins, leaned forward in the saddle, and gave him a gentle nudge. The message delivered by her heel:

This way. I'm certain now.

The riders in front of Elizabeth split off this way and that, their horses' tails flicking and flowing in the wind as, one by one, they went around the wall—as if it were the wreathed tomb of some woman unknown, something to be revered, something not to be trod upon or leapt over.

Someone rode up on Elizabeth's right flank, driving his horse next to her, too close, on his way to overtaking her. William Titcomb, dressed in his best pinks for the hunt, his perfect pedigree hovering about his shoulders like a gold-tinted mist, ever proud to be a friend of the prince, to be such an eligible bachelor in a field of suitors that had been all but decimated by the war. He'd been too young to fight, and Elizabeth felt she could read his very thoughts: the England that had survived was his for the taking.

Elizabeth was his for the taking.

Mama's hopes for their union were as obvious as her fears about Elizabeth's . . . constitution. Inscrutable, her mother had told her once. Not often seen in girls of her stature, that strange constellation of preferences Elizabeth had—a love of politics, of hunting with caked mud on her pants, of keeping her hair short and wild and out of place. Nothing that defined a woman could hold her interest—so said Great-Uncle William—neither gloves, nor shoes, nor gowns. Except for pink ones. She didn't mind a pink gown. But that was as far as it went. She wouldn't even try her hand at needlepoint. And Bach! Those mind-numbing fugues. She preferred Beethoven. He was so confident. Especially his Ninth.

Inscrutable.

Elizabeth was inscrutable.

The Dalloways would be lucky to get her married off to William; they'd be lucky to get her married off at all.

Now as William thundered next to her on his horse, she felt as though he wasn't on a foxhunt but stalking deer instead. And she was a doe, one of the last.

Their eyes met as they rode beside one another, and in his was a dare.

Which path would she take?

Would she go over the wall, or around it like the others?

She would go over; of course she would go over. It didn't matter that William looked so strong, so experienced on his horse, that boys like that started in the saddle before they could even walk. That he'd spent his childhood bouncing between his family's London home and their country estate, that he'd always had a slew of dedicated stable hands at the ready. Elizabeth had been riding only a few years.

But she could do it.

She would make it over the wall.

She was certain.

William went first, crouching low on his glistening Irish Draught, and up they leapt, he and his magnificent horse, higher and higher they arced into the sky, daring the wall to be as tall as the highest bloom, tempting the very vines to entangle and trip them both, tip them toward the earth and break their necks as they came to rest.

William was over.

Safe.

His horse landed on the other side, all hooves rooted squarely to the earth. On he rode. On and on. Ahead.

It was her turn now.

The wall was mere meters away.

But her horse didn't leap. She didn't feel herself pushed into the air. She felt herself falling. She and her horse were both falling.

She hadn't seen the hole in the ground, the entrance to a burrow, the home of some large rodent, some snake, some hare. Brixby's hoof fell directly into it; he careened desperately to the side. His legs gave way horrifically, like tree limbs breaking in a violent, sudden storm. Elizabeth pitched forward, sailed through the damp air; all sounds of hooves and hounds were silenced. There was only blackness.

Thick, silent, suffocating.

CHAPTER 4

Octavia

STROUD, GLOUCESTERSHIRE

Septimus was dead. He had to be.

That must be the news her father had; what else could it be? If Septimus was alive, he'd have written, she thought. He would have come home after the war. To see her. He would have let her know he was all right. Of course he would.

Octavia walked slowly toward the house.

"How did it happen?" she asked, stopping at the bottom of the stoop. "Tell me when."

Her father gripped the railing; was he drunk? She thought he looked unsteady, like his spirit was a bit of a blur. Mum stood behind him, white flour covering her hands, clinging to her hair, making her look older than she was. Older, even, than a mother who'd already lost five children and just learned another was in the ground.

"By telegram," Pop said. "From the War Office, just this afternoon. I sent another inquiry. After all this time, I was sure nothing would come of it, but they said they'd misplaced his record . . ." He trailed off. Mum reached out her hand, took the telegram from her husband. She tucked it into the front pocket of her apron. She wiped her hands on the gingham as if she were finishing something, something she'd been baking for years and was just out of the oven.

Burnt to a crisp.

She went back inside.

The chickens cooed and clucked beside the steps, picked at the ground like this day was no different from the rest. Octavia wanted to put off knowing the details of her brother's death for one more moment. Terrible, she thought, how a life could end, how a loss could ruin her, her hope, her worth, and yet the rest of the world would go on, picking at their feed, clucking about their lives like nothing had happened. Nothing at all.

"No," Octavia said, her feet still rooted to the ground at the bottom of the stoop. "Not how did you hear. How did he die? When? Was it at the Somme?"

"At first I thought the telegram was good news," he said. "But then I read it again."

"What did it—"

"He's alive." Her father's face did not match the news at all. Not at all. It was flat, expressionless. Sorry.

"Alive? What do you mean, he's alive? How could that be bad?" Octavia said. "He must be ill, that's why he hasn't come home, why he hasn't written. We'll just go get him and take care of him. Bring him here to get better—"

"There's nothing whatever the matter with him." Her father wobbled a bit now. Yes, Octavia was sure of it—he was drunk. And that phrase, it sounded posh. So formal. "That's what the War Office said. Just like that. 'There's nothing whatever the matter with him.'" He made his way down the back-porch stairs without falling, but just barely. Octavia quickly stepped out of his way. His large hand gripped the warped wooden railing, his dry, cracked knuckles turned a bit white. He kissed Octavia's cheek. "I wanted to tell you myself. Not sure what kind of man doesn't tell his children about being left by their own brother." He patted her head, but a little too hard. As if his hands were carved from limestone, heavy, cold. "I'm sorry Septimus is a coward. You don't deserve it." He turned and walked toward the brewery on the hill.

Octavia dropped her pail of flowers and went into the house. Her mother was pressing a marble rolling pin over dough splayed on the counter;

it squeaked as it rolled up and back. Up and back. The dough became thinner and thinner, a crack appeared on the side closest to Octavia. "He's in London," her mother said. "And married to an Italian girl. Married! Imagine that." She peeled the dough off the counter, dipped her hands into a bowl of water, and kneaded it back into a ball. She was starting over.

Married? And in London?

It couldn't be, Octavia thought. It just couldn't. He would have come home to see her. At the very least, he would have written. Sent her one of his beautiful poems. Surely the war had inspired dozens.

"He must be hurt," Octavia said. "Maybe he's lost his memory." She was starting to lose her breath now; she could barely stand the news. "We must go to him, Mum. Today. Today! We must take care of him. When is the next train to London?"

Her mother laughed—a false, cold sound. She sprinkled flour onto the counter, tossed it round like feed for the chickens, and smacked her dough ball in the middle. "You heard your pop," she said. "He's all in one piece. Telegram said it. *The doctors say there's nothing whatever the matter.*"

Octavia stepped back. "I don't understand," she said. "Then why wouldn't he—"

"You can guess, can't you?" Her mother went back to pressing the dough. She looked out the kitchen window at Ronnie climbing a tree. "He hates me. For what I did."

"No. He doesn't. And he wouldn't do that," Octavia said. "He wouldn't leave us not knowing after the war. Go on living in London. He would have sent word to one of us, at least."

To me, at least.

Her mother tossed the rolling pin in the sink, the marble hitting the cast-iron side with a loud crack. She untied her apron. "Forget him, Octavia."

The look in her mother's eyes chilled her; it had changed so fast. It reminded her of the days and months after Ronnie was born. Octavia had been ten. She'd never forgotten it, the way Mum had looked at her from the birth bed like an owl eyeing a field mouse from a tree, like suddenly she could see exactly where to strike, to kill Octavia with one blow if need be. Octavia's aunt had called it maternal melancholia; Pop believed it was an evil spirit Ronnie had brought upon their house. Had made Mum not want her baby, had made her abandon him alone in a field soon after he was born. Lie to everyone that he'd been taken. Snatched. A farmer had found him before it was too late. Mum had come to after a few weeks, claimed to be horrified by what she'd done. But she wasn't the same. Haunted. That's what Pop always said. Mum was haunted. That was Octavia's future, she knew. This heavy business of birth. And what comes after.

But now Octavia couldn't help herself; she had to keep pressing, even if she summoned the evil spirit into the kitchen that very moment with her words. Even if she summoned the mother owl that would plunge her beak into the veins in Octavia's neck.

"Something must be wrong, Mum," Octavia said. "Did the telegram give his address?"

"You can't go," her mother said. "People steal young girls like you in London. You'll never find your way. There are street gangs! The Hoxtons. The Tolmas. They make the papers, you know. They're evil."

Her mother was right; Octavia had no idea how dangerous London was. How she could survive in the streets, how she could even afford a train ticket to get there in the first place. Septimus had gone to London so many times, had told her all about it, made it sound like a magical place full of markets and fancy ladies, music and sweets and poets on every corner. But then again, Septimus was a man. A tall, strong man. Not a country girl like Octavia. A girl who only knew how to pick flowers and roll dough and rock babies. The most sophisticated thing she'd ever done was order some hops for her father from a merchant in town. Pop had given her the money and everything; she'd had to sign a slip. She'd trembled the whole time, so afraid of the men behind the counter, how they looked at her, leered at her like they wanted to laugh her out of the shop or were imagining untoward things. Like the nasty drunks who sometimes hung about the brewery. They looked at her just like that. But still, that's all she'd done in life. Order hops.

Octavia Smith? In London?

And what if Septimus really was there in the city, happily carrying on in the streets with his Italian wife? What if the War Office was right, that there was nothing wrong with him? Maybe he wanted nothing to do with his family ever again. Octavia pictured herself finding him, standing on his London stoop, clutching her book of pressed flowers. She imagined saying his name. She imagined him slamming the door in her face.

Death. It would be her death.

And then a verse came to her. By Shakespeare, the man Septimus had told her to turn to in times of need. Another line from *Cymbeline*:

> *Fear no more the heat o'th'sun,*
> *Nor the furious winter's rages.*
> *Thou thy worldly task hast done,*
> *Home art gone, and ta'en thy wages.*
> *Golden lads and girls all must,*
> *As chimney-sweepers, come to dust.*

The funeral verse that celebrated death, the peace of it. And to stay in Stroud and not know Septimus's whereabouts was death to her. But to go and find him hating her, not caring, would be death just the same.

So.

There was nothing whatever to lose.

She tucked a few strands of her brown hair back into their pins, ran her hands down the faded bodice of her cotton dress. She glanced out the window again at Ronnie, who was making his way down the tree now. "Give me the telegram." Octavia said it in a voice she'd never heard come from her throat. As if it had come from the future, a time when she was an older woman, a woman who had learned lessons unimaginable today. She could tell it frightened her mother. Octavia frightened herself.

Her mother slowly slipped her hand into the front pocket of her untied apron and pulled out the telegram. "Here," she said. "But you'll die in that city if you go."

Yes, thought Octavia. I might.

But I'll surely die if I don't.

CHAPTER 5

Elizabeth

Elizabeth opened her eyes.

And heard a voice. She recognized it, but only just.

"Yes, open those curtains there," a woman was saying. The room filled with pale morning light. "That ought to rouse her. And bring that tray. I'll give her water."

Lucy.

The maid Mama had hired when Elizabeth was born, the one who treated Mama like a queen and Elizabeth like a pest flying about the crown. Lucy's hair was pulled back in a tight bun, dark and glossy; she wore her perennial black dress—a crow perched on Elizabeth's bedside. Elizabeth had a taste for theater, but Lucy made her feel as if she were always trapped in scene, commedia dell'arte, harassed by a trope. The devious servant.

"Drink a bit of this," Lucy said, holding the glass of water to Elizabeth's lips. Stiff with judgment, she brushed a bit of dried mud from Elizabeth's hair. "I'm happy that you are all right, of course, but your mother is under such pressure," Lucy said. "This is the worst time of all to pull one of your stunts."

Stunts.

Elizabeth managed to sit up. She could see now that she was at home, in London, in her bed, her sheets and blankets tucked around her. Several other staff milled about the room. Elizabeth took another sip of water. It was all coming back now—Brixby, William, the fall. That Lucy had just called it a stunt.

"I assure you I did not fall from my horse on purpose." Elizabeth smoothed her blankets, trying to regain a bit of dignity. She touched the back of her hair, a bit stiff with dirt, but her head seemed to be in one piece. Pounding, but in one piece. She must have missed the wall. She didn't even remember coming home. "Brixby was sabotaged. By the home of a snake. Or a rabbit. I'm not sure."

"Be that as it may, tonight is your mother's first party of the season. The prime minister is coming. And most likely the prince." Lucy ran a finger along one of the folds of her black dress. "And not just that. There's your mother's visitor today."

Elizabeth took the last sip from the cup, stared at Lucy over the rim. She hated it when Lucy fished like this. "All right, Lucy—who is Mama's visitor today?"

"Mr. Walsh. Mr. Peter Walsh. He's in from India. You've met him several times. He comes round every few years. Of course you know of him."

Elizabeth didn't. Mama had so many visitors, they were like foxhounds, each bark and tail like the next. Elizabeth put the empty glass back on the tray. "I can't keep Mama's stream of visitors straight, Lucy. I believe it comprises half of London."

"He's your mother's . . . childhood friend. From her days growing up at Bourton. The one she writes to all the time."

It was true that Mama sat at her writing desk every day of her life— seeing to things. That's what she called it. Seeing to things. Mama spoke of friends in all sorts of places. But never India.

Elizabeth's bedroom door swung open; Lucy scurried away.

"Good morning, Elizabeth! Good to see you bright-eyed!" It was a man. In thick spectacles and a houndstooth suit. He came to her bedside, squeezed her arm just above the elbow. Elizabeth didn't like it, not least of all because it hurt.

"How d'you do?" she said. "I don't believe we've met." She gently pulled her arm away from his grasp. "And pardon me, but that hurts. I'm quite sore from my fall."

Someone else leaned over the bed then, peering down at Elizabeth intensely.

"You don't remember him?"

Mama.

Her beloved Mama.

In one of her perfect morning-errands dresses, the one the color of buttercups, a matching feathered hat perched on her head. She looked like a grand and curious bird, an ostrich in a traveling circus, eyeing Elizabeth like she was a bit of popped corn on the ground. Mama—dignified, perfect, powerful. And yet—Elizabeth always thought—hollow-bone thin. A strange and inexplicable mix of the grand and the frail. In other words—all that a woman should be. Strong. But not.

"This is not a good sign," the man said. "Not at all."

"Do you remember your fall at least? From Brixby?" Mama looked so concerned, so frightened, as if Elizabeth were twelve again and Mama was eyeing her, looking for signs of the Spanish flu. Desperate not to see any. Mama nodded at the man. "This is Dr. Bradshaw. I had to call him in last night. He's been caring for you."

The doctor gave her a half smile. "Pleased to meet you. Again."

"I apologize, I simply don't remember," Elizabeth said, confused. She looked at Mama. "I met him last night?"

"He's the finest psychiatrist in London," Mama said. "You were quite out of your mind last evening, darling. Quite. Saying all sorts of things I won't repeat."

For any other girl, this might be frightening, confessing secrets to one's mother without knowing which one may have gotten out. But Elizabeth didn't have any secrets. It was a thought that made her a bit sad, but there it was. She was a young woman with no escapades, no diaries under lock and key, not even a wayward friend who might bring a bad influence.

"You didn't break a bone," her mother continued, "so I called Dr. Bradshaw in to examine your mind. Now rest, dear." She placed her cool hand on Elizabeth's shoulder. It was so delicate, so kind, as if the gesture had shrunken Mama somehow, from an ostrich to a tiny finch, as if Mama had curled into the little hollow above Elizabeth's collarbone, warming herself, nesting there. "And tonight is my party. The first of the season you know. Hopefully, we can get you up and about for it."

A blistering pain registered then, thumping at Elizabeth's temples, grubbing at the roots of her mind. She didn't know if it was from her fall, or from Mama's mention of the party tonight.

Mama's parties.

Always, always, she was thinking of her parties. Her parties and the summer of her youth at Bourton when she was eighteen. They were both Mama's obsessions. This first party of the season always worked her into a lather. Of course she would mention it even now, even at Elizabeth's sickbed.

"Mama," Elizabeth said, pinching her eyes closed, trying to contain the pain. She had memories of the hunt, of Brixby's thundering hooves, William's obnoxious bravado, that awful feeling of falling. She vaguely remembered coming home now, being put to bed. "Mama did Brixby—"

"I'll begin my examination," Dr. Bradshaw said. He leaned close to Elizabeth's face, his eyes much too wide behind his thick spectacles, his expression deadly serious—as if he were about to unleash his finely tuned medical mind upon Elizabeth. "Where are you right now?"

"London," Elizabeth said flatly. "At home. In Westminster, of course, but—"

"And the year?"

The thumping in Elizabeth's head was replaced with the sharp pain of annoyance. She wasn't sure which was worse. This was what great medical minds trained doctors to ask? This was how they tested mental competence? This was how they examined the brain?

"1923," Elizabeth replied.

"And the prime minister?"

"Prime Minister Law, but can you tell me—"

"I'm afraid you're wrong there," Dr. Bradshaw said, clearly taking delight in her mistake. "It isn't Law any longer."

Mama cleared her throat as if embarrassed by Elizabeth's error. "She's typically quite good with politics," she said. She stared down at Elizabeth with—pride? Embarrassment? What was it? "I started forgetting those sorts of things at her age too. And now I have the hardest time remembering names and dates!" Mama's polite laughter was strained, even for her. "Music too. I can't even care about Wagner! And all I read are silly memoirs these days. Baron Marbot. That sort of thing." Mama's expression was clear now—pity. She was looking at her daughter with pity.

Elizabeth waited for her mother to keep talking, to engage in her typical theatrics:

Oh, memoirs!

Marbot!

This sharp chord of Tristan und Isolde*!*

Mama always said things like that. Theatrical. Really, she was so theatrical.

Dr. Bradshaw smiled. "Indeed! We'll chalk her error up to a natural loss of interest in world affairs rather than to a fall from a horse."

Elizabeth was so angry, she feared his comment would be the cause of her death—not the fall from Brixby. She could hear Mama explaining the tragedy to her guests tonight.

It's terrible, Mama would say. *Dr. Bradshaw said Elizabeth wasn't interested in politics and she dropped dead on the spot!*

"It's Stanley Baldwin," Elizabeth said curtly, managing to pull herself up now. "Prime Minister Baldwin. Former chancellor of the Exchequer and just home from settling our war debt with America. And perhaps most interestingly, he's a relative of Rudyard Kipling. He took office on the twenty-second of May." Elizabeth glared at Dr. Bradshaw. "I momentarily forgot because *I fell from my horse yesterday.* Whose fate, by the way, is of extreme importance to me. Can someone please tell me—"

"*Elizabeth*," Mama hissed, clearly disturbed by Elizabeth's tone with the great doctor. But despite her scolding, was there a little smile on her lips? Had she delighted in Elizabeth's irreverence? Elizabeth wasn't sure she'd ever seen her mother react that way to her—liveliness.

"That's a promising sign," the doctor said. "That bit of knowledge. Very encouraging."

"Excellent news," Mama said. "I do have my party tonight, and people are expecting Elizabeth. Prime Minister Baldwin himself is coming. The prince even. And several gentlemen who are friends of the prince."

"And the flowers, m'lady," Lucy said, stepping forward from the edge of the room. She'd been lurking. She always lurked. "Shall I get them?" She nodded at the small clock on Elizabeth's mantel. "The time is getting away from us, I'm afraid."

"Thank you, Lucy," Mama said. "But I'll get the flowers myself."

Mama always said that, and Lucy knew it. She shouldn't have bothered to ask. Mama would likely say it ten more times before she left for Miss Pym's—that she'd get the flowers herself. She'd mend her dress herself. She'd talk to Miss Walters about the salmon herself. Herself. Herself. Herself. She could do it all.

"Shall I call the car, ma'am?" Lucy asked. "For your errands?"

"No, no, I'll walk to Bond Street," Mama said. "Really, I love walking in London. It's so much better than the country." Mama turned to Elizabeth now. "I do wish you felt well enough to accompany me, darling."

There were few things Elizabeth detested more in life than shopping with Mama on Bond Street. Mama would drone on and on as they walked, proclaiming how she loved the swing, tramp, and trudge of it all. She would point out the sandwich men, the omnibuses. The little shop that sold glass bowls. (*"When I was eighteen, a visitor at Bourton cut the heads off all sorts of flowers and set them floating in little bowls! Just like those glass ones there! Aunt Helena was so shocked."*) And a stall that displayed water cans, of all things. And the smoke shop that sold little cigars, the ones that sat in the window like chocolates with round golden seals. (*"A friend smoked those at Bourton! How we laughed!"*) And there, the salmon on ice blocks, the rings and brooches in eighteenth-century settings. Every shop, every item, every bit, and every bob seemed to transport Mama to the past, to the beloved summer of her youth.

Oh, life!

London!

This moment of June!

It was always the same.

The theatrics of a shopping trip on Bond Street.

It was exhausting.

"Mama," Elizabeth said. "Is Brixby all right? Tell me he didn't—"

"He's just fine." Mama had never seemed to understand Elizabeth's love of horses and dogs, the guinea pigs she insisted on raising. She even accused Grizzle, Elizabeth's beloved fox terrier, of smelling like tar. And having distemper, even though he'd always been healthy as an ox. "Your father said they've got Brixby standing in the cold creek every other hour. Icing his ankles. Said you and that horse must be the luckiest pair in all of England. You missed the wall by a hair, and Brixby emerged with all of his legs in good working order."

"Elizabeth." Dr. Bradshaw snapped his medical bag shut. "I think you will be just fine. My medical advice is that you not think of this fall. Not one more time. Simply don't let your mind dwell on it." He glanced at Elizabeth's window and then at Mama, pointed at the potted plant on the sill. "I'd worry more about that plant than I'd worry about Elizabeth. Is it a peace lily? Looks more like one of war." He had a chuckle at his joke.

Mama looked at the sad plant, certainly near death. "She doesn't have much of a green thumb, I'm afraid, despite Mr. Garrick's tutelage," she said. "And he's the best gardener in all of London, with me since the day I married Richard. If he can't teach her, I'm afraid no one can."

"Be sure she gets a lesson in botany when she's back at full speed." Dr. Bradshaw nodded to Elizabeth and then to Mama. "Good day to you both."

Mama showed him to the door and followed him out. Before she left, she cast a glance back at her daughter. "See you this evening, darling."

Elizabeth slumped against her pillows, her sore muscles registering a vigorous complaint. She closed her eyes. All was quiet for a moment. Then she heard the swish of a skirt, the tinkle of glass upon a tray. She'd forgotten—Lucy was still here.

Lucy walked to Elizabeth's cupboard now, pulled out a gown. One of the many that were blush pink. "I think she will want you to wear this one tonight. You do feel up to it, don't you? You wouldn't want to disappoint her because the—"

"Prime minister is coming," Elizabeth finished Lucy's sentence. "And the Prince of Wales. And William Titcomb."

Lucy smiled as she held up the pink dress. "It's beginning, you know," she said. She ran a hand down the delicate pink bodice. "Lady Bexborough saw you in Regent's Park two days ago, said you were lovely as a crape myrtle. Soon, you'll be compared to hyacinths. To fawns in a meadow." That last comment sounded unmistakably ominous. "That's what your mother says of you."

"What's so wrong with fawns in a meadow?" Elizabeth smoothed her blankets over her lap. "I rather like—"

"Ask your mother. And what is this?" Lucy asked, running her finger over something pinned to Elizabeth's pink gown. "Is it a—"

"It's nothing," Elizabeth interrupted, reaching for the dress. Lucy stepped back, keeping it out of Elizabeth's grasp.

"It's a . . ." Lucy paused and pursed her lips into a thin, unhappy line. "Dandelion." She shook her head. "You're pinning them on your *gowns* now too?"

It was a brazen comment, even for Lucy. It seemed as though she couldn't help herself; her judgment was boiling over.

"I wear them because—"

"Really, Elizabeth. It upsets your mother a great deal. It's so odd. I've heard your mother say that herself." She ran a finger over the dead brown weed.

She means I'm so odd.

The habit did in fact drive Elizabeth's mother wild. But the world was snobbish about flowers; Elizabeth preferred wild varieties. She had a special soft spot for the weeds of London, rebelling in parks and lawns, taking advantage of every hard-to-reach, impromptu place. Purposefully and boldly thumbing their noses at the precise gardening plans of fine women all over the city.

"I like dandelions, that's all. And you didn't answer my question," Elizabeth said. "Why did Mama compare me to a fawn in a meadow? What's so bad about that?"

"Like I said, ask your mother." She came to the bedside and examined Elizabeth's unkempt hair. "I'll help you with the new curling iron—to put in your waves. But *do* leave the dandelions behind when you speak with William and the Prince of Wales this evening. Hm? I really don't want to be consoling your mother long into the night."

The party. Elizabeth slid down a bit into her bed linens, pulled her blankets to her chin. She looked at Lucy, at her piercing eyes, unmistakably delivering Mama's expectations—

That Elizabeth would rise to the occasion.

Entertain the Prince of Wales with ease.

Begin a formal courtship with William Titcomb.

Take her turns around the room tonight, hide the ache in her bruised limbs, impress William with benign chatter about silly things, acceptable things, cultured things. Bach's cello suites. Botany. Needlepoint. And most of all, listen to him prattle on about himself for the better part of an hour. Overconfidence naturally made one loquacious, she supposed. Perhaps he'd explain why he'd been too busy to call and check on her well-being after her fall.

Yes, Elizabeth knew exactly who she was expected to be:

Daughter.

Dalloway.

CHAPTER 6

Octavia

Why did the brewery have to be so high on a hill? Up such a steep path, lined by this uneven stone wall? Had the masons been drunk when they built it? Had they known it would one day lead to the Stroud Brewery; had they celebrated with too much pale ale while laying the stones?

Out of breath, Octavia silently cursed her long skirts, the tight laces of her leather boots, her thick hair swirled into a bun that wouldn't stay in place no matter what she did. But most of all, she cursed the heat. Everyone was talking about it—how oppressive it was, how it must be the hottest summer in history, how the very old and the very young might drop suddenly, breaking under its yoke.

Normally when she hiked up this godforsaken path, stray dogs would run ahead of her, cheery, with stronger lungs than she. But even the burly hound who'd claimed this hill as his home (she'd named him Mr. Brown) was dragging himself along beside her, barely keeping up, tongue wagging, tail down like a limp flag. She stopped halfway up the hill, leaned against the crooked wall. Mr. Brown sat at her feet. She pulled the telegram out of her pocket. She read the last bit again.

His last known address is a Bloomsbury lodging house.

No, it wasn't magically offering any more information since she'd read it last. It hadn't changed after she'd slipped out of her mother's kitchen, small purse in hand and a summer shawl tucked under her arm, the smell of Ronnie's sweet cheek still lingering. She hoped it wasn't the last kiss she'd ever give him.

"Do you know London, Mr. Brown?" she asked the dog now. "Where's Bloomsbury?" She knelt in front of him, feeling sorry for the both of them, wishing she had a lemon pop to offer, a parasol to give shade. She ran her hand over the top of his head, over the dirty golden fur of his neck, past the dust clinging about his ears, baking in the sun. "Is there only one lodging house there, you think? Will it be easy to find?"

The dog half-closed his eyes; she could have sworn he smiled at her, sat back a little on his haunches, a friend. She wished she could take him to London with her. Maybe he could guard her, protect her from the men who supposedly trolled for young girls in the streets. She could pop into Spratt's before she boarded the train and buy Mr. Brown a dog cake, a puppy biscuit. Maybe she could convince the shopgirl to "loan" her a collar and leash. A fancy one she could lead him around with in the city. Did ladies take their dogs for walks in London? She suspected she'd feel stronger with him by her side somehow.

But she'd need money to buy him a dog cake at Spratt's. She'd need money to get to London. Quite a bit of it.

A train whistle blew—a hollow, ominous sound from the station down in Stroud. She had to hurry. She had to catch the next train to London; she couldn't delay. Not while Septimus haunted London in some sketchy lodging house, perhaps in a weakened condition, preyed upon by a money-grubbing girl. Probably married him after the war, hungry for what his meager pension could provide if he didn't survive.

For that was the story; it had to be. Septimus was recovering from some awful injury. Maybe every bone in his body was broken. Maybe he was learning to walk again. Maybe he didn't want his family to see him this way. That's what she'd discover when she found him. That the War Office had been wrong about his health. They were wrong. She was sure of it.

The train whistle blew again. A man pushed a cart up the hill, bags of bread hooked on the sides, long baguettes jostling like the stocks of rifles. Mr. Brown ran toward him.

"Hello, me 'ansum!" the bread man said. He knelt down to pet Mr. Brown as the dog circled the wheels of the bread cart, his limp tail now suddenly coming to life, waving like mad. He ran about the man's legs affectionately, cunningly working his way into good graces. The bread man smiled as if visited by an old loyal friend, ruffled the dog's fur once more, and tossed him a piece of crust he pulled from his pocket.

Traitor, Octavia thought. *Leaving me for a bread crumb. Probably has a hundred names from a hundred strangers in Stroud.*

So much for her daydreams of being accompanied by a hound in London.

She trudged on. Up, up, and up. The white brick sides of the building came into view, the three chimneys, the thick, darkened panes of glass. Large curly letters her father had painted on the side came into focus:

THE STROUD BREWERY

CELEBRATED ALES & STOUT

WINES & SPIRITS

The words were high up, just under the roof, three stories in the air. And next to them was the thing that had always terrified Octavia: the dark, open doorway cut into the side of the building, the one that had been used to bring sheaves of hay into the loft long ago, the one her father had always warned her about as a child. She'd stand on the attic floorboards, the stale smell of ale floating up from below, and stare at that doorway, blink at the rectangle of light, walk to its edge and push the dusty toes of her shoes just over it. She'd stare down, down three stories to the ground, and down once more, down the steep slope of the hill. If she fell, she knew she'd hit the ground and surely tumble all the way into the heart of town. All the way to Spratt's. All the way past the butcher shop, come to rest with a lifeless thud outside Foster Brothers, a dead body beneath their window full of women's dresses.

Sometimes, when she thought of living and dying in Stroud, living her whole life here without Septimus, she was possessed by a fear that she would jump. That she wouldn't even think it; she wouldn't say to herself, *jump, now.* Her body would do it of its own accord. Or would it be her mind? It hardly mattered. It wouldn't be a choice, somehow. It would just be. Her. Leaping through that portal of light in the brewery attic.

She reached the top of the hill and the brewery's front door. She pushed it open, the bells above her jingling; she was ready for the musty darkness, the haze of smoke, the gray figures of drinkers she could see as her eyes adjusted. The front room was a pub, while the brewery, with its barrels and brewing vessels, was in the back.

At least it was cooler in here.

That was where the pleasantness of the place ended, at its coolness. She immediately drew the attention of the men perched on barstools in the front. There was a group tucked around a booth in the back as well—scruffy crows clinging to the same branch, feathers skewwhiff, bellies too thin, eyes dull and flat like old blackened coins. They noticed her too. She could feel their eyes crawling up her skirts, up her neck.

She stared at the bartender. She knew him well; after all, they shared the same surname.

"Tertius," she said, giving the smallest of nods to her brother. He was the largest man of the family, bigger than Septimus, bigger even than their father. "Where's Pop?"

"Where d'you think?" Tertius barked. He ran a damp white cloth over the bar in angry circles.

A heavy man perched on a stool turned toward Octavia, ran a thick finger under his nose. He patted the empty stool next to him.

"I'll get you a shandy," he said, smiling. "She can have that, eh?" The man looked at Tertius. "Even a girl as young as this one here could have lager cut with lemon soda, couldn't she?"

"That's my sister, you twit," Tertius said. "Come round here, Octavia." Her brother was cruel to be sure, but not so awful as to feed her to the wolves. Octavia gratefully ran around to the other side of the bar. She eyed the till, shut tight. The thick-fingered man had taken offense at his rebuffed shandy; he plunked a few coins on the bar top and got up to go.

Octavia reached for the money.

"What are you doing?" Tertius swooped in and grabbed the coins from her.

"Pop lets me practice with the till," Octavia lied.

Tertius didn't look convinced. He tucked his rag in his back pocket and carefully counted the coins. He yanked the till drawer open; the bell rang out its warning. Tertius shoved it closed with his hip. She felt defeated; she'd never manage to get it open without alerting the entire place.

"What you can do is go check on Pop," Tertius said. "He's bad off . . ." He plucked two empty ale glasses from the bar, their sides covered in foam like waves from the sea had come and gone, left only dirty, salty suds in the dark of night. Tertius put them in the sink beside the pulls. Octavia eyed the till again, certain now she'd never be able to pilfer it in time. She'd have to get the money for a London train ticket another way.

She pushed open the door to the back, relieved when it closed behind her. She took a deep breath and looked at the high ceilings, the cobwebs clinging, dust motes filling the shafts of sunlight pouring through the east windows. The large room was filled with copper and oak vessels, stores of malted barley, crates stacked in uneven towers. A mouse scurried from one vat to the next. The stale smell of fermenting ale made her feel poorly; she'd never gotten used to it even though she'd grown up with it, the stink. The rot.

"Pop?"

"Over 'ere, love." He was in his little office, just off the back of the great brewing room.

She hurried past two large copper vessels, caught sight of her reflection in their round metal sides, scratched and pocked with dents. She'd never liked the way she looked, not in mirrors, not in the shine of old copper.

She reached her father's office door.

"What a sight you are! My girl," her father bellowed, effusive, as if he hadn't seen her in days.

The late-morning light came through the office window, through the dust and dirt of maybe a hundred years. She certainly had never seen the panes clean in her lifetime. His desk was piled high with ledgers, empty ale glasses, his favorite old pewter tankard. She walked in, kissed his cheeks. Then she saw it: the drawer that held his locked box of pounds.

"Hello, Pop," she said.

"Hello, my dear." The smell of stout on his breath was strong. He rarely drank all that much, just the regular evening pint he saw as the God-given right of any working man. But on the rare occasion he drank too many, it made him loud like this, kind and demonstrative in the extreme. She wanted to talk of Septimus, to get her father on her side, to convince him that they all must go to London and search for him. Her father took a swig from an old-looking clay bottle with no markings. "Want a sip?"

Octavia shook her head no. "What is it?"

"It's from before! Brewed up to snuff. I knew I had a crate of them somewhere, and lo and behold, I found it." He held it high, a toast to the free-rein brewers used to have to concoct whatever strength ale they liked before the war. Now there were rules. But as his arm came up to salute the past, he knocked two of his ledgers off the desk. Stray papers flew about; the books landed with a clatter on the stone floor. He leaned over to pick them up; she feared he'd topple over in his state.

"No, no, Pop." She gently stopped him from leaning any farther. "I'll get 'em." She crouched down, a little bird gathering up twigs, straightening her father's nest, eyeing the undersides of his desk as she worked, looking for a hidden key to that drawer.

She stood and put the ledgers back on the desk. She told herself to be brave. They never talked of things. Of real things. Other than her mother's moods, of course. They both watched those like they were tarot cards foretelling their futures.

Say the name.

Say it.

Septimus.

She summoned her courage. "Are you—"

"You're a very good girl, Tave." He cut her off like he'd understood before she could speak. Like he knew she was going near something very hot. And he didn't want either of them to burn. He patted her on the head a little too strongly again; his hand landed on her a few times, heavy, thumping in her ears. He looked at her, took her in as if she were a doll, every eyelash painted in its place, every feature just like it was yesterday and the day before. Like her value was in those frozen fine details, in the fact that they wouldn't change, that he could find comfort in that face from here to the end—a collector's item, to be sure. "Yes, you're my good girl."

"I love you too, Pop." She felt guilty for the idea that came to her then, but she couldn't resist. There was a space there, between the two of them, and in it was her father's gratitude—that she was a girl, that she had always been impossibly good, that she was never surly like Tertius, that she'd had a simple birth, one that didn't ruin her mother's mind like Ronald's had. That she hadn't abandoned the family like Septimus, run off on his selfish mission to be a poet in the city, returned from battle without so much as a word. She felt that what she was about to do just might be the worst thing she'd ever done in her life, the thing she'd likely have to answer for when she met her Maker.

But she was going to use what was between them. She was going to use her father's gratitude for what she was. His trust that she would never change.

"Pop?" she asked. "Could I borrow . . ."

"What, me love?" her father urged. "You can have my whole kingdom as far as I'm concerned."

She dared a smile. "Some money?"

His face changed. Apparently, she could have anything in his kingdom—as long as it didn't involve any actual money. "Why? Did your mother spend it all on—"

"No, no," she said, now wildly searching her mind for something she could reasonably need money for that didn't involve a train ticket to London. "Flowers," she blurted. "I want to buy flowers for Mum. From a proper shop. I think they might . . . help. The situation."

That was as close as she could get to saying her brother's name, to naming what was happening here, that Septimus was living without them, thumbing his nose at the very hearts of his family—*the situation*.

Her father leaned back in his chair. He trusted Octavia to be his loyal court cosmologist of sorts, to help him read and interpret his wife's mercurial moods and any misguided plans that might spring from them. If Octavia said her mother needed flowers—she needed flowers.

"How much do you need?" he asked.

She had no earthly idea how much flowers would cost. Or a ticket to London.

"I . . . don't know. I've never bought them before. But . . ." She paused, trying to come up with an extravagant amount. She lost her nerve. "But I think they might be very expensive."

He reached into his favorite old pewter tankard, fished around the bottom of it with his fingertips, his tongue sneaking out the side of his mouth as he searched. He pulled out a key. It dangled from a worn strip of leather.

"Here," he said. He yanked open his desk drawer and stuck the key into the metal box. He turned it, and the top popped open. He reached in and counted out six pennies. "That should do it." He put the money in her hand, locked the box, and slid the drawer shut with a thump.

While it was true that Octavia didn't know how much flowers cost, or how much a train ticket to London would cost, or lodging or enough food to last her once she was there—she knew six pennies wouldn't come close to covering it. Nowhere close.

"Thank you," Octavia said, hiding her disappointment. "I'm sure this will buy a nice bunch."

"Good. You're certain? It's enough?" He must have noticed the disappointment on her face.

"Oh, yes," she lied.

"All right then." Her father patted her on the head again. "You're my good girl, Tave. And thank God for it." He stood, listed to the side. He caught himself with a hand against the wall, laughed a little. "A bit wobbly on my pins today!" He smiled at her. "Now let's go make sure Tertius ain't about to burn down the place, eh?"

Octavia eyed her father's ratty desk chair, with its stains and ripped fabric, a scratchy print covered with mauve-and-yellow roses. He always joked that it was too Victorian for the place.

"Would you mind if I sat here a minute?" she asked, nodding at his chair. "It's so hot outside, I'm not ready to start for . . . the flower shop just yet."

"You stay back here and cool off as long as you like." He lurched off toward the bar.

Octavia leaned forward, the chair springs whining as she listened to her father's footsteps fade.

One. Two. Three.

She sprang from her seat. Surely, her father wouldn't be speedy—checking on Tertius's doings, placating the crows, having another drink to drown the news of Septimus. She'd have enough time. Plenty of time.

She plunged her hand into the pewter tankard and found the key. She put it into the lock. It stuck. It wouldn't turn a bit. She pulled it back out, blew on the end of it for luck like she always did to the poufs of weeds she found in the Stroud hills, making a wish as the feathered seeds took to the air, chancing a great voyage to sprout stalks of their own. She slid the key back into the lock, carefully, slowly. And heard a click, felt something inside give way.

It was open.

She reached in, grabbed a handful of pounds, and stuffed them into her small purse.

She'd done it.

But then she thought of London. The ticket. The food she'd need to buy. The lodging. What if she had to stay for several days? A week? What if she became ill? Needed a chemist?

She heard a noise. Whistling. Footsteps. Someone was coming. She heard a clanging sound, probably one of the copper vessels. Her father or her brother must be checking something, the priming maybe. She looked back at the cash in the box.

And took it all.

Every last shilling. Every last pound note. She left the box hollow, empty.

The footsteps started again.

She locked the box, put her hands on the drawer to slide it closed—

The doorway darkened. It was her father. Clearly one more cup of ale in him, staring at Octavia's hand on his cash drawer. "I know what you're doing," he said.

Octavia thought her lungs were seizing up, the air just like that key—not budging an inch, in or out. Rusted shut. "You do?"

"Yes." He reached in his pocket. "You're looking for this."

Dangling in front of Octavia was her very favorite thing in the world. Her father's pocket watch. Its gold chain sparkled in the shaft of sunlight coming through the window. Her father flipped open its case. She knew the watch well. Coventry-made. From Percy House of Holyhead. Family lore was that it had been given to her grandfather in the eighties when he got to meet with a member of Parliament about the state of the wool trade in Stroud.

Octavia stared at the watch face, at its fine roman numerals spread all the way around it. In capital type, just above the center where the golden hands met:

CENTRE SECONDS

CHRONOGRAPH

He rarely carried the watch with him; it was usually in his desk drawer. Said he only wanted to count the minutes when he was counting his money. Other than that, he didn't care to know the time, felt freer without it. Figured it was made up just like money was, just like banks and notes and debt and all the rest of it. It wasn't natural, the time. As a young child, whenever Octavia had come to visit her father at the brewery, he would let her sit on his lap and hold the watch, flip it open and closed, watch the dials mysteriously move, marking this thing her father cursed as a false measure.

She loved it.

"Yes," Octavia lied now, taking the watch he held out for her. "I was looking for this. I just wanted to hold it. Check the time."

He knelt down, looked at her intensely. It made her think of the last time she saw Septimus on that hill above Stroud, how her brother had looked at her in a way she'd never seen before. She'd learned to fear men of the family looking at her in any serious way after that, fearing their plans. "I want you to have it," her father said. "For not being a bit like your brothers. Not a bit."

Octavia stared at the golden hands of the watch. "I couldn't," she said.

"I insist on it."

She flung her arms around his neck, so sorry. So very sorry. She felt him rest his heavy head on her shoulder. She couldn't be sure, but she thought she felt his chest heave a little, the tiniest movement, a bit of air pulled in too quickly, and then out, a silent sob caused by her brother. The brother who'd run off to London. Like she was about to do. This might be the last time they were together; she knew she might be lost in the city forever, taken by a mob, stolen and sold to a wild caravan of pirates, or just run over, turned under the hooves of horses and carriage wheels, ground into the streets like a brewery mouse running between copper vats.

She pulled back from her father and gently flipped the watch open. If this was their last moment, she wanted to remember it, the time of day she last saw her father's face.

It was half past ten.

She had less than thirty minutes to get down the hill in the heat to the station, buy a ticket, and board the train to London.

"I love it," she said, closing her hands around the watch. "Thank you."

He smiled. "Now off you go. To get those flowers for your mum, eh?"

Octavia nodded and headed for the door. But she paused just before she reached it and looked back.

"Goodbye, Pop," she said, feeling her courage waver. *Fear no more the heat o'th'sun.* She willed the blood in her veins to beat not red but azured-harebell blue. Flowers. To beat like flowers. "Goodbye."

CHAPTER 7

Elizabeth

"When the party begins, your mother will probably still be rattled from her visit with Mr. Walsh," Lucy said. She was still in Elizabeth's room, still admonishing Elizabeth not to wear dandelions on her dress tonight, not to do anything that would trouble Mama during her first party of the season. She laid the dress on Elizabeth's little settee. "Mr. Walsh will be visiting midday, just hours before the event. I hope it's a pleasant meeting with those two. And I *do* hope she saw my note that he was coming. She was at her desk writing to him just yesterday. Her drawers are getting full of his notes! I'll have to clean them out before long."

Lucy was famous for letting messages from visitors slip.

Elizabeth didn't like the way Lucy said his name—*Mr. Walsh.* She didn't like the way she was talking about him at all. *"A pleasant meeting between those two."* Elizabeth couldn't imagine her mother having a conflict with anyone, let alone an old childhood friend coming to call. And drawers full of his notes from India?

Well. Elizabeth could use a bit of morning reading.

"Bond Street," Elizabeth said. "Mama is going to Miss Pym's?"

"Yes, you know she likes to get the flowers herself. And Rumpelmayer's men are coming."

"When?"

"Rumpelmayer's men?"

"No," Elizabeth said. "Bond Street. When is Mama going to Bond Street?"

"Right away, I believe. I need to go down and help her prepare. Why, do you want to accompany her? To the glove shop perhaps? New cream gloves for this evening would be lovely."

"No, I have a few things to do while she's out."

If Lucy knew what Elizabeth was suggesting, she didn't show it.

"Very well," she said. "I'll leave you to it."

———

Mama's writing desk. The one from the time of the Georges. Mama's people were courtiers once; this desk was what remained of all that. And perhaps Mama's overly dignified comportment—a relic.

The first drawer Elizabeth opened held Mama's leather sewing case, the one the color of almond skins. Mama was forever mending something herself that Lucy could do much faster. But Mama insisted. On mending herself. Getting flowers herself. Writing invitations herself—

Here they were.

Letters.

Stacks of them.

Here were a few that were finished, signed, tucked in unsealed envelopes, ready to post. One to Lady Bruton, a woman Mama claimed had the air of a general in the army. Her relatives had been involved in a peace treaty once, and Lady Bruton didn't let anyone forget it. Mama's letter to her was dry as a stick. All about the weather and luncheons and fundraisers. A widow's fund.

I heard of your plans to write a letter to the paper about young veterans. About finding them work in Canada? How smart about politics you have always been! I would love to hear more, daft though I am about these sorts of things.

Here was one to old Lady Purvis, their neighbor next door, its message thinly veiled. Lady Purvis had not let Mama know of her family's travel plans last season. Or any season prior. The Purvis family would depart for the Falkland Islands or Mallorca without so much as a word.

If you'd be so kind as to let us know before you depart this season, we'd be happy to assist your staff should they need us.

Again, it was ready to post.

Elizabeth opened another drawer. So many letters! Here were several Mama had received years ago from her father, Elizabeth's Grandpapa Parry, Justin Parry. Urging Mama to help her brother, Herbert, take care of the old place. To take care of Bourton. Herbert was letting it rot to the ground, Grandpapa said. The grass around the lake was waist-high! The water was practically hidden from sight! What a travesty.

And here was a letter to Mama's aunt Helena, a former botanist who had supposedly discovered a rare form of orchid.

Dear Aunt Helena,
 I received your letter about the trouble with the butterflies. It sounds as though they aren't what they used to be at all. They used to carom around Bourton in colorful hordes! You must be correct that their flight patterns have been disturbed.
 Affectionately,
 Clarissa

Clarissa.

It was jarring. Elizabeth so rarely heard her mother's first name. And she wasn't sure she'd ever seen it in writing. Mama was Mrs. Richard Dalloway when introduced. She was Mrs. Richard Dalloway on invitations. She was Mrs. Richard Dalloway on every envelope Elizabeth had ever seen. Not Clarissa.

One more drawer.

Letters to Peter Walsh.

All addressed to him in India. Bengal. Dacca. The Central Provinces. Nagpur and Poona.

All addressed.

Never sent.

Some were recent, some a few months old. Others went back years.

Elizabeth pulled one out and began to read. It was different from all the others. Very, very different. It wasn't dry. It wasn't a stick. Elizabeth tried to read it, but it was—difficult. It was a difficult letter. Mama's thoughts ran in long, looping sentences, each one barely disconnected from the last. All about their summer. The summer of 1889. The summer they were eighteen. The mornings were *"fresh as if issued to children on a beach."* Mama wrote that she would always remember Peter's comment that he preferred people to cauliflower. His claim that she loved the country more than society, but that she'd end up marrying a prime minister in London anyway. His prediction that she'd give up her talent for debate, for reform. How strange it was, thinking that Mama could love the country. Could debate.

Elizabeth read letter after letter. She couldn't really make much of them. They were all similar, all full of vague references to their summer. What had happened there. By the lake. Something had happened by the lake. Or was it by a water fountain? Not a single letter was direct. They were full of formalities, vagaries and hints. At rumors, at "disasters," all about one single summer at Mama's childhood home. About her friends Sally Seton, Joseph Breitkopf. Hugh Whitbread. Of Papa. He was there too. That summer.

The only thing that was clear was something momentous had happened. Something that involved Peter Walsh, something Mama still wanted to write about more than thirty years later. Elizabeth couldn't imagine her mother carrying the weight of a secret. The course of her life seemed nothing if not perfectly smooth.

What happened, Mama?

The phone rang; Elizabeth jumped, her guilt simmering a bit. She heard Lucy answer, take down a message of some sort. She heard the telephone click back into its cradle. Elizabeth went back to the letter.

And read the clearest part of all.

Mama had consulted Dr. Bradshaw.

Oh, Peter, I went to see him. Just to ask him, you know. And his answer was so dreadful! Really, it was. He kept droning on about keeping everything in proportion. To rest at midday. That a woman like me shouldn't be thinking of these things. That summer. I left feeling that he is a disgusting man, I think. But they say he's the best. So perhaps psychiatrists are disgusting. Perhaps that's it. Perhaps I'm wrong about it all. I should be happy with it. I know I should.

Grizzle barked in the hallway. Again. And again. Elizabeth leaned forward in the chair and looked out the drawing-room window. Mama. In her yellow dress and matching hat, coming up the path through the garden, past her favorite wrought-iron garden chair. The one without a cushion. Her arms full of flowers from Miss Pym's. Mama looked so lovely amid all those blooms. Were those peonies? How long had Elizabeth been reading letters?

Mama was home from Bond Street.

Elizabeth shoved the letters back in their drawers, but they were all mixed up, half-bent, some out of their envelopes altogether. This would never do. Mama would know right away. Elizabeth yanked the drawers back open, pulled out Mama's leather sewing case to make more room. Her hands trembled as she slid the letters back into envelopes, as she tried to fold them neatly along their creases, stack them back in their places.

The front door's hinge began to squeak. Elizabeth heard Lucy's voice now, welcoming Mama in.

"What are they looking at?" Mama asked Lucy. Elizabeth heard the high hum of a plane, knew it was probably a skywriting plane, puffing an ad for something in the sky. Toffee. Women's shoes. A brand of cough syrup. The sound rattled the windows. Elizabeth guessed that was what Mama was asking about, the plane, what it was writing. What everyone was looking at. Elizabeth heard Mama's parasol land in the umbrella stand by the door, a Bond Street–errand soldier laying down her sword. She waited to hear Mama tell Lucy about her shopping excursion—about the glove shop, the salmon on ice blocks, the little cigars in windows, the glass bowls, the flowers.

But Mama didn't have a chance; Lucy cut her off before she had the opportunity. Lucy told her mother about a telephone call, a message. About Mama not being invited somewhere. Only Mr. Dalloway. Only Mr. Dalloway was invited to Lady Bruton's luncheon. The luncheon about Lady Bruton's proposal for the veterans.

"Oh dear," Mama said.

There was a long silence.

Elizabeth shoved the last letter to Peter in its envelope and slid the drawer shut. She stood, smoothed her blouse, her hair. Waited for Mama to come into the drawing room. To sense that something was dreadfully amiss. Mama would sense a thing like that, the air being displaced by the flap of a letter.

Instead, Elizabeth heard footsteps. Mama's footsteps. Ascending the stairs.

"Fear no more," Mama said to Lucy.

Fear no more?

As Mama's steps receded, Elizabeth heard an awful noise. A loud one.

A scruffy brown bird had flown into the windowpane beside the writing desk with a horrid smack. It seemed a bit dazed as it found its footing on the sill. Grizzle went mad, wriggling his little bread box of a body. He barked as if the bird intended to break in, to carry Elizabeth off in his beak, to violently kidnap her in broad daylight, the tiniest bird of prey. It began flapping its wings now; Elizabeth was worried it was going to beat itself to death.

But it settled, suddenly accepting the limitations of the glass. Elizabeth stared at its unremarkable brown coat, a female for sure. Its job in life wasn't to attract, to shine; in fact, it was quite the opposite. Her job was to blend in, to be camouflaged in plain sight. To wear a plain brown coat day in and day out.

And then Elizabeth knew.

If there was anyone who understood something about Peter Walsh, about what had happened that summer long ago, it would be someone with the greatest interest in rumors about Mama. The one who made it her business to dig for any negative crumb. The one who resembled that dowdy bird on the sill, that frumpy, camouflaged female, the one who wore the same old unremarkable green coat, a mackintosh, day in and day out. The coat Mama despised. The woman Mama despised. Two women who'd taken drastically different paths through the world. Mama—who'd stopped her studies with Fräulein Daniels at a young age, become a mother, a socialite, a kindler of nights. And the other—a woman who'd studied history, become a tutor, a reformer, an activist.

Miss Doris Kilman.

Elizabeth's history tutor.

And Elizabeth knew exactly where to find her.

CHAPTER 8

Octavia

The train began to move. The lush hills and thatched roofs of Stroud were gone in a blink; all too soon her home was behind her. The green slopes of the Cotswolds gave way to the flat as the train passed station after station. Swindon. Reading. Maidenhead. Slough.

Clack. Clack. Clack.

The land changed rapidly outside her window. Patches of countryside cut into squares, some straw-gold, some green, some lying fallow, brown. They passed a canal, long boats crowded at the locks. The train pushed on and on, and the land itself started to gray, to crowd with buildings, brick and steel. Towns and stations went by, one after the other.

She pulled out her father's pocket watch; she'd pinned it underneath her bodice. She couldn't bear to keep it in her purse; she didn't want it any farther from her heart than need be. She flipped open the case. Yes, she'd been on the rails for several hours now. Her family would be wondering where she was. It would be dawning on her mum that she'd meant it about going to London. That she'd taken that telegram, taken her family's trust, and run. Would they come looking for her? Was London a place where she could be found? Or would it be far too big for that? Or perhaps they wouldn't look. Perhaps her mum would just throw another roll of dough into the waste bin, smack her rolling pin in the sink, another child gone bad. Another in a ruined batch.

She must hurry. Surely London was close, and she still had no idea what to do once she arrived. Octavia leaned across the aisle and got the attention of a woman in a white hat with the widest blue band Octavia had ever seen.

"Excuse me," Octavia ventured.

"Yes?"

"I need to get to Bloomsbury. To the boardinghouse there. And I wondered if you might know—"

"Bloomsbury?" The woman's eyebrows plunged low. "What business have you got in Bloomsbury? It's unsavory, that part of town."

"My brother is—" Octavia stopped, unsure how much to tell. "He's hurt. I'm coming to collect him and take him back home. Do you happen to know where the boardinghouse is?"

The woman's face softened. "There isn't one."

Octavia's eyes went wide. "There isn't a boardinghouse?"

"No," the woman said. "It's that there isn't *one*. There are hundreds. Thousands, even."

Thousands?

Before Octavia could respond, the train slowed and stopped. Every passenger on the train began moving, gathering things in their seats. One by one they stood and moved toward the exits.

Paddington Station.

"God bless you," the woman said. And she was gone.

In a rush, Octavia followed the crowd out of the car, stood on the platform.

She looked up.

It took her breath away, the grandness of Paddington. The ceiling was a giant rib cage of steel and glass; birds zoomed through the bounded indoor skies. There were stone archways as far as Octavia could see, large signs above each: Cloak Room; Dining & Tea Room; Bookstall. She moved with the crowd and the exit sign came closer and closer.

She was through it. The exit.

Outside the station, dust flew in her eyes, her dress lifted in the breeze. She heard the honking of motorcars, the whistles of policemen.

London.

She was on the streets of London.

There were fancy hotels with porters in fine jackets out front hailing taxicabs, opening doors. An omnibus clogged the intersection in front of her like a giant slice of red cake, its top decorated with women holding parasols, their shoulders covered in furs—furs in heat like this! Shop awnings stretched down the street as far as Octavia could see.

EVANS RESTAURANT

JAMES STEPHENS COMPANY

WHITTIER'S TAVERN

Where were the poets standing on each corner, reciting Shakespeare or brilliant original works? Where were the divine smells of chocolate shops and flower shops and cinnamon buns on every block? This was London, Octavia knew. But it was not the one she'd imagined. The one Septimus had described. Not by any stretch. This was just a busy, dusty, loud . . . *jumble*. How could her brother possibly write poetry here? How could he even hear himself think in this din?

"You lost?" It was a boy, a little younger than Octavia, his cap jauntily tipped to the side. His blond hair peeked out over his ears.

"Excuse me?" Octavia asked, even though she'd heard him just fine.

"You look lost, that's all," he said, smiling. He had kind eyes, bright. "Can I help you get somewhere?"

Octavia hesitated. She knew she must look like a poor frightened brewery mouse, whiskers twitching, too scared to scurry. But the boy smiled at her, and it was such a warm smile that she decided he was charming, really, in his cap and suspenders. His boots looked a little worse for wear, one of his laces was frayed and held together with a chunk of glue, but other than that, he seemed put together all right.

"Well," Octavia heard herself saying, "I'm lost. And it'll get a bit dimpsy soon enough. So I need to find—"

"Here," the boy said, offering her his arm. "Just tell me where you're headed."

Relief washed over Octavia, and she slipped her arm through his. She thought of her mother's warnings about men stealing young girls off the streets. But this nice boy would do no such thing. He couldn't be more than fifteen, Octavia decided. Just a sweet-mannered city boy who must have been brought up right.

"Why thank you," Octavia said. She was thankful for an arm to hold; all those coins in her purse were heavy. "So, I'm looking for my brother, Septimus Smith. He's a veteran, and he's living in Bloomsbury."

The boy looked a little surprised. "Bloomsbury, eh? Some weird sorts going about in that part of town. Artists and poets and the like."

Octavia brightened. "Oh, I don't mind that at all," she said. "My brother's a poet. That's what brought him to the city at first. Before the war, mind."

"A poet, huh?" The boy looked skeptical. "Lucky for you, Bloomsbury is not far at all. By Underground, that is. Just go back to Paddington." The boy leaned in close and pointed. His shoulder touched hers, and Octavia noticed the smell of tar or coal—something burnt like that— some sort of fuel, coming off the boy's shirt. She glanced at his suspenders and saw for the first time that they were quite stained, that his finger-nails were caked with dirt.

"And then?" Octavia asked.

"Get a ticket for the Circle Line. Get off at Euston Square. Walk down Gower a bit and there you have it. The heart of Bloomsbury!"

Hope rose in Octavia's chest, a little city bird, realizing it just might be able to fly above all this mess. "You've been too kind," she said, feeling color come to her cheeks. "Really, really kind." She let go of his arm and adjusted her hat as a few girls her age passed by. She realized for the first time that she was completely out of fashion. The girls on the street had bobbed hair and wore drop-waist dresses she'd only seen in news-paper advertisements left around the brewery. They had long necklaces draped around their necks. Octavia's dress was plain cotton, tight in the bust and gathered high on her waist. From there it flowed out like a bell. Like a dress from before the war. Which it was.

"My pleasure," the boy said. He tipped his hat and gently put a hand on her shoulder. "Good luck to you, Bloomsbury Girl. Now, off you go."

"Goodbye and thank you again." Octavia felt triumphant. She'd already made a friend, a connection; she was finding her way in this mad throng. Despite the jumble, no one looked ready to nab her from a street corner, like her mother had warned. She felt perfectly safe. Oh, what did Mum know anyhow? Now, how much would an Underground ticket cost, she wondered? She reached for her purse. She knew she had plenty of money. It couldn't be more than the ticket to—

Octavia stopped.

She put a hand on her right forearm. Then her left one.

Her purse.

It was gone.

She spun around and stared into the crowd, looking for the boy, his cap, his dirty suspenders.

He was gone.

And then she knew.

That lovely boy wasn't lovely at all; he'd seen her coming from a mile away, a young girl from the West Country, leaving Paddington Station in her plain old dress, with a purse stuffed fat with cash and ignorance.

He'd stolen them both.

CHAPTER 9

Elizabeth

A ride on the Underground, a short walk from the station, and Elizabeth arrived.

First Church of Kensington, its two tall spires reaching, proud.

The one Mama disliked intensely. It was her experience, she often said, that church was too rigid, that it often made people callous. Cold. All in the name of love and religion, she said. Love. Religion.

Elizabeth hurried up the front steps and went in. It was offensive to slip in after the service had started; even the St. Giles Mission girls—thirteen-year-old workers who came from the factory—knew that. But this couldn't wait. She had to know who this Peter Walsh was, and the only woman who might know would be here, sitting dutifully in one of the pews.

The church was nearly bursting with congregants. Even the expansive balcony seating with its honey-colored wooden railings, its milk-white pendant lights was completely full. There wasn't an empty seat in the house. The congregation was dressed in its finest. Even the Bloomsbury wool shop girls wore fancy hats. In the pew behind them, the Young Maiden's League sat side by side in dresses with out-of-date lace and long sleeves, but still—usually they came in plain muslin. And there were the husbands of the Women's Choir sitting pin-straight, alert, unlike their usual sleepy and duty-bound postures.

What on earth was going on here today?

Elizabeth scanned the crowd, looking for the person she needed to see, for that signature green mackintosh coat, that sensible chestnut hair, those lean and dignified shoulders squared like a great bookshelf filled with books about history and religion.

There she was.

Miss Doris Kilman. Elizabeth's private history tutor. The one Papa thought had such a keen historical mind, the one he entrusted to impart the past to his daughter. The one Mama thought was too strict, too demanding, sanctimonious about her choices. Papa had won that battle; he refused to let her go. Miss Kilman often dragged Elizabeth to church as part of her "education." It was history Elizabeth loved; religion bored her to tears. What irony that Mama and Papa feared she was becoming devout.

Elizabeth walked to the end of Miss Kilman's pew and caught her eye. Room was made and Elizabeth sat. Miss Kilman laid a hand on Elizabeth's forearm and gave it a squeeze. It was gestures like these that made Mama fear Elizabeth had *feelings* for Miss Kilman. How absurd. Elizabeth respected the woman's mind. Her keen historical mind. Couldn't a woman admire another for her intellect without it being romantic? Taboo? Besides, Elizabeth would pick a tutor more vivacious than this one to have feelings for. Or at least one with better taste in coats. And Miss Kilman was *ancient*. Thirty-nine. Or was it forty?

The reverend went on and on; Elizabeth couldn't focus. She couldn't wait for the service to end. She gently nudged her tutor, lowered her voice to the tiniest whisper she could manage. "Do you know who Peter Walsh is?"

A look of disapproval crossed Miss Kilman's face, a storm cloud coming off the Channel.

"Never mind him," Miss Kilman hissed. Then she waved her hand in Elizabeth's direction as if to shoo Peter's name away. "*Pay attention.*"

"What do you know about him?" Elizabeth whispered. "He's coming to visit today."

Miss Kilman looked angry now. Angry but resigned—she knew

Elizabeth was not going to give this up. "Peter's a cad," Miss Kilman said. "That's all—a cad. Always in trouble with women. Always has been. Now pay attention." She gestured to the front of the church. "The *Gage family* is here."

Elizabeth looked at the front pew. Bunches of white blossoms hung on the ends, purple ribbons tied around their stems. Four people sat in the center, and Elizabeth could see only their backs. One was a man, presumably Mr. Gage, with a head of slightly graying hair arranged around a roaring bald spot. He sat very upright as if an iron rod went the length of his back and prevented him even a moment of slouching.

Next to him was a woman Elizabeth guessed was Mrs. Gage, wearing a cheerless black hat. And next to her, slouching a bit, was someone else. Someone younger. A tall boy with a full head of very light brown hair, straight as pencils sharpened to the nub, jutting this way and that. It needed to be combed. And next to him, a girl in a white hat, a peach dress. A perfect color of peach, Elizabeth decided. She couldn't be sure, but they both seemed to be her age.

"And who are the Gages?" Elizabeth whispered.

"The largest donors to the church," Miss Kilman explained. "From Pennsylvania. Iron fortune. They want to make sure Presbyterians prosper here. They say he hates Catholics and Anglicans in equal measure."

So those were the Gage children.

Daughter Gage.

Son of Gage.

They had to be.

Elizabeth wondered if gray was the family's unofficial color: the boy was in a gray pin-striped suit that matched his father's, and he was nodding at nearly every single word Reverend Whitaker was saying. The girl nodded too. So perfect they seemed, so dutiful. Elizabeth imagined every detail about this Gage pair: heirs of an iron fortune, charmers of their parents' contemporaries, bearers of well-bred smiles. They were probably perfect in their parents' eyes, the type of children Mother Gage would have ordered from a menu if she could have. Ones who lived up to expectations. A Gage Daughter and a Gage Son in the Gage Family.

Children who didn't careen into stone walls, fall off horses, argue about politics, or pin dandelions to their dresses.

Elizabeth immediately hated them.

After the service, the congregants filed out of the church and gathered on the steps, shook hands, chatted. Elizabeth turned to Miss Kilman, finally having her undivided attention.

"So," she began. "Peter Walsh. Can you please tell me who he is? Anything about him and Mama?"

"Doris!" A woman came toward them, waving a hand. "How are you, dear?" she asked. She was in a nauseating purple dress; Elizabeth was worried she might drown in it. "Do tell me about the luncheon you've planned? Wednesday next, is that right?"

Miss Kilman turned toward the woman and was immediately consumed in conversation. Elizabeth gently tugged on Miss Kilman's sleeve, hoping to capture her for just one more second, but it was useless. She'd have to wait.

She heard something.

Something soft. Lovely. Coming from the shaded alley beside the church.

A ukulele?

She rounded the church, held a hand above her eyes to see better. She saw something halfway down the alley beside a pile of horrid bloody pelt trimmings cast out from the nearby fur shop. Atop a heap of trash in a bin overflowing with all manner of things—potato peels, wet newsprint, a broken chair, a few mice weaving in and out of the mess—she saw a smear of pure pin-striped gray.

A suit coat.

A perfectly ironed, perfectly stylish suit coat. Sitting on top of the rubbish, trying in vain to imitate one of those cast-off, bloody pelts.

The jacket she'd seen on the Gages' son.

It was in the bin.

And there he was, Son of Gage himself, leaning against the sand-colored stone of the church building, strumming a ukulele.

Elizabeth couldn't be sure, but she thought she saw the boy gesture with a nod for Elizabeth to come closer. Then he looked up and down the alley, checking for who knows what, and then—yes, yes, there— he did it again. He didn't miss a beat of his little ukulele song. He was motioning for Elizabeth to come close.

The last thing on earth Elizabeth wanted was to get a lecture from some pious American boy about the evils of London's youth. Or to answer his ridiculous tourist questions about England, which he would surely have. How old was Big Ben, anyway? Was it true that Westminster Abbey was haunted by Chaucer's ghost? Were the Crown Jewels on display real or fake?

Elizabeth could pretend she hadn't seen this Gage boy. Or pretend she hadn't understood his invitation to come chat. Just give a polite wave and go on her way.

She started down the alley.

"I saw you come in late," the boy said as Elizabeth approached. Not hello. Not how d'you do? But—*I saw you come in late.* He strummed his ukulele as if to punctuate his accusation, a few ominous chords to mark her tardiness. "You got a bit of the evil eye from the reverend, you know." He smiled. But not a pious smile. Not a smile that suggested Elizabeth should kneel, pay penance.

No.

The boy's smile was . . .

"How d'you do?" Elizabeth said, holding out her hand. "My name is Elizabeth Dalloway. And you are?"

"Oh, right. English form and all that." The boy made a show of a little bow. "How d'you do? I'm Calvin Gage."

Unfettered.

That was it.

His smile, his whole demeanor—unfettered.

Elizabeth had been right; Calvin looked to be about her age. She'd been right, too, about his outward perfection. His smile, his height, even the way he stood seemed to announce something, something no one would want to miss. Calvin offered his hand—an odd American habit, to shake a woman's hand so stiffly. But Elizabeth took it and thought she felt something, the tiniest American steam train traversing the lines of her palm—small but made of iron, bound to take them both clear across a continent.

"Pleased to meet you," Elizabeth said, letting the train rattle past.

"Nice brooch." Calvin eyed the dandelion pinned to Elizabeth's dress. His peculiar smile was back.

"It's just my . . ." Elizabeth adjusted her dandelion boutonniere. She didn't want to explain. Suddenly it felt very private, the way she felt about flowers. "It's just something I wear."

"Oh, I feel awful," Calvin said. "I've made you blush. I meant what I said about liking it." He took a closer look. "I think it's smashing. Very avant-garde." Calvin placed his ukulele on the ground now, leaned it against the church. He reached for something in his back pocket. "So you belong to this church?"

"No," Elizabeth said. "I mean I do attend occasionally, but only with my tutor. To indulge her, really. She's forty. And all alone. But so keen about history. She's fascinating, really. I came to see her today, I have something urgent—" She was explaining too much, talking too fast. And now she'd all but insulted his family's church. But she couldn't stop. "Most Brits are Church of England. My family goes once a year to St. Margaret's, but my mother doesn't really—"

"You don't actually believe any of that garbage, do you?" Calvin eyed Elizabeth through a few bits of brown hair that had fallen in front of his eyes.

"Garbage?" Elizabeth asked, confused. "You mean the Church of England? Or Presbyterians? Do I believe in . . . which one exactly?"

"In any of them," Calvin said. He pulled a flask from his pocket, unscrewed the cap. Took a swig. "But I bet your parents do."

Elizabeth could practically feel the shock on her own face—her eyes wide, her mouth slightly agape. She looked up and down the alley, checking to make sure Reverend Whitaker wasn't stalking about, or Calvin's father, or even Miss Kilman, for that matter. Calvin didn't seem worried in the slightest about drinking in an alley in the middle of the day.

"No," she stammered a bit. "My mother doesn't quite fit the church.

She says spirits are mists among the trees. That sort of thing. She's quite poetic, actually." Elizabeth glanced down the alley again. Calvin took another drink. "Are you sure you should be—"

"Sure as the sky is blue." He drew out his American accent dramatically and took another long sip from the flask, its curved pewter bottom glinting in a ray of sunlight that had pierced the alley shadows. His shoulders relaxed, eased a bit. He leaned against the church building and looked at the sky, resting the back of his head on one of the cool stones. "Yes, this is just the thing. The very thing." His voice had a raspy quality to it, as if he'd been sipping brandy and reading long, lyrical poems for hours. Poems about throwing suit coats in the bin, about tossing your head back like that, about how it feels to stare at a sliver of English sky.

"You're not worried your mother will see you?" Elizabeth asked. "Or your papa?"

"My *papa*?" Calvin asked, aping Elizabeth's accent. Then he winked (winked!) at her. "How fabulously English. I don't call him *Papa*." He took another sip. "I call him Father when I want something, and Grim when I don't." He held out the flask. "Better than communion wine, I'll say."

Elizabeth was well and truly dumbfounded now. But perhaps the thing that surprised her most wasn't even the flask—but that she was grinning uncontrollably. Her cheeks aching from it. Who on earth *was* this boy? Calvin was still holding the flask in Elizabeth's direction, offering.

"No, thank you, I don't—" Elizabeth stopped. She was about to say that she didn't drink—which was mostly true. Sipping wine out of those tiny crystal goblets at Mama's parties hardly seemed to count. At any rate, she certainly didn't drink from *flasks*. How vulgar.

"Don't mind if I do," Elizabeth found herself saying.

"Welcome to summer," Calvin said. "So glad we both made it."

Elizabeth took hold of the flask, put it to her lips, took a drink. She fought back a cough at first; she felt like retching. But then without warning, as if summoned by the burn of the liquor, one of those vulgar, direct questions only Americans ask slipped from Elizabeth's British lips: "So why are you drinking in an alley and throwing perfectly nice jackets in the bin?"

Calvin grinned. "What's the real reason you pin dandelions to your dresses?"

Elizabeth looked down at the weed still valiantly clinging to her chest. "To be honest, I'm not sure I know." Elizabeth searched for words. Maybe an American would say that Elizabeth was mad, insane, nutty? Americans said those sorts of things. "It drives my mother positively . . . nutty."

Calvin's unfettered smile returned. "Well, that's reason enough to wear them every single day and night if you ask me. If dandelions bothered Grim, I'd tuck them in every pocket. I'd bathe in them at night." Calvin screwed the cap back on the flask. He eyed Elizabeth's ratty weed as if he wanted to hold it between his fingers, spin it around as if it were a fine yellow rose. A knot of topaz. "Smashing," he said softly. "Really smashing."

"I believe you may be the first to think so."

The side church door burst open.

"The first to think what?" A girl came out, all smiles and bright eyes, like a cheerful grenade, meant to ignite the alleyway. A grenade in a peach dress, a blond bob, and a white hat perfect as a china plate.

"My sister," Calvin said, gesturing toward the girl. "Frances. Frances Gage."

"How d'you do, honeybunch?" Frances dipped in what she must have thought was a proper curtsy. Or did she know it was so improper as to be comedic? It was unclear. "Isn't that what you do here? Curtsy? And do I kiss your hand? The hand of . . . ?"

"No," Elizabeth said quickly. "No need to kiss my hand. I'm Elizabeth. Elizabeth Dalloway."

Frances swiped the flask from her brother and took a swig. A long one. Not ladylike in the least.

"So." She seemed to be studying Elizabeth, rapidly making decisions about her. "I'd peg you for an aristocrat, but the dandelion is throwing me off. What does your father do?"

There was another of those vulgar American questions. Elizabeth had heard this before, asking what "people do." It was strange; British people would never dream of asking such a thing. Besides, most fathers Elizabeth knew didn't really *do* anything aside from managing estates or being in politics. "Papa is a member of Parliament," Elizabeth responded. "House of Commons."

Frances straightened up, looked giddy. "I knew it! I knew you were *something* like that. That's like being a senator's daughter, isn't it?" Yes, she was giddy now. "So you must know the Little Man, then."

"Little Man?" Elizabeth asked. "I have no earthly idea who that is."

"The Prince of Wales, silly. That's his nickname in the press. Americans just *die* for news of him. Can you get us an invitation? To one of his parties? There are rumors in the States, you know."

"Rumors?"

"Being an MP's daughter and all that, surely you can swing it," Calvin said.

"Oh, say you can!" Frances took one of Elizabeth's hands and gave it a little squeeze. As if they'd known each other all their lives, little bunnies that had tumbled about in the same burrow. Elizabeth had never had a friend do that. Be demonstrative like this. Even her own mother wouldn't squeeze her hand. Frances's energy was so . . . remarkable.

"I don't think I can, I—" A noise interrupted Elizabeth. It came from inside the church, booming. Thunderous. The noise grew louder. Someone was calling. Someone with a commanding voice, impossible to ignore.

"Damn," Calvin said. He picked up his ukulele. "It's Grim. He's on our trail." He gently tugged on his sister's arm. "We've got to run. Elizabeth, send a message to the church if you can. If we can meet up." He winked again. Elizabeth wondered if all of them winked. All the American boys.

"Grim always spoils our fun," Frances whispered to Elizabeth. "You can count on him for it." Frances pulled the door open. And another girl stepped out. She was in the plainest muslin dress Elizabeth had ever seen in her life. So plain it almost looked like underclothes. Barely any seams, barely any lines, barely any shape. She had faintly red hair done in a thick braid that hung over her shoulder like a tower bell's rope.

"Your father is looking for you both. I believe we are going for the picnic now," she said softly. She looked at Frances with hopeful eyes. "Are you coming?"

"We'll be right there, honey," Frances said flatly. The girl nodded and went back inside. "She's allergic to fun, that girl," Frances said. "Awful. Just awful. Her daddy's the pastor. Grim is making us socialize with her all damn summer long. It's going to kill me!"

"I'll die before you do," Calvin said. "Last night she showed me her stamp collection. Claims King George loves them too. Stamps. Death by boredom! Who knew a page of stamps could take a man down?"

Grim's voice bellowed again from inside the church.

"I guess this is bye for now," Frances said. "But you'll let us know? About the party invitation. You know where to find us."

Calvin waved at Elizabeth. Awkwardly. She did wish Americans knew how to greet one another. Each one did it differently. A handshake. A kiss on one cheek. A kiss on two. And now—the awkward wave. America needed a national consensus on this matter. "It was a pleasure," Calvin added, dipping his head a bit. Then he disappeared inside, his sister close behind.

The door was almost shut.

As if acting on its own, Elizabeth's foot stopped it.

"Wait," she called after them. "He's coming to my house tonight."

Frances froze and pulled Calvin's arm. They both came back outside. "The Little Man?" Frances asked. "The Prince of Wales? Is coming to your house tonight?"

Elizabeth nodded.

"You must be joking!"

"No," Elizabeth said. "My mother is having a party tonight at our home in Westminster. The prime minister is coming, and the Prince of Wales is supposed to attend as well, and several of his friends . . ."

"Tonight?" Calvin asked. He was beaming. Well and truly beaming. "So where's the after-party?"

Elizabeth furrowed her brow. "The what?"

Frances and her brother shared a silent note of shock. "The after-party, silly!" Frances said. "Where you escape to after being a dutiful daughter all night."

Calvin studied Elizabeth's face. He raised his eyebrows. "Wait," he said. "You don't actually think the parties our parents throw are *parties*, do you?"

Elizabeth didn't know what to say. The only parties she'd ever been to were hosted by her mother or her parents' associates. She wasn't really allowed to go anywhere else in the evening. That's why she spent so much time with Miss Kilman, why she traipsed to this very church; it was the only way to get away from her parents without a big fight. She didn't—as Mama presumed—really even like her tutor all that much. And Elizabeth surely hadn't attended late-night parties. She was supposed to dance with William Titcomb and get engaged, but she ran from social things, really. She preferred the country to London, truth be told. Elizabeth shrugged an admission.

"Oh my god!" France squealed. "How have you *survived* all this time? You poor thing! Have you ever had a stitch of fun in your life? Have you?"

"Well, I like to ride horses—"

"No, not that type of fun. I mean *fun*, fun," Frances said.

Calvin shook his head as if he'd just encountered the rarest of creatures on earth—the seventeen-year-old girl who'd been cloistered in London with the adults.

"Tonight," Frances said. "Just ask the Prince of Wales or someone from his cohort where the after-party is. There might be a British word for it, I don't know. Just ask him where he is going *after*. Will you? Oh, say you will! We'll be ready as soon as we can get away from Grim and the pastor's dreadful children. Nine o'clock? You have a driver, don't you? Can you come get us?" Frances hopped a little, light on her toes.

Elizabeth wanted to say she couldn't do it. That it simply wasn't done—asking to be invited places. It was something her poor relations would do—Ellie Henderson and such. That wing of Mama's family.

But that way Calvin had about him, how he had leaned against the church. How he was making her forget about Peter Walsh for all this time now. And that swing in the hem of Frances's skirt.

Unfettered.

They were so unfettered.

She'd met so few boys like this, and she'd certainly never met a girl like Frances.

"I'll talk to him," Elizabeth said. "But I can't make any promises."

"Fabulous." Calvin opened the church door again.

"We're coming, Father!" Frances called into the darkness.

Calvin turned to Elizabeth, leaned close. "See how she did that?" he whispered. "She's about to ask him if we can go to a party tonight. So it's *Father* all the way."

"You're the berries," Frances said, still beaming. She blew Elizabeth a kiss. (A kiss!) "You're just—the berries. We'll see you tonight."

And they were gone.

The church door swung closed, and Calvin and Frances Gage disappeared inside—Frances's peach dress, her blond bob, Calvin's ukulele, his smile, all of it. Gone. If it weren't for Calvin's cast-off suit coat still sitting among the flies in the garbage bin, Elizabeth would think these two American siblings had been specters she'd imagined. A wild American daydream.

Elizabeth stood in the cool shadows of the alleyway, engulfed now in the sounds of the nearby street—an organ-grinder, the bark of a dog, the honk of motorcars, a vendor shouting about warm peanuts for sale.

She didn't move. She didn't start for the street. She didn't even glance down the alley to see if Miss Kilman was looking for her. Instead, something on the ground caught her eye, just next to her feet. There, next to the church door was something Elizabeth had missed entirely.

A flower pot.

A stone one.

Filled with a tangle of flowers, their petals spotted with black dirt, a bit of splashed mud from the alley. Even a few weeds peeking out.

Elizabeth didn't know why, didn't have a clue on earth why, but as she stared at those flowers, she knew something as sure as she'd known anything in her entire life—

Something wonderful was about to happen to her. Something was beginning, something had arrived.

And then, as if she had never noticed the passage of time before this moment, Elizabeth felt the day stretch before her, an endless expanse that might take years to cross. An eon between now and nine o'clock. Between now and the moment she was to see Calvin and Frances again.

She walked back down the alley, begging for Big Ben to chime.

Thinking of the hours.

For the first time.

Feeling, like she'd heard her mother say, that the hour Elizabeth had just passed through was going to leave its mark.

CHAPTER 10

Octavia

So Mum had been right. Octavia was easy prey on the streets of London, low-hanging fruit for men with dark motives. Now she was penniless in this city—without food, without water, without a ticket home, without a plan for what to do once it got dimpsy. She hadn't been in London for an hour and she'd lost all her father's earnings. What would happen in another hour, another ten minutes, even? She wondered if she'd even make it that long.

A woman caught her eye. She was some distance away, and Octavia thought she looked old—thirty at least—with lips like red helleborines, brave, proud. She looked fancy, all done up, maybe a lady or a duchess. She stood out in the crowd, hanging about the door to a men's hat shop. Probably cooling off under the shop's awning, silver-green like the belly of a fish. Octavia's spirits rose a bit. Maybe this woman could help her. Maybe Octavia could beg for a spot of change to help her get to Bloomsbury. Octavia went toward the woman. She smoothed the bodice of her dress, gave her pocket watch a gentle tap, thankful she'd decided to pin it to her dress and not keep it in her purse, or it would have been gone with all her dosh. Thank goodness for that.

But as she got closer, the woman came into better focus. Her orchid-red lipstick was creeping at the corners of her mouth, upward, almost like a clown's tiny smile. The makeup around her eyes was smudged, and her dress was too tight, ratty in bits, with a tear in the hem. Her hair was one gust of wind away from falling out of its pins; it looked heavy like it needed a good scrub. The woman caught the eye of a man coming toward the shop and raised her brows, suggesting. She parted her too-red lips in a sickening grin.

Octavia stopped, began to back up.

I'll die here. I'll die on the streets of this city or end up selling my body like that.

The sight of the prostitute was too much. Octavia hurried down the street, tears streaming from her eyes. A woman carrying a basket of bread saw Octavia, noticed she was crying; Octavia was sure of it. But the bread woman walked past. She didn't even slow down. And another stranger and then another made eye contact with Octavia, looked a little disturbed by her tears, but not enough to so much as pause.

Was she really so common a sight? Did crying girls in out-of-style dresses haunt the streets on a daily basis? Were the people of London this harsh, this cruel, too busy to stop and help a stranger? She felt as a pigeon must, pecking along, cooing for crumbs, a street pest to be tolerated. Barely counting as a bird.

Octavia sped up, pushed past the crowds. She raced faster and faster, not knowing what to do, where to turn for help. She decided she needed to find the police station. Surely if she threw herself on their mercy, one of them would help her. Wasn't that what they were supposed to do? To help? But they would be crooked too. Who knew what they might do to her—

Something struck her toe.

She didn't have time to see what it was.

She tripped, let out a cry as she fell, her palms burning as they struck the sidewalk. Sharp chips of gravel bit her cheek; she tasted the iron of her own blood on her tongue. The whole world came to a crashing halt as she lay there like a biscuit thrown in the bin.

"You all right, Miss?"

It was a boy. About her age, leaning over her looking concerned. His shoulders seemed sturdy, his face marked by sun and city smoke. He seemed steady, moored to one spot here beside her. He seemed good.

Another thief.

"Stay back!" Octavia shouted, scooting herself away from him. It hurt to bend one of her knees as she moved. It was skinned; blood was seeping through her skirt. But she forced herself to keep going, inch by inch.

"Easy there, Miss," the boy said. He held a rag ball under one arm, and the sleeves of his white blouse were rolled up above his elbows. His cheeks sported a damp red glow. "I'm not going to hurt you. More than I already have anyway." He smiled sheepishly and held up the rag ball. "If I'd blocked that goal properly, the ball wouldn't have rolled under your feet like that." He gestured toward the street behind him. She saw a gang of boys and makeshift football goals made of overturned bins in the street. They must have been playing and she'd tripped over their ball.

"Get away from me," Octavia said. "Just get away. My father is here," she lied. She looked up and down the streets as if she were looking for him, expecting him to show up any minute. "He will be none too pleased about you talking to me, tripping me. I promise you that. And I have brothers! Very tall and strong and we're going to Bloomsbury to find—" She stopped. Thought of Septimus.

Septimus. Where are you? I need you. I so desperately need you. I can't survive without you.

The boy looked at her, as if he knew how awful she felt, coiled in a ball on the pavement, bleeding like an alley dog who'd been tumbled under the wheels of a motorcar. Like he knew she was lying about her father being nearby, like he was very concerned about the reason she felt she had to.

Kindness. He looked at her with kindness.

"Well, I tell you what," the boy said, backing off a bit, giving Octavia some room. He turned and looked toward his mates in the street. "You lot! Catch!" He tossed the rag ball toward them and turned back to Octavia. "Why don't I help you up and get you something to drink while you wait for your pop, eh?"

Octavia kept inching away. "I don't have any money," she said. She put a hand to her cheek; it was scraped, and painful too. "If that's what you're thinking. I don't have a penny for you to steal. So it's not worth your time. I'm not worth your time. So just get on your way."

He crouched down. Reached out a hand. "My name is Redvers," he said. "And I don't want your money."

"Then what is it you want?" Octavia asked.

"It may be hard for you to believe, Miss. But . . ." He stopped and looked over each shoulder as if he wanted to make sure no one was within earshot to hear the secret he was about to tell her. He looked back into her eyes, leaned a little closer. Spoke in a whisper, grinning all the while. "I'd like to help you. If you need it, that is."

"Like I said, my father is—" She stopped and looked down at her hands, brushed the grit from her palms. She stared at her thin veins, branching underneath the pale skin of her wrists.

Blue. Like azured harebell.

She thought of the hill behind Stroud. The ribbons of cold limestone. The orchids, helleborine-red. The blanket where she'd sat with Septimus, where she'd listened to Shakespeare for the very first time. She thought of the letter he'd left her.

"But you, sister, have veins like the azured harebell—fine, blue, and sturdy. You will bloom, I know. Take root."

She thought of the telegram her mother had given her, the news that Septimus was in this very city, at this very moment. Haunting some boardinghouse in Bloomsbury, waiting to be rescued by his loyal sister.

Who he had mistakenly assumed had sturdy veins.

She would have to fake it. She had no choice. She would have to pretend she was as strong as Septimus thought she was. She would have to make this boy think she was made of limestone, that she wasn't someone easily crushed. Because she needed help. She desperately needed help.

Octavia looked up at Redvers. Took his hand.

"If you hurt me," she began, leaning close, making sure there was no room for misunderstanding. She locked her blue eyes on his. "I'll kill you."

Redvers looked a bit shocked. But a small grin returned, without condescension. He looked like someone does when they've been threatened by an equal, sure of the danger, but impressed because of it. Up for the challenge.

"Duly noted, Miss," he said. He put an arm around her waist and slowly helped her to her feet. "Duly noted."

————

"Who you got here, Red?" It was a little boy, no more than seven. He'd come running from the street game. Red had helped Octavia to a bench to cool her off. Rest her pins.

"Pardon his manners," Redvers said, nodding at the little boy. "This bloke here is George. Otherwise known as my baby brother." Redvers put his arm around him now, ruffled his hair. "Got to watch him, now, he'll take the piss."

"No, I won't!" George protested. "And I'm no baby either." He skipped over to Octavia and doffed his too-big cap. "Pleased to meet you, me lady."

"Hello, George. I'm Octavia." She smiled at him, deciding on the spot he was the dearest boy she'd ever seen, aside from her own little brother Ronnie, of course, whom she missed desperately. In an instant, she loved everything about George—his spunky blue suspenders, the ratty cuffs on his pants, the brightness of his smile, his cheeks, his eyes sparkling and sugary as if sweetened with a bit of Tate & Lyle's Golden Syrup. As if, to him, being too poor to own proper-fitting clothes was the greatest thing in the world. "And no need to call me lady. I'm a far cry from that. Just a girl from Stroud."

"Georgie, it's about time to go. You ready?"

"Where are we going?" he asked.

Redvers looked at Octavia. "We're accompanying this fine lady to Bloomsbury."

"No need," Octavia said, trying to hold herself up, fake a bit of dignity. "I can get there on my own." She'd told him of Septimus. He'd guessed her predicament in this city. Octavia felt that being alone in London broadcast itself, as if one of those skywriting airplanes followed her every move, advertised her situation.

"It's no trouble, Miss!" George said. He held out his hands and helped her from the bench. The three of them started down the street, George skipping beside her, moving, she thought, like the freest creature on earth. Freer than even the breezes that blew across the Stroud hills. "And you can call me Georgie! That's what they all do, anyway." He pointed over his shoulder at the gang of boys behind them, who were still kicking the rag ball between the makeshift goals. Several of them looked up, noticing now that Redvers and Georgie were leaving. A redheaded boy with a pigeon feather sticking out of his cap ran up behind them.

"Hey," he said. He touched Redvers on the shoulder. Octavia thought it was less of a tap and more of a shove. "You doing a scarper or what?"

Redvers didn't slow down. He didn't even look back at the boy. "No. We'll be there, don't worry your pretty little head." Redvers held up his hand, gave the gruff boy a half wave. "Now bugger off."

The boy stopped in the street as Redvers, Georgie, and Octavia continued to walk away. "Belgrave and Eaton. At sunset," he bellowed. "You better turn up!"

"I said we'll be there," Redvers answered. "Piss off!"

The redhead made a little sound like a chuff and returned to the football game. Octavia turned her head and watched the boy go, shocked by the language between these two. "Who was that?" she asked.

"My best friend." Redvers shrugged.

"Your *best friend*? And that's how you speak to each other?"

"Oh," Georgie piped up, taking Octavia's hand now, "Tom and Red say much worse than that, Miss. *Much* worse."

Redvers ran around Octavia and playfully grabbed his brother away from her, boxed him about the ears. Georgie giggled as his cap fell into the street.

"Don't listen to this fool." Redvers gave Georgie one more soft punch on the shoulder and picked up his brother's cap. He brushed it off, put it back on Georgie's head, and winked at Octavia. "I promise you I'm a perfect gentleman through and through."

Octavia laughed in spite of herself. She'd become distracted by these two; they were melting her resolve to be cautious, to feign city-girl smarts. And why was Redvers meeting Tom at sunset?

The pain came back, too, from her fall. The cuts on her knee, her scraped hands, the gravel bite on her cheek. She thought of that awful thief who'd taken her purse. She reminded herself that Redvers could be a boy like that, after all. Just because he was clever and clearly loved his little brother to bits didn't make him honorable. Maybe he was leading her to some dark alley where—she couldn't even imagine what.

"Is this the way to Bloomsbury?" Octavia asked, her worry returning full force. "I need you to take me there straightaway." She walked a little taller once more, told herself to broadcast a bravery she knew she didn't have.

"You got the Underground fare to get there?" Redvers asked. "It's four pennies each return. Because at a pace like this, it'll take us till we're fifty to walk."

Octavia flushed, stopped in the middle of the busy sidewalk. A few people in the crowd bumped against her. She stood her ground. "No, I don't have the fare," she said. "Like I told you before, I have no money. So there's nothing for you to steal. And you promised me you'd get me to Bloomsbury."

Redvers smiled and offered her his arm. "What I meant was, I'm going to show you how to get there. How to get the fare, I mean. And then I'll send you on your way."

Octavia refused his arm. The prostitute she'd seen in front of the men's hat shop flashed in her mind. What did Redvers have in mind? Surely, he couldn't mean he was going to make her *earn* her fare in some dark way. She glared at him. "If you hurt me, if you have any ideas . . . I'll—"

"You've scared her, Red!" Georgie said, swatting at his older brother. He took Octavia's other arm. "We're not like that, me lady. What my brother means is, it's an awful long way to go. And your gams are all beat-up." He nodded at the bloodstain on her skirt from her gashed knee. "So we just need to help you drum up the fare, that's all."

"And I'd like to send you with more dosh in your pocket than just the fare. You're going to need it in this city," Redvers said. He became quiet. He looked at the ground and gently kicked a piece of gravel with his boot toe. "I'm not very good at this, you know."

"Good at what?" Octavia asked. She let Georgie keep hold of her hand and lead her down the street. "Getting train fare?"

Redvers smiled softly now; Octavia was sure his hazel eyes were pooling with a bit with feeling—but what feeling?

"No, Miss. I'm an ace at getting train fare," Redvers said. "But not so good at talking to pretty girls."

"Oh," Octavia said. The feeling she'd seen in his eyes, she knew what it was now—shyness. Yes, that was it. He was shy. Behind all that confidence was a boy who was a bit shy. And no one had *ever* told her she was pretty. "You're too kind."

"There are a thousand ways to get a bit of dosh in your pocket in this city," he said, his spirits picking up after her compliment. "And I know all of them. But first . . ." He stopped abruptly in front of a shop. He held his hand up at the sign as if he were a circus ringmaster introducing his first act.

BOOTS PHARMACY

LARGEST RETAIL CHEMISTS IN THE WORLD

He glanced at the cut on her cheek. "We need to get those scrapes fixed up."

Georgie gently pulled Octavia toward the shop as Redvers pushed the door open, the bells above it announcing their arrival.

Octavia stiffened as they entered, intimidated, her shoes tapping on the black-and-white tile floor. The shop looked lovely, shiny even, and most everything seemed expensive. She gazed at gleaming glass bottles—brown, blue, red, green—all lined up like exotic fruit on the shop's walnut shelves. There were elixirs for melancholy, for the liver, for women's hair. In a glass case near the register, she spotted tins of brain salts, tonics for lice, chest creams for tuberculosis. Carved into the molding above a large section of cabinets was the word *prescriptions*.

On a counter underneath, several marble mortars sat patiently, their pestles at the ready.

Stroud had a few shops that sold medicines and such, but they certainly weren't fancy like this and they weren't called pharmacies at all; they were called chemists. And Octavia had rarely gone in; Mum made most of the medical remedies they needed from their garden—elixirs made from milk thistle and goldenseal. Lavender and honey.

Ladies strolled about the fancy pharmacy in stylish dresses—waistlines dropped, their fabric almost gauzy, loosely cut, so heavenly, Octavia thought. Some were studying the adverts on the walls, big posters proclaiming miracle products for all sorts of things.

DR. WILLIAMS'S PINK PILLS FOR PALE PEOPLE

ASPIRONAL: BETTER THAN WHISKEY FOR GRIPPE AND COLDS

BEECHAM'S PILLS. THEY MAKE LIFE WORTH LIVING!

Octavia eyed Redvers from across the shop. If he didn't have any money for Underground fare, just how was he planning on buying anything for her from this place? Was he going to nick some bandages? Pocket a tube of cream for her cuts? She envisioned them all spending the night in jail, locked up for being petty thieves.

"Hello, Mr. Lewis!" Redvers called to the man behind the counter.

"Redvers!" the man said. "What brings you in on a Wednesday? Nothing serious, I hope?" Mr. Lewis wore a cream-colored smock cinched at the waist. "Pharmacist" was stitched over his breast pocket, and Octavia could see his bright-white shirt and dark tie underneath. His small nose and round spectacles made him look distinctly like an owl.

"No, no, nothing too bad," Redvers said, leaning against the glass case by the register. George stood on tiptoe beside him, watching his brother intently. Redvers cleared his throat and scanned the shelves behind Mr. Lewis. "What have you got for some pretty rough scrapes?"

Mr. Lewis moved his spectacles down his nose a bit and eyed Redvers over the top of his frames. "You don't look scratched up to me." Then he looked down at George. "And Georgie, you're looking sharp as ever."

Octavia ducked behind a rack of cigarettes, pretended she was studying a poster for Calvert's Anti-Mosquito Soap. She feared Redvers was about to make his master move, to perform some sleight of hand while the pharmacist looked poor Georgie over, nick a handful of cash from the till.

"It's for her," Redvers said. "Octavia?"

Oh, no.

She had no choice but to peek from behind a large box of cigarettes. Mr. Lewis looked her up and down. She knew her manners; she should've walked straight to the counter, offered her hand, a proper greeting. Instead, she just stood there, still half-hidden like a distrustful alley cat being offered a bowl of milk.

"Well, why didn't you say so, Red?" Mr. Lewis came around the counter and approached Octavia, looking very concerned. "My dear girl, you look dreadful. What happened?"

"I—I . . . fell." She kept her eyes on the toes of her shoes, not daring to meet Mr. Lewis's gaze. She so wanted to be strong, to be stoic, to know exactly what to do. How was she going to find Septimus in this maze of a city when she couldn't even stop these awful tears in her eyes in the middle of a chemist?

"May I?" Mr. Lewis gestured toward her cheek, and Octavia nodded. He gently turned her face to get a better look at her gash. "Ah, well, that's awful-looking, but I don't think you need any stitching. But we need to get you cleaned up and properly bandaged. You don't want an infection." He smiled sweetly. She wanted to fall into the kindness in his eyes, but then she remembered—

"I don't have any money," she said. "I can't accept your—"

"It's on the house," Mr. Lewis said, still with that smile. He gently led her behind the glass case, behind the register. They stopped next to the countertop littered with mortars and pestles. He asked her to sit on a metal stool. "Any friend of Redvers is a friend of Boots."

Georgie plopped on the floor at Octavia's feet, cross-legged and gazing up at her like he couldn't bear to be more than a few feet away from her for any time at all. Not even while a pharmacist dabbed her wounds with a cotton ball covered in antiseptic. Not even while she winced as it stung her cheek, her palms, her knees. Mr. Lewis carefully covered her cuts with a salve that felt heavenly. He bandaged her knees and two little places on her hands, but she refused a bandage for her cheek. She was too embarrassed. A scab was better than looking like she'd just come out of an army hospital with her face wrapped up.

When he was finished, Octavia said again how sorry she was that she didn't have any money to pay Mr. Lewis for his time or his treatments. She even asked Redvers if he had anything he could give the pharmacist; she would find a way to pay him back.

"My money is no good here," Redvers said, helping her up from the stool. "Even if I had it, he wouldn't take it. Isn't that right, Mr. Lewis?"

"That's spot-on." Mr. Lewis went to the register to assist a gentleman who was waiting. The customer had a giant tin of herbal asthma rub and a box of cigars. He was coughing terribly. "Now, off with you. I've got customers waiting," Mr. Lewis said. "And, Redvers, make sure your lady friend doesn't overexert herself."

Outside the shop, Octavia moved gingerly. It felt strange to walk with the bandages on her knees; she could feel the gauze pull and bunch with her movements. Redvers and Georgie weren't rushing her, though; they seemed utterly content to limp along the streets of London with her, however long it took.

"So how did you manage that?" Octavia asked. "Are you some sort of heir to a chemist fortune you haven't mentioned? Is your name Redvers Boots?"

"Nah," Redvers said, chuckling. Octavia couldn't be sure, but she thought he was blushing. "I don't have a penny to my name, really. And any I do get, I give to my mum. But . . ." He paused and stuffed his hands in his pockets as they continued their stroll. "I like to think I'm somebody in this city. Or at least a few leagues from a nobody."

Octavia felt a tug on her sleeve. It was Georgie. He was pointing back at Boots. "See those boards there?"

Octavia turned. Leaning against the side of the pharmacy were several large sandwich boards with leather straps hanging from them. Octavia couldn't read all the words painted on the black boards, but she could make out enough of the white lettering to see they were advertisements for Boots Pharmacy.

"On Saturdays, Red and I wear those and walk the block here." Georgie spun around, pointing up and down the street. "BOOTS IS THE SPOT!" he shouted. "FIX ANY ACHE YOU GOT!" He kept it up, yelling at the top of his lungs, pointing back to the pharmacy, and tipping his cap to any person who stopped to listen to him. His charm and joy were magnetic; even without wearing the sandwich board, he pulled in several ladies with his Boots chants.

"First-rate salesman, that Georgie," Redvers said, admiring his brother. "I worked this out with Mr. Lewis right after Georgie was born, in fact. My mum says babies ought to come with a stocked medicine cabinet. So, I got her one. I got her the entire Boots Pharmacy." He smiled and gently plucked one of Georgie's suspenders, letting it snap back against his brother's chest. "And we haven't paid for so much as a bandage since, have we, Georgie?"

"That's right!"

"I think that's so . . ." Octavia paused, searching for words to describe these two brothers. "Resourceful. So very clever, really."

"And we're just getting started." Redvers's chest puffed up a bit. "I promise you that."

"Just getting started?" Octavia asked. "What do you mean?"

"Well," Redvers said, "between here and Bloomsbury, I'd like to show you a few things. If you'll let me, that is."

"No, no," Octavia said quickly. "I've *got* to get to my brother, to Bloomsbury. I can't be clucking about this city like a chicken in a coop! I haven't got time."

"All right, all right," Redvers said, holding his hands in the air as if to surrender. "We'll just drum up a little dosh for Underground fare and go straightaway. Won't we, Georgie?"

Georgie grinned. "We sure will."

"We won't show Octavia even one nice thing in this city," Redvers added, gently shaking his head. "We won't treat her to even a bit of fun. Noway. Nohow. Isn't that right, Georgie?"

Georgie squeezed Octavia's hand. "Sure thing, Red. We won't treat our lady a bit."

Octavia couldn't help but smile. Again.

"Our lady."

And off they went.

CHAPTER 11

Elizabeth

She stood at the garden gate. She was back home. Back on Hyde Street. Miss Kilman had left after the church service; Elizabeth had missed her. Elizabeth looked down, plucked the now-wilted dandelion from her dress, and tossed it on the sidewalk. She'd need to get a fresh one for tonight.

Tonight.

In eight hours she'd be soliciting the Prince of Wales for an invitation he might not extend. In ten she'd be picking up Calvin and Frances. Time! It was as if it had entered her life today for the very first time, arrived with a horsewhip and fury, chasing the hours, driving them ahead, now yanking the reins, bringing life to a halt. And carrying Peter Walsh closer and closer to Mama. He should be here anytime now.

She opened the gate.

Mr. Garrick was kneeling next to a large sack of soil, scooping trowelfuls into the phlox bed, looking at the pink flowers as if they'd just insulted him. His gardener's apron was smeared with dirt, his gray hair looked almost white in the sun. Grizzle was at Mr. Garrick's side, keeping a watchful eye on the apron pocket where he kept crusts of bread and spare seeds for the birds. Grizzle was quite attached to Mr. Garrick, and it wasn't due to his pocketful of crumbs. Mr. Garrick was as much a part of the Dalloway family as the very Dalloway house itself. He'd been with Mama since she was first married; Elizabeth simply didn't have any memories of home without him and neither did Grizzle.

"Hello, Mr. Garrick," Elizabeth called, surveying his plants. "Are the phlox planning a mutiny?"

"Afraid so," he replied. Grizzle tore through the garden and leapt at Elizabeth's knees. "But the good news is that Grizzle behaved as a perfect gentleman in your absence."

"Is that so?" She knelt and rubbed the warm spots behind Grizzle's ears.

"Other than making a ruckus when Scrope and—pardon me—Lord and Lady Purvis were departing, that is," Mr. Garrick said, wiping his brow with his garden glove. He gestured at the Purvises' home next door. "Must have been six staff out front of the residence with all that luggage. I believe Lady Rose had six trunks at least! So we can't blame Grizzle for that, really. It was quite a sight."

Elizabeth glanced at the Purvises' home. She was relieved Rose was gone for the season. She was so perfect with her blond curls and pristine dresses. Elizabeth knew she'd grow up and be all the things—all the perfect things. And Rose didn't like horses or dogs. Elizabeth never trusted anyone who didn't like at least one of them. Through a side window on the first floor, she could see the furniture had been covered with white sheets, a parlor full of ghosts assembled for afternoon tea. The curtains were drawn on the second and third floors. "They've gone for the rest of the season, then?"

Mr. Garrick nodded. "Mallorca, I believe. That's what the society column announced. Lady Purvis never tells your mother anything, you know. Really, it's very awkward." He glanced at Elizabeth and held his gaze for just a moment. "You're looking rather pink. I'd venture to say chipper, even. Where were you off to in such a hurry this morning?"

"Chipper?" Elizabeth asked. She wasn't sure anyone had ever said that of her. That she was pink. Lively. Lucy often said Elizabeth was a pale hyacinth, a flower in need of sun. But then again, Elizabeth knew full well Mr. Garrick loved her like a grandfather; if anyone was to pay a compliment like that, it would be him. "I just came from seeing Miss Kilman, at that church in Kensington, but of course, don't tell Mama that. But the most extraordinary thing happened. I met these . . . siblings. From the United States. Pennsylvania, I think? They were so strange. So . . ."

"American?"

"Yes." Elizabeth smiled. She sat in the wrought-iron garden chair, her mother's favorite. It was so uncomfortable, so stiff, as if it were designed to keep people out of it. "Yes, that's probably it. American." She ran her hand over Grizzle's warm back. Gave him a gentle scratch at the base of his tail. How calming it was, to pet a dog. "And they were . . . oh, I'm just not sure how to describe them, really."

"Americans are often beyond description," Mr. Garrick said. "You won't be the first to notice that, I assure you." He set his trowel in the phlox bed and began the task of standing up—a job that, in the last few years, had started to give him considerable difficulty.

"Don't get up on my account," Elizabeth said. "Take one eye off those treasonous flowers and they may very well have your head." She looked at the blooms sternly, a momentary coconspirator against the unruly plants. Mr. Garrick grinned and sat back on his heels, wiped his brow.

"Indeed, they might," he said. He winced and rubbed a knee. "I miss the joints of my youth." His laugh was thin.

It was difficult to see him age. Mama loved to tell the story of how she had hired him the very week she was married; how he had helped her assemble her household, decide what went where, which flower bed should abut the next. If he was a grandfather to Elizabeth, he was a near parent to her mother. In fact, Mama often seemed almost girlish in his presence, she trusted him so.

Which gave Elizabeth an idea.

"Mr. Garrick, might I ask you a question? About one of Mama's acquaintances?"

"Of course, my lady," he said. "How may I be of service?"

"Well," Elizabeth said, looking at the delicate, helmet-shaped bloom of wolfsbane. She stood from the chair and plucked the flower. "It's nothing, really. I just wondered if you knew someone in Mama's . . . orbit, shall we say. A Mr. Peter Walsh?"

"Ah," Mr. Garrick said with a sigh. "You must have seen him on your way home from Kensington."

"Seen him?" Elizabeth asked. "He's here already?"

"Unfortunately," Mr. Garrick said. "I wish he'd stay in India for once. He pops in here every time he's home. Every five years or so. As if this is some sort of public house for transients from the Indian subcontinent. A pub one ducks into for refreshment after a long journey!"

"Lucy told me I've met him, but I don't remember—"

"Lucy?" Mr. Garrick said. "Lucy was talking to you about Mr. Walsh?"

Elizabeth was taken aback; she couldn't recall a time Mr. Garrick had interrupted her like that.

"Who is he, Mr. Garrick?"

"He's one of your mother's childhood friends, nothing more," he said, casually brushing a bit of dirt from his sleeve. "From her Bourton days. And of course, we all know how important Bourton is to your mother. They were in the same social circle just before your mother married. When she was just about—"

"My age?"

"I suppose that's right. I'd never considered that. They were just about your age that summer—1889, it was."

"So Peter and Mama were friends? Childhood friends?" Elizabeth eyed Mr. Garrick. In particular, his shoulders. Had they tightened up at the mention of Peter's name? Grown closer to his ears?

"Mr. Walsh is one of the old crowd," Mr. Garrick continued. "Even after your mother was married, he and several others used to hang about the house when I was first hired on. Hugh Whitbread, Peter, Joseph Breitkopf, a Miss Sally Seton. Her best friends from her youth. But they all trailed off as time wended its way, you know, as childhood friends tend to do. Their paths diverged. But Peter's seems to lead him back here every few years." Mr. Garrick reached into his apron pocket and held out a crumb for Grizzle. "You've met him a few times, when you were a little one. And if you ask me, you are quite lucky if you don't remember it."

"Lucky?"

"A gentleman should not speak ill of anyone, my lady." He struggled to his knees and went back to his work.

Elizabeth knelt beside him. "But it's me," she whispered. His eyes softened under his graying eyebrows. He was an owl. A dear, sweet owl who dedicated himself to perching over the Dalloway grounds. Chasing off rodents. Standing guard. "You don't have to be a gentleman around . . . family," she continued. "Do you?"

A melancholy but satisfied smile crept across Mr. Garrick's lips. Like it was a burden to adore Elizabeth so. He glanced at the sky. "May heaven forgive me," he said. He looked back at Elizabeth. "It's well known in London society that Peter wanted to marry your mother, and that there was a . . . well, your father was the suitor who prevailed. That is all. Please don't search further than that."

"Mr. Garrick," Elizabeth said, leaning closer. "Tell me what you know."

"Elizabeth," he said. He was stern now, more than he'd ever been with her, his face closing like a sealed letter, ready for the post. "I've said enough, and I ask that you release me from this uncomfortable inquiry."

She felt remorseful now for pressuring him. "I'm sorry," she said, rising from her knees, wiping a few blades of grass from her dress. "I won't tell anyone we spoke of this, dear Mr. Garrick. I won't say a word."

She kissed his cheek just before running off, Grizzle at her heels.

"Where are you heading now, Miss?"

Elizabeth stopped and turned.

"To talk to Peter Walsh, of course."

She dashed up the front steps and disappeared into the house.

———

The drawing-room door was closed tight.

Elizabeth held Grizzle in her arms and pressed her ear against the cool wood.

It was no use. Mr. Walsh's and Mama's voices were too muffled; she couldn't make out what they were saying. She looked at the handle of the door, the brass knob kept shiny and clean by Lucy at all times. She wondered if she should turn it, open the door just a crack. Mr. Garrick had all but confirmed there was some secret Mama shared with this man. She eased the door open.

"I often wish I'd got on better with your father," Peter was saying. He was settled on the blue sofa next to Mama, a small horn-handled pocketknife in his hand. Strangely, he was flipping it open and shut.

Open and shut.

Elizabeth stared at him, at his checked suit, his weathered skin, his slightly graying hair and sunburnt cheeks. He really was handsome, Elizabeth thought. Handsome in a way that most of Mama's acquaintances weren't. He looked as though he had money, had come from a prosperous family, but had chosen to spend his life out of doors all the same. Which was very strange. All the guests coming and in and out of Mama's drawing room were as white as paper, the occasional foxhunt not being nearly enough to leave a kiss of color on their faces.

No, this man was . . . different. Vaguely familiar somehow. Was that it? Yes, as if she had seen him before, and had remembered it too. Somewhere beyond memory, an impression left on her childhood mind, one she couldn't see but could sense only the outlines. She felt as though she knew him.

"But he never liked anyone who—our friends," said Mama. There was a long pause in their conversation then. Much too long of a pause.

Peter snapped his pocketknife shut and edged closer to Mama on the sofa. Mama's silver-green dress was on her lap, her sewing box beside her, the leather one. She must have been mending when Peter arrived. And there, beneath the dress, Elizabeth could see something else.

Peter's thigh was touching her mother's leg.

Touching.

They were touching.

She'd never seen such a thing: Mama sitting so close to a man. Mama *touching* someone like that. Mama barely touched her own family, for God's sake. Elizabeth had seen Mama entertain countless guests, but there was always a stuffiness that pervaded those visits, particularly those that occurred before midday. Stuffy, boring morning callers. Elizabeth had seen hundreds. Maybe thousands.

This wasn't one of them.

Peter put out his hand as if to take Mama's but let it fall back to his lap.

"Herbert has it now," Mama said rather abruptly. Too loud or too forced, Elizabeth couldn't tell which. A non sequitur for certain. Elizabeth knew Mama was talking about Bourton, how Uncle Herbert had it now and was letting the estate rot to pieces. Elizabeth had been there only a handful of times growing up. "I never go there now," Mama added. Another terrible pause filled the room. "Do you remember the . . . lake?"

Lake.

The way she said it was . . . disturbing. As if her voice were crumbling, her throat collapsing around the word. Was she about to cry? Elizabeth had never seen her mother cry. Ever. Not even at Grandpapa Parry's funeral. It was almost unbearable to see her mother saddened like this.

"Yes," Peter said, leaning in. "Yes, yes, yes." His face looked almost pained when he said it. Yes, it was pain Elizabeth could see. Had she ever seen a man look this way? She'd seen men bored, angry, impassioned, or just plain cheeky. But never in pain—the kind that wasn't physical, anyway. Elizabeth wasn't even sure men felt things like that. Pains of the heart.

Mama wiped her eyes. Was that a tear? Peter still looked distressed, glanced about the room now, as if he wanted to see something else, *be* somewhere else. His eyes moved over the inlaid table, the crystal dolphin and the candlesticks, the chair covers and the old, valuable English tinted prints. He clenched the handle of his closed pocketknife.

Elizabeth heard something.

Behind her.

Coming up the staff stairway, the unmistakable clinking of silver on a tray.

Lucy.

Coming up from the kitchen below, undoubtedly bringing things for tonight's party. Elizabeth dashed into the library so as not to be discovered eavesdropping. Lucy entered the drawing room without so much as a knock or word. Which was odd. Lucy always knocked. She always asked for permission to enter. Did she *want* to interrupt Peter and Mama? Elizabeth heard a bit of shuffling, the tinkle of glass being gathered, and finally, Lucy's footsteps descending the staff stairway. Elizabeth eased back to her spot at the drawing-room door.

"Well, and what's happened to you?" Mama was asking Peter now, taking a needle and thread from her leather sewing box. She began mending the bodice on her silver-green dress ever so calmly. Ever so slowly. Even in the midst of this strange encounter, this closeness with this man, Elizabeth recognized Mama's composure. Mama had summoned it somehow, even after her voice had nearly broken to bits earlier at the mention of the lake at Bourton. Here it was, even here with this man: Mama's sameness. Her coolness. Her staid and steady way.

"Millions of things!" Peter exclaimed. "I am in love. In love with a girl in India."

"In love!" Mama said. "And who is she?"

"A married woman, unfortunately," he said, "the wife of a major in the Indian Army." Peter was in London, he explained, to see about a divorce from his current wife. So he could set about marrying this new woman—who was also married herself.

It was shocking. Multiple marriages, multiple divorces—that sort of thing didn't happen to the people Elizabeth knew. To the people Mama knew.

And with that, Peter burst into tears.

Tears.

Streaming down his face.

Tears streaming down the face of a . . . *man.*

Elizabeth could hardly believe her eyes.

Peter's shoulders quivered as he sobbed. Elizabeth expected Mama to recoil, to go cold as Elizabeth had so often seen her do when she was made uncomfortable by some vulgar display of emotion. Mama had taught Elizabeth to strive for equanimity. She extolled the virtues of always appearing the same, always being the same. Maintaining control of oneself.

"Lady Bexborough opened a bazaar with the telegram in her hand, John, her favorite—dead. What character she has."

Those sorts of things.

But now Mama didn't appear cold.

She didn't recoil.

As a flock of birds is driven from the safety of a tree's branches by a sudden sound, by the backfire of a motorcar, the rifle shot of a huntsman, so Mama's composure flapped and fluttered from her every limb, a cacophony of freedom and fear, birds of paradise on the loose.

She kissed him.

She kissed Peter Walsh. On his cheek, but she lingered. Much too long. It was intimate, that kiss. More intimate than if she had kissed his lips, as if there was some secret there, a secret shared when they touched. A secret remembered.

Then, as if nothing whatever had happened—Mama sat back against the blue sofa cushion, looked almost pleased. Almost happy.

Peter stood and went to the window, flicked his bandanna handkerchief from side to side. Elizabeth wondered if Mr. Garrick was still in the garden below, if Peter was looking down at the perfect flowerbeds, not a weed in sight.

Mama gently placed her thimble, needle, and thread in her leather sewing box; she snapped it shut, stood, and slid it into a drawer in her writing desk. She went to Peter. He placed his hands on her shoulders, faced her, his eyes still rimmed with red from his tears.

It was obvious.

This man was in love with Mama.

The woman in India was not his first choice. Neither of his wives were.

Mama was the one.

The one he desperately wanted.

The one he'd wanted since their youthful days at Bourton.

Elizabeth was sure—she could *feel* it in the room—if Peter could have his way, he'd go back in time and marry Mama. He would choose a different path, one that would erase Elizabeth's life entirely. She simply wouldn't exist. This man, this Peter Walsh, would do away with her, do away with Papa, with this house, with Mr. Garrick's gardens, would create an entirely different past and present if he could.

And Mama, would you do the same? Take an entirely different path? Is that it?

"Tell me," Peter said, still holding Mama's shoulders, "are you happy, Clarissa? Does Richard—"

Richard.

Papa.

It was too much. The mention of her father's name on this interloper's lips. Elizabeth could stay still no more. She opened the drawing-room door, brazenly stepped inside. Peter and Mama quickly parted.

"Here is my Elizabeth!" said Mama. Histrionically, Elizabeth was sure. Perhaps it made sense now, the reason Mama always called Elizabeth that—*her Elizabeth*. Was Elizabeth a possession, evidence Mama trotted out to convince herself she'd chosen the right path in life? Was that it?

"How d'you do?" Elizabeth said to Peter. Flat, chilled.

Ring. Ring. Ring. Ring.

Ding. Ding. Ding. Ding.

Big Ben struck the half-hour.

"Hullo, Elizabeth!" cried Peter, as if he and Elizabeth had met thousands of times. Had seen one another only yesterday. Such familiarity he had with her, like he *knew* her, like he really knew her. He stuffed his bandanna handkerchief in his pocket and crossed the room. He glanced at Elizabeth once more as he passed but did not look back at Mama. "Goodbye, Clarissa," he said over his shoulder.

Elizabeth heard his footsteps as he ran down the stairs.

"Peter! Peter!" Mama cried. She ran past her daughter, out to the landing. She leaned over the banister. "My party tonight!" she called after Peter. "Remember my party tonight!" The front door opened; the roar of London traffic nearly drowned Mama's voice. "Remember my party tonight!" Mama cried again. He was gone. The door shut behind him.

Mama turned and faced Elizabeth. Looked at her as if she suddenly remembered Elizabeth was in the room. Suddenly remembered she had a daughter at all.

"Care to tell me who Peter Walsh is, Mama?"

CHAPTER 12

Octavia

"Is that an . . . elephant?" Octavia asked. She heard a loud trumpeting sound as she followed Redvers and Georgie through Regent's Park. Or rather, along the backside of a large building and a tall fence in the park. They'd left the wide-open lawns without stopping.

"Sounds more like three of 'em to me," said Redvers. "For two coppers, you can ride one." He put his hands between two tall evergreen bushes and pushed them apart, clearing a path for Octavia. Beyond the bushes was a closed gate covered with creeping vines. They curled around the wrought iron, blocking the view of whatever was behind it. It was padlocked. And topped with intimidating spikes.

"Where on earth *are* we?" Octavia asked.

Georgie ran through the opening in the bushes and stood on the other side, holding his hand out for Octavia, offering to help her through. Redvers gestured toward the dirty backs of the buildings and the fence.

"Welcome to the Regent's Park Zoo, my lady," he said. "The pride of London for nearly a hundred years now."

"Yes," Octavia said slowly, looking at the intimidating iron gate. "I assumed it was a zoo of some sort, but . . ." She paused, interrupted by the trumpeting of elephants again. "Aren't we *behind* it?"

"Depends on how you look at it," Redvers said, motioning for her to go through the bushes.

Octavia took Georgie's hand and made her way between the evergreens. Redvers followed and stood beside the padlocked gate. He grabbed the handle and shook it, making a terrible clanging sound. Then he started whistling, low and steady.

Nothing happened.

He climbed to the top of the gate, stopping just below the iron spiky bits. He whistled again, louder this time.

"Hold yer horses!" A man's voice came from the other side. Octavia saw a hand reach through the vine-covered gate and pull the padlock around to his side. She heard the clicking of a key, and the gate swung open. A man in dirty blue overalls held it open with his foot. "Hey, Red."

"What took you so long?" Redvers said, ushering Octavia and Georgie ahead of him. "Piss-poor service, mate."

The man smirked and gently slapped Redvers on the back. "I'll try better next time." He held out his hand and Redvers shook it. The handshake seemed odd to Octavia. The man quickly stuffed his hands in his pockets. Then he leaned against a few sheaves of hay that lined the fence. He eyed Octavia. "And who's this?"

"Octavia," said Georgie, beaming. "She's our new friend."

"Please to meet you," the man said.

"Hello," Octavia replied. She felt embarrassed. She couldn't imagine how bad she looked. She tried to tuck her hair back in its pins, but it was useless. Nearly all of it had fallen out of the nice bun she'd had at the start of the day. Wispy strands were hanging down all over. "Pleased to meet you too."

The man kept looking at her as if not sure what to make of her. He seemed confused. "You from London?" he asked.

"No," she said. "Stroud. Cotswolds."

"Cotswolds? A nice farm girl?" He turned to Red. "Don't muck it up, mate." He smiled. "Now off with you lot. Before we get caught." He picked up a large sheaf of hay from the pile and tossed it onto a waiting cart. It landed with a loud thud; a spray of straw pieces and dust exploded around them. The honey-colored bits stuck to Octavia's skirts; she sneezed.

"I never get caught," Red said. He took Octavia's hand like it was the most natural thing in the world. Like he'd taken it hundreds, maybe thousands of times before. He gently pulled her along. "Come on, you've got to see the big cats. They've got a lion and even one of those jaguars."

Octavia's hand started to sweat as if she and Redvers were holding a hot coal between their palms. Georgie skipped ahead of them, and she softly pulled her hand out of Red's. She lingered by a cage, pretended to be interested in a large iguana that was slow-crawling up a branch. Redvers came to her side. She glanced at him out of the corner of her eye.

"What did you give that man back there?" she asked. She kept her eyes on the lizard, pretending to study its every move.

"What do you mean, what did I give him?" He stared at the iguana as it opened and shut its multilayered eyelids.

Blink. Blink. Blink.

"I meant just what I said. What did you give that man?"

"Just a gentlemanly handshake for opening the gate is all," Red said. "No crime in that, is there?"

Octavia turned to face him, raised her eyebrows. "He put something in his pocket. You gave it to him. What was it?"

"All right, all right," Redvers said. He leaned a shoulder against the lizard enclosure. "Two pennies. For letting us in. It's our arrangement."

"Two pennies?" Octavia asked. "If you were going to pay to get in, why didn't we just go through the front zoo gate? And buy proper tickets?"

"Because those cost six." Redvers grinned and offered her his arm. She didn't take it.

"I don't have time for this rubbish, you know," Octavia said, walking on. They passed a few peacocks strutting freely along the cobblestones. Two little boys chased one right across their path. She felt faint for a moment; she was so angry now, and hot to boot. How she wished she wasn't wearing her old heavy dress, with its full skirt and suffocating neck. She would give anything to be wearing one of those gauzy drop-waist numbers all the girls in London wore. She wiped her forehead. Determined to stay the course. The hours were passing too quickly. What if night fell as soon as she arrived in Bloomsbury? Where would she stay? What would she do? "I've got to get to—"

"Bloomsbury," Redvers said. "I know, I know. This is the quickest way."

Octavia glowered at him. "I may not be a London girl," she said, "but I surely know that the quickest route between two points in this city is *not* through an illegal zoo crossing."

Redvers opened his eyes wide like he'd been falsely accused of some great crime. "Who said anything about illegal?" He sped up a bit and pointed to a crowded plaza. "And besides, we're going to get our money back."

A large crowd was gathered in a cobblestone square, faint sounds of music coming from the center of it. Hippos and zebras and a few ostriches stared from surrounding enclosures.

"You don't want to miss this." Georgie tugged her quickly across the plaza. "Excuse us! Make way! Lady coming through!"

People parted immediately for Georgie. A few seemed to get a chuckle at this little boy commanding them like he owned the entire zoo. They split the herd like lions lazily dodging a whip.

Finally, Octavia could see what all the fuss was about: A man with a head full of tight black curls held a box organ in the center of the square. A little monkey was perched on his shoulder wearing a grand plumed hat and the tiniest formal jacket that looked like a military coat. It had brass buttons. Ranking stripes. The monkey's long tail curled and twitched to the sound of the cheery organ music. Children pushed in close to get a better look. A girl whom Octavia guessed to be six years old pressed ahead of her.

"Please dance, little monkey!" the girl cried. "Can you dance for us?"

The organ man moved his shoulder, nudging the monkey. "You heard them, Olek," he said. "Dance."

The monkey did not dance.

He just sat there on the man's shoulder. Octavia thought he looked bored. Like he'd heard this box-organ tune so many times it was enough to put him to sleep.

"Alex!" Redvers moved to the center of the crowd, waving at the organ-grinder. "Privyet!"

"Privyet, Red," the man replied, still playing.

"That's a Russian way of saying hello," Georgie said. He tugged on Octavia's hand. "Watch this," he whispered, giddy.

"Step up, step up!" Redvers called over the crowd. "Come see Olek, the Waltzing Monkey." Redvers made some sort of clicking sound with his tongue, and Olek climbed off the organ-grinder, swinging his way to the ground as if the man were a giant tree. Olek stood in front of Red as if awaiting instruction. Just the sound of Red's voice had snapped the monkey out of his slumber, given him a bit of a jolt. "May we have a waltz, Alex?" Red asked the organ-grinder.

The first notes rang out. Red took the monkey's hands, and as Red danced, the monkey jumped about, following Red the best he could. Around and around they went, Redvers and the monkey, as if they were at a grand ball. Octavia heard a ringing sound and eyed the crowd, trying to see who had begun to play a tambourine or perhaps some bells.

It wasn't an instrument. It wasn't bells.

It was the sound of money.

People were tossing coins into the organ-grinder's upturned hat on the ground.

Clink. Clink. Clink.

The hat was filling up as the children cheered and giggled. A few joined hands and tried to imitate Red's dance.

Octavia watched until the song was over. Redvers waved at the crowd and knelt down for Olek to hop onto his shoulder. He gently touched the monkey's nose. "Thanks, mate. A good show, that."

The crowd tossed more coins into the hat as they began to move on.

"I wish I knew your secret." The organ-grinder put his instrument on the ground. He picked up the hat and started counting the money. "And here's your half." He handed Red a handful.

"My pleasure." The monkey swung down from Red's shoulders. "See you later, Olek." Redvers sidled up next to Octavia. "I told you we'd earn our money back." He pointed toward a large exit gate on the other side of the plaza. "We've almost got enough to get the three of us to Bloomsbury and back."

It was all Octavia could do to keep her mouth from hanging wide open. "How did you do that?" she asked, following him toward the exit.

Redvers shrugged. "Animals trust me," he said. He offered his arm once again. "And you should too."

Octavia looked at him suspiciously. Georgie tugged at her hand again.

"Red carries sugar cubes in his pocket," Georgie whispered. "From the racetracks. He mucks horse stalls on Saturdays. They've got buckets of them there. And Olek loves 'em."

Red was still offering Octavia his arm.

This time, she took it.

DECEMBER 8, 1952

CHAPTER 13

Elizabeth

The fog was thickening now; Elizabeth could barely see Rose in front of her. They reached the gate to the Purvis home. Rose opened it, and they went through.

The path to the front door was obscured, nearly impossible to find. It was covered in a bit of black sludge as well; Theodore said it was happening all over the city as the soot settled out of the air—everywhere paths coated and concealed. They reached the stoop. Started up the stairs. One. Two. Three.

Elizabeth doubted herself now, her ability to follow through with this errand. She wished she'd sent Theodore in her place. All this talk of Mama, of her leaving things behind—it was stirring it all up. She felt as though swift waters were rising, edging toward the tops of their banks.

Up the last three steps. Four. Five. Six.

Rose stopped. She didn't open the front door. She must have noticed Elizabeth's . . . hesitation.

"I'm afraid I've been inconsiderate," Rose said. "Mother heard you were very ill just last week. I should have spoken with Theodore about this earlier."

Ill.

Had Elizabeth been ill? She supposed so. How had it started this time? Ah, yes. The child. The child in Regent's Park.

Last week Theodore and Elizabeth had bundled up for a stroll. Days before the fog settled in. The dark evenings and gray days had been weighing on her; she needed to get out. Theodore said she'd been playing far too much Bach. He was always concerned when she played Bach. How she used to hate his overthought fugues; she preferred Beethoven as a young woman. Beethoven was so confident. It was pure communication, she said. She couldn't remember the last time she had played the Ninth.

They'd walked to the park. It was lovely that day, a winter park. So still. The trees unmoving, the pouched birds waddling, the ducks flaunting the miracle of their feathers—warm even on the frigid lake. Her breath was a mist. She'd held tight to Theodore's arm.

A girl.

A little girl.

She'd run up to them, a long bird's feather in her hand.

"Look what I found!" she squealed. Her brown curls bobbed a bit; she was jittery with joy. Her mother was close behind, shaking her head, silently apologizing for her child's intrusion.

Elizabeth knelt in front of the girl and smiled. "How amazing this is! A feather. Wherever did you find it?" How delightful, Elizabeth thought, that a child sees every person as a friend. In league with them all.

"Just over there," the girl pointed to a tangle of stiff cattail stems by the pond. "I think it's from a hawk, don't you?"

"I do. I certainly do," Elizabeth said. From a pigeon, more like. It was gray. A plain gray feather. But to this girl, it came from a hawk, so from a hawk it was.

"Do you know how old I am?" the girl asked. She flitted from one topic to the next as a grasshopper leaps from place to place, leaving each completely and utterly behind her. "I'm six! My birthday is in May. The tenth! When's yours?"

Elizabeth didn't answer. She couldn't answer. The girl's mother looked a bit concerned. She took her child's hand and gently guided her away. "Come now, sweetheart." She looked at Elizabeth and Theodore. "So sorry. Good day." Mother and daughter walked away.

"Elizabeth," Theodore said gently. He put a hand on her shoulder. Elizabeth didn't look at him. She stayed down, kneeling as if the girl were still there. She stared at the water. "You mustn't let this affect you," he said. "Let's go have tea. Warm up. Get our minds off things."

She kept staring at the water.

For years, there was just the bleeding. Each month, the bleeding. She was convinced some months were the marks of life. Little children who couldn't hold on. And then one did. Her daughter. Her daughter held on. Elizabeth had gotten to see her, to cradle her for two hours. Her lips blue. Her beautiful lips so blue. Like sapphires. Like night diamonds. And she was gone. Something about her heart. Her heart was not formed. It was the universe that had a faulty heart, Elizabeth felt. Not her daughter.

She'd been born in May.

Like the little girl she'd just met in Regent's Park.

After that day in the park, Elizabeth had spent five long days going from the bed to the garden chair and back again. So heavy her limbs. So weak. Food was abhorrent.

You must have done something wrong. Eaten something wrong. Been too active. Or perhaps not active enough.

You aren't strong like other women, like Rose. Three sons! You're a bit faulty. You've known it always, haven't you? You're being punished. You deserved it somehow. Losing her. Losing her after you lost your mother. You must have done something terribly, terribly wrong.

You're making it all up now—this being Elizabeth Dalloway. Acting as though you're happy. Living in your mother's house. Being a history tutor. Holding your chin up. You're a fraud, really. A fraud.

A fraud who'd be better off—

"I'm fine, Rose," Elizabeth said now. On the stoop of the Purvis home. "I'm fine. I spent a week resting, that's all. So tired of this winter! It's been awfully cold."

"You're certain?" Rose raised her eyebrows. Elizabeth resented her tone, as if Elizabeth were a little papery thing. Something passed around with great care—so easy to rip, so easy to dissolve and drown if gotten wet. Would Elizabeth ever feel like an adult? Did she have to be a mother with six sons at Eton? Was that it?

Not enough. You are not enough. You never will be.

"Yes, I'm certain," Elizabeth lied. She clutched the small wooden box. "My mother left this behind, and I want to know every single thing about it."

Rose touched Elizabeth's arm, a little gesture of camaraderie. Or schadenfreude. Elizabeth couldn't be sure.

Rose opened the door.

SUMMER 1923

CHAPTER 14

Elizabeth

"Peter Walsh is a childhood friend." Mama said it casually, effortlessly, as if Elizabeth had just asked where she'd gotten a new dress or bracelet. As if Mama hadn't just kissed him moments before in this very room. Mama went to the end table by the sofa, picked up her scissors. She'd forgotten to put them in her sewing case. She slid open her writing desk drawer and retrieved it, placed the scissors inside. "He's simply a childhood friend, that's all."

Elizabeth stood next to the blue sofa, placed one hand on its soft velvet. She knew what she'd seen. "What happened that summer, Mama? The summer you were my age. Is that man—"

"Have you settled on a gown for this evening?" Mama interrupted. "I do hope you choose the pale pink. The one with that lovely neckline." With a graceful swoop, Mama gathered her silver-green dress from the sofa. She held it up in the afternoon light, studied its delicate beading, its unique color, its pleats, ran a finger across the small tear in the bodice she hadn't fixed completely. It was odd, Elizabeth thought, the way Mama was holding that gown—tenderly draping it across her forearms like the dress was a limp mermaid she'd pulled from the sea. She laid it on one of the chairs against the wall, straightened the engraving above it, the one of a little girl holding a muff.

"I saw you and Peter—"

"You were eavesdropping?" Mama's face, her gaze, her beaked nose, all coalesced into one fixed point. One sharp tip pointed directly at Elizabeth. "You were spying? While I had a guest?"

"I was walking past and I heard voices and I . . ." Elizabeth suddenly felt defenseless. Mama was gentle and mild—except when she wasn't. Trying to spar with her was like trying to pin a mosquito with a blunt sword; Mama was too delicate, too fast, a nearly invisible brute with a tiny stinger capable of killing. With dengue. Malaria.

"That is the most vulgar thing you have ever done, Elizabeth. Worse than all the rest." Her comment struck like a bell, like Big Ben had decided—for the first time in history—to ring at the wrong moment, to confuse the whole city, unmoor London from the very minutes, to slam its giant clappers against Elizabeth's head and pound her attention away from Peter Walsh.

"The rest?" Elizabeth asked. "What vulgar things have I done?"

Mama lowered her gaze. "I think you know," she said. The bell was quiet now; Big Ben had marked the moment. Mama's mosquito wings began their high-pitched buzz; she soared toward the dining room. "Our meal is ready," she said, her back to Elizabeth. "Shall we go through?"

Dutifully, Elizabeth followed her mother to the dining room. She eased herself into a chair, her hips still aching from her fall from Brixby. The butler came in for midday service. Elizabeth summoned her courage.

"I promise you I don't know what vulgar things you are talking about, Mama." Elizabeth stared at her mother. Mama seemed stiff now, completely closed, unwilling to say one word more.

Mama held her hand up to let the butler know that, yes, she would like a piece of the fish. And a serving of carrots. But not the parsnips. She prattled on now about how Miss Walters had been able to cook tastier dishes in the last year or so, but nothing like she could before the war. Oh, how Mama missed the fancy ices Miss Walters used to make, she said, especially the terribly complicated ones shaped like swans. Elizabeth poked at the lukewarm parsnips on her plate, felt she might be sick as she watched her fish sit limp in its own juices. She looked up at Mama, asking. There was an awful pause.

"The dandelions on your gowns," Mama finally said. "Never caring a straw about a glove or a dress or even an obligatory polite conversation. The thousand hunts you have to your name and yet zero courtships. It's clear to us what you're doing. We aren't blind, darling."

"Clear about what I'm doing?" Elizabeth asked. She didn't care about the impudence in her tone. Not a straw. "What is it exactly that I'm doing?"

"Throwing your life away."

And with that, Mama stopped her fine mosquito wings, lit on the table. Still. Somehow it was more chilling than being stung. Elizabeth opened her mouth to protest. No words came.

Mama's face softened like she had an unexpected wish to heal the very wound she'd just inflicted. "I think if you would take a bit of time with him. There are things you don't know that may change your—"

"With whom? Take my time with whom?"

"William. William Titcomb."

William. That brash, perfect boy who had nearly killed her just yesterday. She supposed her parents had chosen him for his uprightness, his good family, his impeccable manners. Though how rude was it to witness a girl knocked from her horse and not call to check on her well-being? To her knowledge, he hadn't telephoned. But it gave her pause, this mention of William. How emphatic her mother sounded. Elizabeth had to admit that Mama did display a certain . . . prescience about things. Her intuition about people, about unspoken conflicts in a room, about connections—her abilities could not be discounted. Beyond William's breeding, what did her mother see in him? There was, Elizabeth had sometimes thought, something memorable about him, something in his demeanor. She couldn't place it. But it hardly mattered—it wasn't Mama's opinion of him that counted; it was hers. And currently, her opinion was low.

"I'm not talking about that today, mother. I'm talking about what I just saw."

Mama took a deep breath, seemed exhausted with this conversation. "What you saw . . ." She paused. "Has its roots in my youth. And I don't want you to do anything in these summers, in this time of your life, that will cause you the type of suffering I have endured. That's what

I meant to say. Your summers. I want you to be very careful with your summers. Choosing your path."

Elizabeth heard something.

A strange, rapid clicking sound.

She wondered if the noise was coming from the small clock on the mantel behind Mama, if it was broken, as if the seconds were tick-tocking away too quickly, as if some gear had slipped inside, throwing its fragile innards off-kilter.

That wasn't it. The clock was behaving admirably. Steadily marking the moments.

Tick. Tock. Tick.

Elizabeth glanced at the window over Mama's shoulder, wondering if the sound was coming from a bird tapping at the glass. Often, like the one she'd seen earlier in the drawing room, birds couldn't see the panes and would fly straight into them. Or stand on the sill and peck and peck and peck at the glass as if they couldn't accept their path was blocked.

The windowsill was empty.

The sound was coming from Mama's end of the dining table.

It was coming from Mama.

As Mama attempted to slice through her food, her knife trembled against the plate, clicking softly against the china. *Click, click, click.* She was trembling. Like a baby bird was at the window after all but wasn't pecking at the glass in a determined way, but instead holding its face, its beak against the pane, gently shivering as if winter had suddenly come. As if it needed shelter.

A giant oil painting—several massive stags emerging from a fog—hung above the fireplace behind Mama. Elizabeth had looked at that painting a thousand times during a thousand meals and always saw her mother as one of those beasts, strong, clear-eyed, with antlers crashing through society with strength and ease. Mama certainly faltered at times, getting lost in memories as she did. Seeming here, but somehow not. But Mama was a stag. She'd always been a stag.

"Mama . . . are you all right?" The question felt so odd on Elizabeth's lips. Mama was the strongest woman Elizabeth had ever known; to ask her such a thing felt absurd.

Her mother set down her cutlery. Put her trembling hands on her lap. She straightened, sitting perfectly upright as if she were about to lift and place a hoof, take an unsteady step through the fog.

"Whatever you may have seen or heard today in the drawing room . . ." Mama paused, ran her finger along the curve of her wine goblet. She was no longer a mosquito plunging dengue fever into the flesh. And she wasn't a stag. She was just a woman who looked as if she was about to say the truest thing she had ever—or would ever—say to her daughter. "It had nothing—*nothing whatever*—to do with Peter Walsh. Do you understand?"

Was she asking Elizabeth to stop prying, to stop searching? Was she asking without words to remain hidden, to remain a mother unknown?

"I understand," Elizabeth said.

Mama returned to her plate.

Sliced into her fish.

They ate in silence. Moments before they finished, Miss Kilman arrived. Elizabeth heard her speaking with Lucy downstairs. Elizabeth could feel Mama's dislike of the woman filling the room. Elizabeth stood and excused herself but looked back at her mother just before leaving. She thought of Mama's shaking hands, her talk of the past, of her youth. Elizabeth expected to still be smarting from her mother's suggestion that she was throwing her life away. She expected to feel angry about that kiss with Peter, enraged on Papa's behalf.

But she didn't feel those things.

"I love you, Mama." It was a phrase she had said perhaps a handful of times. Once when she was twelve and Mama lay dying of the Spanish flu. Once when Elizabeth had caught her mother crying after a rare spat with Papa. And this moment, Elizabeth felt, was just as momentous. It deserved that word. *Love.* "And whatever happened to you, I—"

"And I love you, my Elizabeth," she said. "I love you so."

With that, Elizabeth left the room, closed the door behind her.

———

"Really, Grizzle!" Miss Kilman was tramping up the stairs, the little dog barking madly at her heels. His paws were leaving bits of garden mud on her skirts. "Cleanliness is close to godliness!" Her bag of books was slung over her shoulder; she was ready for Elizabeth's afternoon tutoring session.

"Miss Kilman, I really can't study now—"

"We've got the rise of the railroads in the American West today!" She kept barreling toward Elizabeth's room. She went in and settled herself in the sitting area just off Elizabeth's bedroom, the place where they did all their history studies together. Lucy had already left them tea. Miss Kilman adjusted her mackintosh, straightened one of its wooden buttons. She pulled a thick book from one of her bags. "The shift in the means of production. The Industrial Revolution." She clicked her tongue and shook her head. "The sad moments in history when man was enslaved by those with capital."

"Really," Elizabeth protested, "this is very urgent. I must prepare for the party tonight, and I'm dreadfully concerned about Mama—"

"The party tonight? How it breaks my heart to hear you speak like this." Miss Kilman snapped the history book closed, held it up. "This fretting about parties. All professions are open to women now. You can be a historian! Study history even more than I have. Or be a politician. Or use that wild love you have for animals and become a veterinarian." She paused, placed the book on the table, and picked up her teacup. Eyed Elizabeth over the china rim. "You're a member of the bright generation. All the doors are open to women now. You don't want to be some outdated socialite standing at the top of a staircase, welcoming revelers, do you? You want to be useful! You don't want to waste your entire life like . . ."

"My mother," Elizabeth finished her sentence for her. "You don't want me to waste my life like my mother has. She tells me I'm throwing it away by ignoring parties and you tell me I'm throwing it away by paying attention to them. I'm the recipient of so many critiques my head spins."

Choosing your path.

The late-afternoon sunlight came through the window, lit Miss

Kilman's face on one side, illuminated her wrinkles. "I wish you wouldn't let your mother upset you." She took a biscuit now. "I told you all I know. There are rumors about Peter Walsh, that's all. Rumors about your mother."

"What rumors?" She thought of Mama downstairs again, that tremble, her cutlery against the plate. Of Mama kissing Peter, sitting so close. Seeming like a different woman entirely. She thought of the strange assurance Mama had given her that whatever Mama's secret was with Peter—somehow it had nothing to do with him. "I need to know everything about Mama's summer. When she was young. In 1889. She was eighteen. What have people said?"

"That you look like him." It was Lucy. Breezing into the room now, picking up the tea service. The china cups clinked as she placed them on her tray. Her expression was flat, unremarkable, as if she'd announced the tea had gotten cold. Or that it was expected to rain before nightfall. "Miss Hilbery saw you in Regent's Park and said the same just a few days ago. How had she put it? Was it that some pirate had been wrecked on the coast of Norfolk, had mixed with the Dalloway ladies, perhaps, a hundred years ago? That pirate blood would explain your lack of resemblance to either of your parents, really. Or perhaps something more recent than that."

My god.

Elizabeth tried to digest it, Lucy's suggestion. She felt as though her mind wasn't working right, like it was suddenly having a hard time understanding simple words. And then, in one horrifying moment, Lucy's meaning became clear.

Someone else's blood in my veins.

"Lucy," Miss Kilman said. It was a snap of the reins. A strong pull on the bit. "That will be all."

Miss Kilman's tone was truly alarming. For Miss Kilman—the working-class sympathizer, the woman who'd been tossed out of school because she waxed on about the plight of the German workers—to speak to a staff member this way was extraordinary. She believed everyone should be doing manual labor, everyone taking care of their own tea. But now, she spoke like the lady of the house. Lucy stopped at the door, her tray filled.

"But aren't all the Dalloways fair-haired?" Lucy asked. "Blue-eyed?" Lucy cocked her head a bit, studied Elizabeth's face. "Your Mama says you bear a mystery about you. *Inscrutable* is the word she uses."

Miss Kilman moved quickly now, gathering her things. "Elizabeth, I'm going to the Army and Navy Stores straightaway. I need a new petticoat before they are all picked through! Do come with me. Get a bit of air, hm?" She was positively tossing the rest of her belongings in her bag. She took Elizabeth's arm. Pulled. And not so gently.

"Pardon me?" Elizabeth glared at Lucy. "A pirate wrecked on the coast of Norfolk? What a dreadful thing to say! And you're suggesting that Mama, that she and Peter—"

Miss Kilman yanked Elizabeth away now, onto the landing and down the stairs. "Oh, who *knows* what goes on with these sorts of things?" she whispered. She glanced back at Lucy, silently admonishing her not to follow them. "People like your mother grow up on fancy estates, come out in society, and gallivant about when they are your age. All summer parties and courtships, like characters in frivolous novels. Hundreds of pages about the mundane daily matters of silly women. No real problems to speak of. Thank heavens you aren't a bit like her. And that you look a bit different. That's all. You simply look a bit different. God's way of telling you that you are to take a different path! To a real profession!" Miss Kilman put on her hat now, adjusted it on her head. It was crooked. She resembled a desperate pigeon trying to arrange her feathers. They reached the next landing, just in front of the drawing room. "Now, tell your mother we are going," Miss Kilman whispered. She looked at Elizabeth as if she was reminding her of her own strength, of her ability to pull herself together for this moment. All she needed to do was go into the drawing room and inform her mother that she was departing. That was all.

"Mother is resting," Elizabeth said. She could barely breathe, let alone step inside that room, face Mama after what she'd just heard. Miss Kilman gave her an encouraging but stern look. She should go in.

There on the sofa, with her head on a pillow, was Mama, resting just as Elizabeth had thought she would be. Elizabeth was overwhelmed with an urge to run to her side, beg for some assurance that her whole life had not been a lie, that there wasn't some dreadful secret that could ruin them all.

But she didn't run to Mama. It simply wasn't done. Running to Mama.

Miss Kilman stepped into the room behind Elizabeth. Mama slowly rose from the sofa. Glowered at Miss Kilman. It was all too much for a moment; Elizabeth thought she might faint.

"I've . . . I've forgotten my gloves," Elizabeth lied. She hadn't intended to wear any in the first place. She slipped out of the room, leaned against the wall; she needed to catch her breath. She gazed in the little mirror hanging on the wall opposite. Did she look like Mama at all? Like Papa? No one had ever said she took after either of them; Elizabeth hadn't thought a thing of it. But it was all clear now. Peter and Mama had fallen in love by the lake at Bourton. Mama had chosen Papa but had not kept her promise to him. She'd carried on with Peter ever since. He'd visited over the years, just as Mr. Garrick had said. Popping in. As if the Dalloway home were a pub. A pub where Peter could catch a glimpse of his true love.

And his daughter.

This was why she never felt that she fit. That she wasn't good at it, being Daughter Dalloway.

Because she wasn't.

She was Daughter Walsh.

She stepped back into the drawing room, back into the chill between Mama and Miss Kilman. "Shall we go?"

They said their goodbyes, and she and Miss Kilman were just about through the front door when Elizabeth heard what was perhaps the saddest of sounds. A voice so desperate. So cloying. So thin.

"My party tonight!" Mama called down to them, leaning over the banister above. Her face pale as always, her hair perfectly in place. "Don't forget my party tonight!"

The same thing she'd begged Peter.

They made their way to the garden gate, to the street. Elizabeth stopped. "So this is what you knew. What Lucy said about Peter."

Miss Kilman put her arm gently on Elizabeth's shoulder. "Tonight," she said. "Your father will be home tonight. For the party. You must talk to him. He will know the real answer." She gently touched Elizabeth's cheek, brushed a strand of hair away from her face. "You must ask him to tell you the truth tonight."

————

Elizabeth accompanied Miss Kilman to the Army and Navy Stores; she didn't know what else to do with herself. She wandered blindly into the tobacco department. Then followed Miss Kilman onto the lift and up to the petticoats. Elizabeth felt as though she were floating above the earth, the petticoats stars in an otherwise empty sky. This one brown, this one striped, this one complicated with lace. She and Miss Kilman had tea, but Elizabeth could barely sit still. She excused herself, left Miss Kilman fretting, she knew. But she had to go; she needed out, needed air. She waited on Victoria Street for an omnibus. Perhaps more than air, she needed movement.

"As if some pirate had been wrecked on the coast of Norfolk, had mixed with the Dalloway ladies, perhaps, a hundred years ago."

Yes, movement was what she needed. The omnibus pulled up, her steed. She paid her penny, took a seat on the top. She watched the crowds pass by, the buildings. All at work, she thought. All of them monuments to work. She would run great enterprises. She could be a farmer, have people under her, visit them at their cottages. Parliament, even, if necessary. She would be through with her mother's world, her horrible world of cities and parties and secret undoings.

She got off at Chancery Lane. She should turn around. She should catch the Westminster omnibus home. Dalloway ladies didn't stroll up the Strand alone; she was venturing. One short walk, she thought. She caught sight of herself in a shop window, a woman unknown. Perhaps she would know tonight. Her father would tell her tonight.

Here it came, the Westminster.

She got on. Ready, she felt, for whatever the night may bring.

CHAPTER 15

Octavia

The lake in Regent's Park was still as the glass of a watch face.

Its shore rambled in a loose circle, dotted with a few wooden piers and rimmed on the east side with boys and their fishing nets. A man pushed a cart with a sign for sausages and mash. Octavia, Redvers, and Georgie slowly walked along the lake. The breeze was just the thing; Octavia was so happy to be cooling off and out of the bustle of the zoo. She was so knackered. This had been, by any measure, the longest day of her life.

"How much more do we need for fare to Bloomsbury?" she asked.

Redvers jingled the coins in his pockets, looked skyward as he worked on his best guess. "I think we've got enough for fare, but Georgie and I aren't going to leave you in Bloomsbury without plenty of dosh. You'll need it. You might need to stay a few days, who knows? I can show you places to sleep that aren't too dodgy."

Octavia stared at the water. She hated to admit it, but the thought of Red and Georgie leaving her in Bloomsbury scared her to bits. How would she get on? She couldn't work the city like he could, making it pour free money into her pockets; she wouldn't know what to do with herself. She wouldn't know how to get a hot meal. How to survive.

"Want to see me catch a fish?" Georgie asked.

"Now, don't go bragging, Georgie," Redvers said. He ruffled his little brother's hair.

"But you've been bragging all day! It's my turn."

Red blushed at that and nodded for Georgie to go on. "Net's behind the—"

"Fourth bush to the left." Georgie finished his brother's sentence as he ran off toward a line of benches along the lake. "I know, I know," he called over his shoulder.

"A net?" Octavia asked.

Redvers didn't answer, he just pointed. Georgie stopped at a bush, crawled underneath it, and emerged with a net and two glass jars. He brought them to Octavia, puffed up so proudly like he'd unearthed a pirate's treasure, as if Blackbeard himself had inexplicably left his loot beside a bench in Regent's Park all this while.

"See?" he said, holding up the net. "I made it myself."

The "net" wasn't a proper net at all. Octavia could see that it was a pair of women's stockings stretched over a coat hanger. A stick was lashed to it for a handle.

"Well," Octavia said, taking the makeshift net in her hands. She whipped it about in the air a few times as if she were trying to catch butterflies. "It's top-notch, Georgie. Really top-notch."

Georgie's eyes sparkled. "Thank you," he said. "I'm an ace at making these."

The three of them walked to the lakeshore and found a spot next to the other young fishermen. Georgie stuck his net in the water a few times and pulled it out. Nothing. He stuck it in again and again. And on the fourth try—it was filled with tiny fish. He held up his catch.

"Do you eat them?" Octavia asked. She thought it must take a hundred or more to make a meal out of those tiny things.

"Nope," Red said. "He sells 'em." He pointed across the lake at the docks jutting into the water. The piers were dotted with grown men fishing with proper poles and wearing nice clothes. Gentlemen enjoying the lake for the day.

Georgie wrangled the little fish into one of his glass jars and ran to the other side of the lake. One of the fishermen reached in his pocket and handed over some cash for the jar. The man unscrewed the cap and began to spear a small fish on the end of his hook.

"Good work, Georgie!" Redvers called. Georgie ran to another part of the lake now, dipping his net in for another haul. "We'll be on the hill!" Red pointed to the grassy slope beside the lake, covered with people having picnics.

"We will?" Octavia asked.

"Well, not until we get our food," said Redvers. He walked to the man with the food cart and ordered several sausages, a piece of fish, and some chips.

"That'll be five," the man said, filling two plates with steaming food.

Octavia waited for Red to greet the vendor by name, to offer him some service in exchange for the food, or to pull some other trick out of his sleeve she couldn't even imagine.

Instead, he pulled out five pennies.

"Thank you, sir," Redvers said, handing Octavia a plate.

It smelled delicious. Octavia hadn't realized how hungry she was. She hadn't eaten since early that morning. But then she felt terrible about how much food there was and how much money Red had paid for it. "You paid full price for this, didn't you?"

Red nodded. "That's one thing that's not cut-rate in London—fresh food. The only way you get a deal is if it's stale, rotten, or recently dead—and you killed it yourself."

———

Octavia was too full and happy to feel any shame about how fast—and how much—she'd eaten right there in front Red. She imagined what her father would do back home if she did such a thing—suck down a whole meal in front of a boy. She'd probably get a lashing. But she wasn't at home; she was here, in London, in this heavenly grass. She spread out on her back, an acceptable two arm's-lengths from Red, and stared at the drifting clouds. One looked like a dragon who'd dropped his tail. Another was a clover losing its fourth leaf in the wind.

The last looked like a house to Octavia, a house with a hole in the middle.

"So." Red rolled on his side, facing her, propped up on an elbow. "Mind telling me what you're really doing in London?"

Octavia shot him a shocked look. As if there were any question. "I told you," she said. "I'm here to see my brother."

Red plucked a dandelion from the grass, spun it between his fingers. "I figured there might be a little more to it than that," he said. "Not often I run into penniless country girls hunting down their brothers in London."

Octavia sat up. "If you must know . . ." She tried her best to sound as icy as possible. Dignified. She smoothed the bodice of her dress, flicked a few hay pieces from the front. "I don't have any money because I was robbed. By a boy who looked to be your type." She regretted it the moment she said it. She could see the comment land in Red's chest, she thought, like an arrow sticking there, its tip quivering.

"My type, eh?" Red flicked the weed across the lawn as if he were pulling Octavia's arrow out of his breast, tossing it away. Like he was accustomed to having barbs fly at him. Accustomed to taking them out himself. Accustomed to waiting for wounds to scab over. "Have I stolen anything from you? Have I?"

"No," Octavia said, her voice low, full of remorse. "You haven't."

"You don't have to tell me a thing about what you're really up to," he said. "But don't go—"

"No," Octavia interrupted. "I want to. Tell you. I do."

Which was true. In Stroud she didn't have any friends to talk to, really. She was too busy to have a friend. She helped Mum with the cooking and cleaning. She fed the chickens and the pigs and the cows. She tried to teach Ronnie his letters, tried to teach him to read, but that was a big old job there. He couldn't sit still for five minutes, and once it started getting a bit dimpsy out, he was no good at all. And when she wasn't doing all that, she was listening to her father go on about the customers at the brewery, the ones who always had a few pints too many and a few coppers short. Or she was listening to her mum squawk about the girls in town who were already getting married, snatching up the boys. So no, Octavia didn't have any friends to talk to. She'd surely never had a friend to waste a day with—to tramp through a zoo or have a picnic by a lake. Septimus was the closest she'd ever had to a friend. Reading Shakespeare on the hill with him when she was a little girl.

Always Septimus.

Looking at Redvers next to her in the park grass, she thought he might be her friend. Keeping her afloat in London like he had, with all his kindnesses. Yes, she decided. He was her first friend ever.

"I have two brothers I love more than anything. Ronnie and Septimus," Octavia said. "Tertius is my other one. The oldest. Him, I could do without." She ran her fingers through the grass in front of her now, as if ruffling the hair of a small child, soothing him after skinning his knee. Telling him to settle. "Ronnie is still back in Stroud. He's seven. He reminds me of Georgie, actually. And I feel awful for leaving him. Just awful. My whole family would likely boot me out if I try to go back. But I had to leave, you see. Because of Septimus. Septimus is here in London. He left me a note before he disappeared. So I've come to find him and bring him home."

Red sat up now too. "He disappeared?"

"He wanted to be a poet," she said. "To be an artist in London. That was his dream. I was seven when he left Stroud. He set out to make his dreams come—" She stopped. Redvers didn't seem to like what he was hearing. It made Octavia want to plead Septimus's case, to make Red understand how wonderful her brother was. What a scholar, what a kind man he was. Then she realized she was thinking of Septimus in the past tense. "He *is* magnificent," she said. "Smarter than any Cambridge man, for certain. Honorable. Funny. The best brother a girl— "

"Then why'd he disappear on you?" Redvers asked. "I mean, no offense or anything. But what kind of brother does that?"

"He left Stroud to be a poet in the city. He couldn't be a poet in our little village. That's what he always said. So he left for London. Then fought in the war," Octavia said quickly as if that could make up for any previous sin. Maybe it did. "I think he may have been injured. The

War Office didn't know his whereabouts. But then we got this telegram. They said he lives in Bloomsbury. That he's married. I have to find him."

"I see," Redvers said. "So he never tipped up in Stroud after he got home from the war. That it?"

Octavia didn't like the way he said it; she didn't like the look on his face, like he knew something. "Yes, probably because he's been hurt," Octavia said. "Doesn't that happen to soldiers? The ones who get hit by bombs or bullets?"

"Course it does," Red said. He spread out on his back again, looked at the clouds. "I've seen . . ."

"You've seen what?"

"Kingdoms," Red said.

"Kingdoms?"

"Lay back with me." He gently pulled her close to him, eased her down to the warm grass. He pointed at a collection of massive, billowing clouds. "Look. See there? A kingdom. There's the castle, the wall 'round it. A moat even. And over there, that's where I'd live, in one of those little puffs outside the wall. A hut. All the posh folks would be on the other side. It's better outside the wall, you know."

Octavia could feel the warmth of his body next to her as she looked up and saw what he did—a cloud kingdom. For a moment, she let herself imagine being its ruler, its queen, filling the moat with terrifying creatures who would stop brothers from running away. She'd outlaw money entirely and give everyone the same amount of everything. In her kingdom, there would no wars of any kind. She simply wouldn't allow them.

They stayed there like that, a gentle breeze rolling over them, carrying the soft sounds of children playing in the distance. The kingdom dissolved.

"What have you seen, Red?" she asked, still staring into the blue. She knew he hadn't been talking about cloud kingdoms. Not really.

"It's just that . . ." Red paused. He turned on his side to face her. "When soldiers come back but don't come back right, it's a tough go. And if that's what you find in Bloomsbury . . . I just know I couldn't see Georgie hurt like that. I couldn't take it." Red took a deep breath, looked at her so solemnly. But sweetly. "I just hope you're sure you want to look for him. Because you don't know what you'll find."

Octavia was quiet for a while. Thinking. Listening to a girl giggle at the top of the hill. A dog barking, begging for a biscuit. She imagined finding Septimus nearly blown to bits. She imagined him perfectly fine and slamming the door in her face. She imagined returning to Stroud without knowing which was true, and that, by far, was the worst of all. She looked at Red. "You'd look for Georgie, wouldn't you? If he'd never come home? You'd look for him. No matter what."

Red picked up his cap, slowly turned it around in his hands. And nodded. Like Octavia had solved a puzzle he didn't know he had. "Sure would," he said slowly. "Sure would."

"I thought so." She looked into his bright hazel eyes. "You love Georgie like I love my brothers. I can tell."

"Your brothers . . . the young one's Ronnie? You looked so sad when you said his name."

"Yes. Ronnie." The thought of her little brother, of him alone at home, hit Octavia like she'd stepped in front of a train. It blew against her, right through her, pummeled her under its heavy wheels. What if mum took to her bed? What if she had one of her spells? Octavia wasn't there to shield him from it. Gather him up, get him outside to play rag ball. Her decision to go to London had put him in harm's way. "After he was born, Mum . . . changed. For months on end. She wasn't herself. She tried to leave him. Leave Ronnie. She left him in a field and lied, told us he'd been snatched." The tears threatened now. And then came. They fell right out of her eyes, the ones Pop always said were so big, so innocent, but so serious all the same. Red reached out and wiped a tear from her cheek; his finger was calloused, rough, but somehow felt lovely. So lovely.

"Octavia."

That's all he said.

Octavia.

She felt like they were both under the same weight—the heavy, heavy weight of loving a brother.

"My father thinks it was the devil," Octavia said. "The devil that possessed my mum. The devil Ronnie brought us."

Red gently shook his head. "Well," he said. "I don't believe in the devil. And neither does my mum. She says having babies is a battle as tough as any other. Except you don't have the weapons you sorely need." He gently smiled. "As for the devil, if there is one, that's my pop. We'd all believe that."

"He is?"

"He's got two problems. Either he's drunk and here. Or drunk and gone." Red shrugged. "So Mum has a little job. And I earn the rest to keep us going. Georgie is real smart. We've got to give him the best."

"That's what I want for Ronnie too. The best. And for Septimus," Octavia said. "The very best."

They were so close now on the grass. Redvers took her hand and pulled her a bit closer. And closer still. It overwhelmed her—the warmth of his skin, his eyes, the love he had for his brother. His cheeks reddened by the sun, by his thousands of trips all over the city he'd mastered. His lips. They were coming closer and closer.

Octavia stopped.

She heard a rustling, then a clinking sound.

She pulled back a bit and saw that money had fallen out of Red's pocket when he'd leaned in. A *lot* of money. A giant wad of bills was in the grass between them, surrounded by a heap of coins. She pushed back. "What's this?" She held up some of the cash.

"Oh," Redvers blushed. "Just a bit of dosh." He reached for it. But Octavia pulled it away.

"It's not just a bit of dosh," she said. "It's more than you earned at the zoo. It's more than you could earn there with a hundred monkey dances."

"I've got a lot of jobs in this town," Redvers said. "I brush the horses at the racecourse. I sell half-bruised fruit. I even—"

"That's not the point." Octavia stood up, tossed the money at Red.

He looked confused. "Then what is the point?"

"That you've had enough to get me to Bloomsbury from the moment I met you! You've had enough to send me there and put me up for a week's time if need be. All this earning a quid with a monkey dance and selling tiddlers at the lake and getting free bandages from Boots—it's all been unnecessary. A ruse! You told me you didn't have a cent. That we had to spend the whole day in the city earning our ticket fare." She angrily brushed the bits of grass off her dress. "Now I understand."

"And just what is it that you understand?"

She glowered at him. "You just didn't want to spend any of your stash on *me*. We had to earn what you'd spend on my ticket and keep your money for yourself. And I thought you might be a friend, I thought—"

"It's not that I didn't want to spend my money on you," he said, standing up.

"Oh, really?" Octavia said. "Then why didn't you?"

"Because I didn't want you to go." Red gently dug the toe of his boot into the grass.

"So you were just—"

"Trying to spend a little time with you. That's all," he said. "I'm sorry. Here." He held out the wad of cash. Then he started gathering the coins from the grass and holding them up for her to take too. "You can have it all. It's yours."

Octavia stared at the glittering shillings and crinkled notes. She thought about taking them, storming across the park, rich enough to get to Bloomsbury and stay as long as she needed. She could see a sign for the Underground on the other side of the hill. Surely someone in the station could tell her which train to catch, where to ride to.

Georgie came running up the bank now, his homemade net dripping with lake water. He was pink-cheeked and out of breath. "Sold both jars of tiddlers, Red! For the most ever!" He pointed back across the lake. "Those blokes there are *posh*. They're about to sail these little teak boats and—" Georgie stopped. He noticed all the money on the ground and the wad in Red's outstretched hand. "What's going on? Why's all the money out like that?"

Red bent down and picked up the rest. "I was just giving it all to Octavia here," he said. "She's about to leave. On her way to find her brother."

"You're leaving us?" Georgie said. "Aren't we coming with you?" He turned to his brother. "And Red, Mum needs most of that this week. The rent's up. We can't just—"

"Yes," Octavia said, looking at Georgie's sweet face. He made her think of Ronnie. He made her think of home. She just realized it, but that was it. This darling boy made her think of the Stroud hills, the spring when the new flowers pushed up, all hope and apple-green stems.

But Red—he made her think of staying away from Stroud forever. She didn't know why, but he did. Away. Forever. "Of course you're coming with me, Georgie," she said, taking his net. She shook it out; a spray of water droplets blanketed the grass. "And I'm not taking all that money. I wouldn't do that. We'll save plenty for your mum." She took Georgie's hand and started leading him across the park toward the Tube station. She looked over her shoulder at Red. "Come on, Red. We don't want to miss the train."

Redvers smiled.

And came running.

"First stop, Westminster!" Georgie said, starting his typical skipping gait.

"No, Georgie," Octavia said. "It's Bloomsbury. My brother is in Bloomsbury. Not Westminster."

"But," Georgie said. He looked at the sky. "It's getting late, we have to get to—"

Redvers cleared his throat, interrupted his brother. "So there's one more little thing."

Octavia stopped. "And what is that?"

"You know those jobs I said I had? The ones that got me all this dosh to get us to Bloomsbury? To keep a roof over our heads?"

Octavia nodded.

"Well," Redvers said slowly. "I have one more job lined up for today. And it's in Westminster. Where all the posh folks live. On Hyde Street."

Octavia sighed. "All right," she said. "One more stop. And that's it. You promise?"

"With all my heart." He smiled.

And this time, Octavia was the one to take his hand.

CHAPTER 16

Elizabeth

Mama's party had begun.

Elizabeth smoothed the bodice of her pink gown, hitched up her cream gloves. She'd dutifully left her dandelion boutonniere in her room, but now she wished she hadn't. It had made her feel brave, and she'd need that tonight in spades. She practiced what she would say, how she would begin.

Papa, I have something I need to speak with you about.

However would she manage it?

She scanned the room for her father but didn't see him. She scanned the room for the prince but didn't see him either. She saw the prime minister moving through the crowd in his official-looking jacket, in his golden tassels. He looked rather silly, Elizabeth thought. In costume almost—a figurehead at best, a child's puppet at the worst. The usual members of society were clustered about the room. And wasn't that Mama's poor relation, Ellie Henderson? And there was Mama near an open window, elegant in her silver-green dress, ready to swim through the night with ease.

A breath of wind sent the yellow curtains aflutter, the ones covered with birds of paradise. Mama seemed delighted as if the birds had signaled success. As if every person in the room—every object even—were part of an orchestra and she the conductor. As if she had raised an invisible baton to a beat only she could hear, and the air itself had responded, lifted those bird-covered curtains, brought the flock to life, swirled and enlivened any stagnant conversations.

Elizabeth spotted William Titcomb next. He was chatting with his friends, several men who had come down from Cambridge, all friends of the prince. Elizabeth had met them before, this coveted group of bachelors everyone said was so handsome. She supposed so. No, she knew so. They were all so . . . *expected*—and so intimidating because of it. But she must pluck up the courage and cross the room. Inquire about a party after this one that she wasn't sure existed.

She started toward William.

"Good evening," Elizabeth said. He turned, looked pleased to see her. Quite pleased.

"Good evening," William said. His jacket was a rich navy, his pocket square gleamed a matching blue, his shoes shined. Come to think of it, he was always in navy. And his shoulders were unbelievably broad, Elizabeth thought. So squared. No wonder he looked formidable on horseback. "Are you well?" he asked. "I can't stop thinking about that dreadful fall. I feel as though I'm responsible."

"I'm well," Elizabeth said. She noticed now that William smelled faintly of peppermint. And . . . bourbon? "I'm bruised, but well. The worst are my arms, must have broken my fall." She gently touched her right elbow, the ache still there.

"May I dare say you look stunning this evening," he said.

"Like a hyacinth? A fawn in a meadow, perhaps?"

William looked confused. "Pardon?"

"Never mind," Elizabeth said, forcing a smile. "Apparently, my mother thinks I'm growing up, being compared to flowers and fawns. According to her, it's a dreadful thing."

"I can't imagine anyone comparing Elizabeth Dalloway to a hyacinth. An oak perhaps. Roots to the center of the earth." It was his turn to smile now.

It stopped her, this compliment. An oak. Rooted. Her mother had always made her feel as if she were a wayward thing, flying off in the wrong direction. But to be a tree, hard to topple. It felt like the most wonderful thing to be. She wanted to thank him for his remark, to say something meaningful about it, but she stopped herself. She didn't want to encourage him. He didn't have a chance in the world with her. Not one chance in the world. The last thing on earth she wanted was to marry someone so sensible. And one fine compliment wasn't going to change all that. That's what her mother had done. Marry sensibly. And look where it had gotten her—having affairs with men from India and droning on about it all in thick letters. Pining away for a summer in her past. No, Elizabeth would not tread that path. But she didn't wish to be mean to William. She really didn't. "How clever. I don't believe I've ever heard someone compared to a bit of the forest."

"I'm afraid I'm known for overusing metaphors." He grinned, but then looked serious once more. "And again, I'm ever so sorry about what happened with Brixby. I telephoned earlier. To see how you were getting on. I left a message."

"You did?"

"Yes, I left word with one of your staff. A woman. She didn't offer her name."

Lucy.

"No," Elizabeth said. "I wasn't informed. My apologies. It happens often, I'm afraid."

"I also left word of an invitation. To my father's July foxhunt. It's a tradition," William said. "It's on the north end of our estate. Really, it's always a fabulous time. My father brings in first-rate dogs." William leaned in a bit. "And I promise no stone walls this time."

"That's so lovely of you," Elizabeth said. "But—" She stopped as the sound of Big Ben came through the open windows, mingled with the birds of paradise still fluttering on the curtains. It was eight o'clock. She was to collect Calvin and Frances in an hour's time.

"But . . . you can't?" William asked, finishing her sentence. "You can't come? Is that it?" An underbutler passed by with a tray full of cocktails. Mama had hired him for the event. William helped himself to a glass. He took it down in one shocking drink. "And who are you looking for?"

He must have noticed her distraction. "Truth be told . . . the prince."

"Edward?" William knitted his brow. "Elizabeth Dalloway is interested in *Edward*? I would have never guessed that, I assure you. And he's not coming. You know he attends events on whims, not plans."

"I'm not *interested*," Elizabeth said. "It's that I need an invitation from him. To one of his . . . after-parties."

"Why, Elizabeth Dalloway, you *do* surprise me."

"So there is one?"

"A party after this one?" William asked.

Elizabeth nodded.

"Of course there is. There always is. And it's not really the after-party. It's the real party." He grinned. "But you never struck me as the type who would want to come. Going about with your zealot of a history tutor and all. Glad she didn't convert you."

"She's really quite knowledgeable," Elizabeth said, feeling defensive. "I admire her, that's all. Mama has it so twisted around. Why are adults so helplessly out of touch? Will that happen to us?"

"Dear god, I hope not," William said. "Take me out and shoot me behind the barn, as they say."

Elizabeth smiled. "Anyway, is it too late to get an invitation? For tonight? I'll have two guests with me. Americans. Calvin Gage and his sister, Frances."

"Oh, now I see. Frances, you say? American girls are all in love with Edward," William said, looking bored with the whole idea. "As if any of them stand a chance. They don't understand how these things work. Although, knowing Edward, he just might break every rule that's ever been."

"No, Frances isn't—" Elizabeth stopped. The thought hadn't occurred to her, that Frances might actually have designs on the Prince of Wales. She thought they just wanted to meet him.

"And anyway, you don't need an invitation, Elizabeth," William said, gently shaking his head at her. "We don't stamp them up and send them to butlers. You just need to know someone and know where the party is. Then you tip up. That's all. Welcome to youth," he smiled. "I thought you'd never make it."

"I just . . . tip up? Tonight?"

"Yes," he said. "Tonight we're swimming. On Marshall Street. Magnificent pool. Enormous. Marble and all that."

"You must be joking. The municipal swimming pool?" Elizabeth was more than a little confused. All the parties she'd ever been to had been in private homes. Gardens. The palace. "Why on earth would someone host a party at a place like that?"

"I believe you'll see when you get there," William said. "And I hope you're prepared to be in the press. They've been poking about our parties this summer. A lot of us think they'll publish a story any day. The *Daily Mail* seems ever so interested in every single thing we do in the wee hours of the night. Calling us a movement of Bright People or some such thing. Bright Young People."

"The *Daily Mail*? I've never even read—"

"Of course you haven't. It's nothing but a postwar rag," William smiled. "Party starts at ten. Come when you can. I suspect we'll still be there when the sun rises. Typically, we finish these affairs with a bit of breakfast."

He looked so hopeful then, William. And Elizabeth felt horrible for it. She felt like she'd just made a date with him for a late-night swim. And that hadn't been what she'd meant to do at all. Not at all. But she didn't know how to undo it. "Tonight, then," she said.

William stood a little taller, his smile broad now. His cheeks filled with a bit of color. "I look forward to it. But I *do* hope you know what you are getting into. And I wouldn't tell your mother a word about it if I were you."

"Not a peep," she said smiling. "Our maid Lucy will love to have something over my head. I'll get her to cover for me." Elizabeth wanted to say something more, something about her shock that William would be doing things that might land him in the *Daily Mail*, things that would upset his family. But she didn't get the chance; she saw her father across the room. She must go to him. She must ask him to tell her everything. He and Mama were speaking to some guests. But Papa was looking at Elizabeth, watching her talk to William. Was he hoping things were going well?

Was he pleased that a courtship might begin? For he did look pleased. He looked proud of her. "I'll see you later this evening," she said to William.

Elizabeth made her way across the room toward Papa.

Her mother and father were speaking to a distinguished-looking gentleman and his wife, the man rotund, in a thick charcoal-gray suit. Elizabeth recognized him right away.

"Dr. Bradshaw," her father said rather loudly, shaking the man's hand. "Doctor to all of London's troubled souls." There were polite chuckles all around. Papa turned to the man's wife. "And Lady Bradshaw."

The psychiatrist. The one who had cared for Elizabeth this morning. The one Mama said she'd consulted about some issue for herself in her letter to Peter. The doctor who had offended Mama told her to keep whatever it was in the proper proportion. Surely Papa didn't know she'd consulted a psychiatrist. Did he?

"How good of you to come," her mother said, extending a limp hand to Dr. Bradshaw and his wife.

"We almost didn't. Just as we were leaving," Lady Bradshaw said, "my husband was called up on the telephone, a very sad case. A young man, one of his patients—killed himself. He had been in the army. Things had gotten so out of proportion for the fellow. So sad. He'd had such a time of it."

A look crossed Mama's face. If she were a stag, her antlers, at this moment, seemed made of a fine, fragile glass indeed. Mama said something to Lady Bradshaw; Elizabeth couldn't quite tell what it was. Then Mama turned and abruptly walked away. Almost rude. She moved briskly through her party, not meeting anyone's eyes, not saying hello, not laughing gaily, not stopping at all, even though several guests were clearly trying to get her attention. She breezed past them all. She looked as if she couldn't bear Dr. Bradshaw's presence, not for one moment more.

Almost rude.

Mrs. Dalloway was being rude. It was like seeing the rarest of comets shoot through the night sky.

Mama went into the empty drawing room and Elizabeth followed, hid herself behind one of the stiff armchairs in the corner. And watched.

Her mother went to a window, lifted it, and stared into the night. On and on she looked. She stared at that square of darkness, a ghost in her silver-green dress, the ghost of a mermaid. Half woman, half fish, one who dives and swims through crowds, flips her tail, and splashes with ease. But in here all her finery looked odd and ill-fitting somehow, like all the flesh had disappeared from her body, every scale had fallen off, as if she were a collection of brittle fish bones perilously perched on the windowsill, about to topple out, hit the pavement. Shatter to dust.

Was she leaning out the window?

She was.

Staring down and down and down to the street.

Elizabeth didn't know what to do. She was so frightened, frozen, her feet rooted to the carpet. Why had Lady Bradshaw's comment about that soldier affected Mama so? Lady Bradshaw hadn't said the name of the poor man, had she?

The curtain in a window of a home across the street moved. An old woman appeared. She was in a robe, about to draw the curtain it seemed. Two women standing in windows across the street from one another, one hosting London's most exclusive party, the other—alone and early to bed. It was strange to see Mama's bracelets, her gown, her hair done up, juxtaposed with that woman in a nightcap. As if they were two different species. Two different animals entirely. On two paths that would never intersect.

The clock struck.

Finally, finally, it struck. Time had sped up; it had begun to move like a quick-flowing river.

Nine o'clock.

The woman across the street pulled her blinds closed.

Mama stepped back. Away from the darkness.

She stood. Quiet. She took a deep breath, ran her hand over the beads of her silver-green dress. She was preparing to reenter the party.

Why had she stayed at the window like that?

"It had nothing whatever to do with Peter Walsh."

Mama smoothed her hair. Elizabeth had the startling thought that these parties were talismans somehow, beloved figurines Mama used to keep something at bay. Something overwhelming.

"It had nothing whatever to do with Peter Walsh."

If not Peter, then whom?

The mermaid dove back into the crowd.

Elizabeth went straight to William. He stood in the middle of his Cambridge crowd, but suddenly she wasn't scared of them. At the moment it seemed nothing could be more frightening than what she'd just seen at the window. That darkness.

"William," Elizabeth said. She was even so brave as to touch his shoulder. "I'm leaving for the party. I will meet you there?"

William handed his brandy to one of his friends—not so much handed it off as forced it on him. "Absolutely," he said, his face brightening. "We'll go immediately."

"No, no," Elizabeth said. "I'd like to pick up my friends first and meet you. If that's all right."

"Of course it is." A song came drifting over the crowd then; a few couples began dancing. It was a waltz. "But perhaps a dance before we go?"

She must have nodded. It was something about the music. She might be all right if she could just listen to the music, to be with it somehow. William took her hand, led her to the center of the room.

Step-step-step.

Step-step-step.

Around and around they went.

It stilled her mind. She thought only of the notes, only the movement of her feet, the sturdiness of William's shoulders. She smelled peppermint again, his shaving cream perhaps. She felt the scratchiness of his suit, tickling her palms. Here. She was just here.

Step-step-step.

Step-step-step.

The music stopped.

She saw her father again; Dr. Bradshaw had gone.

"Thank you, William," Elizabeth said. "I'll see you shortly." She kissed his cheeks. She started across the room.

She heard her name.

"There's Elizabeth." Someone said it in a hushed voice. But Elizabeth heard it. Her name. "She feels not half what we feel, not yet."

Peter Walsh.

It was Peter Walsh. Talking about *her*. To a woman in red next to him. They were a bit too close to one another on the love seat. Peter wore the same checked suit she'd seen him in earlier that day, but now he wore a fresh pocket square. Elizabeth studied his face, its creases, its . . . adventurousness. Yes, that was it. He had the face of someone accustomed to long journeys across seas, treks with elephants through the Indian countryside, nights spent in canvas tents, sleeping in the hush, the buzz of wings, the lion's roar. He had the face of a man who preferred to be outside. Who preferred the country to the city.

Like Elizabeth did.

Elizabeth pretended not to hear; she kept walking in the direction of her father.

"But one can see they are devoted to each other." The woman in red was looking at Papa. She was watching Elizabeth cross the room to Papa. Was this woman talking about them? Elizabeth glanced at the woman's dress, tried to be inconspicuous about it. The red was wild, like it had spent the day catching butterflies, tramping over hills, a thick leather strap of a collection box flung over the shoulder. The dress was perfectly respectable, but . . . a bit loud, Elizabeth thought. Yes, loud. Brave, even. Elizabeth was certain she had never seen this woman before. And she wasn't sure why on earth Mama would have invited her on a night when the prime minister was coming. A lady in red like this.

She heard Peter say something to her. Did he call her Sally? Another of Mama's childhood friends from Bourton. Mama had mentioned her in that letter to Peter. Mr. Garrick had mentioned her too.

Sally Seton?

The woman in red is Sally Seton.

Elizabeth reached her father.

"I—" her father began. He looked so happy to see her. "I wanted to say something." He took a sip of his drink. "It's the Hungarian tokay. It's going to my head a bit tonight!"

"What is it you wanted to say, Papa?"

"Just that—I saw you across the room. And at first I didn't know who you were, dancing with William. And I wondered, who is that lovely girl? And then it hit me—my daughter! It is my daughter."

And it did make her happy.

True or not, it did make her happy.

She heard poor Grizzle locked upstairs, howling. She saw Peter, still on the sofa, looking at something. On his face was an expression Elizabeth couldn't discern. Hope? An encounter with a longed-for wish. Elizabeth followed his gaze—it landed on a woman who was moving across the room.

There she was.

Mama.

Hostess. Here. But not.

"Thank you, my sweet papa." Elizabeth kept her eyes on Peter. She must ask. She had to. "Papa, who is that man?"

He followed her gaze. "Peter Walsh," he said. "That is Peter Walsh."

"No," Elizabeth said. She turned to her father now, summoned every bit of courage she had. "I know his name. But who *is* he?"

Her father took a sip of his tokay. "Elizabeth, your mother doesn't have anything to hide, do you understand?" He looked at her sternly. "Nothing at all. She only thinks she does."

"Yes, Papa."

"Rumors are part of your mother's problem." He put his arm around Elizabeth. Gave her a gentle squeeze. "And I don't want my dear daughter falling prey to them."

It was something about the way he said it: *"my dear daughter."* She believed him.

"Thank you, Papa. That means more than you know."

CHAPTER 17

Octavia

The house was dark, but in the late-afternoon light, Octavia could see through the first-floor windows; the furniture was covered with white sheets. The warm glow of the sun coated the covered sofas and settees. A house full of golden ghosts. The curtains on the second floor were drawn.

"It looks empty," Octavia said, gazing up at the grand Westminster home. "Are you sure this is where Lord and Lady Purvis live? It doesn't look like anybody's there."

"Sure am," Redvers said, ushering Octavia down the sidewalk. They lingered in front of the house next door to the Purvises'. A little wire-haired fox terrier frantically barked at them from behind a wrought-iron gate. An old gardener was on his knees working in phlox beds. He eyed Red, Georgie, and Octavia with suspicion. Red doffed his cap.

"Evenin'," Red called to the gardener.

The gardener pushed up from his knees, an action that clearly caused him trouble, and came to the gate.

"Do you have business at this house?" the gardener asked, his brows furrowed.

"Just passing through," Redvers said. He put his hand on the small of Octavia's back and gently pushed her along. She didn't budge.

"Redvers," Octavia hissed. "Your manners." She looked up at the gardener. "Hello," she said. "My name is Octavia Smith. Of Stroud." She held out her hand.

"How d'you do, Miss," the gardener replied. "My name is Mr. Garrick. Gardener to Mr. and Mrs. Richard Dalloway. Is everything . . . quite all right?"

She knew what he was asking. He was eyeing Red and Georgie, wondering if anything bad was happening, if she needed help. She wanted to tell him not to worry his head.

"Oh, yes," she said. She looked behind him, at the grounds. "And those are gurt big gardens you have. How pretty." She glanced at the Purvis house next door. "We're just about to do a job for—"

"Well, Mr. Garrick, it's been a pleasure," Redvers said, interrupting Octavia. "A real pleasure. But we're just passing through. On our way to get my little brother here some of his favorite biscuits." Red gently tugged on Octavia's arm, a bit more forcefully this time. Georgie took her other arm.

"*Octavia*," Georgie hissed. "*Let's go.*"

Octavia could feel the gardener's judgment blister their backs as they walked away. "I don't think that man liked us," she whispered to Red, scanning the homes and lawns around them. "Everything here is so fancy. That man was *angry*. And why didn't you tell him we have a job next door? For the Purvises?"

"He can bugger off. We're free people, ain't we?" Red snapped. "These posh folks always need an explanation for everything. It's none of his business." The tone of Red's voice was different than it had been all day.

"But . . ." Octavia glanced back. Mr. Garrick was still watching them. "Why did you tell him we were getting biscuits?"

"Because it's the truth," Red said. They passed out of the neighborhood and came to a long row of shops. "We're early yet for the Purvis job. So we'll pop in here and get a biscuit." He stopped in front of a store. Octavia looked up at the sign.

LIBERTY OF LONDON

"What's this?" she asked. There weren't any biscuits in the window. There wasn't any food at all in Liberty of London's shop windows.

Only fabric.

Loads and loads of fabric.

Octavia pressed her face against the window. It was unlike anything she'd ever seen. The shop was filled to the brim with colorful cloth, each print more beautiful than the last. Some of it was draped on mannequins and on dress forms. A line of fabric bolts leaned against the front window, all pressed together like a row of fine books, a library of color. Some of the designs were tiny floral prints, the blooms modern somehow, like they were flowers but only just. Like they straddled a line between actual blooms and mere suggestions of them, whiffs of the feeling you get when standing in a field of poppies. They were red and purple and bursting in splotches, petals touching as if they were all banding together to hide some secret behind their blossoms.

Some luscious secret. One they were protecting with their very lives.

Next to the floral prints were swatches of paisleys, and next to those were fabrics covered with complete abstractions. Shapes like triangles or uneven squares, circles of brilliant and shocking yellow. Indulgent yellow. Vulgar yellow. The bravest yellow she'd ever seen. Braver even than the color of wildflowers flouting the limestone in Stroud. Braver than the yellow-green of early hops waiting to be ground to death in her father's brewery. Braver even than the color of the sun itself.

"What *is* this place?" Octavia asked Red, almost breathless.

"You've never heard of Liberty?" Red looked shocked. He cracked a smile and slowly shook his head. "You're a strange bird, I'll give you that. Must be the only girl in the world who's never heard of this place."

Octavia was still staring at that yellow. "Uh-huh," she said, not caring enough to say anything back. She couldn't take her eyes off the place.

"And I mean that in your favor," Redvers added quickly. "Like you blew into London from another world entirely."

"Uh-huh," Octavia said again.

She went in.

The shop reminded her of a beehive, a glistening honeycomb

crawling with insects, buzzing, buzzing, buzzing with purpose, with work, with life. Shelves were stocked with endless bolts of prints, tables were scattered throughout the shop, posh ladies gathered around them, barking at grim-looking clerks in black—*cut this much; no, that much,* and then, *no, on second thought, could they have one yard more of this?* The rip of fabric and the clink of scissors filled the air. The clerks stationed at the tables kept so calm, Octavia thought, carefully taking orders from their customers, holding their positions, steadfast against the demand.

All save for one, that is.

One clerk's table was different. Very different.

A woman was cutting fabric there. Her brunette hair was done up in the most fabulous and frantic bun, wisps falling freely around her face and neck as if blown by the wind and never meant to be shielded from it in the first place. Like Octavia's. Her hair was just like Octavia's. The woman wasn't serious like those other clerks in black, either; she was laughing, loud, the unapologetic center of a sunflower. She was wearing a bright red-and-yellow dress that had to have been made from a Liberty print. It just had to be. Octavia had never seen that yellow anywhere else but here.

"Mum!" Georgie ran to her side, let himself fall among the folds of her skirt. A skirt blanketed with those blooms, tight-lipped, hiding something behind them; Octavia was sure of it now.

"Georgie, my darling," the woman said. She asked a customer if she could be so kind as to wait just a moment. Then she tapped the arm of a male clerk nearby who was measuring a dress form, holding straight pins in his pursed lips, had a tape measure hanging from his neck like a domesticated snake who wouldn't dream of biting.

"Maeve," the man protested, his words a bit mangled from the pins in his mouth. He pulled them out. "I'm really too busy to take your table at the moment. I—"

"Then I will be all the more grateful when you do," Maeve said. She looked at Redvers and then at Georgie. "So that a mum may have a bit of time with her sons."

The clerk rolled his eyes, defeated, vanquished. He took the scissors

Maeve held out for him and began to slice through a purple paisley print on the table. He granted a duty-bound smile at the customer waiting on her fabric.

"Come with me, boys," Maeve said. She eyed Octavia. "And bring your guest."

They followed her through the store toward a back room. Octavia almost tripped over several bolts of fabrics, mesmerized by the swish of Maeve's dress; its beauty made it difficult to focus on where to place her own feet.

The room was dark, lit only by a few milk-white pendant lights that looked ancient, their glass blooming with hairline cracks. The floor was littered with chunks of fabric, tangles of thread, tape measures, a stray pincushion here and there, dotting the floor like fat rodents who fed on string and fabric scraps.

It was a mess.

Octavia loved it.

The four of them stopped in the middle of the room beside a large cutting table.

"Mum, this is Octavia," Redvers said. "Octavia, this is my mum."

"Pleased to meet you, Octavia," she said. She pulled a little wooden stool over. "Please, call me Maeve."

"Hello," Octavia said, her eyes still wide. "This is . . . well, it's the most beautiful place I think I've ever seen!" Octavia wasn't sure where her bravery had come from, to be so loud. She couldn't help it. She really couldn't.

But Maeve didn't seem offended in the least; she tipped her head back and laughed like Octavia was a pure delight, like she'd danced an unexpected waltz, right there by the cutting table, a monkey let loose in a fabric shop. "Tell me you've *never* been to Liberty?" Maeve asked as she eased herself onto the wooden stool and took a deep breath. "My, how my pins hurt by this time of day. No break to speak of! Wish you had all popped in a bit earlier." Maeve looked at Octavia. "My boys come once a week, my excuse to take a rest," she whispered.

"Guess what?" Georgie piped up.

Maeve leaned against the cutting table and smiled wearily. "Tell me, dear."

"Octavia's from the country!" Georgie said. Maeve motioned for him to hop on her lap. He did, nestling like a bunny burrowing in a field of Liberty flowers. "She's from Stroud. She's never even been to London before. Not once!"

Maeve raised an eyebrow, her expression changing. "Is that right?" She looked suddenly serious. "Stroud's in Gloucestershire. Cotswolds?"

"Yes, ma'am."

"Where is your family? Your mother? She's with you in the city, yes?"

Octavia wasn't expecting that. A question about her mother. About her family. The one she'd abandoned and would likely never welcome her home again. Her face bloomed red, a vibrant flower print. She couldn't tell the truth; Maeve wouldn't believe her. She'd think Octavia was just some vagrant who'd cottoned on to her sons, a street urchin with no home. Octavia took too long to drum up a lie.

"They're all back in Stroud," Red interjected. He said it with concern like he was alerting his mother to the facts.

"I see," Maeve said slowly. "So you're in the city . . . alone?"

"I'm looking for my brother," Octavia said, feigning courage. "Septimus Warren Smith."

"He was in the war," Red explained. "Never came home. War Office says he's in Bloomsbury somewhere. So Octavia here is going to find him."

"Hmm," Maeve said. She gently shooed Georgie off her lap and leaned toward Octavia. "Well, Octavia from Stroud."

Octavia held her breath. Waited for Maeve to ask her to leave, to stop leeching off her boys, to stop tagging along. Treat her like the street orphan she was.

"I promise I'll pay Red back for all his help. I'll pay him," Octavia said, defensive now. "I just didn't have any money, see, and . . ." She paused, ordered the tears she could feel in her eyes to retreat. "Once I get to Bloomsbury and find my brother, he will care for me, or I'll get him home to our parents, my father has a brewery, and he can—"

"I'm so very glad my boys found you." The look on Maeve's face—Octavia didn't feel judged somehow. Maeve's eyes, her dress, her wild, beautiful hair, and now her tone of voice—they all did that, made Octavia feel at ease.

"You're glad of it?" Octavia asked. She felt shy in the face of kindness, looked down at her skirt, which now seemed more out-of-date and faded than she'd ever realized. Next to these Liberty fabrics, her dress was a corpse, she thought. A corpse from long ago that desperately needed a burial.

"Of course I am," Maeve said. She reached for a green tin on the cutting table and pried off its lid. It was filled with biscuits. She handed one to each of her sons. Then to Octavia. "Now, boys, go to Mr. Kirby's office. Tell him I sent you. And that I need a bottle of lemon squash from his icebox. For a very special guest."

"We can't stay here that long, Mum," Georgie said, whining a little, his mouth full of biscuit. "We've got quite a little earner up the—"

"Marbles," Redvers interrupted. He wiped the crumbs from Georgie's mouth. "We've got quite a little game of *marbles* set up. Just up the street. Right here in Westminster. Georgie's hoping to earn a pile of glass glarnies by the end of it."

Glass glarnies. Those marbles that reminded Octavia of the berries on juniper bushes back in Stroud. The marbles the boys there were always trying to get her to buy. Red and Georgie were going to play marbles?

Maeve narrowed her eyes at her boys, first at Georgie, then at Red. Her warm smile fell flat. "Marbles, hm?"

Red nodded. "Yep, a right old tourney, Mum! Just up the street. Must be ten boys on their way for it. We'll clean up for sure."

"Go get the bottle of lemon squash," Maeve said, her voice as flat as her smile. The boys ran off as if they'd just escaped some horrible fate.

"That's awfully nice of you," Octavia said. "To send for lemon squash." She was still holding her biscuit, too nervous to eat it in front of this marvelous lady. This woman, a type of person Octavia had never dreamed existed. So bright, so colorful, so . . . alive. And working. A woman working. A woman who'd had children, even. Who—and this was truly the most extraordinary thing—seemed almost happy.

A happy mother.

How odd.

"I hope," Octavia continued, "it isn't a bother to—"

"Don't mention it," Maeve said, waving a hand in the air. Octavia could see now that Maeve's hands were rough. A large callous was on her right hand, just at the place where her fingers went through scissor loops, and her fingertips bore tiny red marks and scars. Octavia guessed they were wounds from unruly straight pins, slices from scissors delivered in moments of distraction. "Now," Maeve went on, "tell me what you like about this place so much. You glowed like the sun when you walked in."

Octavia couldn't believe it—she had expected Maeve to start interrogating her about her family back in Stroud the moment the boys disappeared. But she wanted to talk about Liberty. About fabric.

How wonderful.

Octavia looked around the back room, eyed the scraps of fabric on the floor, the bolts lining the shelves. She was determined to find perfect words to describe what she was seeing. Because that's what Septimus would do. He would describe something he loved with a poem on the spot. With a comparison that would inspire. "These prints," Octavia finally said, "they make me feel at home. Like I'm with the flowers back there."

"What a lovely thing to say." Maeve looked delighted again, like Octavia was still some sort of exotic animal performing in a zoo. But concerned a bit, too, like maybe she wanted to pick the lock on Octavia's cage and let her out. "So they remind you of Gloucestershire? These fabrics?"

Octavia nodded.

"And you want to go back there?" Maeve asked. "It's a good place for you?"

Yes, of course, Octavia thought. She wanted to go back. She *would* go back. She *must* go back. She would collect Septimus, and together they would return to Stroud. To their family. Nurse Septimus back to health if he needed it. And Octavia would be taken care of by her father until some bachelor scooped her up. Then he'd take care of her. They'd live in Stroud, close to their family. People didn't live apart from their families. Not by choice anyway. Not unless they were ill or angry or running away from something dreadful. Or poetic geniuses who were too important to stay home. People didn't just choose to be somewhere else because it was an idea they fancied.

Did they?

Octavia would go home.

"No," Octavia said. She wasn't sure the answer had come from her own throat.

"No, you don't want to go back home? And why is that?"

Octavia felt a rush then, like some secret door had opened a crack and she'd stuck her toe out. Just a toe. But then she pulled it back. "I mean, no, I don't know when I'll go back. But I'll go back. I'll surely go back. Once I find Septimus. That's when I'll go."

"One bottle of lemon squash! Fresh from the icebox." Red came in holding it above his head like an award at a fair. He popped the top and held it out to Octavia. She smiled.

"Thank you," she said and took a sip. The drink was tart and cold and sweet. And to Octavia, it was perhaps the finest thing she'd ever had. As if it were much more than a drink. Much more than a soda. It was a whole world in a bottle, she thought. A whole world.

"All right, Mum," Red said. "Just wanted you to meet our Octavia, here. But we've got to get to that—"

"Marble tournament," Maeve said, completing his sentence for him. "Yes, I know."

Georgie ran to his mum and gave her a kiss. Red followed. There was such warmth, such familiarity among the three. Sweet, Octavia thought. Sweet like a bottle of lemon squash. But tart too. The taste of envy on her tongue.

Red gently ushered Octavia and Georgie toward the door. "We'll see you, Mum!"

Maeve stood up and followed them. "Wait," she said. "Octavia."

The three stopped just before they went out to the shop floor.

"Yes, ma'am?"

Maeve looked at her, still kind, but a bit stern as well. "Don't let my boys get you into anything. And you can always come back here if they do. Do you understand?"

Octavia nodded.

Maeve leaned a little closer. "You said my boys have been helping you. And that when you get to Bloomsbury, your brother can care for you. Or your father can care for you at home."

"Yes, ma'am," Octavia said. "I promise, I won't bother your sons when I—"

"Just because you accept help from all those boys doesn't mean you aren't surviving on your own wits." She reached down and smoothed the collar on Octavia's dress. "Making it on your own is not the only measure to go by. And don't listen to those who tell you it is. Can you remember that?"

Octavia nodded again even though she wasn't sure at all what Maeve had meant. But she felt like she'd partly understood it somehow, understood it with some piece of herself she didn't know she had. But wherever Maeve's comment had landed, whatever place in Octavia it had struck, it made her feel something.

Something unquestionably good.

Something strong.

"Yes, I will," Octavia said. "I will remember."

"Good," Maeve said, smiling now. "And you know where to find me."

Octavia smiled. "Yes ma'am," she said. "I certainly do."

CHAPTER 18

Elizabeth

The building was dark.

The car pulled up; Frances took Elizabeth's hand as if she'd done it a thousand times. Take her hand. They stepped from the motorcar onto the lamplit street. Calvin was close behind.

They stood, the three of them, in the shadow of the Marshall Street building. Several stories high with grand arches in front, giant windows reflecting blinking stars.

"Your mother doesn't have anything to hide, do you understand?"

"My dear daughter."

She wanted to believe her father. Just for tonight. That she was his and his alone. Could one do that? Choose to believe something?

"Looks like we're the only ones here," Elizabeth said. "And it's half past already. William must have been making me out to be a fool. Sending me on a wild-goose chase for a swim party I'm not welcome to."

"Don't talk like that," Frances said. Did all Americans have indefatigable hope like this? An endless supply of lilt for their voices? "We're early yet." She gently tugged Elizabeth's hand again, pulled her forward. They went up the marble front stairs, pulled on the giant copper handle of the front door.

It was locked.

"Oh, let's just go," Elizabeth said. "William has had his fun. I'm sure he's telling the prince all about the stiff Dalloway girl who wanted to go to her first real after-party. How he sent her racing off into the night."

"His loss, I say." Calvin joined them on the top stair. "Who wouldn't want to invite two beautiful girls from either side of the pond?"

Elizabeth wasn't sure anyone had ever called her beautiful. Just this morning Mr. Garrick had called her chipper. Lady Bexborough had compared Elizabeth to a crape myrtle.

But not beautiful.

Frances adjusted her gold hairband. Twirled in front of Elizabeth and Calvin in her white dress. "But don't I look dressed for a party? Be honest."

Elizabeth smiled. "Of course you do."

"Well, then," Frances said. "Let's have a party." She dashed off into the darkness, disappeared around the side of the building.

"What are you doing?" Calvin chased after his sister, that slippery little fairy in white. Elizabeth had the impression that Calvin had spent much of his life chasing after her, trying to guard her from herself. He rounded the grand brick building and disappeared. Elizabeth followed.

"See?" Frances pointed at an open window halfway up the side of the building. Two stories at least. "I knew there had to be a way in."

"But there's no way we can reach—"

"Want to bet?" Frances hiked up her dress, stepped over a bit of garbage on the sidewalk and took hold of a copper-green downspout. She hoisted herself up and up, a spider determined to climb to the faucet.

"This isn't safe!" Elizabeth called after her, watching the hem of Frances's dress swing this way and that as she climbed in the darkness. Elizabeth suddenly felt terribly responsible for these two Americans; she was their shepherd through the wilds of London.

"I know!" Frances answered. Still climbing. Up and up and up.

"Can't you do something?" Elizabeth looked to Calvin. "Convince her to come down or threaten to tell Grim? Something! She'll fall."

Calvin looked up. "Have you met her—my sister? Do you think anyone can get her to do something she doesn't want to do? I just assist with the consequences of her actions."

She was there. Frances had made it to the window. She pulled herself through.

And was gone.

Elizabeth stood there in the darkness, surrounded by the sounds of traffic and a few people chatting as they passed by. She stared at the black square of open window, waited for Frances to peek her head back out, to let Elizabeth and Calvin know she was okay. But everything was still.

Had she fallen?

What if the window was several stories above the pool, what if Frances had cascaded down and down and landed on the tiles below? Slipped down the inside of the wall like someone had turned on the water, flushed this little white spider back down the drain.

Elizabeth heard the creak of hinges.

A few meters away, a side door opened. Frances peeked out.

"Come on!" Out of breath, joyous. "I've broken in!"

"Besides," Calvin said, walking toward the open door, "she usually pulls it off."

The building was massive, dark—a grand cavern of marble and tile, lit only by the moonlight coming through the windows. A large pool shimmered a silver-blue under an enormous arched ceiling; tiles covered the walls, the floor. A second-floor balcony was above, its decorative railing rolled along like waves frozen in iron. Elizabeth could just make out the ladders leading into the water, passageways to whatever secrets were in the deep.

Frances was pulling off her shoes.

"What are you doing?" Elizabeth asked. "I don't have my swimming costume, I—"

"Sure, you do," Frances said. She took Elizabeth's hand and pulled her across the tiles. Closer and closer to the edge.

"Frances, where are we—"

"Hold your nose!"

And they were in.

Shocked by the cold, completely underwater, still holding hands. The sounds of bubbles filled Elizabeth's ears, and then a muffled sound, an entrance, a soft rumbling. Calvin had jumped in beside them. Under the water she could just make out the shape of him, his shirt clinging to his chest, his suspenders holding tight to his shoulders.

And then a delicious silence, that stubborn, thick silence of water. As if the entire world had been completely forgotten, shut out. All of life above them, all its expectations commingling, teeming, thrashing, waiting. But just now, just this moment, they were safe below the surface.

Just stay down.

Let's just stay down here forever.

She felt the pull of Calvin's hand. Heard the swish of his arms and legs slicing through the water, pulling them both to the surface. They burst into the air with gasps. Frances was already clinging to the side, sputtering and laughing. She pushed away from the wall without warning, began swimming laps, doing the backstroke down a lane of the pool.

Elizabeth reached for the cool steel rails of the ladder, Calvin beside her. They let their toes sink toward the deep, caught their breath. Calvin shook the water from his hair, droplets clung to his eyelashes like the tiniest of marbles. She felt brave; this night made her feel brave. Seeing her mother like that at the window, hearing the rumors about Peter Walsh, about her father. Ending up submerged in a pool in a gown with an American boy. This night. What on earth did she have to lose?

"Could you hold me up?" Elizabeth asked. Brazen. She felt brazen. Like she wanted nothing more than to be like Frances. Unafraid. Unfettered. "I want to float." She pushed away from the ladder, turned on her back. She kept sinking. Her blush-pink gown felt as though it had pockets filled with stones. Calvin swam over, put a hand under her back. She stared at the grand tiled ceiling far above them, at the moonlight coming through the open window. She didn't know this boy in the least; she should talk of sensible things, light things—Bach cello suites. Needlepoint. She didn't want to. "Do you think it will be terrible to grow up?"

He was still holding her up. Gently. "I think it depends."

"On what?"

"On which direction you go, I suppose," Calvin said. He took his hand away and playfully let Elizabeth sink. She splashed him; he reached for her, helped her float again.

"Direction?" she asked.

"Do you know any adults who are happy?"

"Happy?" Elizabeth had never thought of it that way. Happiness. She wasn't sure she'd ever contemplated the topic at all. She thought of her mother standing in front of that window, hiding in the drawing room, kissing behind closed doors. Peter bursting into tears beside her. She thought of that elderly woman in the home across from theirs, alone and ready for bed before the night had even begun. Papa who perhaps knew and hid all of Mama's horrible secrets. Elizabeth thought of Mr. Garrick. His aging knees. Lucy, her spitefulness. "No," she said. "I suppose I don't. A happy adult. I'm not sure I've ever seen one."

"Not your mother?"

"Especially not my mother. I think something dreadful happened to her, in her youth, and I still don't know what. And yours?"

"Who knows? She barely says a word. I've a theory she's some sort of amoeba—no capability for preferences." Calvin took Elizabeth's hand, intertwined her fingers with his. Pulled her to the side. Elizabeth could barely think of anything else, the feel of his hand on hers. She must try.

Keep talking.

"And Grim? Is he happy?"

"Oh god, no," Calvin said. "I'm not the son he ordered off the menu. I'm supposed to be a teetotaling future preacher."

Frances swam up now, climbed out of the pool. She stood above them, dripping. "I'm going on the hunt for some towels," she said. "And hopefully there's a locked bar I can break into." She blew them a kiss and trotted off.

Elizabeth dared. She touched Calvin's arm under the water. Floated a little closer. "If you aren't what he wanted, then what are you?"

He looked up as if searching for words, like he was trying to pull them down out of the damp darkness. "I'm a man who loves to play the ukulele and drink bourbon. I do all right in school and sports. In any other family, that would be enough for a lad, wouldn't it?"

"Well, you seem like a lovely boy to me."

He smiled. "And what about you, Elizabeth Dalloway? Are you the daughter your mother ordered?"

"The great Mrs. Dalloway? The greatest hostess in all of England?" She asked it dramatically, as if her mother were about to emerge from the depths, burst out of the water like a mermaid who'd been there all this while. Breathing. Breathing under the water, just waiting to be announced. Elizabeth looked down at the water, at the faint, wavy outlines of her feet. "Hardly. She's a bit of a trope, I'm afraid. And she wants to take me down the same route. A stifled upper-class society wife and all that. She wants me to take my turns about the same room. Secretly, I think she wishes she'd chosen a different path in life entirely."

Calvin reached for her under the water. Wrapped one arm around her waist. "Then don't choose the path she did. Don't become a socialite." He pulled her close. "And I won't become a preacher. We'll do it all differently. We'll be free."

Did all Americans do this? Swim so quickly, dive so deep?

"Free?" Elizabeth whispered.

"Like this."

He kissed her.

She could feel the brush of his legs against hers, the warmth of his body, the caress of his cotton shirt. The cold water rippling around her shoulders. There was nothing else in the world but this warmth, this water. Nothing. She wrapped her arms around his neck; he pushed her against the side of the pool. She could feel his body; she wanted it closer, close as the water, touching every part of her, leaving no air, no space between them.

He kissed her again. And again. He was reaching now; one hand moved along her waist, to her breasts. He ran his lips along the side of her neck. Now he was reaching again. For the hem of her dress. He was pulling it up. She could feel his hand on her leg, on the inside of her thigh.

But then—lights. All of them. The whole grand room lit up. Doors opened. The night air rushed in, raised a chill on Elizabeth's arms. Elizabeth blinked in the horrific sudden brightness, heard singing and laughing and . . .

Was that a ukulele? One like Calvin's?

A crowd flooded through the front doors, all clamor and color and cacophony. A young man in a suit led the crowd, strumming a ukulele. His suit was a nice one, except the legs were cut a bit too short. He kicked off his loafers and sat poolside, dangled his bare feet in the water, and strummed away on his ukulele. And sang a bit. Elizabeth didn't recognize the tune. Some song about being lost at sea. About being far, far out to sea. About not knowing the way home. The rest of the crowd filled the room around him.

Elizabeth and Calvin quickly pulled apart and watched, dumbfounded, as the rest of the near circus entered the building. Two men in golfing attire were carrying a large vat full of liquor bottles and beer. Another carried one full of champagne. Gorgeous women of all varieties were in tow—some glamorous in lavish gowns, their hair pressed into perfect Marcel waves, and others in pants and button-up blouses, their hair in rough-cut shingles. Elizabeth even saw a few wearing men's ties.

"I'm telling Lord Lordsome about the lot of you!" a man shouted over the pool, holding his finger up and wagging it at the whole crowd. He—or Elizabeth *thought* it was a he, she couldn't be certain—was wearing a maid's dress just like Lucy always wore: black, thick, a high, sensible neckline. He had a hunk of iron keys, so large as to be comedic, hanging from a chain around his waist. And he was wearing lipstick. Was that a wig? A man in a dress and a wig? He swooped around the pool, gently prodding people on the shoulders, jabbing others in the ribs. "Naughty, naughty!" he squealed. "Yes, Lord Lordsome will hear of this first thing in the morn!" Laughter erupted all around.

Elizabeth swept her eyes about the room, hoping to see a table full of bath towels or something—anything—to wrap herself in. She couldn't get out of the pool like this: her pink gown was soaked through; it would cling to every inch of her body, reveal its every curve, its every secret. She was mortified.

"I see you came for an early swim," someone said.

William Titcomb.

He was on the edge of the pool near Elizabeth and Calvin, smoking a cigar. He was in his suit from earlier, but now his bow tie was loose, a few buttons of his shirt undone. He wore a beret on his head, cocked to the side. He seemed to notice Elizabeth looking at it. "Borrowed this from Harold."

"Harold?" Elizabeth asked.

"I'll introduce you." He pointed across the room. "That's him, there. Curled up in that chair like a goblin. He'll sit there all night watching every little thing. God only *knows* how many of us will end up in his novels."

"Could you point me to the towels?" Elizabeth whispered.

"Of course." William extended his hand. Elizabeth took it and climbed out of the water. "There are a few on that little table by Harold's chair."

Elizabeth immediately felt naked. Positively naked with her wet dress clinging to her body like this. It was dreadful.

"A novelist? Say you'll introduce us!" Frances was back now, still dripping wet, a rat in a wedding dress. She must have missed the towels. "I've never met a novelist. And my name is Frances. Frances Gage." She held out her hand. "And you are?"

"William," he said. "William Titcomb. And this"—he waved a hand at the crowd still pouring through the doors, at the slew of girls who had already jumped in the water, gowns and all, at the novelist hunched in his chair, at the man strumming his ukulele—"is the most exclusive party in all of London." He took a long puff on his cigar and exhaled a massive cloud around the three of them. "Hell is empty, and all the devils are here."

Shakespeare.

The Tempest.

"And if I were you," William said, smiling, "I'd prepare to have the best evening of your lives."

CHAPTER 19

Octavia

The redheaded boy spoke first.

"What's *she* doing here?" he asked, pointing at Octavia. It was Tom, one of the boys she'd seen when she'd first met Redvers, when she'd tripped on his rag ball. The one Redvers said was his best friend but talked to like an enemy.

Octavia stood behind the Purvises' home with Red and George and watched as Tom and two other boys approached. She thought they looked a bit dodgy in a group like that. Like a pack of dogs she'd seen in Stroud, all homeless but healthy, plump, eating well because they'd decided to band together. To scavenge as a cluster.

Night had fallen, but all the Westminster homes around them were lit like Christmas trees, each window a bulb of golden light. Octavia eyed the lawn next door; she hoped that cranky gardener, Mr. Garrick, didn't reemerge from the house. How suspicious he was. Was it the way she looked? That must be it. She was so out of place in this wealthy London neighborhood. So out of place. And now it was dark; she felt her chances of finding Septimus diminishing by the second.

Redvers leaned close to Octavia, whispered in her ear, "Just follow my lead."

"What do you mean, follow your—"

"You ever seen a rozzer suspect a girl?" Redvers asked Tom. Tom didn't respond; he just stood there sizing up Octavia. He looked bested.

"Guess I haven't seen a bird in cuffs, come to think of it."

"That's what I thought," Redvers said. "We'll back slang it, and she'll keep an eye on the front."

Tom continued his close study of Octavia; she could feel his eyes on every part of her. "You ever done this before?" he asked. He motioned toward the Purvises' home. "How's your whistlin'? Better if it sounds like a real bird, you know. Like this." Tom pursed his lips and started to blow. The noise that came out didn't sound like a bird. It didn't even sound like a whistle. More like air escaping a tire.

"You call that a whistle?" Red asked.

"Why d'you think I'm the screws man?" Tom gave up on the whistling. He looked back to Octavia. "Go on, then. Let's hear it. Your best bird whistle."

"Why on earth do you want me to whistle?" Octavia asked. "And besides, I'm not very good at it anyway."

"Red, you meater!" Tom threw his hands in the air. "You weren't even man enough to tell her?"

"Never mind that, she's workin' for me, so bugger off," Red said. "She'll get part of my cut, not yours. And you sure we got the right place?"

Working for Red?

She wasn't sure exactly what was happening, but she knew enough to know it wasn't good. It wasn't good at all. And it was happening much too fast. One of the other boys, a short one with several unfortunate moles on his nose, stepped forward and dug in his pocket. He pulled out a folded paper and held it up for Red to see. He pounded a stubby finger at a block of text. "Read it yourself."

Octavia peered over Red's shoulder as he read. It was one of the quality papers, the society column.

SOCIETY NEWS

JUNE TRAVEL

Lord and Lady Flint will depart London on the 2nd of June for their tour of Northern Rhodesia. They will return for the final month of the season, in time to attend the palace ball.

Lord and Lady Ellsworth will depart London on the 10th of June for their maritime tour of the Falkland Islands. They will return in August to host a celebration in honor of Lady Ellsworth's niece, Abigail Duckworth, who will be completing her first season.

Finally, Octavia saw Lord and Lady Purvis's listing, the third in the column:

Lord and Lady Purvis will depart London with their daughter, Rose, on the 13th of June for their journey to Mallorca. They will miss the remainder of the season.

Octavia scanned the rest of the page, name after name, place after place, gobsmacked by the summer travel plans of the wealthy. She'd never seen such a list of exotic-sounding places. She didn't know where any of them were, but she knew they weren't in Britain. "But why is it in the paper?" she whispered to Red. "Their travels?"

The short boy heard her and yanked the newspaper away, folding it and returning it to his pocket. "Why do they do anythin'?" he said. He looked at Octavia like she was thick as a barber's block. "To look good, that's why. Not a true bone in their bodies. And we make sure they pay for it."

"Too right," Tom said. He glanced around the neighborhood and then back at his best friend. "You got the putty knife?"

Redvers nodded and pulled a small knife from his pocket. He handed it to Tom, who—Octavia now realized—had quite a few tools on him.

A small sink plunger hung from one of his back belt loops, and a pair of pliers hung from another.

"Sure it's time?" the short boy asked.

"Best time for it," Redvers said. "Trust me. They're smack-dab in the middle of their parties, now. Not a one of them is thinking about anything that ain't in a champagne glass."

"Who is having parties?" Octavia asked. She was starting to feel chilled now, despite the warm summer night.

"The posh folks," Tom answered. He gestured around at the Westminster houses. At the one next door where that angry gardener had been, Mr. Garrick. And the barking fox terrier. "Best time to start a job is this time of night, when every soul in every house is working up a lather over themselves, counting up their sons at Eton."

"Get on with it," Red answered. "Octavia, just stay with me for a bit, eh?"

The rest of the group dispersed all at once as if they'd rehearsed their movements. Tom pulled a bit of ivy from a drainpipe that ran down the entire side of the Purvises' house and began to shinny up. The putty knife was in his mouth now, and his plunger swung from his belt loop like a stiff foxtail. The other two boys ran to a side door and leaned against the house. Georgie disappeared around the other side. Redvers turned to Octavia.

"All right," he said. "Now you go round front. If you see any rozzers lurking about, do your best to whistle, like Tom said. If you can make it sound natural, even better. But if you can't manage that, just make some sort of noise so we know they're coming." Redvers squinted his eyes and watched as Tom made it to the top of the drainpipe to a little terrace. The glow from the house next door provided enough light for Elizabeth to see. Tom pulled the putty knife from his teeth and started working it around a windowpane. "And keep an eye on these neighbors," Red added, nodding at the house next door. "If you see that nasty gardener, sound the alarm. Or if that ratty little dog starts barking. Or any other servants for that matter."

"He's . . ." Octavia wasn't really listening to Red. She was watching

Tom finish with the putty knife and start working his pliers around the window. "He's taking out the window tacks, isn't he?" Octavia took a few steps forward, held her hand up to shield her eyes so she could get a better look. Tom pulled the plunger from his belt loop now, stuck it to the windowpane. And then, quick as you please, without a sound Octavia could hear, the pane came right out of the window. Tom gently set it down on the terrace, put his hand through the opening, jimmied the latch. Up went the window.

And Tom was through.

"My god," Octavia said, clapping a hand over her mouth. She'd known it all along, hadn't she? Hadn't she just hoped against hope this wasn't happening? But she'd known. "He's . . ."

Breaking in.

Stealing.

Robbing the home of a family gone for the season.

In a flash, Tom opened the side door where the other two boys were waiting. They disappeared inside. Octavia could see their dark shadows as they moved through the first floor now, pulling things off shelves, searching drawers. A siren sounded somewhere close by.

"The front!" Red hissed at Octavia. "Get round to the front! I'll check the back!" He took off toward the streets behind the house.

Octavia ran. Her hands trembled as she raced into the front lawn. She opened the gate and swung it shut behind her, told herself to slow down. She tried to scan the streets, the intersections, be a good lookout, but her blood drained toward her feet; she felt light, like she might float up and up and over this posh neighborhood, over the top of Big Ben. Just as she'd passed its giant clockface, she would cascade down like she was finally falling out of the window in the brewery attic back home. She blinked her eyes, tried to calm down.

Just walk. Look normal.

She looked for the police, to see if she could spot the source of the siren.

Wouldn't want anyone to catch us.

Us.

Octavia was one of *them*. A thief. A member of a street gang. One in a pack of wild dogs. She saw the source of the siren. It was an ambulance speeding down the street. It went around the corner and disappeared. Octavia glanced back at the first floor of the Purvises' house. She couldn't see the boys now; she could only imagine what they were taking from the second floor. Red came around front, out of breath.

"Nothing in the back," he said, heaving. "Did you see it? Was it a rozzer?" He was looking up and down the streets wildly, the intensity in his eyes making him nearly unrecognizable. He didn't look like the savvy boy she'd met near Paddington Station, the one who moved through London with swagger, with charm, with connections and friendships that seemed to cover the whole city.

He looked like an animal.

She thought of her father, how ashamed he would be if he could see her now, helping these boys break into the home of a fine family. Becoming a common criminal on the streets of London. She thought of the street gangs her mother had warned her about. The Hoxtons. The Tolmas. Was Red a member of one of them? Was that who he was?

"Get away from me," Octavia said, backing away from Red. "You're a criminal." The tears came now. She didn't want them to. Oh, how she didn't want them to. But they came.

"Octavia," he said softly, taking a step toward her.

"I said, get away from me."

"Octavia," Red said again. "It's just a job. I need it for Mum. For our rent. Landlord keeps raising it on us, and we don't have enough this month . . ." He stopped. There was a sound, a small explosion from across the street. They both jumped.

It was a motorcar backfiring, stalling in the middle of the road. A puff of black exhaust hovered over the pedestrians and the other motorcars, their drivers shouting, the traffic becoming snarled. The broken-down car looked fancy. Mysterious even. Some seal was carved into the back window. Was it royalty? The queen? Someone above all this, someone who was worth something, really worth something.

Octavia didn't care.

The moment Red was distracted by the commotion in the street—

She ran.

————

She went as fast as she could until the sound of Big Ben stopped her. The booming bells sounded like warning shots, funeral hymns, dark pronouncements of failure. She could see the clock's face now on its mighty tower; she could feel the clanging of its bells on her skin, between her ribs, down her back, as if some stranger had come up behind her, had surrounded her with his arms, held her against her will. Held her while she wondered what fate he had in store for her.

She kept her eyes on Big Ben. On the time. She couldn't bear to pull out her father's pocket watch. She couldn't bear to think of her father at all. Seeing her like this, helpless in the city, running away from a boy she'd met in a street gang. And maybe the worst—she'd used Pop's hard-earned money to get here.

She looked away from the tower and saw a small group of boys night-swimming in the Thames, the water glimmering and darkening in turns under the streetlamps. The boys were splashing and giggling and dunking one another under the oily surface. On the shore, a sign warned of drowning in the tides. She thought for just a moment about running into the river with those boys, slipping into the water, feeling it cool her skin, numb her exhaustion, push and push and push her past the city. To the sea. Far, far out to sea.

She saw a woman, a stylish woman. She wore a very sharp summer trench coat, a brilliant-red hat on her head. She was leaning into the street, waving her hand, hailing a cab. A book was tucked under her arm. Octavia wondered what the title was. Was it a novel? A mystery? Maybe the biography of a king? Or maybe it was the master, the genius:

Shakespeare.

The one Septimus had said Octavia should always turn to.

Fear no more the heat o'th'sun,
Nor the furious winter's rages.
Thou thy worldly task hast done,
Home art gone and ta'en thy wages.

Octavia looked at the woman again. At her hat. At its delicious red. It reminded Octavia of the orchids back home. And the band on the hat was yellow, like buttercups in the Stroud hills. The fine-flowered fabric of her dress peeked out beneath her coat's hem, colorful and carefree.

Like a Liberty print.

Shakespeare came back to Octavia again as she thought of Red's mother, Maeve. More of the poem from *Cymbeline* that Septimus always read to her. The last lines now:

Quiet consummation have,
And renownèd be thy grave.

It was a funeral hymn. One that celebrated the end. The end of struggle. One that rejoiced in death.

Or was it?

Thy worldly task.

The work. The struggle. The toil. Maybe the verses were marking all the efforts that came before the end. Naming them before they turned to dust.

The cryptic words from Maeve came back to Octavia then. About there being different ways to measure one's wits. That just because Red and Georgie had helped Octavia, she was also surviving on her own power. Her efforts were getting her through this city alive. Her instincts. Then she thought of the soldiers' honored graves back in Stroud, how she'd always known her own life wouldn't—couldn't—ever be remarkable like that. How Septimus was the one who had greatness in him—to write, to create, to set off, to fight.

Not Octavia.

Big Ben quieted, the peal of its bells receded from the streets, the leaden circles of sound drifted over the waters of the Thames, dissolved over the heads of those swimming boys who were somehow still afloat. Octavia looked again at the woman on the curb, at the busy Liberty flower print on her dress, at her hat the color of orchids, at her butter-cup hatband.

And then, as if all those flowers, all those colors had suddenly de-cided to mingle like madness and then part ways, disperse in a hundred directions, leaving the fabric exposed, revealing the secret they'd been so carefully hiding:

Octavia knew *exactly* how she was going to get to Bloomsbury.

And she knew *exactly* how she was going to find Septimus.

CHAPTER 20

Elizabeth

"Is it her?" Frances hopped up and down on the tips of her toes next to the pool, the white gauze of her dress still drenched and firmly pressed against every inch of her body. Her dip in the pool had changed her from an ethereal fairy to some sort of ebullient mummy. "It is. It's *Tallulah.*"

Elizabeth had never heard of her.

"I read she was moving here this summer," Frances continued. "To do a stint at the Wyndham. I even asked Grim if I could go. And of course, he said no. Even though I called him Father!" Frances was running her fingers through her wet hair now, shaking water droplets all over Elizabeth, trying to look presentable. "I just never *dreamed* I'd meet her."

"I have no clue who on earth you are talking about," Elizabeth said, running her hands over her short locks now too.

"Oh, you and Grim," Frances said, wrapping some of her gown around her fingers, wringing out the water. "What a pair. Do you live under rocks?" Frances pointed across the pool. "Tallulah Bankhead. She's the one who looks like a purebred cat in a bad mood."

Elizabeth saw her. And Frances was right—she did look like a feline. Her eyes were rimmed with dark liner and looked drowsy, half-closed as if she felt surly and already exhausted with this party. She was wrapped in a dark silk gown with a shockingly low neckline. She puffed on a thin cigarette. Several men flocked around her, pigeons hoping for a crumb.

"Who is she?" Elizabeth asked. "The name sounds vaguely familiar, but I really don't know. I'm not being cheeky, I promise."

"*Tallulah Bankhead*. American actress. Silent films. And Broadway. This is her first time in England! To do the stage here. She's only a few years older than we are, you know. I'm still holding out hope I can make it into the pictures somehow. And tonight just might be my entrée." With her hair shaken out, her dress slightly less wet now but hopelessly wadded and wrinkled, Frances started off in the actress's direction. Elizabeth didn't follow. Frances turned back. "Aren't you coming?"

"Absolutely not. I need a—"

"Drink." William interrupted her.

"I was going to say towel," Elizabeth said.

"We'll get that next." He thrust a glass of champagne at her.

Without so much as a thought, Elizabeth took it and drained the entire glass. She was so thirsty. Starving too. When had she eaten last? And if the bubbly could take the edge off the feeling of being naked in the middle of a public pool at ten o'clock at night—well. "Can you get me another?"

William smiled. "But of course."

"Don't trust me to get the drinks!" It was the man dressed as a maid again. He went careening by with an evil laugh. "Who knows what I may put in them!"

"Who is *that*?" Elizabeth asked.

"A walking trope," William said, laughing a bit as he watched the man prance away in his black dress. "Commedia dell'arte. It's back in fashion you know. He's the devious servant. There's a know-it-all doctor running about here somewhere as well. Quite a few tropes in our midst."

"I know a few of those in real life," Elizabeth said. She thought of her mother. And Dr. Bradshaw. Lucy. And him, really. William. The golden boy with the perfect pedigree she was supposed to marry. But now—his beret, his bow tie undone, his delight in irreverent tropes— she was a bit confused. She remembered thinking once that there was something about his demeanor she couldn't place. And now she thought she might know—was there a little spot of joy in his eyes, maybe a joke about it all? All this—being who you were expected to be. Was that it?

"Tropes certainly come from somewhere, don't they?" William asked. "I'll get you another drink." He dashed off toward the champagne vat on the other side of the pool.

And then Elizabeth spotted them—the towels. A pile of deliciously dry, fresh-looking white towels. They were neatly folded on a little table by a few chairs, chaises. The aspiring novelist who William had said looked like a goblin was curled into one of them. Harold, was it?

Elizabeth hurried over and snatched a towel off the top of the pile. She wrapped it around her, squeezed it tight. She felt warm and a little protected now; she realized she was completely exhausted. And the champagne was going to her head. There was an empty chair next to the novelist.

"Do you mind?" she asked, motioning toward the empty chaise.

He looked at her without moving his head, knitted his brow as if she had just appeared on stage, suddenly burst in from the wings for her audition. He was deciding whether or not to cast her. "Let me ask you something," he said. Rather gruffly.

No greeting. No introduction. Just, *let me ask you something.*

Elizabeth took his strange question as a yes. That she could sit.

"What are you thinking right now?" he asked.

He *did* look like a goblin, Elizabeth decided. His nose was rather bulbous, his skin pocked and pale as if he spent his days lurking in secret hollows under tree roots.

"Pardon?" she asked.

He leaned closer. "Don't think about your answer," he said. "If you think about it too much, you'll miss it. What is running through your thoughts *at this very moment?*" He hungrily drank from a bottle of . . . whiskey, was it? Something golden. No glass. No pouring. No pretense. He took another.

Elizabeth wasn't sure how to answer him. She wasn't sure she'd ever stopped to think about what she was thinking. How odd his question was. If it weren't for his British accent, she might assume he was American.

I suppose I'm thinking that you look like a goblin. But I'm not prepared to say that. So I'll say something else. Something acceptable. Like—

"I'm thinking that I'm rather cold," she said. "That it's a bit chilly in here."

The novelist waved a hand in the air as if in supreme frustration. He pulled his knees up to his chest, coiled himself tight, and leaned against the back of the chaise. "So you're not going to play," he said. "I see. I can hardly get anyone to play."

"Sorry, I don't think I understand," Elizabeth said. She pulled the towel tighter around her shoulders and shivered. She wished she'd grabbed another. "I didn't mean to offend you. It's just that I don't quite know what you're asking."

"Harold, are you harassing this poor girl?" William was back. He sidled up behind her chair and lowered another glass of champagne over her shoulder. She took it.

"Not in the least," Harold said. "I'm merely working, that's all. Can't begrudge a man that, can you?"

"Look what I borrowed," Calvin arrived now, strumming a ukulele. "From that nice chap Eagan over there. He told me not to let Harold take the piss. So who's Harold, anyway?"

"That would be me," Harold said. "And you can tell Eagan he's a bastard."

"Harold's been *deeply* disturbed by *Ulysses*," William said, as if that explained anything. "Unfortunately for all of us, he was able to get his hands on a copy in Paris in May."

Harold sat up now, swung his feet around, and put them on the cold marble floor. He leaned toward Elizabeth as if fighting William for her good opinion. She had the distinct feeling that she'd just been thrust into a bit of tug-of-war. "Don't listen to him," Harold said, motioning toward William. "His most prominent thought is that he won't be able to spend his six-thousand-pound-a-year allowance. It's simply too big." Harold took another swig from his bottle. Cast a devious smile. "His allowance, that is. Not his brain."

Elizabeth felt even more awkward now; they were flat-out insulting one another. She felt the pressure to choose sides. "I'm not sure I—"

Harold interrupted her. "It's just that I've spent the past *year* working out the plot of my new novel," he said desperately. "And now I'm not sure it even matters any longer! I came up with a roaring twist about a man plunging over the Cliffs of Dover." He pulled a cigarette from his breast pocket. He put it between his lips without lighting it. "It's already passé and I haven't even gotten it down on paper yet."

"Harold," William said. "Give it a rest, eh? For one night at least."

Harold locked eyes with Elizabeth. Lowered his voice to a hoarse whisper. "James Joyce. The bastard follows every single thought a character has," he said. He was so close to her. Much too close. "And the entirety of the story happens in one single day. It's an unrelenting stream. A stream of—*consciousness*. And word has it Woolf is about to break the entire form of the novel wide open. *The mind. She's going to crack open the mind of a woman. And that's the story.* The whole of it. *The mind!* My career is dead before it ever really began. Plot is dead! Story is dead! Just when I think I've mastered it."

You're a madman.

An absolute raving lunatic.

Elizabeth looked at Calvin for help. He was still strumming his ukulele. She looked at William.

"Joyce," William explained. "James Joyce. He wrote *Ulysses*. He's become Harold's nemesis. And he's in terror about Virginia Woolf. What she's working on now. Word has it, it's another novel that happens in just one day. About a woman. One woman."

"Too right," Harold said, searching his pockets now. "It's me that should plunge over the Cliffs of Dover."

"Nonsense," William continued. "I think it's rubbish, these books. It's only old people who live their whole lives in one single day. Because by and large, each day is the same as the last by that point, isn't it? The die is cast." William had a hand on the back of Elizabeth's chair. "I, for one, don't live in one day. I live in summers," he said. "In summers like this one." He smiled. "At least I will until I'm old."

"Here, here!" Calvin said, strumming enthusiastically. "To the summers of our youth!"

Harold attempted but failed to light his cigarette. "However you look at it, Joyce is a bastard," he said. "He's wrecked my whole life. I've been a mess. A pure mess since I read the last page."

He stood up.

Elizabeth's mind flooded with thoughts. How Harold was so like a goblin. And shorter than she thought. And his shoulders, how thin. She thought he should eat something. And how could a novel upset a person like that, anyway? Hadn't he been alive when the Germans dropped their bombs? Hadn't he been a little boy when it happened, like she had been a little girl? Hadn't someone in his family gotten the Spanish flu? Those were things to be troubled by. The things of importance. Why was he thinking about *the mind*? Books about the *mind*? Woolf was writing about the mind of a single woman?

How frivolous.

"So which is it?" Harold asked, as if he could hear Elizabeth's thoughts. He looked at her and then at Calvin and William and then back again. "Is the story what's actually happening?" he said. "Or is the story what we're thinking? What we're all thinking about what is happening? Where do those thoughts even come from? And what about thoughts about things that aren't happening at all? Thoughts about the past. Thoughts about the future. Which story is even real? I don't even know what *matters* anymore."

William took a sip of his champagne and came around Elizabeth's chaise. "My dear chap," he said to Harold. "I'm afraid none of us know what matters any longer. You're not alone in that." He held up his glass to make a toast. "To the whole of England not knowing a damned thing about what is happening. And to having a fantastic summer in spite of it."

Calvin strummed along as if to accent the toast.

Harold harrumphed. He tossed his unsmoked cigarette on the wet floor and lurched off into the crowd. He looked so unsteady, Elizabeth thought. She worried he might slip.

"Are all novelists like that?" she asked William.

"Afraid so. It's a terrible affliction, really. To be a writer."

"There's a fantastic little balcony I just spotted, Elizabeth," Calvin said, pointing up. "Fabulous view of the pool and all the ruckus going on. Care to join me?"

"I know a better spot," William said. "Takes a key to get up a staircase to the roof. Which I happen to have." He smiled his golden smile. "Best view in the house."

"I'm—" Were they competing for her attention? Yes, yes, they were competing. These two boys she didn't know at all, really. "I'm not sure I—"

"I've met her!" Frances swept over before Elizabeth could respond to either William's or Calvin's invitation. She was still drenched, but her face was glowing. "I've talked to Tallulah." Frances took Elizabeth's hands and pulled her up from the chaise, away from William. Away from Calvin. She spun her around. "She's invited me backstage after her first show at the Wyndham! Can you imagine it? Backstage! You should come, Elizabeth! We'll be starlets. I can just see it, can't you? You'd be smashing as the lead!"

No, Elizabeth couldn't see it. No one had ever suggested Elizabeth could be the lead. Not on the stage or on a screen or at all, really. It was Mama who was theatrical. It was Mama who shined.

Frances began a barefoot waltz, leading Elizabeth in the dance. Calvin caught on immediately and began accompanying with ukulele music.

Step. Step. Step.

Step-step-step.

Around and around they went, Elizabeth laughing, her towel cascading off her shoulders. Frances smiled at her, twirled even faster with a look on her face as if she could die at this very moment and be happy.

And somehow, Elizabeth thought—

I could as well. Die this very moment. Die happy. In this feeling. What is it?

Feeling . . . unfettered.

This girl dancing with her was so free. Elizabeth hadn't known a woman could be like this. Dream of being in picture shows, dance like this, squeal like this. Frances pulled Elizabeth close to the pool's edge now; they turned their backs to the boys. Elizabeth knew what came next. She was about to be pulled in.

I didn't know that a woman could leap like this.

But Frances stopped, her toes just on the edge. "Be careful with my brother, darling," she whispered. "Love's not his strong suit."

And with that, she let go of Elizabeth's hand, took one grand spin right on the marble edge, teetered, and—

Fell in.

Elizabeth stayed where she was, there on the side.

"Be careful with my brother."

She thought about the alleyway beside the church. When she met Calvin. His jacket in the bin, a flask in his back pocket. How he'd stared at her dandelion, called it smashing. Smashing. How they'd talked tonight. How they'd kissed.

Elizabeth wanted to jump in; she wanted to go after Frances, to ask her to explain. She wanted to leap; she needed the cool water on her face, a little stubborn silence all around her.

She couldn't jump in.

She wasn't sure why.

But she just couldn't.

How stupid I am. How silly.

"You see?" Harold was back. He sidled up next to Elizabeth. "You're gazing at the water. And what are you thinking?"

How she hated this little goblin. The devious servant raced along the tiles behind him. Tallulah Bankhead looked bored on a chaise. Two men in suits wrestled in the water. Several girls with perfect hair and swimming costumes sat on the pool's edge like little yellow finches. Elizabeth glanced at Calvin. Sitting behind her. Still playing his ukulele. She thought of his hands reaching for the hem of her dress, his hands running up her thighs. How it felt to be pressed up against the side of the pool like that. What bliss she had just felt in this very water.

How stupid I am.

"I'm not thinking," Elizabeth lied. "I'm not thinking at all."

"Impossible!" Harold said. "If you weren't thinking you'd be dead. I bet you're wondering if you should jump in. Weighing the pros and cons as they say. Water too cold? Or maybe you're thinking of some time you were swimming in the past. When your evil brother tossed you in when you were six years old. Is that it? You still hate him over it."

"No," Elizabeth said flatly. "I'm an only child. I don't have a brother." She didn't like this game. She didn't like thinking about what she was thinking. It was disturbing. Frightening. How many thoughts had she had in her life that went completely unnoticed? What had they all been about? And were they coming from her? And if so, who was listening to them? Who was the one inside herself, listening to her think? Accepting messages, rejecting others. "You are wrong. Completely and utterly—"

"But nevertheless," Harold said, his shoulder gently touching hers, "you're standing here thinking about something related to swimming. To water. Something about yourself. Something negative. Then positive. Then negative again. I know that much." Harold put his arm around her, and she could smell the sickening sweet whiskey on his breath. He was practically purring. "But you're not in the water. You're just thinking of it. And you want to know the worst part?"

"No," Elizabeth said, looking him straight in the eye. "I really don't."

"The worst is that if you did jump in," Harold went on, "you'd probably be thinking about it still. Past swims. Future swims. Are people judging your swim? Should you be swimming at all? Should you let your hair get wet or leave it dry? And on and on. You'd be missing it, the water, the swimming, even then, even as you drown in it, you'd be missing it. Your thoughts keep you pinned to the sideline, no matter where you are. And that's what they do."

"What *they* do?" Elizabeth asked.

"Our thoughts. They keep us pinned to the side of life. And we miss actually living it. We live our entire lifetime in our memories, in our wounds, in our little shoulds and should-nots. And we miss out because of it. They can drive us to all sorts of things. To hang it up, even."

Elizabeth didn't like him next to her. She didn't like him at all, she decided. He felt full of darkness somehow. He was churning something inside her, some awful feeling she didn't want to have. "To hang it up?"

"Kill yourself," he said. "Hang it up. Toss your last shilling into the Serpentine. Your thoughts can drag you under. And keep you there."

DECEMBER 8, 1952

CHAPTER 21

Elizabeth

"Rose? Is that you?"

Lady Purvis. Elizabeth peeked over Rose's shoulder and saw the old woman in the drawing room. She sat in a wheelchair, very upright, a thick afghan tucked around her lap. Her gray hair sat on her head like a flock of dead pigeons, her face the owl that had slain them.

"Remember, let's keep things . . . in proportion," Rose whispered as they went into the room. "Mother's heart."

"But what topics shall I—"

"History," Rose said. "Mother does think it so interesting that you dabble in history."

"I teach it actually, I tutor all over the—"

"Mother!" Rose entered the drawing room before Elizabeth could finish. "I've brought Elizabeth!"

"Hello, Lady Purvis," Elizabeth said. She leaned down, kissed the woman's cheeks. How papery they felt. But they were healthy-looking, pink. Quite lively. Rose was right; her mother certainly wasn't on death's doorstep. And delicate she was not—her nose sharp, beaked. Made for cracking through rodent bones. "It is a pleasure to see you."

"I'm so glad you've come," Lady Purvis said. "How are you dear? I heard how ill you were last week. And you're not off to the country and out of this mess?"

Who'd told her? Elizabeth wondered. Surely not Theodore. Perhaps she'd assumed when Elizabeth hadn't emerged from the house for six days straight other than to sit in her mother's garden chair and stare off. Or maybe it was someone else entirely or no one at all. Rumors were like a disembodied presence in London; they stalked about without the need of a source to carry them, it seemed.

"Not yet," Elizabeth said, taking a seat on the sofa. "I keep hoping it will lift."

"Your mood or the fog?" Lady Purvis asked. She was being sincere. But it sliced, her comment.

"Both, I suppose," Elizabeth forced a smile. "I'm staying in London until it all lifts."

"Good girl. I'm not budging either." Lady Purvis's beak lowered. Her head turned around, her eyes centered on Rose as if appraising her as possible prey. "Which I have repeatedly told my children. They can bury me in the garden, for all I care. I'm staying with this house until my last breath. Which is likely on its way."

"Now, Mother. Your heart," Rose patted her mother on the shoulder then turned to Elizabeth as if they were the only two in the room. "She's never gotten over that looting in the summer of '23. It's quite hard to get her to leave the house for any length of time."

"I do remember that," Elizabeth said. "I believe Mr. Garrick spotted one of the boys climbing the drainpipe. He summoned the police. I don't believe the thieves were ever caught."

"Some awful street gang," Rose shook her head. She sat on the sofa opposite her mother. "Broke in the day we left for Mallorca. After that, Mother simply refused to leave. That's why I came in this morning. To persuade her to come with me out of the city."

"Which is pointless. I won't leave my house to be looted again." Lady Purvis tucked her afghan a bit more tightly under her legs. "History does repeat itself, doesn't it, Elizabeth? You should know better than anyone else. With your study on the subject."

"Speak to the past," Elizabeth said, "and it shall teach thee." She was dreadfully uncomfortable now. She couldn't go on like this much longer, swimming in this banter. Drowning in it, really. "I've come to ask about—"

"How clever. That saying. I'm unfamiliar with it." Lady Purvis grinned. "I love that you've made a hobby of it. Good for you."

A hobby. Elizabeth was used to this sort of thing. These comments about her career. Though the sting hadn't lessened over the years. She'd studied. She was a history tutor now, just like her old tutor Miss Kilman. But Doris would have been disappointed in her, Elizabeth knew. Elizabeth had been supposed to reach higher than this. There were bigger opportunities for her generation. The bright generation. But still. Elizabeth tutored so many sharp students in London, and she'd even taught a day here and there at the school when teachers were ill. It didn't matter; it wasn't worth saying all that now. She'd made missteps; she'd told her father to let Miss Kilman go after Mama left. Elizabeth hadn't done serious study since, not really. Enough to become a tutor, that's all. She'd stopped so many things after that summer. Riding. Reading. Arguing about politics. The facts and dates just wouldn't stick in her mind any longer. As if her mind had become an upturned china plate: everything slid right off. Elizabeth hadn't known then how important it was to take all the correct steps when one was so young. The die had been cast at the age of seventeen, it seemed. One must know their path straightaway—or land on another one entirely.

"Thank you," Elizabeth said graciously. "I do enjoy tutoring."

Lady Purvis cleared her throat, cast a glance at the small box Elizabeth held. "I see Rose gave you the medal."

"Yes," Elizabeth said. She lifted the lid, flipped the medal over, and stared at the inscription once more.

For the bravery of
S. W. S.
All my love to you, C. P. 1923

"Your mother gave that to me in June of that summer," Lady Purvis said. She took the box with unsteady hands. "She wanted me to give it to the family of a soldier. I was so terribly involved with all the veterans' affairs, you know." She picked up the medal. "I never found them. I gave up and tucked this away, thinking if I ever came across them in my work, I'd have it handy. I didn't think of it all these years until this morning. I came across it in that cabinet there. I feel terrible about it. I really do. I should have returned it to you long ago."

"Did she say how she knew Septimus Smith?" Elizabeth held out her hand, took the medal back. Looked at the bit of blue ribbon hanging from it.

"No. She just said it was terribly important to deliver it." Lady Purvis shifted in her chair with a bit of a grimace. "She said it meant a great deal to her. I feel awful. Just awful."

"Were there other medals she gave you?" Elizabeth asked. Perhaps it was just a bauble, Elizabeth thought; perhaps she had left ten such gifts for ten such soldiers and their families throughout the city.

"No," she said. "Just this one. For the family of Septimus Warren Smith."

"For his family—because he died in the Great War?" Elizabeth ran her hands over the initials. *S. W. S.*

"That's the odd thing," Lady Purvis said. "That's what I assumed when she told me to give it to his family. But when I inquired at the War Office about him, they had no record of his death. They said he returned from the war and there was nothing whatever the matter with him. I even checked the War Graves Commission. All veterans are buried in military cemeteries. But they have no record of a tombstone." Lady Purvis sighed as if remembering her valiant effort. "Once I learned he was alive, I went looking for the man himself. But there was no Septimus Warren Smith in any directory I could find. So very odd."

"But if Septimus were alive in '23, and Mama knew him, why would she want you to give something to his family?"

Lady Purvis cleared her throat. Her papery cheeks flashed pink. "That's why I feel so terrible, dear," she said. "Because I haven't a clue. I don't know why she would give me something for the family of a living soldier."

And it could have helped us find her. If his family knew something. If they know something still.

"What about his family? You couldn't find them?"

"Either he didn't report any when he enlisted, or the commission lost the record if he did," she said. "They couldn't give me a single person to be contacted. Do you how many Smiths there are in England? I didn't even know where to begin."

Elizabeth paused, looked once more at the inscription. "Thank you, Lady Purvis," she said. She placed the medal back in its box and snapped the lid shut. She stood. She felt a bit unsteady, had the impression of being on a boat far, far out to sea. The idea that Mama could be found. Elizabeth felt caught in the undertow of it. "And Rose. I appreciate you coming this morning. I appreciate you both for returning this. But I must take my leave." Elizabeth didn't stop to make proper goodbyes. To kiss cheeks. To wait for Rose to stand. To wait for her to wheel Lady Purvis to the front door. She left.

Rose trotted after her. "We're ever so sorry about all this," she said. "Where are you off to? The country after all? The air is quite clear if you can get far enough out. But the roads are blocked—"

"No," Elizabeth said, opening the front door. "I'm not going to the country." She stepped into the fog. "I'm going to find a relative of Septimus Warren Smith."

SUMMER 1923

CHAPTER 22

Octavia

Octavia spent the night crouched beside a bin in an alley. A group of boys congregated around the back door of a bakery near her spot; the baker threw out old buns and pastries in the morning. She waited until the horde of boys had their fill, then she took what they'd dropped on the ground or thrown out.

With a belly full of stale buns, she made her way down the block to a sign. It was hanging from an ornate iron arch:

PUBLIC SUBWAY

UNDERGROUND RAILWAY

Crowds moved up and down, passing her on either side; one man bumped her shoulder so forcefully she worried she would tumble down the stairs.

I can do this.

Just venture down. Below the surface.

She could hear the clacking and rumbling of the mysterious underground trains. Dank, humid air wafted out of the stairwell as people came out.

She took a breath.

And went down.

It wasn't very bright. The ticket platform. But bright enough. She saw a sign; she was in Westminster Station. There was a row of ticket windows, clerks sitting behind panes of glass. People were lined up to buy tickets; others were perusing magazines and newspapers from several newsstands along the passage. There was a little cigarette shop too. Octavia saw packets of mints, all kinds of tobacco.

The train fares were posted on signs in the hallway. She didn't have to read them; she knew she didn't have enough money. She didn't have *any* money.

She spotted a gate at the end of the hall where a man was taking tickets. Standing as tall as she could on her tiptoes, she could just see the platform beyond him; a train was pulling in. She heard its roar, the grind of its wheels on the track. A surge of people exited the cars like the whole world had tipped and spilled them out. A new crowd surged back into the train as if the world had tipped yet again, in the other direction, and in the water ran once more.

She looked away from the platform.

And saw her spot.

It was perfect.

On this side of the ticket gate, just between two newsstands, there was a little alcove. And it was empty, save for a small trash bin and two men who leaned against the walls reading papers and smoking. But other than that, it was empty.

She walked to the alcove, smoothed the bodice of her dress, reached under her skirt.

And took out what she kept pinned there.

The watch.

Her father's gold pocket watch.

She opened it, stared at its face. Thought of her dear Pop back at home. What was he doing? Was he sick with worry? Was he angry? First Septimus had run off to London and now Octavia. He was probably wondering what had gone wrong, what he had done in life to deserve this. His children running off, his wife going mad with melancholia after the birth of their last.

Oh, Pop.

She snapped the watch shut. She thought of Red getting bandages at Boots after her fall, how Georgie had told her they walked around with advertisements for the pharmacy in exchange for free medicine. She thought about Red rattling that gate behind the zoo, getting them in at a cut-rate. She thought about him slipping a sugar cube to Olek the monkey, getting him to dance, smiling as an upturned hat on the ground filled with sparkling money. It was as if he shook the gates of the entire city until all its jewels tumbled out of its pockets and into his.

Just by shaking it.

Octavia thought of Maeve. What she'd said about accepting help. How it didn't mean Octavia wasn't using her own wits. Just because Red had shown Octavia how he worked his magic didn't mean Octavia didn't have magic of her own. Red was resourceful; Octavia was too. She could get through this city. She could get to Bloomsbury.

"Magic watch here!" she called. But not very loudly. It was the volume she would use when saying "excuse me" as she moved down the sidewalk, not wanting to cause a stir.

No one looked.

She tried again. Louder this time.

"Pocket watch magic!"

Still, nothing.

She eyed the crowd and saw a little girl. About seven or eight years old, Octavia thought.

Perfect.

Octavia walked over. The girl was holding her mother's hand and eating a pink lollipop. They seemed middle-class enough. They certainly weren't fancy enough to be riding in a private motorcar up above on the street; they were down here with the rest of the masses. But still, dressed well. Clean.

"Hello," Octavia said, approaching the girl. "Would you like to see my magic watch?"

The girl's mother frowned and pulled her daughter away. She looked frightened. Frightened of Octavia. "Come along, Penelope," she said. "Don't bother with that."

Octavia didn't give up. "It predicts the future," she said. "It really is magic."

The girl stopped, pulled on her mother's hand. "Oh, Mummy! I want to see! I want a magic watch."

Octavia held out the watch and flipped open its golden lid.

"How much?" the woman asked, her brow furrowed now. The fear had been replaced by annoyance. She looked up at the ticket man, at the platform beyond.

"Pardon?" Octavia said.

"How much do you want for the watch? Our train will be here shortly."

Octavia shook her head. "Oh, no," she said. "The watch is not for sale."

"It isn't?"

"No," Octavia said. "But for two pennies, it will tell your daughter about her future."

"Oh, please, Mummy! Please!"

Reluctantly, the woman dug into her purse and pulled out two pennies. She handed them to Octavia. Octavia realized she didn't have anywhere to put her earnings; the awful boy at Paddington had stolen her money, purse and all. So she tucked the coins into her bodice. Slipped the cold pennies against her chest. The woman's eyes went wide at the vulgarity. She probably regretted handing over the coins, Octavia was sure of it. But Octavia chose to ignore what this woman thought of her. Had she ever done this before? Ignored someone else's opinion of her? Of what she should be doing or how she should be acting, looking? Surely not. Trying to survive had a way of cutting through all that. What a thrill this was. Octavia crouched down to the girl's level. She held out the watch.

"All right," Octavia said. "Do you see that hand there? The second hand? The one going very fast?"

The girl nodded.

"I want you to close your eyes," Octavia said. "And when I tell you to open them, I want you to guess how much time has passed."

"How fun!" The girl jumped a little with excitement and handed her lollipop to her mother. "Hold this, Mummy. I must concentrate. I've never counted *time* before!"

Her mother smiled, conceding.

"All right, close your eyes," Octavia said. The little girl did as she was told, pinching her eyes shut so tight her face started to turn red. Octavia waited. Seven seconds passed. "Open them up!" Octavia said. "How much time went by?"

"Um," the girl said, thinking hard. "Ten? Ten seconds!"

Octavia smiled and shook her head. "So close you were! Seven."

"So what does that mean?" Penelope asked, looking very concerned. "What does that mean about my future? Am I doomed because I got it wrong?"

"No, no," Octavia said. "Quite the opposite. You were three seconds off, which means you will have three children."

"*Three children!*" Penelope said, hopping up and down. "That's perfect! Oh, I hope they're all boys! No. No, I'd like one girl. One very sweet, lovely daughter. I'm very good at doing hair, you know." She pointed at her own curled locks.

"I see that," Octavia said, smiling. She tugged at the strands of her own unkempt bun. "I'm not very good at it at all! Now would you like to know who you'll marry?"

"Oh, yes! Yes!"

Octavia told her to close her eyes again. And the girl did. And she waited. Only five seconds this time. "Open them up," Octavia said. "How much time passed?"

"Oh, let me think," Penelope said. "I think ten! Ten seconds passed."

"Penelope," her mother said, shaking her head. "That's what you guessed last time. Why don't you try another number?"

Penelope looked at her mother sternly. "There are no rules in *magic*, Mummy. You have to *feel* it." The girl looked back at Octavia. "Ten! That's my answer."

"Five seconds off this time," Octavia said. "And what's the fifth letter of the alphabet?"

Penelope scrunched her nose. "A, B, C, D," she said, holding up a finger for each letter. "E! The fifth letter is *E*."

"And that's the letter the name of your future husband begins with. *E*."

Penelope looked mesmerized. Her eyes opened wide. She looked up at her mother. "Do you know what this means?" she asked. "Could it be?"

"Could it be what?" her mother said.

"The only boy we know whose name starts with an *E*!"

Her mother crinkled her brow again. "Elliot? The fishmonger's son?"

"Yes! Elliot!" Penelope looked back at Octavia. "He's very nice, but I've never thought of him much. I mean the fishy smell is quite awful and some of the girls poke fun at him about it. But I never have. Well, once. When he'd been handling scrod. But I *certainly* never will again." She stared at the watch face intensely, marveling. "He's my husband!"

The rumble and clack of a train filled the air. Octavia could feel the crowd begin to move down the passage; last-minute riders hurried from the ticket counter and pushed toward the gate.

"Penelope, we must go," her mother said. "Our train is here."

"Oh, thank you," Penelope said to Octavia. She gave her a little hug. "I'll be Mrs. Elliot Bates with three children. It's the best news of my life! And all from a magic watch!"

Her mother took her daughter's hand and gently led her away into the crowd.

Octavia waved.

And patted the two coins in her bodice.

She turned and faced the next wave of people streaming down the steps into the station.

"Magic watch here!" Octavia called. Very loud this time. Very loud. "Fortunes! Two pennies a piece!"

She would be buying a ticket to Bloomsbury in no time.

No time at all.

The thief who had taken her money had at least left her something: directions to Bloomsbury. He'd told her to get to the Euston Square station and walk down Gower. Now, she kindly asked the ticket man how to get there. Yes, yes, she could get to Euston Square from this station. Circle line.

She boarded the train; she was on her way to Septimus at last. She knew obstacles lay ahead: it would be dark, there would be thousands of boardinghouses, and she had no place to say.

No matter.

Octavia Smith could survive in this city by her wits.

Euston Square. The train stopped and she got out. Up the steps and into the darkness. Motorcars zoomed past, their lights shining bright. The streets were still full of people despite the hour. She glanced this way and then that, looking for the sordid people she'd been warned about. She saw no such thing. She saw an organ-grinder like the one she'd seen at the zoo. A man carrying a canvas and a worn leather satchel. A woman who looked on her way to something fine—a theater perhaps? There was, however, a suffocating smell of fried fish. And a row of grimy houses, some windows broken, stuffed with paper to keep the wind out. Did Septimus live in one of them? Did he have paper stuffed in his windows?

I'm coming, Septimus. I'll get you home.

What street was she on? She was supposed to walk down Gower. Yes, there was a street sign. Gower. She walked on and saw a formidable building, an ornate sign proclaiming that it was University College. She passed row after row of houses, people coming in and out. She saw a sign pointing toward the British Museum. She followed it. She found herself in front of great wrought-iron gates, a marble palace beyond them. The museum.

She was at the British Museum in the middle of Bloomsbury in London.

And had no earthly idea how to find her brother.

She should get to a street corner, ask for help, do what Red did—make the city dole out its money and its secrets. She should use time to tell fortunes.

She couldn't.

She was so tired, so very tired. Exhaustion overwhelmed her. She had to sit. She leaned against the museum gates and slid down to the pavement. She knew passersby would think she was a street urchin, no home to her name.

But they were wrong. She had a home. It was with Septimus, and he was here. Somewhere. He was here.

Sleep, she needed sleep. Did street urchins sleep on the street? She supposed so. Here was the pavement, offering its services. For free, no less. She wished a blanket would appear, or even a newspaper for warmth. She noticed for the first time that the air had a bit of a chill. But she could sleep here, just fine. After all, she was the sister of Septimus Warren Smith. On her way. And that was something. Really something.

CHAPTER 23

Elizabeth

"Do you think it will hurt?" Frances sat in the window of the barn, no pane of glass in it, just an open square cut into the wood. Elizabeth couldn't believe she'd known this wild girl for over a month now. That it had been nearly five weeks since the first swim party. And most of all, she couldn't bear the fact that it was July, that the summer was ripening, headed for the rot of August. That it would end.

"Will what hurt?" Elizabeth asked. She was brushing Brixby. She ran stiff bristles over his massive shoulder. Now down the center of his chest. She wiped her brow. Not only was July a harbinger of summer's end, there was also something different about its heat. June always blew in, the start of something, the sun a novel thing, silly, a group of children arriving after a dreaded winter speech from the adults. But July was different. The heat. It seemed to slow the air, bully its way through open barn windows; it seared. Frances seemed impervious. She had one knee pulled up, her foot on the sill, her other leg dangled over Brixby's large oat bin. She flipped through a magazine.

"This. Will this hurt?" Frances asked.

Elizabeth didn't look up. She assumed Frances was pointing to Brixby. "Riding?" Elizabeth heard footsteps coming through the grass, someone approaching the stall. "Riding only hurts when you fall off."

"No, not riding," Frances said. She held the magazine between her thighs now, pulled a cigarette from her tiny bag. She lit it. The cloud of smoke mingled with the dust motes and horsehair suspended in the July heat. Frances looked at Brixby now. "Though I can't *imagine* being up on that beast, let alone *falling off.* Have you? Fallen off?"

"A hundred times," Elizabeth said. "But the last one almost killed me. I was headed straight for a stone wall hidden by two tons of flowers. I blame William. He was showing off."

"Speak of the devil." Frances was craning her neck out the window. "He's walking across the field, headed straight for us."

He'd been underfoot all summer. They'd had parties all over London. One all-night affair at William's country estate. The Guinness girls had tipped up at that one. Telling some story about a prank they'd pulled on Asquith's wife. Burning a dress.

Of course, Elizabeth never told her parents what went on at these things; surprisingly, they didn't ask. And even more of a shock: they let her go. Stay out as late as she liked. Elizabeth knew Mama wanted her to attend parties, but she was sure Mama meant stuffy society parties, not late-night affairs out of sight. But Mama seemed almost delighted each time Elizabeth went out. And Papa looked at her with the same pride he did during the first party of the season.

"My daughter."

He'd been treating her so tenderly since that night she'd asked him about Peter. She wasn't sure if it was to assure her or to apologize for a rumor that was true. But there it was. Her father's tenderness.

"Your summers. I want you to be very careful with your summers. Choosing your path."

Elizabeth had adored each party—not for the drink or the chatter or the presence of fame. But for the mixture of it all. The wonderful chaos of the mixture. People thrown together like a shocking bouquet—dandelions, wild clematis, pristine roses and peonies. None considered weeds. All proper blooms. All equals. Novelists, poets, royalty, politicians' daughters, American actresses, men dressed as maids. It was intoxicating. It was the new future, they said. When all titles would dissolve.

When women and men could swap and swap again. Do any jobs. Be anything. No rules. No straitjackets. This generation was to be free. The war had shown them that proper proportion and posturing hadn't saved a soul. Not one single soul. The youth—England was theirs for the remaking. Perhaps the rumors were right that the *Daily Mail* was following them, Elizabeth thought. Perhaps her generation was bright after all. Bright Young People.

And of course, there was Calvin.

She loved these parties and the attention she received from Calvin. Perhaps the brightest part of it all.

"William is so delightful, I think," Frances said. "He's in love with you. You have to know that."

"He's lovely, it's just that—" Elizabeth stopped. What was it that held her back from William? He was funny and charming and always tipped up with a lovely metaphor pulled from Shakespeare. "But I worry about the path he'll choose."

"The path?"

"That all this talk of being bright, of being a new generation, is just that—talk. In the end he'll want a society wife and three sons bound for Eton. He'll become every single thing a person is supposed to be. Aren't we all running from tropes at a gallop? I'm worried he'll turn his horse back toward the barn."

Frances hopped down from the sill. She cautiously made her way around Brixby, gave him a wide, wide berth. "A trope made you fall off your horse?" she asked. "That's a rather thin excuse."

"Besides, he can do better than me," Elizabeth said. Brixby's side twitched, shuddered; several black flies took to the air. "He's his father's grand prize. And I'm Mrs. Dalloway's sad entry at the fair."

"Not me," Frances said. She put the cigarette to her lips; the tip glowed. "I'm exactly what my parents want me to be—in part, I guess."

"In part?"

"Never mind," Frances said. She held up her magazine on the other side of Brixby's massive neck. "What I meant was—will it hurt?"

Elizabeth ducked under Brixby to see the magazine. Frances held it open to a full-page advert for a child's cough tonic. There was a pen-and-ink drawing of a mother cradling a tiny baby in her arms.

"Coughing? Does coughing hurt a baby?" Elizabeth asked, utterly confused. "I'm sure it's uncomfortable for the child, just as it is for adults I suppose—"

"Oh, good lord, do I have to spell every single thing out for you?" Frances said, exhaling another cloud of smoke. She was wearing a thin blue top that reminded Elizabeth of a sailor's shirt. Like she was about to board a ship at any moment. Leap through the barn window and chart a new course. "To have one of *these*. A baby."

"Oh."

Frances looked back at the advert. "And . . . you know. What it takes to have one."

"*Oh.*" Elizabeth was about to duck under Brixby's neck and return to brushing. But she saw something. In Frances's eyes. Something sad, wistful. "Are you . . . quite all right?"

"Will you show me how to pet him?" Frances was looking at Brixby now.

"Here," Elizabeth said. "Just rest your hand here, just at his shoulder."

Frances put her hand on Brixby like she was trying to pet a bomb. Like any minute he might roar to life and blow her to bits. Was she shaking? Was Frances, this bon vivant, this wild American—trembling? It made Elizabeth think of Mama. Trembling. That awful day in June. That awful luncheon.

Elizabeth rested her cheek on Brixby's side, on the grand curve of his body. So warm. So divine. Frances leaned against Brixby now too, both girls facing each other, the horse their pillow, their faces close.

"How will we pick the right one?" Frances asked.

"The right horse?"

"The right husband." Frances looked frightened again. Elizabeth couldn't believe she was capable of fear. She'd wondered if it was an emotion Americans didn't experience at all. "Isn't that the secret to everything?" Frances asked. "Picking the right husband?"

Choosing the right path.

"My mother certainly thinks so."

Frances smiled. Relaxed her body a little more, her cheek resting more deeply on Brixby's side. "We should be able to try out several, don't you think?" Her unfettered smile returned. "Like dresses! We should be able to try them on like dresses! Everyone knows you can't tell a damn thing about them when they're still on the rack. We should be able to wear a few!"

"Wear a few what?" William had made it to the stall. He strode in now, his saddle flung over his shoulder. He was in his hunting pinks. His jodhpurs.

"Nothing," Elizabeth said. She and Frances stood up, pulled their faces away from Brixby's warmth. "Nothing at—"

"Sex!" Frances said with glee. Her fear vanished as if it had never been there in the first place. She returned to her spot on the windowsill, nonchalant, like a cat leaping back to a warm spot in the sun. "I was just asking Elizabeth what it might feel like to have sex."

Oh, it was awful.

Simply awful.

Elizabeth loved flouting the rules just as much as the next bright girl, but still—*sex*. Said so directly like that. As if Elizabeth knew—

"Why were you asking Elizabeth about it?" William smiled, lifting his eyebrows. He hoisted his saddle onto a rack. Began rubbing a cloth over the leather. "Does she have firsthand knowledge of the subject?"

Frances evidently thought this was the most delicious and hilarious comment anyone had ever made in her presence. "I wouldn't be surprised!" She swung her legs happily over the sill. "I think there's an ocean behind Elizabeth's eyes. Leagues of mystery! I keep telling her she could be an actress! Famous on the screen." Frances flicked her cigarette out the window.

"I think she could be a champion rider myself," William said. "You should see her on a hunt."

A famous actress.

A champion rider.

Add to those Miss Kilman's predictions: a veterinarian, a master of large enterprises, a professor. And to Mama's: Elizabeth would be Mrs. William Titcomb, hostess of prime ministers, a woman who had chosen the right path.

"Frances!" Elizabeth nearly dropped her brush in frustration. She looked in the direction of the discarded cigarette. "Go get that right now! Put it out! In case you haven't noticed, this place is mostly comprised of hay and hundred-year-old wood."

"My apologies. About the cigarette, I mean." She winked, slipped down from the sill, her cream-colored shoes landing in manure. "And I can't believe you love to stand in shit." She lifted one foot and then the other. "I'll go put it out." Frances paused before leaving the stall, looked back at Elizabeth with a sweet smile. And turned to William. "And William, you shouldn't think ill of Elizabeth. I had just been saying that I have become what my parents want me to be—in part."

"And which part is that?" William asked.

"I'm supposed to get married and have babies. I don't really want to get married, and I don't really want to have babies. I just want to make them!" She seemed so pleased with herself. To shock. She didn't even blush. Just moments ago she'd seemed so afraid. Elizabeth felt so naive. Did everyone her age feel comfortable talking about these things during their summers? Had Mama talked like this during hers? Had she and Peter gotten lost in all of it? Was that what had made Mama tremble? Remembering the path she hadn't meant to go down one summer night?

"I'll go get the cigarette," Frances continued. "But I'm going to take a circuitous route about the place, lingering in the vicinity of that gaggle of stable boys we saw earlier." She did one of her signature incorrect curtsies. And left.

Elizabeth felt small droplets of sweat gather under her arms and in between Brixby's brush and her palm.

Americans.

My god.

"Are you coming to tonight's festivities?" William asked. He cleared his throat a bit. Was he trying to help her? Steer the conversation back to safer ground? His tone—it felt like an olive branch. *Let's pretend none of this happened.*

"Where is it tonight? Will we swim? Or invade your father's country house until morning?"

"Not this time." William leaned against the wall now. "Edward says he has a smashing surprise tonight. He's sending cars to pick everyone up. We'll be a full-on caravan."

Elizabeth reached for a new brush, the one with the tines now, began on Brixby's mane. William was still leaning against the wall. Staring. Waiting for an answer.

"So will you join us?" he asked.

"Well, yes. We'll come. Of course we'll come."

"We?"

"Frances and me, of course."

"And Calvin?"

"No," Elizabeth said. "Well, I mean yes. I mean Frances and Calvin and I go to these things together. So we will all be there tonight. For Edward's surprise."

"Has he been out here?" William picked up his saddle again. Hoisted it over his shoulder.

"The prince?"

"No, Calvin. Has he been out here?"

"Calvin doesn't ride." Elizabeth pulled a particularly gnarled mat from Brixby's mane. The horse huffed and stamped a hoof. "At least I've never heard him mention it."

"Has he ever met a horse?"

"I don't know. I presume so."

"They're herd animals, you know." William nodded at Brixby. "They live and die by reading people. Sussing out threats. If you're afraid and try to hide it, a horse will know. Same goes for anything you're trying to hide. A horse will know."

Elizabeth stepped back from Brixby's half-done mane. "Don't lecture me on the senses of a horse. Or assume I don't know what you are suggesting." Elizabeth pulled Brixby's hair from her brush. "And don't try to tell me a horse knows what a person is hiding."

"They won't know *what* you're hiding, but they'll know you're hiding. And *that's* what worries them." William looked at Brixby, at his wet-black eyes, with a look of admiration. Yes, Elizabeth thought, William was admiring the horse. His abilities. "Because if you're trying to hide, a horse can't tell who you really are—friend or foe." William stepped out of the stall now. Looked back over his shoulder. "You should bring Calvin out here. Introduce him to Brixby. See what happens. That's all I'm suggesting." He walked away.

Elizabeth marched after him. Swatted at a few flies. She felt angry. Like she'd been challenged to a fight, and she was determined not to lose. Not here. Not next to her own horse. Her own army. She'd come to be very fond of Calvin. She felt sure he was going to live a better life, one freer and livelier than the staid one William was likely headed for. "So every horse adores you, I suppose," she called after him. "Because you're not hiding anything. Is that it?"

William stopped, adjusted the saddle on his shoulder. The hunting party was assembling in the field behind him. The hounds had begun to bark. "Of course I'm hiding something," he said. One of his hunting companions called his name, motioned for him to hurry. William looked back at Elizabeth again. "But there's one thing a horse will always forgive you for keeping close to your chest."

"Which is?"

"That feeling that you just don't measure up."

Elizabeth paused. His words landed in her chest, someplace deep, someplace true. "What could you possibly—"

"Nothing big," William said, shrugging his shoulders. "Just a little problem—that being alive counts against me."

"Pardon?"

"If you're a young man walking around these days it means one of two things: you were either too young to fight or you didn't die in battle." He looked at the gravel and matted hay beneath his feet. Softly kicked a tiny rock to the side. Looked back into her eyes. "Either way, you don't measure up."

"Never measure up to whom?"

"The heroes. The ones six feet under," William said. "Like my brother." He adjusted the saddle on his shoulder. Looked directly into her eyes. "Good day, Elizabeth Dalloway."

She watched him go, held up a hand to shield her eyes from the sun. The stirrups swung from William's brown-black saddle as he walked toward the field. She felt silenced. So stunned she wasn't even sure what to ask. She never would have guessed. Not in one hundred years. Not in three more wars. Or two more influenzas.

William felt he didn't measure up.

CHAPTER 24

Octavia

She sat in the grass in a little Bloomsbury park. Under a tree in Russell Square.

Oh, the heat. The July heat.

She'd been looking for Septimus for weeks. She'd tried everything. She'd been to the War Office. They'd told her what she already knew. No record of his death. Nothing wrong with him. No known address. She'd asked strangers. She'd knocked on doors up and down the Bloomsbury streets. Most had slammed their doors in her face. She couldn't blame them; she knew she looked a fright, living on the streets as she'd done. She'd seen military men in uniform, run to them, and asked. No one had heard of him.

Her wounds from falling over Red's rag ball outside Paddington were faint red scars now, one clear across her cheek. She still had only the one sad dress, out-of-date, tattered, stained with grass from her lay-about in the park with Red. Bits of hay from the zoo stubbornly clung to the laces and crevices of her boots. She thought of Red often, imagined what it would be like to have him here. To have Georgie bouncing along beside her in Bloomsbury's gardens. Red would show her a thousand new ways to earn some dosh here, to get some better food, find better shelter. But she tried to stop herself when she thought of him like that. When she remembered the moment they first met, when he'd helped her up after she'd fallen, how kind he'd looked, how sweet he'd been when he seemed shy, when he'd told her he wasn't good at talking to pretty girls. She chastised herself. He was a member of a street gang, nothing but a thief.

Octavia had survived by using her watch. Using time. Her fortune-telling earnings were enough to buy fresh food once in a while, and she supplemented with scraps she'd learned to find. She followed the street urchins. They crawled all over Bloomsbury like fleas. Hopping. Hungry. Fast. She saw them in the alleys outside the butcher's. Outside the grocery. She learned which days the stale biscuits were cast out. The rancid meat. The rotted fruit. If she was determined, she could cobble together a meal that wouldn't make her sick. Not for long anyway.

Now she patted the tattered purse she'd gotten at a charity shop and sighed at the meager amount of jingling money inside. She hadn't been able to earn enough for a place to stay. Not one she'd feel safe in. She'd rather be out in the rain and the dark than stay in any of the rooms she'd seen. Prostitutes came out of them, men so drunk they couldn't walk. She'd heard fights through windows. Things being smashed. No, the streets were better than that. So she found overhangs to shelter under, little caves among the branches of pine trees in the park. Once she'd slept in an overturned canoe someone had left by a little pond. It was the best she'd slept since she'd gotten to London.

She was hungry. She didn't want to give up this shady spot in Russell Square, this lovely bit of shade under a tree. So she did what she'd learned to do: crawl around the base of nearby bushes. People often tossed things at the bushes as they walked past—leftover food, half-smoked cigarettes, all sorts of things.

She spotted something.

Something red, tucked at the base of a juniper bush. She went closer. An apple. A half-eaten apple, withered in the heat, browned and shrunken.

But only on one side.

She could get a bite or two out of the other.

She picked it up. A sweet bite of fruit would be just the thing. It would buoy her spirits, give her the strength to search for Septimus for one more day. She raised it to her mouth and out slid a white maggot, a squirming grain of rice. And another and another. All defending their prize.

She dropped it; she thought she might be sick, might faint.

Give up. You awful brewery rat. Street urchin. Silly. Stupid. Girl. Give up.

Just as she thought she might break into sobs right there in the middle of the park, something else caught her eye.

Two women walked by in strange uniforms. They wore dark jackets with gold braids, official-looking caps. She'd seen plenty of men in uniforms, but women?

Women? In uniforms?

She shouldn't bother them. They'd probably throw her in some home for girls and lock the key. Besides, all she'd done since she'd gotten to this city was beg for help. She was so tired of it, of the way people looked at her, such a weak, sad little thing. Learning to make some dosh from a watch and haunting alleys like a ratty cat. Wishing she could be riding Red's coattails, feeling lost without him. It had always been this way, hadn't it? As a girl she'd clutched onto Septimus like a bur begging for a ride to a different spot on the hill. Then she'd clutched onto Red. And now she was running to these ladies.

Maeve.

Something about these women in uniforms made her think of Red's mum.

It was their clothes. How the color was a Stroud-night blue. Made from such a posh-looking wool. And the creases were so crisp, you could slice a finger on them.

She thought of Maeve in that Liberty shop full of fabric, full of color. A woman. Happy. A happy woman. Octavia remembered what she had said. She remembered again.

"Just because you accept help from all those boys doesn't mean you aren't surviving on your own wits."

Maeve had adjusted Octavia's high collar. Her faded, old-fashioned collar.

"Making it on your own is not the only measure to go by. And don't listen to those who tell you it is. Can you remember that?"

Octavia had promised she would.

Asking for help didn't mean she wasn't navigating under her own power. Running on her own steam. Maybe that's what had kept Octavia alive, asking for help. Taking it. Maybe that was worth something. Made her worth something.

"Excuse me!" Octavia called. She ran beside them.

"Yes?" one of the women asked. Chestnut-brown hair peeked from under her cap. Her nameplate said Claire. The other was a blonde. Marta. "How may we help you?" asked Claire. They didn't look at her with pity. They didn't seem afraid of her. They didn't seem to judge.

Octavia took a step closer and read the tiny print below their names.

SALVATION ARMY

Women? In the army? Octavia had never heard of a women's army. A women's *salvation* army.

"Are you . . . soldiers?" Octavia asked.

The women smiled. Marta laughed softly. "We *are* soldiers of a sort. Soldiers for good, I like to say."

Soldiers for good.

Octavia felt a little hope rise in her chest, buoyed by relief. She shouldn't hope, she knew that. But she couldn't help it. One last try, she thought. Just one last try. Ask for help. It was her power, after all. Her best and strongest power, asking for help. "I'm looking for a boarding-house in Bloomsbury."

"Oh, no, no," Claire said. She looked older. Fifty? Octavia was so bad at guessing ages. "You won't be able to stay in one of those, dear. They are quite dodgy for a girl your age. Besides, you'd need *money* for that."

"Yes, I know," Octavia said. She patted her purse. "I almost have enough. But that's not what I meant. I'm looking for a specific board-inghouse—"

The women looked suspicious now. Worried. "And pray tell, *how* did you get that money? I hope you have not been—"

"I earned it," Octavia said. "I worked for it. And not like you think." She reached for her pocket watch and held it up. "I'm a fortune-teller. I use time to tell the future."

The women looked at one another, still disapproving. "Well," Marta said. "There's a relief centre just down this way. That's where we are headed. It's in that council building there." She pointed down the street. "We can get you a ration of food coupons for the time being and get you to some appropriate shelter."

"But I don't *need* lodging," Octavia said. "I need to find my brother."

"Family? In the city?" Marta asked. "You have family in London?"

"Yes. Family. He's staying in a boardinghouse here in Bloomsbury. I just don't know which one."

Claire turned and looked down the street, the gold braids on her jacket shining a bit in the sunlight. "There's a post office just a few blocks away," she said. "The Marchmont. Turn that corner there, then your next right, and then a left."

"A post office?"

"They'll have a directory, dear," Claire said. "With names. And addresses. It's not perfect, the city changes so fast these days. But your brother just might be in it if he's lived in the same spot for long enough."

Octavia's face fell. "I don't think he'll be in it, you see," she said. "I already checked with the War Office. They said they had no known address for him."

"The War Office?"

"Yes, ma'am."

"Not to disparage our fine military," Marta said, "but there were just so many . . ." She paused and looked at the sky as if sending a prayer to the clouds, to whatever was above them—or wasn't. She looked back at Octavia. "So many men were lost or missing or just simply unaccounted for. The War Office really can't keep up. I'd ask the postmaster if I were you. If anyone knows your brother's address, it'll be him."

The Marchmont was an unremarkable brick building. The heavy wooden doors were unlocked. Inside were rows and rows of small locked metal boxes, tiny mausoleums holding mail in a sprawling cemetery of communication. And in the middle of a large hallway, sitting on a wooden table, she saw it. A very thick book that was open. A directory.

She scanned the names.

Smallridge. Smead. Smetzer. Smith.

So many Smiths. Eugenes and Harolds and Victors. Edwards and Geralds and Daniels. But no Septimus. She looked again. And again. It was no use. She shut the book. It was over. She would never find him. She thought of the day ahead of her, the night. Picking among rotten food for dinner, sleeping on pavement, consorting with vermin. All for nothing. This whole summer in London. All for nothing.

"Can I help you, Miss?" A man came down the hall wearing a brown postmaster's apron. He was carrying an armful of letters. There was that look of pity Octavia had seen so often on people's faces when they saw her. He'd probably run away from her too.

"I'm looking for someone," Octavia said. "But he's not in the directory. I'm afraid he may not even be on this earth, truth be told."

"Oh, my," the man said with softness. The first she'd seen in a man's face since she'd arrived in this city. Softness. Save for Redvers. Until she'd learned who he really was. "I hope that's not the case," the postmaster continued. "And you can't count on that directory there. It doesn't have a hope of keeping pace with this city. It's out of date the moment it comes off the press. What's the name you're looking for?"

"Septimus. Septimus Warren Smith. His wife is Italian and he's a veteran, living in Bloomsbury."

The man seemed to be searching his memory. "Come with me."

Octavia followed him down the hallway, her dirty shoes so worn they didn't even tap any longer on the tiled floor. The man ducked behind a large oak counter, pulled out a thick book, started flipping through it.

"Bloomsbury," he said. "Seems an Italian name is ringing a bell to me. A woman comes in for mail. Here. Could his wife be Lucrezia? Lucrezia Smith?"

"I don't know, I know only that—"

"Because there's a woman—she goes by Rezia, from Milan, I believe—who stops in at the counter almost every day to pick up the mail for her husband. She often brags that he's a veteran. Very proud. But a nervous sort, if you ask me. She always seems so nervous about something. And dreadfully thin. Her husband has come a few times with her."

"What did he look like?" Octavia could barely get the words out. Hope. Here was hope. She could barely stand it.

"I haven't seen him for a bit, but I think he was a tall chap. Nose a bit pointy? Dark hair. A little pale, really. A pensive sort."

"Eyes? Do you know what color?"

"Sorry, Miss. I didn't pay that much attention."

It could be him. Everything fit. The Italian wife. His dark hair. Pale skin. Septimus always spent more time poring over Shakespeare than he did out in the sun. And his favorite pastime was thinking, mulling.

Octavia could barely keep her feet on the ground; she wanted to leap over the counter, throw her arms around this man. She managed to keep still. But only just. Just long enough to ask—

"Do you know the address?"

"52 Tavistock Square."

And yes, she could walk from here.

CHAPTER 25

Elizabeth

"Where *are* we?" Elizabeth looked out the window of the motorcar. Frances was by the other window, and William was squeezed between them in the back seat. Calvin sat in front with the driver.

"Covent Garden," William said, peering into the dark streets. "The seedier bits of it. Just on the edges, I think."

The parties Elizabeth had been to this season involved swims and estates and great lawns. Not dark places like this.

"Tallulah is in front of us," Frances said, staring past the driver. She couldn't stop fawning over the actress. It was readily apparent to everyone that she was driving the actress batty. She was too much. Even charm can become grating in the wrong proportions. "Yes, yes, I'm sure of it."

Abruptly, the motorcar ahead of them stopped, and Tallulah and her friends spilled out of it and onto the dark sidewalk. Elizabeth saw glimmers and flashes of gowns in the light from the streetlamp. Elizabeth's car stopped as well. And then the car behind them and the one behind that. There were nearly twenty people in the caravan. Frances immediately hopped out.

"Come on," William said. He held out a hand for Elizabeth. "We don't want to miss this one. I have a feeling about it."

"Miss what?" Elizabeth protested. She slid across the seat and allowed William to help her out. "I still don't understand what we're even doing tonight."

The crowd milled about aimlessly on the sidewalk. What kind of party was this? All they'd been told was that a car would collect them in Belgravia at eleven o'clock. A whole stream of cars had shown up, the usual crowd Elizabeth knew from the other parties. Then they'd caravanned across the city to the purlieus of Covent Garden.

"Do you think it's going to be a street party?" Frances whispered. "I'm too embarrassed to ask. I feel as if we should know somehow."

"Doubt that," Calvin said. His ukulele was slung across his back. Dear Calvin and his little musical instrument; his songs had delighted her all summer. Somehow they represented everything he was: light, lovely, faintly comedic. She looked at him under the streetlight. How glad she was he was here. "I don't spot any drink," Calvin said, scanning the sidewalks. "So this can't be our final destination."

"I happen to know," William said. He looked rather pleased with himself. "I've been letting on like I don't. But I'm not telling, so don't even try."

All the women were dressed in their finest, which struck an odd note on this dark and dirty city street. White boutonnieres on men's coats popped in the night; women's heels ground into the grit and muck. Calvin stood out for his casualness. His slacks that weren't tailored properly, the collar on his shirt that wasn't ironed. But it didn't matter. Really, it didn't. That was the thing about this summer. The wild mixture. Rules like crushed glass at their feet. Everyone seemed to fit. The ratty novelists, the off-kilter Americans, the Dalloway girl who'd rather be in jodhpurs.

Now, several people started peering into darkened storefronts as if they were looking for someone or something. A few even knocked on windows. On doors. A dress shop. A butcher's. A store that sold fine papers and inks. All of them were closed. The wail of car horns and angry shouts of passing drivers took Elizabeth's attention from the strange scene on the sidewalk. Several men in their party were practically daring cars to run over them, dashing into the street in front of the traffic. The closer they got to being hit, the louder they whooped and laughed.

Frances stared in horror. "They're going to get themselves killed—"

Tallulah Bankhead squealed from about half a block down. "I've got it! I've got it!"

The crowd ran to her and gathered around. Tallulah had dropped on all fours right there on the filthy sidewalk, her dress smeared with grime, her gloves blackened as she peered at something on the ground. A symbol. Drawn with chalk.

PMB 22.05.23

And below that, a circle, drawn with deep gold.

"He's outdone himself this time." It was Harold, the aspiring novelist, the goblin. He was next to Elizabeth now, peering down at Tallulah, his hands in his pockets.

"Who's outdone himself?" Frances was breathless. She was thrilled by whatever mystery was unfolding. "Tell me! Do tell me."

Harold resisted Frances's pleas and offered Elizabeth a cigarette instead. She refused one. She was still bristling over what Harold had said to her by the pool several weeks ago. "Edward," Harold said. "He's outdone himself. This looks to be the best treasure hunt yet."

Frances's eyes went wide in the darkness. "Edward? You mean—"

Harold gestured across the street. To a closed newsstand. The Prince of Wales was leaning against it.

Edward.

"*The Little Man.*" Frances beamed. Elizabeth worried her American friend might die on the spot. The headline: *Most Optimistic American Alive Dies at the Feet of the Prince.*

"For God's sake," Harold said, in a near hiss. "Don't let any of this crowd hear you call him that."

"Oh," Frances said. "I'm sorry. I'm American. I don't know these things."

"That's what the press call him," William explained. But his tone was a bit kinder, as if he were trying to cover for Harold's gruffness. "You'll get tossed out on your ear if you say that nickname out loud. The filthy press. But mind you, this whole crowd would love to make the papers with our escapades. Don't believe anyone who tells you something different. They're lying when they say they mind the *Daily Mail* sniffing around. By this time next season, I imagine these little treasure hunts of ours will be the talk of the town. The Bright Young People and all that."

"Why on earth would the papers—even the *Daily Mail*—be interested in this?" Elizabeth asked. "A bunch of us crawling through Covent Garden, playing some sort of game?"

Harold pulled a flask from his jacket and took a swig. Frances didn't even wait for the invitation. She took it from his hands. Took a long, long drink.

"The answer is simple, love," Harold said. "No one wants to be who they are." He took the flask. "Everyone wants to read about people who are doing better, living lives they can't ever hope to have. It gets them out of their own reality, out of their own heads. Escape. It sells papers. And lots of them."

Elizabeth hated Harold, she decided. She hated him.

Elizabeth eyed the prince. She'd met him before, at her coming-out. A few times at a party with Mama and Papa here and there. He'd been lurking about this summer; Elizabeth had seen him. But she'd never thought he was interesting in the least. She didn't care if she met him or not. The party-boy son of the boring stamp-collecting king. Wasn't it all so predictable? If commedia dell'arte was so in vogue, well—here was as fine an example of a trope as one could hope to see.

Except.

She looked at him again, across the street. Standing as he was in a circle of lamplight.

There *was* something about him. She could sense it now, even from a distance. Something about the way he was standing. The way he was leaning. Apart from everyone. With his jacket all buttoned up, his collar tight around his neck. He wasn't smiling. Just watching. He was—a thing apart. Yes, that was it. And she could feel it. His separation.

"And *he's* so happy?" Elizabeth asked, gesturing toward the prince. "Living the life everyone wants to read about in the papers?" She looked at the crowd still gathered over the chalk drawing. She motioned at

Frances. At William. At Calvin strumming his ukulele. At the crowd. "And all of us? We're the ones people want to be?"

Harold took another drink from the flask. "Well, there's no one doing better than us, is there?" He turned to walk away but paused. "And that's the frightening thing. When your life is supposed to be the good one. And your own mind is as much of a torture as everyone else's." He wrinkled his nose as if he were about to say something terribly distasteful. He lowered his voice to a whisper. "So we have to make it up a bit, don't we? That we're all so damned happy."

He walked away.

Elizabeth stood there.

She wasn't sure why, but Brixby came to mind. Dandelions. The howl of hounds on the scent of a fox. Grizzle. His fur. The warmth of it. The damp, earthy smell of it. The dust in the stables. The leather of the reins. The sound of bubbles when she jumped into a pool, gown and all. Frances twirling on the tiles. *Step-step-step.* Calvin taking her hand, reaching for her dress.

Summer.

Elizabeth thought of Mama's childhood friends, that awful Peter. Miss Sally Seton. The lake she always spoke of. The flowers. The bowls.

It had ended.

Mama's summer.

It had ended.

She'd chosen a path; apparently, she felt it was the wrong one.

And from then on, she had to make it up. Being happy. Talking about the perfect flower combinations. The perfect guest lists. All the while remembering—

Her summer.

Was this Elizabeth's? Elizabeth's summer? Her Bourton? Before she tumbled down an unsatisfactory road?

And then Elizabeth knew. She marched up to the symbol drawn in chalk.

"I know what it is," Elizabeth said.

The crowd—Tallulah Bankhead, William Titcomb, Harold, Frances, Calvin, the man who'd been dressed as a maid at the swimming pool—they all turned and looked at her as if she'd dropped from the heavens. Some gargoyle who'd flown down from the top of a castle wall.

"What is it, sweetheart?" Tallulah asked, her American accent thickened with drink. "It's a date," Elizabeth said. "The twenty-second of May, 1923. And PMB is Prime Minister Baldwin. It's the day he was instated. And that, right there in the circle"—Elizabeth stooped and pointed at the golden circle—"is a cigar label. My mother always stops at cigar shops. I've seen hundreds of them. She likes to look at them because someone smoked them during the best summer of her life."

The one that makes her tremble, the season that holds her secrets.

"The prime minister?" the maid-man asked. "And a cigar?"

"The girl's a genius," Harold said, his eyes glinting in the streetlight as he looked at Elizabeth. "I bet it's the brand Baldwin smokes. And the next clue will be in that smoke shop there. My hunch is that Edward has arranged for it to be unlocked."

The crowd let out a whoop and a cheer. A few kissed Elizabeth on the cheek before hurrying toward the smoke shop. Even Tallulah looked giddy.

"Thank you, darling!" she said. "You've saved the day!" She ran off toward the shop, her dress fluttering behind her.

Harold looked at her. "Brava," he said.

"Indeed," Calvin added. He bent down to get a better look at the chalk drawing. "You're sharp as a knife to figure that one out. I would've died before I had the answer."

She'd never had this type of attention—a celebration of her wits. Mama seemed to think one's brain would rot by womanhood, and the only other woman who'd praised Elizabeth's mind was Miss Kilman. But here it was—recognition.

Frances ran up, giddy, out of breath. "You're the talk of the night! The genius Dalloway girl who solved a clue!" Frances took her hand and tugged her toward the cigar shop. William and Harold and all the rest walked on. Calvin stayed behind.

"Don't go," he said.

"I—"

"Don't listen to my brother." Frances glared at him and tugged on

Elizabeth harder. "Elizabeth just saved the night! She solved this clue! She needs to go see the spoils of her labor. She's coming with me to the smoke shop. To be celebrated."

"Please stay?" Calvin asked. "I just want to tell you something."

Elizabeth looked at the crowd rushing into the smoke shop. It was her moment in this little famous group. Her time. This wild hour in Covent Garden on a treasure hunt with the prince.

This time.

What feeling was this? What was it?

Some hours leave their mark.

She knew what this time was.

This was her lake. Her row of beautiful glass bowls. Her wild puff of a skinny cigar.

"I'll be there in just a minute, Frances," Elizabeth said. It was an apology. "I promise."

"You're missing out," Frances said. She dropped Elizabeth's hand. "I did my best."

Elizabeth couldn't tell what crossed Frances's face, but it was something she hadn't seen there before. Like Frances was going to miss Elizabeth, as if Elizabeth were leaving, right now, right here on this Covent Garden street corner, boarding an omnibus they couldn't see. As if the society page had already announced her departure to the far reaches of the earth. A tour of the Falkland Islands. An excursion to Mallorca. As if the end of the summer had come and a great ocean already lay between them. Two beautiful girls on either side of the pond.

"Her specialty is spoiling all the fun," Calvin said, taking Elizabeth's arm. "She's really fabulous at it. Learned it from Grim."

"Piss off," Frances said. She looked at Elizabeth. "Bye, sweet girl."

She didn't look back.

———

The alley was desperately dark. A slice of moonlight barely squeezed between the buildings. A few mice skittered away from Elizabeth's feet; one crossed the toe of her shoe—a little tickle, a tiny ghost. Water dripped from the gutters above. Calvin stopped. Reached in his jacket pocket for his flask. They both took generous drinks. How divine it was to feel the bourbon slide down her throat, reach her fingertips, her toes. How it made her care just a bit less about where they were. The edges of Covent Garden. In the middle of the night. A bad hour in a bad part of the city.

She didn't want to be anywhere else.

"Can I tell you something?" Elizabeth asked.

"Anything."

"Do you remember what you said in the pool?" Elizabeth pressed her back against the cold damp stones of the building. "About choosing something different? Being something different?"

"So we have a shot at being happy in life?"

"Yes. So we have a shot. So we don't start making it all up. That's what makes women like my mother unhappy, isn't it? They stop being bright?"

Calvin didn't answer; he put his arm against the building, just above Elizabeth, leaned close. She didn't look in his eyes or at his lips or at any of those things that would make them a sad trope in this alleyway—the upper-class British girl falling for the self-made American. No, her face didn't flush, her heart didn't pound, she didn't look at his strong jaw-line, how the shadows fell just so.

She looked at his shirt collar.

How it wasn't pressed correctly. It wasn't even the right proportion. It was all out of proportion. Out of style. So American. So . . . different. She decided it represented everything, that shirt collar. It wasn't a trope. It was the end of them.

She kissed him.

And kissed him again.

Elizabeth should have stopped, she knew she should have stopped. But she was going to do it differently, life. Live it completely differently than her mother had. She would not live one last June, one last July, and then collapse into a sensible marriage. She wouldn't do it. And that would fix the problem, wouldn't it? The problem of growing up?

A different path. Different choices. That would fix it—save her from being a socialite staring out the window into the darkness.

Calvin's hands moved down her sides now, lower and lower. Over her hips, then to the small of her back. She felt as though her body was roaring to life, as if she'd been dead all this time and hadn't known it. Craving. She was craving him. She felt so small next to him. How much taller he was, sturdier than her. Anyone could tell how strong he was by looking, but to feel his body was another thing entirely. Perhaps they were a trope after all. A dreadfully delicious trope.

She kissed him again and again. She arched her back against the building, ran her hands through his hair now. Perhaps Lady Bexborough had been right; Elizabeth had pirate blood in her veins.

But.

A bit of shock registered. His hands. Was he pulling her dress up? He was. She felt the dank alley air rush up the front of her legs. And now he was unfastening his pants; she heard the clink of a belt buckle. And her underclothes. He was tugging at those, pulling them down. Harshly. Much too quickly. They had lace. They had ribbons. She heard a rip.

Then the strangest thing happened: a torrent of thoughts arrived. All sorts of thoughts. All the pleasure, all the roar, all the whip of the seas on her pirate ship—vanished. Stopped. All at once, it stopped. It was as if she'd been riding Brixby and they had run into that stone wall. Smashed right through the clematis, crushed the petals between her body and the obstacle. She felt flat; she felt so—

Aware.

So terribly aware now. She came out of that blissful, misty, murky cloud of pleasure and was suddenly aware of every thought. As if each one were a judgment, a voice from a tribunal.

You should stop.

What kind of a girl doesn't stop?

You should keep going.

Why are you thinking of stopping?

Really, you aren't any fun. To stop now. All the forward-thinking girls would keep going. All the fabulous ones would love this. You should be like them. You should try.

You should stop.

He was inside her.

It burned; it was sharp. As if she were undergoing some terrible surgery, some cold scalpel hollowing out her body. Out. She wanted him out.

But he was inside her. Again and again. And as Elizabeth's mind seemed to fly a thousand miles away from her body, he felt gone too. His eyes closed. They fluttered a bit. His face had an indescribable look, as if going inside Elizabeth had made him go inside himself, to someplace in the deep, unreachable, unknowable. Not a place to be shared.

Elizabeth was alone.

Physically closer than she had ever been to another human being.

Elizabeth was alone.

What's wrong with you? Enjoy this. Flowers of any sort, snip them and mix them up, let them float in little glass bowls. Chaos. Let it float. Live. Be free.

Calvin moaned.

Is the story what is happening or what we're thinking about what is happening?

Harold. Elizabeth thought of Harold now, of all people. About the stream he'd mentioned. The stream of—consciousness.

Something is wrong with you, thinking like this. This should be fun. Isn't this fun? You just need practice. You're so sheltered.

You can be anything. Even this. A woman like this.

Another deep pang. Another push. Another dreadful sound from Calvin, a far-off sound that made her feel like nothing, like a cold iron section of train track he was returning to.

It was over.

Calvin stopped moving, went slightly limp against her. She felt a sickening wetness between her legs, now down her thighs. Thick. Cloying. He looked at her for the first time since it began. He had returned to her, to his own body. His eyes were open now; he felt here, in this alley with Elizabeth, awake. Aware. Here.

Elizabeth wondered if it had happened at all. In her mind, she'd traveled to a thousand places. Thoughts of her parents, expectations, something about flowers, little glass bowls, the generation after the war. She couldn't even remember all the thoughts she'd had in such a short time. Maybe that's what had happened. Elizabeth had just been in an alley thinking.

Is the story what is happening or what we're thinking about what is happening?

Calvin looked at her now. She thought he would say something about what had just happened. They would make plans. Discuss this monumental night. Instead, he looked at her dress. At the spot just below her collarbone.

"Your dandelion," he said. "Your smashing dandelion is still holding on for dear life."

Elizabeth forced a smile. He saw her, she thought. He really saw her. He understood her strange need to pin these little rebels on her dress. It was going to be all right.

It was going to be all right.

She liked him.

She liked this.

She did.

Calvin looked at her now as though he were about to apologize. To say he was dreadfully sorry for how far things had gone. That he would never want her to suffer any ill consequences or rumors. That they would sally forth together somehow. Slay all the dragons ahead. Fend off any gargoyles attacking them from castle walls.

"Dandelions," he said. "I'll never look at one the same." He fastened his pants, pulled his belt tight. "They'll remind me of this summer. Forever. They'll bring me back to this summer."

CHAPTER 26

Octavia

She was running now. The city moved by her quickly. She passed shops, men washing windows, their cloths leaving rainbow streaks of soap on the glass. The scent of stale beer wafted out of open pub doors. It was a blur of movement, of noise, of smells. Octavia felt a chill on her skin despite the July heat. As if it were all a dream, this race to Septimus, that last bit of a dream just before waking. The part that makes you bolt upright, gasping.

That part of the dream.

She passed 42 Tavistock Square.

44. Then 46.

The next building didn't have a number. It was just one in the long row of nondescript brick buildings all three stories high, connected to one another. Distinguishable only by their front stoops. 48? Octavia hoped it was 48. So the next, that one there with the wet newspaper on the path, the bicycle with a flat leaning against the fence, was 50. That one was 50 Tavistock Square.

She stopped. She looked at the next, the next brick building, the first in its row, at its white shutters, its wavy panes of glass. A gauzy, yellowed curtain fluttered from the open third-story window. A low wrought-iron fence ran along the front; there wasn't a yard to speak of. Three plain stairs led up to the front door, itself a grungy white. A ragged cat slept just beside the stoop.

52.

The number above the door said 52.

She was at 52 Tavistock Square. The home where a Septimus Warren Smith had possibly received mail.

She rang the bell. And waited. A dog barked next door. She rang it again.

No answer.

She took a step back and looked at the third-story window once more. She saw something move, she was sure of it. Someone was home. She tried the bell again. And again. But still, no one answered. Next door, a woman emerged with a broom. She was heavyset, a red apron tied at her waist. She began sweeping her stoop. She looked kind enough.

"Excuse me," Octavia ventured.

"Yes?"

"I'm sorry to bother you," Octavia said. "But I'm looking for someone who lives here." She pointed to the door. "At number fifty-two. His name is Septimus. Septimus Warren Smith. Do you know him?"

The woman stopped sweeping, leaned on her broom handle. She didn't answer the question. "Pardon?" she finally asked. Perhaps she was extremely hard of hearing.

"Septimus Smith," Octavia said. Louder this time. "But never mind, I'm sorry to have bothered you. I'll go to another neighbor." Octavia turned back to Septimus's door. Prepared to knock again.

"Are you a friend of his?"

Octavia turned, her hope rising. The highest it had been since stepping foot in London. The highest. "More than that, ma'am," she said, smiling. "I'm his sister. I'm his little sister from back home in Stroud. You see, Septimus was the seventh. And I'm Octavia, the eighth. We're siblings. Family."

The woman slowly came down the steps of her stoop and walked to the low fence between them. Octavia could see now that she was much older than she'd realized. She seemed very kind, very much like a grandmother. There was something about the woman that was comforting. So comforting. Like she wasn't part of London; she was part of the country somehow. A little piece of the country in the middle of all this mess. She wasn't looking at Octavia like she was a street rat carrying fleas. She really wasn't.

"You don't know, do you?" the woman said.

Octavia shook her head. "Know what?"

"You see that window there?" The woman pointed at the third story. At the window with the curtain still fluttering. The open window of 52 Tavistock Square.

"Yes," Octavia said.

"Septimus threw himself out of it."

CHAPTER 27

Elizabeth

She hadn't been able to see him for a week. He'd telephoned and said Grim had him in a veritable prison. Something about a prominent guest; they were entertaining an important family. He missed her, he said. Desperately. He wanted to know if she was wearing a dandelion. He told her he'd seen a gaggle of them pushing through a crack in the path at their home in Belgravia; he wasn't letting the gardener near them. He was saving them for her. He couldn't wait to see her again. But that family. That important family. His father would have both of his children's heads if they refused these dinners. These awful evenings.

Father.

He called him Father.

The invitation arrived a few days later.

THE PRESENCE OF
ELIZABETH DALLOWAY
IS REQUESTED BY
MR. AND MRS. BERNARD GAGE
OF
368 SOMMERS COURT
BELGRAVIA SQUARE
JULY 18, 1923
12 O'CLOCK

It was odd. Elizabeth had had no notice. Calvin hadn't telephoned, hadn't said a word about this.

Could it be?

Usually, formal invitations came at least two weeks prior to an event. Maybe this was just another of those American customs, Elizabeth thought. Whipping up invitations that didn't give the guests enough time to even get dressed.

Or.

Maybe Calvin had told Grim everything. Confessed his feelings for Elizabeth. They were inviting her into their home, into their family. This was the beginning. It was beginning. What happened in the alley—Elizabeth had just done it wrong. Sex. She would get better. It wouldn't frighten her so much next time. She would be ready. The joy wouldn't skitter away like it had. Besides, Frances had mentioned it herself—that it might hurt. It probably always did. Elizabeth would like it. She would learn to like it. Other women, fabulous women, liked it.

Elizabeth sent the reply that yes, she would attend. She smiled when she realized her greatest fear wasn't about meeting his family, or even impressing them—she was terrified she would call Calvin's father the only name Elizabeth had heard all summer long:

Grim.

Elizabeth could just hear it now.

How d'you do, Grim?

Thank you for the invitation, Grim.

Grim, what is the weather like in Pennsylvania this time of year?

There was also the complication that this luncheon was falling on the very same day as Mama's mid-July party. One of Mama's favorites. She always said summer wilted after mid-July, started to faintly stink of rot. For this party the Dalloway house would be filled to the brim with members of Parliament, the prime minister, high-ranking government officials, and of course, all their wives. And flowers. So many flowers.

Elizabeth must ask her mother's permission to attend a luncheon on such an important day. Mama would have her head if she failed to show.

Elizabeth went to look for her, sure Mama would be flying about the house, ordering this to be done and then that. Lucy would be beside herself; Mr. Garrick would be flummoxed. Rumpelmayer's men were probably already on their way; the doors were likely off their hinges. The July party was the one that required the most work, the most fretting, the most flowers. Elizabeth searched the house. The drawing room, the library, even the kitchen where her mother sometimes went to instruct Miss. Walters on the suitability of the salmon from the previous evening. Finally, Elizabeth ran up to Mama's forbidden bedroom. She didn't know where else to look. She knocked on the door.

No answer.

Elizabeth heard Grizzle whining at the foot of the stairs. She went down, pulled on her wide-brimmed hat, and stepped onto the porch, Grizzle in tow. It was a lovely day. The sun itself seemed to have ripened. The leaves had aged into a sturdy green, a valiant green, a green that was putting up its last fight of the summer, preparing for the battle it always lost against the reds and golds of fall. Calvin's invitation felt like this day, this day right here: full of vigor, full of bravery. Perhaps together they'd win against winter.

There she was.

Mama. In the garden. Hunched over the roses. Cutting them with a pair of shears.

Snip. Snip. Snip.

Elizabeth went to her side. "Mama, I've never seen you in the garden like this." She adjusted her hat in the sun. "Picking roses, are you?"

Her mother stood up, clutching thorny stems in her gloved hand. Beads of sweat covered her forehead; her shears glinted in the sun. Mama seemed oddly at ease here, in the garden, surrounded by plants. It was the strangest thing Elizabeth had ever seen, really. Mama with her hands in dirty gloves like that, sweat ruining her hair, plucking flowers from her own garden and not from Miss Pym's perfect pots. Mama went to one of the garden chairs, the wrought-iron one without a cushion. She sat. But not in her typical upright way. This time she . . . slouched. Could it be? Yes, that was it—Mama was *slouching*. A thing Elizabeth was certain she had never, ever seen. Not once. Not even that morning in 1918 when Mama had come down with the Spanish flu. She'd been perfectly upright in her dining chair one moment and took to her bed the next. One does not slouch. Even when dying.

"Roses are the only flowers I can stand to see cut," Mama said now, ignoring a fly buzzing about her head. "I prefer someone else to cut the others while I'm not looking." She held up her bunch of miniature pinks and reds. "Aren't these lovely? I think they're just perfect."

"Yes," Elizabeth finally said. Did Mama look younger? Was that it? "They are lovely. For the party tonight?"

"Hm?" Mama asked, still admiring the roses. Elizabeth's question had been drowned a bit by the chiming of Big Ben. The time. She was sure now that summer had started a clock that had been slumbering through Elizabeth's childhood. She needed to prepare for lunch with Calvin in Belgravia. She needed to ask for permission to go.

"The flowers. The roses," Elizabeth said. "Are they for tonight?"

Mama shook her head no and smiled. "No," she said. "They aren't for tonight."

"Oh." So odd. Mama was being so very odd. But Elizabeth must go. The time. Look at the time. "Speaking of tonight. I'd like to attend a luncheon today. In Belgravia. But I promise to be back in plenty of time for the party." Elizabeth braced herself. Waited for Mama to look worried, to fret about Elizabeth being late. To make sure William would be in attendance. To issue another ominous warning about caring for people in her summers. About keeping things in proportion. About not throwing her life away. Choosing the right path.

"All right." Mama looked at her daughter. A long look. One that made Elizabeth feel terribly uncomfortable. "Have a wonderful time."

Have a wonderful time?

"All right? It's all right if I go?"

"Yes, is this with William?"

"No, it's with some wonderful—"

"The religious friends, then? Miss Kilman told me weeks ago you have made some American friends. Religious ones." Mama leaned her head back, took in a bit of sun. "Other than her smugness about it, I don't mind a bit. Really, I don't." Mama looked at Elizabeth. "I'm terribly happy that you've had your summer. To watch you gad about has been the most marvelous thing. To see you. In a summer like this."

"Thank you," Elizabeth said slowly. "Enjoy . . . your roses. And I'll see you—"

"One more thing," Mama said. She still held the thorny stems in her leather glove. "I'd like you to get the flowers for this evening. Could you do that for me?"

"Me?" Elizabeth asked. "You'd like me to get the flowers? For the party? All of them?"

"Yes, dear." Mama laughed as if she'd just asked Elizabeth something as simple as pouring a cup of tea. "You've certainly seen me choose them a thousand times. haven't you?"

"Well, I suppose I know, but . . . it's your July party," Elizabeth protested. She came closer to Mama's wrought-iron chair. She was focused on her roses again. So intensely. Elizabeth needed her full attention. "There are *so many* flowers we'll need for tonight. I'm not ready to pick flowers for an entire party! Truthfully, I don't know which flowers go with—"

"Get whatever you like," Mama said flatly. She didn't bother to look away from the blooms. "Go to Mulberry's. Miss Pym will help you."

Get whatever you like?

"But Mama." Grizzle started barking like mad now—at who knows what—as if even he knew how odd this afternoon had become. "Are you . . . angry about the luncheon? In Belgravia? Are you angry about anything? Has someone said something about . . ."

Mama turned, exhaled. "Not in the least," Mama said. "Do you understand? I'm not the least bit upset about your lunch. Summer is almost over. It's all a riddle after this. And I want you to solve it. I won't stand in your way." She wiped a bit of dirt off her dress. "Just tell Miss Pym you'd like the usual flowers of midseason. Bring them home and put them about. All right, Elizabeth? I haven't asked you for anything all summer. Can you do this for me?"

"Yes, of course." She felt terrible now. Terrible for complaining about being asked to do one thing for a party. Mama was right. Elizabeth never helped prepare for these things. Not once.

"Good," Mama said. She looked directly at Elizabeth. With . . . kindness. Was that it? A softness? "And I mean it. Enjoy yourself."

———

Mr. Gage. Mr. Gage. Mr. Gage.

Elizabeth slowly made her way to the gate of the Gages' Belgravia summer home.

Not Grim. Not Grim. Not Grim.

She was ready for this; she could feel it. She opened the gate, started up the path.

"She said no." It was Frances. She was sitting on a swing that hung from a large tree in the garden. "Just like that. No."

"Who said no?" Elizabeth went to her. Frances pumped her legs back and forth, swinging. Her day dress was a lovely cream, but it was too thick, the hem wasn't buoyant enough; it wasn't flirting with the air. It seemed too heavy for the heat.

"Tallulah," Frances said. She dragged her feet along the ground. Came to a stop. "She said she can't help me get an audition."

"I'm so sorry. I'm sure that—"

"She said she doesn't help anybody." Frances leaned her face against the swing's rope. "It isn't me. It's just that she doesn't help anybody. That's what she said."

"I'm sure that's it," Elizabeth reassured her. She sat in the grass now at Frances's feet. "Can you imagine how many requests she gets? If she said yes, she'd fill the audition rooms with a thousand girls each."

Frances leaned back a bit in her swing. Looked up at the leaves. At the sun blinking through them. "I'll be on the stage. I'll be on the stage in America. Won't I?" She looked at Elizabeth, so desperate. Her voice so little. It reminded Elizabeth of something.

"Don't forget my party tonight! Don't forget my party!"

Mama. Frances was reminding her of Mama.

"I can't wait to see you in the pictures," Elizabeth said. "I'll be the first to get a ticket."

"And you, sweet girl. What about you?" Frances hopped down, sat in the grass next to Elizabeth. "You're the daughter of a member of Parliament. In the States, senators' daughters do all sorts of things. All sorts. They write letters! They have causes! They start foundations. Some are actresses. You'd have all the right connections."

Elizabeth smiled. "I don't have a cause to my name. Who on earth would I start a foundation for?"

Frances stared into the sky again. She squinted a bit, thinking. "I've got it!" She clapped her hands. "For lovely British girls who don't know how talented they are! How bright their futures are." She took Elizabeth's hand and gave it a squeeze. "That's who you'll start a foundation for."

Elizabeth smiled. It really was lovely, to be believed in like this. For Frances to believe Elizabeth could be on stage. Start a foundation. Calvin thought Elizabeth was bright, avant-garde, ready to cut whatever path she liked. And sweet William thought her a champion rider.

"Frances!" It was Grim. Standing on the stoop of the Belgravia home. Elizabeth recognized him from church. His strangely straight spine, his sensible gray hair, the suit that matched. He was rotund, his voice loud. He gave the impression that he'd just arrived from some long-ago time—he'd brought the outdated mores but left the fashion behind. His gray suit was quite a fine one. Quite modern. "Don't delay our guest!"

Elizabeth hopped up from her spot on the grass, madly brushed the little bits from her dress.

Mr. Gage. Mr. Gage. Mr. Gage.

Not Grim. Not Grim. Not Grim.

"How d'you do, Mr. Gage?" Elizabeth said hurrying to the stoop. Where was the footman? A butler? Even a lady's maid to answer the door. Not—

"Come along, Frances!" He motioned for his daughter and put a hand around Elizabeth's shoulders. It was so familiar. *Too* familiar. "So pleased to make your acquaintance, Elizabeth Dalloway. Welcome, welcome."

Frances hurried to the stoop and softly pushed past Elizabeth. But as she did, she whispered in her ear, "I'm sorry." She squeezed Elizabeth's hand once more. "But I told him." She raced ahead and disappeared down a hallway.

It was all happening too fast now. That beast, time, had begun to gallop. Horsewhip and fury. Grim ushered Elizabeth inside. The walls were dripping with paintings, every furniture surface was laden with sculptures, fresh flowers. Yet he seemed so . . . austere. "I'm sure you were surprised to see me open the door!" he said as he walked. "We don't keep much staff, and I sent the few we do have home already."

"You sent them home?" Elizabeth asked. "But how will you get on? There's over a month left in the season. Perhaps my mother could spare a few—"

"But doors *aren't* difficult to open, are they?"

Elizabeth didn't know how to respond. How to dredge up some appropriate comment about the opening of doors. Their ease. Or their difficulty. The dignity one may gain or lose by opening them. "Yes. Doors do open. Without challenge, really."

It was the best Elizabeth could do.

They continued down a hallway, past one marble-topped side table after another.

"Now," he said. "Let's go through." He pushed open a door to the dining room. "And I say we just get right down to the business of eating, shall we?"

This was so strange. It wasn't proper to arrive at a home, meet your host at the door, and be shuffled into a dining room and forced into a meal. Initiating conversation with the first bite.

Elizabeth went in.

There were four people already at the table.

Mrs. Gage.

Frances.

Calvin.

And a young woman.

"Elizabeth," Mr. Gage boomed. "This is Mrs. Gage. And of course, you know my children, Frances and Calvin."

Mrs. Gage stood, nodded at Elizabeth, sat back down.

"And Calvin," Grim said, "why don't you introduce Gretchen?"

Calvin gave Elizabeth a bit of a helpless look. This must be what it felt like to be imprisoned by Grim, Elizabeth thought, being barked at like this. "Elizabeth," Calvin said flatly. "This is Gretchen. Gretchen, Elizabeth."

Gretchen looked familiar. She had braided red hair. A plain dress. So plain it almost looked like underclothes. She wore a wooden cross on a long chain around her neck. Where had Elizabeth seen her? Where was it?

The alley.

Beside the church.

Gretchen had popped her head into the alley when Elizabeth had first met Calvin and Frances. They'd said she was the pastor's daughter. That they were forced to socialize with her. She was allergic to fun, they'd said. She collected stamps.

Gretchen stood and nodded to Elizabeth. She was so dainty, so pale, rather gangly. And she had a terrible complexion. Unhealthy-looking, Elizabeth thought. Far too much time spent inside. But she had kind eyes. Very soft, very kind eyes.

"How d'you do?" Elizabeth said.

A small clock on the mantel chimed the hour.

Elizabeth sat.

The table was set simply. There wasn't a centerpiece. Just several bowls full of steaming food with large spoons sticking out. There was no staff for service. Elizabeth tried to get Calvin's attention, tried to silently communicate how awkward this all was. To smile at him. To be in league with him. To exchange a small roll of the eyes.

Isn't Grim so awful?

Isn't Gretchen so plain?

After this, we'll swim. And splash. And dive.

That's what Elizabeth was trying to say. But Calvin kept his eyes on his plate.

Grim sat at the head of the table. "I'm so happy I could attend this

luncheon at all," he said. "Here at the end of the season, it seems every
church in the country has found a need for more money."

Elizabeth wanted to correct him; it wasn't the end of the season.
Not even close. It was the middle.

"Well, Mr. Gage, you are so generous," Gretchen said. She picked
up a bowl of small red potatoes and forked a few onto her plate. Elizabeth had never seen such a thing, serving one's own potatoes like that.
They landed on her plate indecorously.

Thud.

Thud.

Thud.

Like little red heads rolling from a guillotine, Elizabeth thought.

"Why thank you, Gretchen," Grim said. "I'm so happy you could
join us this afternoon. What a delight." He leaned toward Elizabeth.
"Gretchen is the pastor's daughter. Raised by one of the finest religious
minds I've ever known."

"How lovely," Elizabeth said.

Now Gretchen began the revolting process of spearing pork chops.
But not before flicking the sprigs of rosemary from them like they were
bothersome insects who'd dared to land on her food. One wouldn't
want any *flavor* after all. The horror! "Father is an angel," she said. "I'm
so blessed."

The dishes were passed. Elizabeth tried to follow suit, to mimic the
habits of these strange Americans, spearing meat, knocking bulbous
potatoes onto her plate.

The room fell desperately quiet. The only sound was the awful scrap-
ing of cutlery against plates. The chewing of food. Gretchen slurping
the water out of her glass. There wasn't any wine in sight. What Elizabeth wouldn't give for William to tip up with a bottle of whiskey or at
least a small goblet of champagne.

"So Frances tells me you ride?" Grim said, quite out of the blue.

"Yes, I do." Elizabeth felt hopeful now. Grim was going to get to
know her. To really become acquainted with the girl his son was courting. And perhaps this line of conversation would light a spark that would

enliven the entire luncheon. Riding. Horses. "I have a horse named—"

"We've been to Kentucky," Grim interrupted. "To see the races there. It was so thrilling, watching those jockeys drive those horses like that. Is that what you do? You race?" He asked it with a polite smile. But it didn't feel polite. Not in the least.

"No," Elizabeth said slowly. She took her napkin out of her lap and set it on the table. She was giving up her conquest of this pork chop. Of these potatoes. Admitting defeat. "I don't ride horses in races. I hunt. Foxes." Perhaps Grim didn't mean anything by it. Perhaps senators' daughters in America raced horses as a hobby? Who knew.

"Oh?" Gretchen asked. She did seem kind, Elizabeth thought. Genuinely interested. Poor girl had been caught in Grim's clutches. Elizabeth pitied her, this pastor's daughter.

"Yes," Elizabeth said. "Foxes. It's terribly exciting. They're awfully hard to catch. You never know where they're going to lead you. Over walls, through streams, straight into the brambles. They hide in the trickiest of places. Take you down the wildest paths."

"Father," Calvin said. "I'm finished. And don't feel well. I need to step out."

Father.

Had Calvin looked at her? Had he motioned for her to follow?

Grim bristled but consented. Gretchen turned her attention to her next round of potatoes.

Elizabeth tossed all but a shred of decorum out the window. "Please excuse me," she said. She stood, carefully placed her napkin on the table, and followed Calvin out of the room. Rude. It was rude and she knew it. Down the hall, into the garden, the breeze made her feel as though she'd been sweltering in a closed trunk, in an airless, dark box this whole afternoon. She followed Calvin down the path; they stopped at the gate under the shade of Frances's tree.

"My god," Elizabeth said, sitting on the swing. "Poor Gretchen. She's probably never had a stitch of fun in her whole—"

"You're not wearing your dandelion," Calvin interrupted. "You're supposed to wear them. For me." He scanned the grass, found a dandelion, and picked it. Held it out. "I've been saving these for you."

Elizabeth took one, twirled the stem between her fingers. "Thank you. And I'm afraid you've caught me," she said. "I just couldn't wear one to meet Grim. I lost my nerve."

Calvin looked at her. "I wish you hadn't."

"Next time," Elizabeth said. "I promise." Elizabeth looked back toward the house, dreaded returning to the luncheon, to that awful dining room, to the sound of the guillotined potatoes. "I know what we'll do," Elizabeth said, a devious grin on her face. "Let's take poor Gretchen to an after-party. Introduce her to a bit of a life for the summer. Eagan might fancy her, actually."

Calvin didn't smile. He looked at the sky now. He stayed like that. For much too long.

"She said yes." He kept looking up as if some great interest were swooping through the blue. The sky was empty. "I asked her last night."

He wasn't talking about an invitation to a party, and she knew it. Everything went still. The London traffic. The twitter of birds. Elizabeth. Time. She wondered if her heart was even beating. She waited for Calvin to say more, to make sense of it. To explain that he hadn't meant what he'd said.

He didn't.

"You asked her—"

"The wedding will be in Pittsburgh," he said. "In September."

"The wedding? You're marrying *Gretchen*?" she said. "I thought you didn't want any of that. The church. Tradition. I thought you wanted to be different. Bright. I thought we were going to be bright."

"Frances told Grim," Calvin said. "About us. He was furious, insisted on inviting you here, to make sure you understood. He was going to announce the wedding during the luncheon. Make a big show of it. I couldn't let him; I didn't want Father to—"

"I thought he was Grim," Elizabeth said. "Grim when you don't want anything from him. And Father when you do." An ambulance siren wailed in the distance. "What is it you want from him?"

"Have you ever been poor, Elizabeth?" He didn't have to ask; he knew the answer. "I haven't either. And I'm not prepared to find out. You knew that. You have to have known that."

The ambulance grew louder and louder.

"Money," she said. "It's about money."

"You think I'd stay in the will if I married outside the church? If I married a British girl from the Church of England? Father says you are all just Catholics with a grudge. And he does dislike Catholics."

"There's no need to be cruel." Elizabeth spun the dandelion between her fingers; the stem collapsed in her grasp, blotting with green. "You're dreadful enough as it is."

He looked hurt, defensive. As if he still wanted her good favor, even after all this. "These British blokes aren't any different, Elizabeth." He stepped close to her, reached for her hand. She didn't let him have it. "If courting you meant William had to give up his six-thousand-pound-a-year allowance, do you think he'd do it?" Calvin asked. "He just wants six sons at Eton like the rest of you."

Elizabeth dropped the dandelion. She stood from the swing. "I don't want that. Six sons at Eton."

Calvin shook his head. "Then what do you want?"

"I already told you that night in the pool," she said. "I want to be happy. After this. After this summer. I want to take whatever path will get me there." She walked to the gate and opened it. "And I don't expect you to understand this," she said, "but Brixby would've hated you."

The gate clanged shut behind her.

CHAPTER 28

Octavia

Octavia wasn't sure how much time passed, how long she had stood there on that stoop. She thought the woman had offered her a place to stay. Or said something about a boardinghouse. Food, maybe? Had the woman offered her food?

Octavia wasn't sure what she had said to the woman, but she must have said something. Octavia felt like she was coming to, awakening here beside this grandmother. Out here. Octavia must stay out here. In front of her brother's home.

The woman said she was sorry. So very sorry. She went back inside.

Octavia looked at the curtain still fluttering in Septimus's window. The window he'd thrown himself from. She stood and watched. It moved, she thought, like water, like tiny waves, untruthful. A tide that was coming and going, hiding its rage, its power to rise up, to drive things from the surface, pull them to the depths.

The cat that had been sleeping under the bush woke now, stretched, and walked toward Octavia. She looked at him.

"Do you mind if I sleep in your spot tonight?" Octavia asked. The cat flicked his tail as if to interrupt her, shook his head like he was casting fleas out of his ears. "Here beside the stoop? Under the bush? Or even here, just beside it." She felt a kinship with the animal. The two survived the same way: stalking vermin, sorting through trash, shaking fleas out of their ears. Staking claim to dry spots under bushes. It was only right to ask for permission.

The cat ignored her. Strolled away uninterested. Octavia walked up the three stairs to Septimus's door, felt the pain push through her now, push through her chest, through her ribs, stick out the back of her. She knelt on the stoop, curled around her wound, laid her head against the cold gritty stone, and wept. She knew she couldn't stay there until nightfall. It was getting dimpsy now, the sun low in the sky. Someone would see her, complain, call the rozzers. She would stand. Somehow, she would stand, a girl without her brother, her hero, the one who made her worth something. She would stand up, walk this city until it was dark, and then come back. She would sleep on the stoop of her brother's home. Near the place where his heart hit the pavement, near where it beat its last blood. She felt close to him somehow. At his funeral. Here on this stoop. His funeral.

And at her own.

———————

Something knocked against her back. Something pointed, a bit sharp.

Octavia opened her eyes. For one murky moment—all dreams and exhaustion and thirst—she forgot where she was.

Septimus's stoop.

She'd slept here all night, curled like a homeless cat. The sun was just coming up.

"Shoo! Off you go, girl!" It was a woman's voice. Shrill. "I almost tripped over you!"

She loomed over Octavia, her arms full of luggage and hatboxes; she was wearing the most peculiar hat. There were beads, tassels, ribbons, the oddest of colors joined together. It was unlike anything Octavia had ever seen. It was lovely.

Octavia remembered more. About what had happened. She was on the stoop. Of the house. With the window. Her brother had jumped from.

"Please let me pass," the woman said curtly, pushing past Octavia now, struggling down the stoop with her luggage. She looked exhausted, pale, thin. Much too thin. Her hair was dark, bits of it peeking from under the hat here and there. And her eyes were dark, too, wet and black and worried like one of the mice that scurried about the brewery. She went toward the gate. Scurrying. Yes, thought Octavia, she was scurrying.

"Ma'am," Octavia called. She pushed herself up from her place on the stoop. "I'm—"

"Are you selling something?" the woman asked. "If so, I'm not buying. Now, off you go."

"My name is Octavia," she said. The woman was down the path now, almost at the gate. Almost gone. "I was his sister."

The woman stopped. A small case slipped from her arms, fell to the stone below. She put everything down, the hatboxes, the luggage, even her slim purse. Her arms hung limp at her sides. She turned.

"My name is Rezia," she said. "And I was his wife."

Their flat was very sparse, but lovely all the same. There was the fireplace, the coal scuttle, a high-backed couch. There was the newspaper on a little table by the door, a few small bags of sweets. A large dining table was just outside the kitchen, but it didn't look as if it had been used for a meal perhaps ever.

It was covered with fabric. Felts. Flowers.

Rezia sat. She adjusted the collar on her dress, smoothed the skirt about her legs. It was an off-white, the dress. Muslin with a lace collar. If Octavia didn't know better, she'd assume it was a woman's wedding dress. A plain one, but still. With a white hat and bouquet, it would do. Octavia looked back at the table that was covered with felt flowers, ribbons, bits and bobs.

"That's where I make all my hats," Lucrezia said. Octavia noticed for the first time how thick her Italian accent was. Octavia loved how her voice sounded, like a song that went up and down. Up and down. Some notes held just a bit longer than others. "That is what I love," Lucrezia said. "They're in the Italian style, you know." She took the one she'd been wearing off her head and held it in her hands. "Septimus helped me with this one. Told me to sew it up *exactly* how he had designed it. He seemed so happy." Rezia held it out for Octavia. Her dark eyes looked like a brewery mouse's again, scared, ready to run. "And then he jumped."

Octavia took the hat in her hands. "It's—" she stopped. She couldn't speak, holding that hat. The hat her brother had designed.

"I'm sorry. I shouldn't have told you all that. You don't look so well," Rezia said. She took Octavia's arm and led her to the sofa. "Mrs. Filmer has left me. I sent her away. But I'll get something. Espresso. Some krumiri?"

Octavia didn't know what to say. She'd never heard of anything like that.

Rezia smiled. "Forgive me. Italian cornmeal cookies. You will like them." She disappeared into the kitchen.

Octavia sat on the sofa and spotted several pictures in frames on the end table. One was of Septimus in uniform. Where was he? A court-house? Rezia was next to him in a very plain dress, one that looked very much like the one she was wearing now. And she was in one of those peculiar hats, holding a group of flowers that looked rather wilted. Their wedding day? And next to that was a picture of four women standing in front of a luscious garden. Each woman had her hair pinned back, but the wind was undoing it all. Curls escaped, wisps blew across faces, smiles unfurled.

"That is me," Rezia said, returning. She placed the tiniest cup of coffee on the table in front of Octavia. Octavia had never seen a cup that small, coffee so black. She guessed it was Italian. "And my sisters. In a garden in Milan. I am going back. Back to Italy."

"Italy?"

"Yes," she said. She took a sip from her cup. "That is where I met Septimus. At my home. In Milan."

He'd been sent to the Italian Front. Lucrezia had met him when he was on leave. They had been so in love, she said. From the very first moment. He'd recited Shakespeare; she could listen to him read poetry forever, she said. She'd never doubted coming to London with him when the war was over. Leaving everything in Milan—her family, her sisters, those gardens. Not like these awful London gardens, she said, no better than fancy patches of weeds. No, they were nothing compared to the Milan gardens. And no, he'd never spoken of his family in Stroud.

"None of us?" Octavia asked. "He never mentioned my name?"

"No. Except," Rezia said, pausing. "Your mother. He said she lied. But he would never tell me about what. He said that's why he left his home."

Octavia looked at Rezia's table again, the one covered with felts and ribbons. "Ronnie," she whispered.

"Ronnie?"

"My little brother. After he was born, my mother lost her mind. Tried to abandon him. She left him in a field. She lied, said he'd been snatched." Octavia looked down at her little cup, at the steam rising. A feeling came, that her body could not hold itself up, that she might drop the black coffee on the floor, burn her legs, shatter the porcelain. That she wouldn't even feel it. "A farmer found him just in time."

Rezia's eyes were wide. "Why would a mother do such a thing? Such an awful thing?"

"My aunt said it was maternal melancholia," Octavia said. "My father said it was the devil." Octavia looked at the window. The large one in the center of the wall. Was that the one? Was that the one he'd gone through? "I guess that's why he never came home. Because he wanted to be done with my mother. Done with all of us, I guess."

"No, no. That's not it," Rezia said. "Your mother was why he left. But he never returned for a different reason altogether." She put her cup down on the table, looked at Octavia very matter-of-factly, very calm now. "It was the war."

"The war?" Octavia said. "But you just told me that you came here from Italy when it was over. That just before he jumped, he was making hats. That you were both so happy. So he wasn't hurt. He wasn't injured in battle. He made it through the war. He survived. He could have come home. And he didn't."

Rezia's eyes filled with . . . Octavia wasn't sure what it was. Rage.

Tears. Grief. "We saw doctors," Rezia said. "And a psychiatrist. Dr. Brad-shaw was the best, that's what everyone told us. The best in London. And he told us there was nothing wrong with Septimus. That he should have a hobby. Get interested in things outside himself. That he had lost all sense of proportion. Dr. Bradshaw said there was nothing wrong with Septimus. He said it over and over."

"I don't understand," Octavia said, shaking her head. "Then how could it have been the war that made him jump? That made him not want to come home. If he was one of the lucky ones? A soldier who survived in one piece?"

Rezia stood and crossed the room to a little writing table. She opened a drawer and pulled out a stack of paper, tied with one of her hat ribbons. She handed it to Octavia. "I think you should read these."

———

The writings were not organized in any way. Octavia went through the stack, page by page. Some held diagrams, designs. Septimus had drawn little figures of men and women brandishing sticks for arms; some had wings on their backs. Some papers had circles on them. Just—circles. It looked as though Septimus had traced around shillings and pennies. He'd made some of them into suns. Some had tails like comets.

He'd drawn a map of the world. Here were continents. Here were mountains with climbers. Here were the seas, filled with little faces laughing, peeking out of the water, menacing faces tucked among waves.

The writings were next. So many writings. She expected poetry, fine, fine poetry. Styled after Shakespeare, littered with Greek, beautiful stanzas from her self-taught brother. Genius of Stroud. Man with a future. Smart as any Cambridge man. The one from the Smith family who was to be something, who *was* something, who was going to live a full, exciting life for all of them.

The writings weren't what she expected. Not at all. Septimus wrote that he heard voices talking behind the bedroom walls. That he couldn't understand why the maid, Mrs. Filmer, thought it odd. Couldn't she hear them? Couldn't everyone? And if not, how mad she was, how deaf. There were people in the walls. Everyone knows there are people in the walls. And here was the Greek Octavia expected, but it was not in a poem. It was not even an allusion to an epic poem; it was not tucked in fancy phrases.

It was in the mouths of birds.

Greek.

In the mouths of birds.

Septimus wrote that they spoke Greek to him in the park. That rooks would sit in the trees, look straight at him, and speak in Greek. They would say all manner of things. The secret of life. The meaning of life. That we should not kill trees. That they were as much alive as we were. That Septimus should tell the prime minister.

Do not kill trees.

The meaning of the world.

Universal love.

Octavia read on. How Septimus had a dear friend in the war, a man named Evans. How he had died in the dirt and the mud. How Septimus had watched his friend die. How Evans would come to him. In London. A ghost. Visit him in the parks. In their home, even. And all the mud was gone! All the dirt had vanished from Evan's flesh! But they were not welcome visits. Evans came to tell Septimus that it was wrong, so very wrong for Septimus to be alive when so many other men were dead. So wrong to live. People were after him, he was sure. Intent on making him pay for his life. No, he couldn't meet with anyone, go to any veterans' charities. He couldn't list his name in a telephone directory. They'd find him. They were tracking him.

Octavia ran a hand over the last sentences her brother had written, more confusing than all the rest:

I do not want to die.

Life is good.

The sun is hot.

Scatter me among the trees.

Octavia clutched the papers to her chest. She thought of the faces he had drawn in the ocean, glaring, criticizing. The voices he heard in the walls. The voices of birds in the park. In Greek. And perhaps the loudest voice of all, from whom she did not know—that it was not right for him to live. That Septimus was a failure. That it is not right for failures to live. There was a voice, a powerful voice, a disembodied voice saying that to him.

Die.

Rezia was at the window, looking out. Octavia joined her there.

"He didn't survive the war, did he?" Octavia asked. An organ-grinder passed below; the whines and whistles of his notes reached their ears. People moved along the street as if Septimus's death were nothing but an imperceptible shift in the air, lost at once in the winds shouldering through the crowd.

"No," Rezia said. "And I think that is what he was trying to communicate. To Dr. Bradshaw. To anyone. But no one would listen. He did not kill himself. *He died in the war.*"

CHAPTER 29

Elizabeth

If Big Ben rang for the next few hours, Elizabeth didn't know it. If it stopped like it had when she was a child during the war, she wouldn't know that either. She walked through the city with no direction. No time. She just walked and walked.

Almost blindly, she took the Underground to Bond Street. She hated Bond Street. Those awful trips with her mother. But now, strangely, she craved its noise, its commotion. She wanted to stare in windows at shiny things, she thought. Yes, she'd like to shop a bit. For the first time in her life—Elizabeth Dalloway wanted to shop.

She took the steps out of the station two at a time, emerged aboveground. She stopped in front of a vegetable market, looked at the gaggles of carrots, knots of cauliflower—then a basket of red potatoes. Like Gretchen's guillotined heads. She quickly looked away. She couldn't bear to see red potatoes ever again, she thought.

Not again for the whole of my life will I be able to look at a red potato.

It will make me sick.

She moved on to the butcher, selling pork. Women were asking for this many chops. No, no, perhaps this many. Then the stall with herbs. There was dried thyme hanging for its sins, branches of cheerful rosemary, optimistic in their reach.

None of that, either. Rosemary. Pork. I can't look at any of that. Ever again.

She strolled on, thinking of this wild summer. This season that had been unlike all the rest. It was an undertow. She glanced down an alleyway and couldn't help but think of the one beside the church. She saw a men's shop and thought of Calvin's suit coat tossed in the bin.

"You don't believe any of that garbage, do you?"

That's what Calvin had said. Elizabeth could almost hear his voice.

She passed a small fountain now and thought of the party at the Marshall pool. The water that had muffled the sounds of the world. The ebullient American girl unlike any other girl Elizabeth had ever known.

"Excuse me." It was an angry woman in an out-of-date black hat. A feather was tucked in the hatband. Elizabeth had bumped her shoulder. "Watch yourself," the woman snapped.

"I'm sorry," Elizabeth mumbled. "So sorry."

Elizabeth hadn't been paying attention. She *couldn't* pay attention. She tried. She came to the fanciest part of the street now, the nicest shops. She stopped in front of a jeweler's storefront. Trained her eyes on the gold. The necklaces, the brooches, the bracelets. There, an old-fashioned piece of mourning jewelry, the hair of the dead woven behind a knot of topaz. It made her think of the war, of all the dead sons her mother talked about, the dead boys, the dead children bombed just outside their school on Upper North Street, the bronze sphinx on Victoria's embankment still bearing pockmarks from shrapnel. She remembered thinking of death when she was eleven. Waiting for bombs as she huddled in her room. She thought of the flu, how she was convinced she'd die then, at twelve, pulling on her mask. She thought of all that. She stared at that piece of mourning jewelry, a brooch someone had made from their loved one's hair. Clipped a lock of it before they were laid in their casket.

The dead.

It made her think of the dead.

Is that what I am to become? The walking dead? It's already happening. July isn't even over and it's already starting. Is this what happens? People

hurt us and leave scars that we return to over and over? Borne into the past.
By the people who've hurt us.

Elizabeth tried again, to look at things. She moved on to a hat shop. If she could just look at brand-new things, she thought. Maybe that would help. New things. All shiny and placed just so.

Impossible.

It was impossible not to sink into the flood, the flow of thoughts. She was so angry. So mortified. How could she have let herself be taken in by Calvin? How could she have become entangled like that? Been hurt like that? Not have seen it coming.

Really, you are such a stupid girl.

An embarrassment. You're an embarrassment.

And everyone will know it.

She thought of the moment he pulled her into that alleyway. What she'd given to him. What he'd taken.

Now, she came to a smoke shop. And stopped. She stared at the cigars that lined the display. Skinny ones like those her mother always spoke of, then the fat, thick ones, made for a man, Elizabeth was sure.

A cigar. The clue from the treasure hunt in Covent Garden.

My underclothes. Ripping.

What you did was sordid. What kind of a girl does that in an alley?
What kind of a girl are you anyway?

Elizabeth wasn't sure how long she had stood there in front of the smoke shop. Staring. Just staring at cigars. A man inside the shop noticed her, caught her eye. He looked at her with suspicion as if he was worried she was working out how to steal a box of tobacco. Or perhaps that she was a madwoman, paralyzed in front of the shop, raving thoughts burning through her mind, like they might drive her to break the window, to cause a scene.

A woman.

Staring in a shop window on Bond Street.

Helplessly carried back and back and back.

To the past. To her memories.

To her summer.

Elizabeth's breath hitched in her throat. Her eyes went wide.

Mama.

Someone hurt her.

Someone desperately hurt her.

Or was hurting her now. It was a wound that unmoored her mind.

What has hurt you? Who was it?

It had nothing whatever to do with Peter Walsh. That's what she'd said.

"It had nothing whatever to do with Peter Walsh."

Then what was it? What hurt you?

And then Elizabeth heard it. Big Ben rang out. Time resumed.

She heard it for the first time since she'd left Calvin's home in Belgravia. Since Calvin had said those awful, awful words—*"she said yes."*

Ring. Ring. Ring. Ring.

Ding. Ding. Ding. Ding.

Elizabeth was late. So very late. For Mama's July party. For Mama herself.

I must go to her. I must go.

Elizabeth couldn't bear to stop long enough to hail a taxi. Movement. She needed movement. As if Brixby were underneath her, as if she were in the saddle, chasing a hidden fox, jumping over flower-covered walls placed all throughout the city.

Leap or die. Leap or die.

She raced to the Underground station, paid her fare. The train could not move fast enough under the streets of London. Elizabeth felt that the very air had conspired against her, as if it had thickened here underground, was pushing back against the train, slowing it to a crawl as if the mud of Flanders had been resurrected, had found its way to Britain, oozed into every tunnel under the city.

Finally, the train arrived; finally, the doors opened. Up the stairs, up and up and up. Onto the streets of Westminster. Down this block here, now this. Past the Purvises' home, past the guard they had stationed there for the season after the theft. Now she was at her gate, her home. She was at the Dalloway home.

Cars were lined up out front. Well-dressed guests were stepping out, a few streamed past the gate, into the house. The front door stood open. The party had begun. Mama's July party.

Elizabeth saw her father in the garden. In front of the rose bushes Mama had trimmed back much too far, their thorny stems sticking out like the remains of a poor haircut.

He looked dreadful.

Elizabeth pushed past the guests, past the gate, rude, so rude.

So be it. So rude.

She ran past the phlox bed, the wolfsbane, the tulips.

Flowers. The flowers! Elizabeth remembered—she was supposed to get the flowers for tonight.

"Papa," Elizabeth said, reaching him. Finally, finally reaching him. "I'm so sorry I'm late." She was breathless from the running. "And the flowers. I completely forgot the flowers. Mama asked me to buy them for the party from Mulberry's. But I didn't. What will we do?"

Papa was looking at the rose bush. Still looking at the stubby stems, the ones without blooms. "I'm not worried about that."

"But . . ." Elizabeth began. "We don't have *any*. Not a single bloom. I suppose Mr. Garrick could clip some from the garden? Will Mama faint if I cover the place in phlox? Mingle wolfsbane and tulips?"

"I'm not worried about that either." Her father didn't look at her. She stepped around to his side. Tried to get his attention.

"You're upset because I'm late," Elizabeth guessed. "I know. I'm terribly sorry, and I'm sure that Mama will be so upset too, and I'll make it up to the both of you. I've just had the most dreadful day. The most dreadful entire summer, really. It's the worst and the best of my life. I really can't tell which."

Did he know? Did he know what had happened in that alleyway? Had someone seen them? Told anyone who would listen?

Papa looked at her then. In a way he never had before, as if his gaze had pinned her there, forced her to be still, there in the fading late-day light. In the garden. She went still.

"I'm not worried about you being late," Papa said softly. "I'm worried about your mother. She hasn't arrived. I haven't seen her since noon. No one has."

Elizabeth shook her head, confused. "No," she said. "That's not possible. Mama is never late. She'd *never* be late for her party." Elizabeth took a steadying breath. "I'll find her. I will. She must be here. She *must* be. Perhaps her green gown has ripped. She's probably frantically mending it with her little leather sewing kit. It tends to come undone at the bodice."

"You'll have to help me," Papa said. "With this party. I can't do it alone. There are so many guests, and your mother has a way with them. She's the hostess. The greatest hostess. I don't have it. Her way. I don't have her gift."

"Don't worry a bit," Elizabeth said. "I will find her."

Elizabeth ran up the stairs of the front stoop and went straight into the house, straight into the party, straight into the middle of the crowd.

The guests stared.

Elizabeth was still in her luncheon dress, her hair unkempt, jutting this way and that from all that running. Her fingertips green from mashing dandelion stems between them. Her face puffy, she was sure, from crying. She'd been crying. She stood in the middle of the room, surrounded by them, all in their finest, all sipping cocktails, some grouped around—yes, the prime minister.

She saw Peter.

And Sally Seton.

She ran to them.

"Have you seen Mama?" Elizabeth asked.

"No," Peter said. "Not at all."

Not since you kissed her.

She felt he should know her whereabouts somehow. He shouldn't be able to kiss another man's wife and then lose track of her completely.

"Have you seen her, Miss Seton?" Elizabeth asked. "I believe you are Miss Sally Seton?"

Sally was not in daring red this time. She was in muted blue. "Yes." Sally smiled. "That was my name a long time ago. Before I married. And

I haven't seen her. Not at all. But Clarissa wouldn't be late. Not even when she was seventeen would she be late."

"We'll start asking the rest of the guests," Peter said. "Perhaps someone has spotted her."

"We're her—childhood friends," Sally said. "We'll help with this party. Just let us know what we can do."

"Thank you," Elizabeth said. But she wasn't comforted. Not really. Peter and Sally looked as worried as Papa.

Elizabeth tore down the staff stairway, looked in the kitchen, in the staff dining room, even in the cellar. She asked every person she could find.

No. No. No. None of them had seen her.

She ran up the little stairway that led out of the kitchen to the back garden.

Mr. Garrick.

The closest person Mama had to a parent, the man who had been with the family since the moment Mama was married. Elizabeth would go to his greenhouse. He would know where her mother was. He would know what to do. He would tell her not to worry. She went into the great glass building. Stepped into its warm, humid air.

"Mr. Garrick," she said. He was watering several tomato plants, checking that their stems were secure on their stakes.

"Elizabeth," he said. He set down his watering can. "Lovely to see you this—"

"Have you seen Mama?" Breathless. She was still breathless. The humid greenhouse air made it worse, made her feel as though she were gasping.

Mr. Garrick peered through the steamy windows back at the house. "Her party has begun," he said, looking a bit confused. "She'll be in the house, of course."

Elizabeth shook her head. "She isn't."

"But her party . . ." Mr. Garrick trailed off.

"*Has begun,*" Elizabeth finished his sentence. "And she isn't at it."

Mr. Garrick nodded slowly. "Then something is wrong. Something is terribly wrong."

Elizabeth did not want to hear that. Couldn't he offer some sensible explanation? Wouldn't he know something, anything? "I forgot the flowers, Mr. Garrick. For the party. Perhaps she's getting those? On Bond Street? Could she be delayed at Mulberry's?"

"Elizabeth," Mr. Garrick said. He gently jabbed his spade into a pot of soil. "Your mother is always on time. If she is anywhere, she will be in her room. In her bedroom. Have you checked it?"

"No," Elizabeth said, shaking her head. "She's always asked me not to go in."

"Go in it, Elizabeth," he said. He touched her arm. So softly. "Go into her room."

———

Elizabeth went back into the house. Went up the stairs. Walked down the hallway. Passed the bathroom with its open door, its dripping tap.

Drip. Drip. Drip.

Closer and closer.

She stopped in front of Mama's bedroom door. And knocked.

Waited.

Knocked again.

No answer.

She put her hand on the doorknob, the crystal one cut like a diamond. Slowly, Elizabeth turned the knob until the latch clicked.

She pushed the door open.

There was Mama's dressing table, her pincushion stuck with hatpins. There was Mama's cupboard that held her dresses, her gloves. There was her side table with the candle. A fresh one, hardly burnt down. Baron Marbot's memoirs. Shakespeare. *Othello.* Elizabeth took a few steps in, onto Mama's plush rug.

She looked at the bed.

The sheets were pulled tight. The pillowcases smooth.

Nothing out of place.

Except for one thing.

What was on it.

A dress.

Laid out as if in a casket, as if a body had just been in it, just moments before, but was now gone. Leaving nothing behind.

But this dress. And the leather sewing case Mama had used to mend it.

Her sea-green gown.

Mama was gone.

The mermaid had shed her skin.

DECEMBER 8, 1952

CHAPTER 30

Elizabeth

She didn't tell Theodore.

She felt dreadful about it, but she didn't tell him.

He wouldn't let her traipse off in this fog on an impossible errand—to find the family of a soldier Mama knew in 1923. With only an engraving on the back of a medallion to lead the way.

It was madness.

And her mind.

There was the matter of her mind to consider.

She could fall into one of those trenches she was famous for. Bombed by all those thoughts, the ones that stung, the ones that were so loud. About what Elizabeth had become. Her little job. Her odd little haircut, her ill-fitting slacks. Her dependence on Theodore's money. Her lost child. All of it. Her thoughts about all of it. So loud.

If she told Theodore, he would try to stop her. And he would be sure she had her mask. He would be so upset with her if she left it behind, taken it off after Rose arrived.

But she traipsed off into the fog without it. The War Office was first. The gentleman behind the counter seemed not only mystified by Elizabeth's request but also peeved that he had to be at work at all. The fog had closed most shops, most places of business. Going out in it could be lethal; the lucky ones were able to stay home. The downsides of being employed by the government had become glaringly obvious; one had to report for duty, fog or no.

He was able to locate Septimus Smith's dusty record. He returned home. Septimus Warren Smith. No address.

Did the man have any information about Septimus's relatives?

"No," the gentleman behind the counter said, "no one is listed. No next of kin."

The Commonwealth War Graves Commission was next. Had he died? Had there been a funeral? Perhaps a family record of that. No. They had no record of his grave. Of his death. He must still be alive. He must be. Septimus Smith was alive. Veterans were buried in military cemeteries. He would be in his sixties now. He could tell Elizabeth something about Mama.

The post office was next, the Marchmont. Perhaps a directory could help. But how many Smiths were there in London? She must try. It was worth that. Elizabeth fought her way through the fog, past the honking motorcars, the snarled traffic. Storefronts were shuttered, the sidewalks coated in thick black sludge now. Everyone in masks. Some wore silk scarves wrapped about the head above a strand of pearls, trying to maintain a sense of style. Others wore masks made of sterner stuff, thick cotton and heavy straps. Elizabeth reached the plain brick building and stepped inside. The clear air was such a relief. She glanced down the hallway at the rows and rows of metal mailboxes, each a little doorway to a life in London. Elizabeth wondered if one of them belonged to Septimus, if perhaps a letter from Mama had crossed its threshold.

Perhaps they've come here together to collect the mail.

The directory was sitting on a little wooden table in the middle of the hallway. She raced to its pages, thumbed straight to the Smiths.

There were hundreds, if not thousands.

Salvatore Smith.

Sean Smith.

Sebastian Smith.

No Septimus.

Elizabeth saw the postmaster's window. She walked to it and found yet another disgruntled government worker behind the counter. It was a thin man this time, no more than thirty, Elizabeth decided. His apron hung behind him on a nail—off with formality it seemed to say. Off with pretense.

"Excuse me, kind sir," Elizabeth began. "But I am looking for someone. I'm looking for the address of a Mr. Septimus Warren Smith. I can't—"

"Check the directory," the man said flatly.

Elizabeth smiled politely. "I've done that and run aground, I'm afraid. I was hoping there might be a record of him, any record at all, that there might be a Mrs. Septimus Smith who is to receive his mail now? Or some forwarding address, perhaps?"

The thin man muttered something incomprehensible and disappeared into a back room. He returned with a large book in his hands. He held it up. "Old one," he explained. He began thumbing through it. "What was the name again?"

"Septimus," Elizabeth said. "Septimus Warren Smith. I believe he is a friend of my mother's." She could feel a bit of light in her eyes; she'd spoken in the present tense. Septimus *is* a friend of her mother's. The man kept flipping pages, running a finger down the names.

"Nothing." The man snapped the book shut. "Can't help you."

There was no Septimus Smith in the current telephone directory, and there was no Septimus Smith in the old one.

Elizabeth thanked him and returned to the fog. It hit her now, the thickness of the air. In her hurry, she hadn't noticed; she'd thought she could breathe. She couldn't. A coughing fit stopped her at a crossing signal; a policeman was there holding a small torch of fire. It was the only way they could see. Each policeman looked like a prehistoric creature who'd crawled out of a cavern with his primitive light. How her lungs hurt. How they burned. How awful she was to leave Theodore like that. Leave him to worry. If she were to become a casualty of this horrible coal smoke, she would hurt him so deeply. She would hurt him as if on purpose. She would have chosen to disappear and leave him behind.

Like Mama had done to her.

She needed something to help her breathe. A bit of fabric. Something to hold over her mouth. She owed Theodore that. To try to keep breathing.

She looked down the street. A tobacco shop. Closed and dark, its little gold-stamped cigars sitting like sticks at the bottom of a lake. Next, a bakery. Shuttered. All the buns and cakes pulled from their shelves, orphaned crumbs in their wake. There, a newsstand. Open. No shouting newsboy, though. Just a gentleman in a mask handing out papers from a tall stack. Elizabeth went over, picked one up.

WORSE THAN 1866 CHOLERA

DEATHS FROM FOG

Magazines lined the racks. She took one of those too.

LONDON IN CHAOS

FOG COSTS £10M

HOSPITALS AND MORGUES FILLING

There, out of the corner of her eye, another light. At first, she thought it was another policeman directing traffic with a torch.

It was a light in the window of a women's dress shop.

Could it be open?

They would have something there. A scarf or something like it. Something to help her breathe.

Elizabeth walked to the door, peered in. Yes, the lights were on; an open sign hung in the window. She thought of Mama shopping on Bond Street, every bit and bauble reminding her of her past. Elizabeth thought of shopping there herself that awful summer of '23 after Calvin had left her. Carrying her heartbreak up and down the sidewalk like an item she couldn't return. Trying desperately to focus on the cigars, on the little glass bowls, the flowers, the water cans, begging them to stop the stream in her mind.

Who hurt you, Mama? Were you hurt? When you were young?

Now, she went in. A shirt caught her eye. It was a women's shirt, the oddest she'd ever seen. It had a wild floppy collar, big cuffs, tiny buttons. Too many buttons. Elizabeth loved it. She didn't know why. She studied it again.

It was all out of proportion. That was it. The proportions were all wrong.

"May I help you?" It was an old woman, her white hair in tight curls. A woman who should not have her shop open at a time like this. A woman who should not be out in the fog. She was frail; she was old. Her lungs were vulnerable. At least she had a mask hanging from her neck.

"You're open," Elizabeth said. "I was so surprised to see the light in your window."

The woman nodded at her little desk against the wall in the back as if someone were sitting there. The chair was empty. "James and I have been open every single day since we began forty years ago. Can't close it now. He'd have my head." She smiled, sparkled a bit.

"James?"

The woman pointed at a picture on the wall. "My husband. He's been gone almost ten years now. Didn't even get to see the end of the second war. Not fair, that. Not fair at all. But I'm glad he's missing this mess." She nodded at the fog outside.

Elizabeth walked closer to the picture. Their wedding picture. The woman was in a very plain dress, holding the smallest of bouquets. Her smile was determined, her shoulders squared to the camera. James looked pleased, happy to have her take the spotlight. There wasn't a church behind them. No altar. Some sort of office? Was that a bookshelf?

"It's lovely," Elizabeth said. "The picture. You were a lovely bride. Where were you married?"

"The Register Office," the woman said. "Good a place as any to be official."

The Register Office.

Official.

An official record of marriage.

"It's lovely, it really is," Elizabeth said. "But I'm afraid I must run. You've been so very helpful."

"How have I helped, dear?" She looked quite confused. "Is there something you want to buy?"

Of course Elizabeth should buy something. The woman's customers had likely all dried up in this awful smoke. Shops like this would go under. Elizabeth reached for the strange shirt. The one completely out of proportion.

"This. I'll take this."

———

52 Tavistock Square.

In Bloomsbury.

Lucrezia Smith lived at 52 Tavistock Square. Septimus's wife. Her maiden name was on the marriage license. And her first. Lucrezia. And that was the name in the directory. Lucrezia Smith. Elizabeth had expected her to be listed as Mrs. Septimus Smith; Elizabeth would have never guessed Septimus's wife would be listed by her own first name. She had never known any woman to officially call herself that after marriage. Her own name.

Elizabeth held the odd shirt over her mouth and nose, tried to contain the spasm of a cough she could feel rising in her chest.

She rang the bell.

Waited.

The door opened and a woman stood there. A remarkable woman. Tall and slender, perched just so in the doorway, a bird who'd decided to light for a moment. She seemed to be Elizabeth's age. In her late forties at least. Her dress was magnificent. The print. Hundreds of flowers, bright and modern flowers. And the cut. It wasn't like the awful boring blue one Rose Purvis had been wearing, the one that jutted out from the tiny waist in perfect pleats like cupcake papers. It wasn't cut in that dreadful fashionable shape at all. It was tailored all the way down to the knee. But it wasn't tight, it was . . . just right. It hugged her body in the most elegant way. The sleeves were a bit puffed at the shoulder, a few buttons at the high neck. Small pearlescent ones, like those found on women's gloves.

And her hair—it was pinned and smoothed tightly all around. Was she from a magazine? She had to be from a magazine. From the cover.

No, this woman did not look like a cupcake in the least.

"May I help you?" the woman asked. Elizabeth noticed now that the only thing normal about this woman was her eyes. They were wide, honest. Serious, as if assuring you that whatever you saw in them was true, that they were too clear to hide anything. It struck Elizabeth that the most elegant thing about this woman might be in her eyes, the simplicity in her eyes.

Elizabeth cleared her throat. "My name is Elizabeth Dalloway," she said. She used her maiden name. Without any thought really. *My name is Elizabeth Dalloway.* "I am looking for a Lucrezia Smith. The wife of Septimus Warren Smith. I'm looking for someone who knows him."

The woman smoothed her flowered dress. She seemed to deflate just a bit, become a little smaller. But her eyes didn't change. They locked on Elizabeth's. Honest. True. "I know him."

"You do?"

"I'm his sister," she said. "Octavia Smith." She opened the door a little wider. "Do come in."

———————

The drawing room was very simple. Here was a coal scuttle. Here, a high-backed chair. Here, a mantel with candlesticks and a small vase. Three windows granted views over the London street below. The middle window was odd, though; flowers made of fabric and felt hung around its frame. All sorts—there a pink felt rose, here a white paper gardenia. A green vine above it all, burdened with . . . clematis? The other two windows were bare.

Octavia took Elizabeth's coat and brought tea. They sat.

"I do love your suit. I love boxy cuts," Octavia said. "Is it Chanel?"

Elizabeth had heard that name in passing—Coco. Coco Chanel. But she really didn't have any earthly idea who it was. Not really. Something about clothes. That's as far as it went. "I'm—"

"People at work tease me that I should wear Claire McCardell." Octavia laughed. "American designer. Casual country-girl looks. Denim and gingham and that."

Elizabeth was completely lost in the conversation. She'd never discussed fashion designers in all her life. Octavia must have noticed.

"I'm from Gloucestershire, you see," Octavia explained. "From a farm there. I'm London through and through now, even my accent is going! A shame, that. I think it's lovely the way we talk. But the city changes you, that's for certain. But I'm a country girl. Always will be. At the core of me."

Elizabeth nodded, attempted a smile. She took a sip of tea and tried not to stare at that odd window, at the flowers all around it. Perhaps this Octavia was a bit dotty, one of those women who collect bits and bobs and hang them everyplace until the walls are covered. Maybe she would regale Elizabeth with tales of knitting doilies, tea cozies, oven mitts.

But that dress.

So sophisticated.

The flowers on it seemed so sophisticated.

Octavia sat upright, very upright. Elizabeth noticed her shoes now too. Very modern. The heels quite high. The proportions interesting.

"How do you know my brother?" Octavia asked.

Elizabeth took another sip of tea; she wanted to delay her answer. "I don't."

"Pardon?"

"I don't know him," Elizabeth said. She put the teacup down, her hands a bit shaky. "My mother does, though. I think they may have been—close. After the war. The Great War."

"Close?" Octavia asked. Elizabeth could tell her suggestion about Mama and Septimus had been communicated. "And who is your mother exactly?"

"Mrs. Dalloway. Mrs. Richard Dalloway. Clarissa Dalloway. Clarissa Parry." Elizabeth feigned a smile. "Women do have so many names, don't they? Makes them terribly hard to find."

"Clarissa Dalloway?" Octavia asked.

"Yes, my mother was—is—" Elizabeth stopped. How could she describe her mother? Mama was a wife. A socialite. An urbanite in the extreme. But as a girl, she had lived in the country. She had become a mother. A London mother. A hostess. A writer of letters. Hider of secrets. Mysterious. But not. In so many ways what she was—was expected. So expected. But she was hurt. Elizabeth was convinced. She was hurt. Someone had hurt her.

"Your mother is a . . . ?" Octavia asked. Elizabeth must have lapsed into reverie.

"A woman," Elizabeth said. "My mother was a woman." She was stammering now.

"She *was*? Or is?" Octavia was being delicate, Elizabeth could tell.

"I'm not sure," Elizabeth said. "She's missing. Since July of '23. No one has seen her since. She never arrived at her own party. I was seventeen."

Pity. Pity crossed Octavia's face. Elizabeth sounded like a fool, a madwoman, and she knew it. What an outlandish story it was. But it was a true one.

"I'm afraid that's not likely, that," Octavia said. "That Septimus and your mother were . . . close."

"I know it seems odd," Elizabeth said. "And the age difference would have been something. But after the war, perhaps in the twenties, they were close. Perhaps they left together. She said something about Italy. Maybe they went there together? She left something behind, a quite personal message for his family—"

"My brother didn't survive the war."

Elizabeth didn't want to hear it; she convinced herself she *hadn't* heard it. "But I checked with the War Office," Elizabeth said. "He came home. He wasn't hurt. And the Commonwealth War Graves Commission. He didn't die; they have no grave record."

"He's not buried there. In a military cemetery. They wouldn't have him."

"Why on earth not? Where is he buried then?"

"He's not." Octavia pointed to the fireplace. The mantel. The small vase Elizabeth had seen when she came in. "He's there."

It wasn't a vase. It was an urn. A life. A life reduced to a little pot of ashes. Elizabeth knew about those. A life reduced to a tiny handful of ashes. "But why wouldn't they have him?"

"Because he threw himself out a window." Octavia nodded at the window decorated with fabric flowers. "That one. The summer of 1923. I was seventeen as well." Octavia put her teacup down now. "You see, his body survived the war. But his mind didn't. He went mad."

Madness.

Suicide.

Mama cared for a mad soldier who had died by suicide. How did she know him? How could she have possibly known him?

"I'm ever so sorry," Elizabeth said. She felt dreadful now. Showing up on Octavia's stoop like this.

Mama cared for a mad soldier who had died by suicide.

"They must have been acquaintances right after the war," Elizabeth went on. "Perhaps they met at a bazaar. Or a fundraiser. She did take part in many charities. Maybe they had long talks or—"

"Birds in Regent's Park spoke to him in Greek." Octavia dangled her foot, the toe of her leather shoe went up and down. Up and down. She was so calm. So regal in that dress. So matter-of-fact. A woman who had stepped from the pages of a London magazine, claiming to be a country girl whose brother had gone mad. "He saw Evans—a dear friend, a fellow soldier—back from the dead in that park. His wounds healed. All the blood and bullets gone. Septimus had watched him die on the battlefield." Octavia shook her head now as if remembering something. Reminding herself. "When Septimus came home to Lucrezia after the war, he didn't come home a free man. He was trapped in his mind. Always in his maddening mind." Octavia stood and went to a small table. She slid open a drawer and pulled out a stack of papers tied with a ribbon. She handed them to Elizabeth. "I'm sorry to disappoint you, but if you read these, I think you'll understand. Septimus was very ill. He didn't have friends. He didn't have acquaintances he spoke with. His wife said she could barely get him to sit still on a park bench for long. I really think it's impossible that your mother ever spoke to him."

Elizabeth opened the first folded sheet of paper.

There were drawings. Dead bodies. Heads in bushes, mouths open, shouting. The wall of a house filled with angry faces. Frightening faces. They all seemed to be screaming. There were writings. There were conversations with Shakespeare, odes to Time, accounts of the dead singing behind rhododendron bushes.

Universal love—the meaning of the world.
Do not cut down trees. Tell the prime minister.

"I'm—" Elizabeth stopped. She didn't know what to say. "I'm ever so sorry I've bothered you. Mama must not have known him, then. She must have left gifts for families of soldiers who—" She stopped again, handed the papers back. "I suppose I won't know. I won't really know. How she knew of your family."

"I don't know where they could have met. He was so ill, Lucrezia couldn't get him to step foot in a veterans' home, to get help. Or attend any event for veterans at all. The best she could do was get him to a psychiatrist. And I'm afraid Dr. Bradshaw made it all worse in the end."

"Dr. Bradshaw?"

"Yes, a Dr. Bradshaw." Octavia tied the ribbon around the stack of papers, pulled it taut. "He was Septimus's doctor. Terrible. He was a terrible man. He told Septimus there was nothing wrong with him. That he should get a hobby. That he should keep things in proportion. That's how he talked—keep things in *proportion*. Meaningless little things like that. That Septimus should try not to be so *self-absorbed*. That his thoughts were—*frivolous*." Octavia put the papers back in the drawer. "My brother saw the dead. He believed there were people inside the walls shouting at him. Birds talking to him. Messages he was getting from all over. And Dr. Bradshaw told him to get a hobby. To think of something outside of himself. That the war hadn't hurt him at all."

"Dr. Bradshaw?" Elizabeth asked again. "Dr. Bradshaw treated your brother."

Octavia nodded.

Their link. Here it was. The link between Mama and Septimus Warren Smith. They'd both consulted the same psychiatrist. Dr. Bradshaw must have told Mama about Septimus, a poor soldier who had gone mad. About his mind. Dr. Bradshaw had told Mama about a soldier who'd lost his mind. A memory rang in her mind, a time when Mama was discussing a soldier. Septimus must have been the soldier Lady Bradshaw had spoken about at Mama's June party. That's when Mama was told that he'd killed himself. That he'd decided to leap to his death. That's when Mama had gone to the window and stood in front of the blackness. Leaned into the blackness. She must have taken a gift, a medallion, to Lady Purvis to give to Septimus's family before she left. She had felt badly for his family. Wanted them to have something. That was it.

"Mama called Dr. Bradshaw dreadful as well. She didn't have a kind word for him," Elizabeth said. "But he was terribly important, she said. Supposedly the best in his field. Mama even had Dr. Bradshaw examine me after I hurt my head in a riding accident when I was young. And my mother saw him. For herself."

"For herself?" Octavia sat back down on the sofa. Her anger at the psychiatrist had passed a bit. She was the one who seemed sorry now. "She saw him? Was your mother mad too?"

Mad?

Was my mother mad too?

"No," Elizabeth said. She was sure. Certainly, Mama was not mad. Not a bit. "She was perfect, really. Well known. A hostess of prime ministers. The wife of a member of Parliament. I believe she regretted who she married, but that isn't uncommon. Is it? I think she wondered about the path she chose in life. If she chose the right one. I think someone hurt her. I think she was desperately hurt as a young woman. I just don't know by whom."

"Then why did she see a psychiatrist?"

The question quieted Elizabeth. "I don't know."

Octavia nodded as if she knew more than Elizabeth did. Elizabeth didn't like it. She smiled and stood. "Thank you for the visit," Elizabeth said. "For the tea. For chatting with me. My mother must not have known your brother, only heard of him. Felt badly for him. I thought finding his family might help me discover my mother's whereabouts. I was mistaken." She gathered her bag, smoothed her slacks. Octavia stood as well.

"You said you were looking for Lucrezia. His wife," Octavia said. "If you'd like to chat with her as well, she'll be home soon. She's at work. We both work at—"

"No," Elizabeth said. "That won't be necessary. But thank you."

"My pleasure." Octavia's smile was warm. Sincere. She showed Elizabeth to the door. Clicked there in her magnificent heels. "And I do hope you find your mother."

Elizabeth looked at the square of white, the fog she was to return to. None the wiser. She'd learned nothing. Nothing from this trip. She glanced at Octavia's dress, those flowers bunched together. Her hair sleek, those buttons just so. Like Octavia had money. She looked like she had money. Money, against the backdrop of this humble boardinghouse. A country girl from a village in Gloucestershire in a fancy dress, in a run-down boardinghouse. Something about it didn't make any sense.

"Octavia?" Elizabeth turned.

"Yes?"

"May I ask you something?"

"Of course."

"How has it been for you?" Elizabeth asked.

"Pardon?"

"How has it been for you . . . since you lost him? Your brother. Since he decided to leave your life when you were seventeen. How has it been for you?"

1923

CHAPTER 31

Octavia

They would go back. Of course they would go back. Rezia to Milan. Octavia to Stroud. For their man had died. Their reason for being here in this city. For being in the middle of London, with its cacophony, its filth, its swing, tramp, and trudge. Their reason for being in the middle of all this. All this life.

Their reason had died. Their reason had not survived the war.

Octavia had been with Rezia for three weeks now. It was already the middle of August. Octavia knew she should go home to whatever awaited her. She should forget her ill-fated summer in London, forget telling fortunes, forget the lovely boy named Red who had turned out to be a thief. But there was something about talking with Rezia, a woman who knew Septimus. It was such a comfort. Talking to her. Like he existed between the two of them, at the meeting of their memories. If they went their separate ways, something would be lost.

Slowly, Octavia had stopped looking like a homeless cat. Rezia gently held Octavia's head over a cast-iron bowl and poured water over her hair. She scrubbed in the soap. Rinsed it over and over. And Rezia made her dresses. Blue ones and yellow ones and even a pale-green. She showed Octavia how to make hats. A Juliet cap with a felt flower over the ear. A circle hat, graduated on one side, punctuated with two round baubles. And no matter the type, Lucrezia loved putting flowers on hats.

Octavia took her to different flower stalls, showed her different types. Rare flowers. Wildflowers. Stroud flowers. Rezia learned how to copy them, how to fashion them out of felt. Big red orchids. Blue harebells. Beads like juniper berries. All nestled in a bit of lace.

At the end of August? Yes, then, they kept saying. They'd each go home then. Octavia to Stroud and Rezia to Milan. Of course they would.

When September dawned, they finally started to gather their things. To go home. Octavia sat at their dining table after breakfast, sewing a pale-blue hat. Perfect for a felt harebell.

"Azured harebell."

Octavia thought of him.

Not of Septimus.

Shakespeare.

Octavia went to the bookshelf. She hadn't packed the books yet. She couldn't bear it. Here were Septimus's books by Darwin. Here were the ones about the body, its musculature, its sinews. Here were his volumes of poetry. Rows and rows of poetry.

She saw it.

Cymbeline. The very book he had held that day in the Stroud hills when Octavia was a little girl. She took it down and searched for the line. The very line.

Turn to it, he'd said. *Lean on it.*

She found it quickly, knew its place in the book by heart, the lines she would never forget:

> *With fairest flowers*
> *Whilst summer lasts and I live here, Fidele,*
> *I'll sweeten thy sad grave. Thou shalt not lack*
> *The flower that's like thy face, pale primrose, nor*
> *The azured harebell, like thy veins . . .*

She closed the book and walked into Rezia's room, saw her trunks, the ones that would soon be bound for Italy. When Rezia went back.

To be with her sisters. To be in Milan, in the gardens. And Octavia went back to Stroud. To be with her own family. To be at the brewery.

Octavia clutched the Shakespeare to her breast.

"Do you know what my brother told me?" Octavia said, standing in Rezia's bedroom doorway.

Rezia looked up, holding a dress in her hands. She was in the midst of folding it, laying it in a trunk. "What was that?"

"It was about a flower. Azured harebell," Octavia said. "Septimus called them the poet of the Cotswolds."

Rezia tucked her yellow dress into her trunk. Picked up a pair of stockings from the bed. "A poet? The flower is a poet?"

"He said they look as if they are about to break, but then—they bloom instead."

"How lovely," Rezia said. "That sounds like my Septimus. On his good days. My poet."

"But then he said I should be like them."

"To be a poet?"

"No," Octavia said. "He said I should bloom where I'm planted. Like the harebell. I took it to mean I should settle in Stroud. Accept the life I had there. Figure out how to bloom there. But now I think it means something else."

"What is that?"

Octavia clutched *Cymbeline*. She looked at Rezia's things. At Rezia, who would leave the life she'd worked hard to build in London. For it was hard to live in London. To make a place. "Why did you come to London?" Octavia asked.

Rezia looked puzzled. Her brow furrowed over her dark eyes. "To be with Septimus, of course. I—"

"Was it? He was the only thing that made you leave it all behind?"

Rezia paused, looked thoughtfully at the things in her trunk. "I suppose it was love and . . ."

"Something that called to you?" Octavia raised her eyebrows. "Something you wanted to follow?"

Rezia slowly nodded, like Octavia had named something true,

brought it into the light. Something Rezia would've gladly kept in the dark. "You can't mean it," Rezia said. "We can't stay here. Septimus is gone, soon the money will be out."

Octavia dashed to the table by the kitchen. Took a whole stack of Rezia's hats in her hands. She went back to Rezia's room, held them up.

"With my flowers," Octavia said. "And with these."

"With those? Money from selling hats? They don't fetch that much, I'm afraid, dear girl."

"We're not going to sell hats." Octavia went to Rezia's side. "Put down your things and follow me. We're going to Liberty."

———————

Maeve was at her table, cutting fabric. Customers grouped around her, held up this bolt of linen, now this bolt of taffeta. Her hair was up and wild as usual. She was loud and laughing, just like the day Octavia had met her.

Rezia followed Octavia through the store, gaping at the fabrics. "They're so lovely," she said. "They remind me of . . . gardens in Milan."

They approached Maeve's table. At first, she didn't recognize Octavia. She seemed confused, seeing a girl like her in the store, and went back to cutting.

But then her scissors stopped.

"Octavia?"

Octavia smiled. "Hello."

"Are you all right?" Maeve put her scissors down and took Octavia's hands. Octavia had forgotten how beautiful she was, how full of life. That's where Red had gotten it, that life in his eyes. She felt as though she were seeing him again somehow. "The boys are all right? They haven't gotten you into anything, have they?"

"Not directly," Octavia said, smiling. "But they taught me quite a bit."

Maeve looked relieved and straightened the measuring tape that hung over her neck. "You never know with those two. So, how can I help you?"

"Well," Octavia said. "I've come to see you about a book."

"A book?"

"When the war began, I started a collection. Of pressed flowers. Beautiful rare wildflowers. All sorts. I picked them in Stroud. The colors all mingled together on gray blotting papers. It was for my brother."

Maeve smiled. One of the male tailors gestured at her to return to work. She held up her finger, silently telling him she was staying right where she was. "A book of pressed flowers," Maeve said. "For your brother. Go on."

"Yes," Octavia said. "But he would want me to use the book for myself now."

"Dear, I'm afraid I don't understand—"

"They would make beautiful Liberty prints. The flowers that I have. The combinations."

Maeve smiled but knitted her brow. She looked as if she were piecing it together. "So . . . you want to—"

"Work here," Octavia said. "As a cutting girl to start. But maybe eventually I could show the owner my ideas. My ideas for designs."

Maeve looked delighted. "Liberty designs."

"So you'll let me?"

"Let you?" Maeve asked, smiling. "I'm a far, far cry from the boss of the place, dear. Although I'm flattered you think I can hire you on the spot. But I can teach you how to measure and cut. And you'll have a chance, then. We can get you as prepared as possible to inquire about a position."

"That's all I want. A chance."

Maeve shook her head and smiled. In just the same way she had when she first met Octavia, when she'd realized Octavia had never stepped foot in a Liberty shop, when Octavia had nervously pronounced it was the most beautiful place she'd ever seen. "I had a feeling you would conquer this city on your wits, I just didn't quite appreciate how right I was at the time." Maeve looked at Rezia then. Raised her eyebrows. "And who is this?"

"Lucrezia Smith," Octavia said. "My sister-in-law. She'll make the hats."

CHAPTER 32

Elizabeth

The authorities weren't called until late that night. They kept waiting for her to turn up. Surely, Mrs. Dalloway was out getting flowers for her party. Or selecting the perfect salmon from one of those ice blocks on Bond Street. Or visiting with one of her many friends. She knew all of London. All the right people in London. Someone would have seen her. She'd been delayed by some sensible thing. That's why she hadn't arrived at her party. Surely, that was why.

There was no message from Mama—only her gown laid out on her bed, her sewing kit beside it.

It was all Elizabeth had.

A dress.

Elizabeth knew it was a letter, it was a message somehow. That dress was meant to speak volumes. The fabric was trying to communicate.

Lucy told her to stop saying things like that. It was dark, she said. Disturbing.

Naturally, the rest of the season's parties were canceled. An eerie silence fell upon the Dalloway home. Rumpelmayer's men didn't come. Doors remained on their hinges. Miss Walters stopped serving salmon. Even Lucy changed; she allowed the brass door handles to become smudged. And other than her mother's absence, the saddest change of all—there weren't any flowers. Mama wasn't there to go to Miss Pym's, to bring home collections of blooms for each week, petals that signaled and chattered about the season. The passage of summer, the passage of time. Without flowers, the house seemed like another one entirely.

Elizabeth told Papa to let Miss Kilman go; she couldn't study history any longer. The dates and names wouldn't stick. Details of British politics used to be magnetic; now, she could barely follow any of it. The rumblings about Asquith and MacDonald. She didn't care a straw. Miss Kilman left her a card.

You are a brilliant girl, such a keen historical mind you have. Don't waste it. Use it. All the doors are open for you. You can be anything. Don't forget that. And don't quite forget me.
—Doris

Elizabeth went to the barn, thought it might help clear her mind. She went to the tack room, brought out Brixby's brush. She couldn't even do that—brush her horse. She sat on an overturned bucket and looked at his beautiful chestnut hair. How tall he was. How formidable. She couldn't imagine that she used to ride him. Really, she couldn't. That was the thing about Mama vanishing like she did—so many things seemed frightening now. It seemed very dangerous, very daunting, to live even one day.

The Bright Young crowd kept inviting her to parties. She went a few times, but all the tinkle and glamour had departed. Besides, their only answer to her sorrow was another drink, another swim, another romp through Covent Gardens. She didn't want to do any of that anymore either.

William.

William telephoned. He asked her for tea. She turned him down. He kept trying. He sent a note of condolence to the house. Didn't he know what had happened with Calvin? Frances said Calvin had bragged to anyone who would listen. He wanted to tell everyone about his big British summer with the daughter of a member of Parliament. What a tale. What a memory it would be. Didn't all of London know? No one sensible would court her now, no one who cared about reputation and standing. Elizabeth had wrecked all that. She was known as wild. The sad, wild girl without a mother. The sad girl whose life had gone all wrong in just one summer.

But gardening.

It was sudden, her fondness for it. She wasn't any good at it. Poor Mr. Garrick kept coaching her. She pulled up dandelions, tossed them on the path like vermin. She felt terrible about it at first, but it became easier. Uprooting those odd things she used to love.

"Hello, Elizabeth!" It was William. Standing at the gate now. Elizabeth was kneeling by the phlox bed. She thought this little plot was small enough—four feet by six—to tame. Surely, she could handle land of this size. She wiped her hands on her skirt. She didn't get up.

"William." She couldn't drum up much cheer in her voice. But she was polite. She waved. "The gate's open."

He came through, stepped around the piles of dead dandelions on the path. "I thought you loved these."

"I did. But I'm growing up, aren't I?" She feigned a smile.

He came close, held something out for her. "I brought these for you." Small sunflowers. A modest bunch. "I told my mother you had a fondness for weeds. She explained that, technically, that's what sunflowers are. Weeds."

"Thank you," Elizabeth said. That did make her smile. Even in the midst of her sadness, her grief. He did make her smile. "Does she think I'm the oddest girl in all of London for liking weeds?"

"Not at all," William said. "She thinks it's rather avant-garde."

Elizabeth smiled. She stood and placed the bunch on the wrought-iron table, glanced at the chair. "I'd offer you a seat, but these chairs are dreadful to sit in, really. My mother loves them. I can't begin to imagine why."

William looked desperately sad for her. "So, no word?"

"No word."

He put his hands in his pockets. "I'm not sure what to do, Elizabeth," he said. "What if we ride? I'm not dressed for it now," he glanced down at his navy slacks, "but perhaps tomorrow? Would you like that? To ride? My father's holding another foxhunt—"

"You don't have to do this."

"Pardon?"

"You aren't tied to a courtship with me. We never really began one. And my reputation is damaged beyond repair." Elizabeth sat in the garden chair now, started pulling off her shoes. It was so rude, to pull off your shoes like that in front of a guest. She didn't care. She couldn't. "I wish you the very best in the world. But I'm afraid I'm not a good match for anyone. I don't think I'll ever be."

William sat in the chair across from her. "I already know what you think."

"Sorry?"

"I know you don't want to be in a courtship with me. Because of what's happened with your mother. But also because of me. I'm not quite what you want."

"Don't speak badly of yourself. I won't have it," Elizabeth said. "You'll find a lovely wife. A beautiful hostess. Someone who can entertain prime ministers and pick the perfect gloves." She paused. Looked at him. "I won't ever be that, you know."

He smiled. "Maybe that's not who I'm waiting for." She felt color come to her cheeks. He gently pulled a sunflower from the bunch. Twirled it between his fingers. "But to pass the time, could we go riding?"

It was the way he twirled that flower. So irreverent. They were talking of serious things—and here he was twirling a tiny parasol.

"I don't ride any longer," Elizabeth said, still blushing, she knew. "I've told Papa to sell Brixby."

"You're selling Brixby? Why on earth would you do a thing like that?"

Elizabeth watched a fat bumblebee carom above the phlox. "It just seems like the thing to do."

"I believe the wisdom in *Henry V* would refute that," he said. "The lines about a horse: 'When I bestride him, I soar, I am a hawk: he trots the air; the earth sings when he touches it.'"

"Shakespeare." Elizabeth grinned.

"Your mother loves him you know."

"Pardon?"

"I spoke to her at your coming-out," he said. "She asked what I liked to do and I was a bit panicked. I'd just gotten high marks in literature, so I talked a bit about my love of Shakespeare. I believe I was your mother's favorite suitor after that. I believe that's why she encouraged you in my direction."

Elizabeth remembered something then. Something Mama had said during that disastrous luncheon after Peter Walsh's visit. Mama had begged Elizabeth to give William a chance, that there was something about him she didn't know.

"She had a great fondness for *Othello*, but *Cymbeline* was her favorite," William said. "'Fear no more the heat o'th'sun, nor the furious winter's rages.'"

"I heard her say that very thing once," Elizabeth said. She leaned forward now, put her chin in her hand. When was it?

"Fear no more."

She knew.

Mama had said it when she came home from her Bond Street errands in June. When Elizabeth was hidden in the drawing room reading her letters to Peter Walsh. Mama had come home, and Lucy had informed her she hadn't been invited to Lady Bruton's luncheon.

"Fear no more."

She had said it right after Lucy gave her the message. She walked straight upstairs and took to her bed.

"What does it mean?" Elizabeth asked. "Fear no more the heat of the sun?"

"I'm not one to claim I know the full meaning of Shakespeare," William said. "But to me, I suppose it's an acknowledgment that life can be quite difficult. And not just from the elements." William looked away then, trained his eyes on a few birds flitting about. Was he about to say more? About the line? "My father hates me for it, you know. Not a very manly thing, to be fond of Shakespeare. I didn't fight in the war. I read poetry, and I'm really not fond of anything that has to do with business. He wants me to be in finance. What a disaster I am."

So that's what Mama meant about William. He loved literature more than business. And was shamed for it. A disappointment to his family. Mama was so good at getting people to open up. They must have spoken of it all at her coming-out. "I think that's a terrible shame," she said. "Do you write as well?"

He looked shy now. "A bit here and there."

"Well, I think you are made for it."

"Made for it?"

"For being a fabulous writer," Elizabeth said. "First, because you aren't at all gloomy like Harold. I imagine your stories would be rather uplifting. And second, you have a wonderful author's name."

"I do?"

"William Theodore Titcomb. It's very erudite," Elizabeth said. "And Theodore makes you sound like a scholar."

"Then will you call me Theodore?" He smiled.

She nodded and couldn't help but smile back. "Theodore it is."

CHAPTER 33

Octavia

Maeve said Redvers was at a racetrack, washing cars. One of his new jobs.

She went straight there. The track was dirty, dusty. Driving lanes arced in a great sloping circle. Men roamed about in racing jumpers, helmets, goggles.

Octavia saw him by a car holding a hose, a cigarette hanging from his mouth.

"Hello," she said.

Red looked up, gaped. "Octavia? How did you—"

"Your mum told me where you were." Octavia walked over to the green racing car. It was low to the ground, had a small windshield. Black dirt and grit clung to its sides. "Is it difficult? To get all that dirt off?"

Red looked at the car. "Not so much," he said. "But they pay me like it is." He smiled, but it faded quickly. "Not that I'm being dishonest with 'em. I'm not. I'm really not. Honest wages for honest work, I swear, I—"

"It's all right," she said. She walked closer to him. His cheek was smeared with a bit of motor oil. All that dirt made his hazel eyes shine, look so clear, like jewels, she thought.

"It was wrong to drag you into that business at the Purvises'," he said. "Stealing. I should've told you. And I'm trying to straighten up. Really, I am. Looking for jobs on the up-and-up. It's just Mum's rent.

It keeps climbing. But I'm doing all sorts. Hauling luggage at the train station, washing these cars, even horses at the track too. Did you know horses needed washing?"

Octavia shook her head and smiled again. But then she looked at him. Straight at him. To make sure he would hear what she was about to say. "You are very brave."

Red raised his eyebrows. "I am?"

"Yes," Octavia said. "You are surviving in this city on your own wits. And it's a bit of a war. Surviving. Hardship changes a person." She looked down at her new shoes. Shiny. Because she'd had a bit of luck, because she'd found Rezia. "My brother taught me that."

Red brightened. "You found him?" He looked so hopeful. So happy for her.

"No," she said. "He died in the war."

"I'm so sorry, Octavia."

"Thank you." She looked into his eyes. "Thank you for everything you did for me. For helping me search."

"It was my pleasure." He said it faintly, like he was desperately sad, like he was letting something go. "So you're leaving? Back to Stroud?"

"Not quite yet," she said, smiling. "I have an idea for us. How we can survive on our wits. And maybe just not survive. Maybe do even better than that. And it's all on the up-and-up."

"For us?"

Octavia stepped a little closer. She reached up and gently wiped clean the little spot on his cheek. And kissed it. "Yes, for us."

Red looked at her like she'd just given him the greatest surprise of his life. That kiss. The most wonderful, most surprising gift of his life. He leaned in. "May I?"

She nodded.

He kissed her. There beside the green race car. By the garage full of oil cans and hoses and tires. He kissed her. "All that day in London I'd wanted to do that. And I cocked it up, didn't I?"

"Yes," Octavia whispered. She smiled and kissed him again. "You did."

"So are you going to tell me what this big idea is?"

"You'll have to wash up first," she said, smiling. "We're going to be planning a trip."

———

STROUD, GLOUCESTERSHIRE

She was wearing a dress she'd made herself.

From discarded scraps of Liberty prints. She'd been a cutting girl there now for over a month. She had her pick of the extras.

Red was in his best brown pants. His best shirt and cap. Walking beside her.

"Do you see what I mean?" Octavia asked, out of breath. "The brewery is so high on this hill. The path is so steep, isn't it?"

"It's not so bad." Red was trying to put up a good front; Octavia could tell. He was just as exhausted by this little hike as she was.

The sun was so hot. Octavia looked down at her lovely Liberty dress. This one was covered with red peonies against a deep-blue backing. Sprays and spots of yellows peeked through here and there. She'd chosen this one, this red one, to wear back to Stroud. It was bold. And so was she.

She remembered the last time she'd climbed this hill, telegram in hand from the War Office, the one that said that Septimus was in London in a Bloomsbury lodging house and that nothing was wrong with him. She remembered cursing her long, plain skirt that day, the tight laces of her leather boots, how they made a hike up the hill so much more difficult.

Now a few people stared at her as they passed. She recognized a person here or there. There was the woman who owned Spratt's, the little shop that sold dog cakes and puppy biscuits. She looked at Octavia but didn't seem to recognize her one bit. Octavia saw the town doctor hurrying by, the one who'd come to their house after Ronnie was born, the one who'd agreed that the devil had gotten into Mum's mind.

He didn't recognize her either.

No one did.

People passed, glanced at her, took notice—like she was some lady unknown. Someone who had deigned to visit Stroud for some mysterious purpose they couldn't even guess at. She looked like a different person, walked differently, even. She decided that steep hills were still difficult, but a little less so when she was wearing a Liberty print.

Then someone recognized her.

"Mr. Brown!" Octavia cried. The stray dog ran straight to her, wound around her legs, wagged his tail madly. She knelt and rubbed his head, his ears, his dusty brown haunches.

"This your dog?" Red asked.

"No," Octavia said. "We're friends. Dear friends. But we had a falling-out at the beginning of the summer."

Red reached down and patted Mr. Brown's head now too. "A falling-out? What could this mutt do to you?"

"Well," Octavia said, looking at Mr. Brown sternly, "I wanted him to come with me to London when I left in June. So that I could act like a lady with her hound in the city streets. But he threw me over for the bread man." Octavia pointed a little way up the hill to a man pushing a cart loaded with long baguettes, baskets of rolls, golden loaves.

"Smart dog," Red said, giving Octavia a cheeky smile.

"Smart?" Octavia feigned offense. "To throw me over for the bread man?"

"See how round his belly is?" Red asked, patting the dog on his healthy-sized sides. "He's surviving in Stroud on his own wits. And looks like he's got it figured from the looks of him. He'd be a fool to leave now. Even for a lady as lovely as yourself."

Octavia smiled. She looked at Mr. Brown in a way she hadn't before, suddenly felt very proud of him. Of his life in Stroud. Through the summers, the winters—on he lived. On he thrived. "I suppose you're right," she said. "He's blooming where he's been planted."

A train whistle blew—a hollow, ominous sound from the station down in Stroud. She was reminded of what lay ahead. The brewery at the top of the hill. Her father. The money she had in her purse to repay him. The story she had to tell. The news of Septimus. Her plan.

The train whistle blew again.

They trudged on. Up, up, and up. The white brick sides of the building came into view, the three chimneys, the thick, darkened panes of glass. Large curly letters her father had painted on the side came into focus:

THE STROUD BREWERY

CELEBRATED ALES & STOUT

WINES & SPIRITS

"My, my," Redvers said as the brewery came into view. "You weren't kidding, were you? What a place! And your family owns it? The whole place?"

Seeing it with Red like this, Octavia felt as though she were seeing her family's business for the first time. It seemed so large, so nice. In London, everything was jammed together, packed in tight, coated with a layer of dirt. The Stroud Brewery gleamed like a white castle on a hill compared to all that. The gorgeous hills of the Cotswolds spread out below, a sweet breeze swirled around them, everything seemed to glow.

"But what's that?" Red asked. He was pointing to the dark, open doorway cut into the side of the building, the one Octavia's father had always warned her about as a child when she would run about the attic of the brewery. The one she used to stand near, push the dusty toes of her shoes over. She'd stare down, past her shoes, down, down. Down the three stories to the ground, and down once more, down the steep slope of the hill, thought that if she fell, she'd hit the ground and barely pause. Her body would surely tumble and roll all the way into the heart of town. All the way to Spratt's. All the way past the butcher shop, come to rest with a lifeless thud outside Foster Brothers, a dead body beneath their window full of children's clothes, women's dresses.

How odd, she realized now, for a little girl to think such dark thoughts. How sad that she hadn't pieced it together in her mind, hadn't realized she was unhappy. That she wasn't looking forward to living her life through Septimus. That it wouldn't be enough—thinking of herself as a girl without some hopes of her own. A girl without any adventures to her name.

The daughter.

Daughter Smith.

"It's an old doorway," Octavia explained. "Used for hay when this place was a barn. It used to scare me, as a girl." She gently shook her head. "It doesn't now."

They reached the front door of the brewery. Octavia pushed it open, the bells hanging above her jingling; she was ready for the musty darkness, the haze of smoke, the gray figures of drinkers she could see as her eyes adjusted.

She was ready for the bartender.

Tertius.

He stared at her, not recognizing her at first. But then—

"*Tave?*" He came around the bar. "Octavia! Pop, come quick, it's Octavia!" He picked her up and twirled her around, held her so tight.

She was shocked. He'd always been so awful to her, really. So curt. Such a bully.

"You're . . . happy?" Octavia asked as he set her down. "Happy to see me?"

He stepped back and looked at her. "You're beautiful!" he said. "My God, we all thought you were dead in a London sewer." Then he knocked her on the shoulder. Gently, but still. The shoulder bump of an older brother. "And *of course* I'm happy to see you, don't be daft. You're my *sister*, Tave."

"What is going on out here—" Her father pushed through the swinging door from the back. Saw Octavia, his daughter. She could tell he was taking her in, like a sudsy drink of ale that had been brewed a thousand miles away. One no one had ever tasted around here. Her smart hat, her shoes, her brave, bold red dress. "My god," he whispered. "My god."

She ran to him. "I'm so sorry," she said. "I'm so sorry, Pop."

Her father pulled away, tears in his eyes. "I knew you'd gone to London to look for your brother, you silly girl," he said. He wiped his eyes. "But when we hadn't heard from you we thought you were . . ."

He looked at her again, like she was a ghost. A ghost in a red dress. A woman unknown. "Did you find him?"

Octavia looked at the gritty floor of the brewery. Inhaled, felt the damp of the air, smelled the sour fermented ale. She thought about how to tell him. That Septimus had jumped. The double shame it would bring: that first Septimus had run away from his family to be a poet, and then he had died by suicide. Dishonorable. Pop should not see it that way, but she knew that's how he would. It's how the world saw it. The message it whispered. A dishonorable death. The military cemetery wouldn't even have his body.

She thought of telling her father that. That Septimus had killed himself. That he was in a little pot of ashes on a mantel in Bloomsbury.

She didn't tell him that.

Because it wasn't true.

She told him the truth instead.

"He didn't survive the war," Octavia said. "The War Office was wrong that he was in London, a survivor. He died. He died from injuries he got in the war."

Her father closed his eyes. Nodded slowly. "So he couldn't," he said. "He couldn't come back to us."

"That's right," Octavia said. "He couldn't come back to us. He was hurt. And he didn't make it."

Redvers stepped a bit closer then and pulled his thin cap off his head. It seemed no one had noticed he was there.

"I'm ever so sorry for your loss, Mr. Smith." Redvers cleared his throat. "From what Octavia's told me, your son was a very brave man. Who fought until he couldn't fight anymore."

Octavia's father looked at Red. Smiled sadly. "And you are?"

"Redvers, sir," he said, standing a little taller. "Redvers Moore."

"Redvers Moore of . . . ?"

"London, sir. Redvers Moore of London."

Octavia's father furrowed his brow. "And you know my daughter how?"

"We're—or we're going to be," Octavia said, "business partners."

"Business partners?" Pop asked. "What business?"

"Well," Octavia said. She smoothed her skirt. Straightened up a bit. "I am at present employed at Liberty of London. I'm just a cutting girl. For now. But I have plans. Ideas. For dresses. I came to get my book of pressed flowers. They're my . . . designs."

"Designs?"

"Yes," Octavia nodded. She turned to Redvers. "And Red would like to start another business. We'll be doing this one together."

"Sir," Redvers said, "I happen to know a lot of people in London."

"A lot of people, Pop," Octavia said. "*A lot.*"

"And?" Her father looked confused.

"A lot of *thirsty* people," Red said, smiling. "A lot of people who might like to drink Stroud ale. And sell it in their pubs too."

"You make the ale here," Octavia said, "but then we can distribute it in London. Our business could triple. Think of it!"

"My god, Tave," Tertius said. He looked at Red. "You sure about this? You think it could work?"

"I do," Red said. "I know it will."

"Our Stroud ale in *London*?" Tertius looked giddy.

"And, here, this is for you, Pop," Octavia said, digging in her purse. She pulled out a wad of cash. "I took this. I stole it. From your till. To get to London. And I'm paying you back. And then some." She held out the money. "I'm sorry I did it."

Her father smiled, looked at his daughter. "I'm not," he said. "Not at all. Let's consider it a loan. A business loan."

A business loan.

A business loan for a *girl*.

She remembered when she'd left for London, how he'd looked at her as if she were a doll, every eyelash painted in its place, every feature just like it was yesterday and the day before. Like her value was in those frozen fine details, in the fact that they wouldn't change. But here she stood before him, every bit of her altered, a new dress altogether.

And he loved it.

He loved his changed daughter.

"How about a shandy?" Tertius said, already pouring beer from the pulls. "For both of you?"

"Yes," Octavia said. "But then, there's someone I need to see."

———

Mum was in a rocking chair. She was looking out the window watching Ronnie muck about with the pigs. Or maybe she was looking far off. Beyond Stroud. Beyond England, even.

"Hello, Mum," Octavia said, stepping into the room. She'd removed her hat.

Her mother looked at her and smiled as if Octavia were a ghost who had come for a visit and she didn't know how long it would last.

"Octavia," she said. Just that. Nothing more. *Octavia.*

"I'm sorry, Mum," she said. She ran to her, threw her arms around her mother's neck. "I'm so sorry. I had to find Septimus, Mum. I had to. And he—"

"I already know." Her mother placed a hand on Octavia's cheek.

"He fell . . . in battle," Octavia said, stammering a bit. "In the war. Honorably. Very honorably, he—"

"Jumped." Her mother's eyes filled with tears. "A veteran found us. One of Septimus's friends. They fought together. He wanted us to know. Said Septimus spoke of us often in the beginning but then . . . didn't anymore. Said he couldn't really talk about anything that made sense." She wiped her eyes. "I didn't tell your father. That his son was a coward twice over." The tears fell and her mother started rocking again in the chair. Slowly. Back and forth. Back and forth. It was the chair she'd rocked Ronnie in after she'd lost her mind and found it again.

Mothers. And their babies. There were several lifetimes on Mum's face.

"He wasn't a coward. He wasn't. It wasn't right that the military wouldn't give him a proper grave," Octavia said. She gripped the rim of her hat in her hands. "He wasn't dishonorable." She looked into her mother's eyes to make sure she was heard, understood. "And neither are you."

The rocking chair stopped.

"I think it's a war," Octavia said. "Surviving." She knelt by her mother's side. "Getting enough money to live on. Fighting for it. And having babies. It's a war. I think surviving is full of them—wars."

Her mother's eyes seemed so clear, so blue. "War?"

"Sometimes a body can survive one, but the mind cannot."

Her mother's lips trembled. "I love my child," she said, looking at Ronnie outside. "I didn't mean to ever harm him. I don't know what happened, and I can't stop thinking of it. Leaving him like that. In a field. All alone. I came to my senses in a few weeks, Octavia. After he was born. Just a few weeks. And I—"

"The body survives some wars . . ."

"And the mind does not." Mum finished the sentence.

"I saw you give birth," Octavia said. "And it was a battle if ever I saw one." She looked at her mother's tired eyes. "And you are both honorable. Septimus, an honorable son. And you, an honorable mother."

"Thank you, Octavia. Thank you." She leaned in and kissed her daughter. She pulled back and shook her head a bit in disbelief. "Do you know what I've been thinking of? All this time while you were gone?"

"What's that?"

"That your father shouldn't have given you his pocket watch," she said. "He told me. That he'd given it to you. And all I could see over and over in my mind was a horrible gang of men stealing it from you, leaving you dead, all because of a watch. All for a bit of gold that keeps the hour."

Octavia smiled and pulled the watch from the little pocket she'd sewn into her dress. She'd sewn little pockets for it in all her dresses. She held it up, flipped it open. Coventry-made. From Percy House of Holyhead. Fine roman numerals spread all the way around it. In capital type, just above the center where the golden hands met:

CENTRE SECONDS

CHRONOGRAPH

"Nobody killed me for it," Octavia said. "It actually kept me alive, this watch. I used it to tell fortunes. I used time."

Mum smiled. "How smart," she said. "Then I'm glad of it. I'm glad your father gave it to you." They both looked at the watch face, at the seconds, minutes, hours flowing right through their hands. "Septimus's time has passed," she said. They heard Ronnie laugh outside, racing after a duck. "But yours has come."

DECEMBER 8, 1952

CHAPTER 34

Elizabeth

Elizabeth was transfixed. Octavia's tale—of a country girl riding a train from Stroud to London when she was seventeen, meeting a street gang, earning a living from her wits, working her way into Liberty, distributing her father's ale all over the city—was astonishing. This woman was astonishing. And now as each neared fifty, Elizabeth had the distinct feeling that they were standing here in the foyer holding the lives they'd made in their arms. Like little bundles of curated goods collected from shops all over the city.

Elizabeth's felt skimpy.

"So do you still work at . . ." Elizabeth ventured.

"Liberty," Octavia answered. Hers was a confident smile. Unapologetic. "I still work in the shops, helping measure and cut. But I've worked up to designs. They've made two of mine now. This is one of them." She touched her skirt. "Azured harebell. And orchids. My brother's favorites. And Lucrezia, Septimus's wife, she makes hats for them. They're quite popular."

"Women of your generation can be anything!"

"A veterinarian! A doctor! A master of a great enterprise!"

A designer.

"I've taken up so much of your time," Elizabeth said. She still held the wadded-up blouse in her hands. The one she'd bought at the shop on her way here. To hold over her mouth as a mask. "Thank you. Truly. For sharing your story with me."

"Please visit again," Octavia said. "I treasure people who were connected to Septimus, in large ways and small." Octavia glanced out the window. "Are you sure you want to traipse through this fog? It's terrible. Do you have a mask?"

Elizabeth held up the blouse. "I bought this on the way. It's the strangest thing. It has the oddest proportions. But I rather like it."

Octavia took the tips of the sleeves in her hands, held them up. "I agree," she smiled. "Whoever designed this refused to keep things in proportion." She let the sleeves drop. "How I admire that."

"Keep things in proportion."

It rang in Elizabeth's mind—an hour announced by the bells of Big Ben. Like one of those hours in the early morning, just as darkness departed. The ones that came on the heels of night, all souls still tucked away.

"Keep things in proportion."

Mama had said that to Elizabeth in 1923. Mama had been mending her silver-green dress before she met with Peter in the drawing room. And after, at that awful lunch, Mama had told Elizabeth that she was throwing her life away, not keeping things in proportion. Mama had written about it in her letter to Peter, the letter Elizabeth had found in Mama's writing desk, telling him that when she'd seen Dr. Bradshaw for herself, he had given her that same dreadful advice—to keep things in proper proportion. Lady Bradshaw had said that of a soldier at Mama's own June party. Septimus. It had been Septimus. Dr. Bradshaw had given the advice to him as well.

"A young man, one of his patients—killed himself. He had been in the army. Things had gotten so out of proportion for the fellow."

That comment had sent Mama to the window in the drawing room. To that square of darkness. It had made her lean into the black.

And now, Elizabeth looked at the wrinkled shirt in her hands, the one with the cuffs and the collar that had been stitched in such odd ways. The one she liked. The one Octavia liked.

"I will never be able to thank you enough, Octavia," Elizabeth said. "You have helped me immeasurably."

Octavia smiled. "That's wonderful, but I haven't done anything, really, I—"

"I'm afraid I must go," Elizabeth said. "I have something very urgent I must get to."

Octavia opened the door. "Goodbye, Elizabeth Dalloway. It's been a pleasure."

Elizabeth held the blouse over her mouth, stepped onto the stoop, and ran down the path. Her feet could not carry her fast enough. Through the fog, she could just barely see the cracks in the little garden path to the gate. And the gate itself was hanging crooked, eaten by rust. Another year and it might fall off.

She stopped.

She'd forgotten. Something she must say. Something she must do.

She turned, walked back to Octavia's door, and rang the bell. Heard Octavia's footsteps. The door opened.

"Is the fog too terrible?" she asked. "Do come back in. You can stay as long as you like. We have—"

"No," Elizabeth said. She reached in her purse. "I forgot to give you this."

The medal.

Octavia took it, turned it over in her hands.

For the bravery of
S. W. S.
All my love to you, C. P. 1923

"S. W. S.," Octavia said slowly. "My brother. Septimus Warren Smith."

"C. P.," Elizabeth said. "My mother. Clarissa Parry. She wanted Septimus's family to have this."

"It looks just like . . ." Octavia whispered, still looking at the message. "Like the medals they give soldiers at their burials. The medals for the families." Octavia turned it over and over in her hand. "He died in the war."

Mama must have known it. That he wouldn't get a proper burial. No one would treat him as if he'd died in battle—not the military, not the public. Dr. Bradshaw least of all. Mama would have felt it, the sorrow of this soldier's family. She would have nearly drowned in empathy. In her ability to sense feelings from miles off. She was kind. Above all, she was kind. She left a little something for the soldier's family.

"Keep things in proportion."

"Thank you for this. It helps me more than you know," Octavia wiped a tear from her eye. She studied the medallion again. The back of it. "But it's so personal. The inscription. As if they knew one another. But I can't imagine they did. Why do you think—"

"No, it's you who have helped me." Elizabeth turned to go.

"But what have I done?"

"You've shown me how to find my mother."

CHAPTER 35

Elizabeth

The sewing case.

Mama's leather sewing case.

The one the color of almond skins.

The one she'd carried about, the one she had used to mend her silver-green gown the day she spoke with Peter. The one she'd often tucked into her writing desk. The one she'd used to mend anything that was falling apart, to repair its seams, to keep its proportions. Herself. The one she'd used to mend things herself.

The one that had been by her bed the day she disappeared. By the sea-green dress.

Elizabeth had never thought to look there. To open it. To look at Mama's needles. Her thread. Her thimbles. What could a woman's sewing kit have to say? Who would open a thing like that, a woman's sewing kit?

Elizabeth came home, went through the cellar door, hurried down the cool stone steps. She knew exactly where it was. She'd put it in a box with all of Mama's favorite gowns. A blush-pink. A muted-blue. The silver-green.

Elizabeth tore into the box, sifted through the silks and the taffetas and the beads.

There it was. The sewing case.

She picked it up, its soft leather cool in her hands. She flipped up
its latches, removed the little tray that held the scissors, the seam ripper.

And there it was.

A letter.

From the summer of 1923.

From the last day Mama had been seen alive.

A letter to Elizabeth.

CHAPTER 36

Clarissa

My Elizabeth,

 I want to tell you the most important thing. I want to tell you about the voice. Loud. Within. How it scolds; how it criticizes. How I have battled it with all my will. I know now where I must go, what I must do. You, my darling, are unmingled. Immeasurable. I know that I am a hindrance, that without me you could find your way. You could be free of everything. Every profession is open to women now. Miss Kilman is right. You will work, I know. You will solve the riddle.

 What I want to say is that you are my greatest joy.

 You.

 And one summer.

 I'd like to tell you about my summer. One single summer that I lived. I was eighteen.

 He was there. Always looking a bit grumpy. It was endearing, really. Caroming about Bourton like a bumblebee, pollinating the grounds with those little sayings of his. He'd see me in the garden, accuse me of musing among the vegetables. He preferred the company of men to cauliflower, he said. It was a jab; he thought I had a talent for politics, that I should devote myself to the state of things, the state of the world, not to gardens or appropriate flower pairings for parties. I should do something with my life that had actual value, he said.

They were delicious, our political arguments. They came to me easily that summer; I could scarcely believe the ideas were mine. Names and dates seemed to stick in my mind with ease. I was as good as Lady Bruton on public matters—Lady Bruton who doesn't even invite me to her luncheons any longer. Doesn't ask my opinion on war issues. How it hurts. "Fear no more," Shakespeare says! In death, these terrible bruises will cease.

We sat by the lake at Bourton one night, he and I, ideas passing between us. He'd flip that obnoxious horn-handled knife open and closed, open and closed. We talked and talked, the crickets joining the chatter. It was riveting. He was jealous; he wanted me all to himself. When Sally rowed up in the canoe, he refused it, waved them off. We lay in the tall, stiff grass by the lake. He always said that was the night he felt closest to me. Beside that lake before the others could come back and harass us again with the boat. There were kisses. A bit of a tumble. He talked of that night. Too much. There were rumors.

But nothing happened beside that lake. Not really.

Except that I was with someone who saw a politician in me, an intellectual. I was with someone who thought I could be something like that. I was with Peter. Dearest Peter Walsh. Did I love him? Or did I love being who he thought me to be? A political woman. An intellectual woman. Capable.

And she was there too, of course. She'd pawned a brooch to get to Bourton. She hadn't a penny. Her parents had quarreled—how shocking! That a mother and father would do a thing like that. She strolled in after dinner, unannounced. How it upset your great-aunt Helena! I'm not sure she ever forgave her.

We sat up all night. Talking. She sat on the floor. We read Shelley. Morris. Plato. We were going to reform the world! We were going to write letters; she wanted me to write a book! She saw that in me, that's who she believed me to be—a writer. A thinker. So many of the ideas were hers, but how intoxicating they were. I didn't know a thing of sex (forgive me, darling, for shocking you, for talking like this, but it's true). The most pro-found thing that had happened to me to that point was that I'd seen a man drop dead in a field. I was ten or so. He'd been fussing with a plow. And I'd seen cows just after their calves were born, which was quite shocking. I grew up in the country, you know. I used to ride. Take my woolly dog for runs through the fields. All of that.

But that's all.

That's all I'd seen, really. Cows and horses and a man dropping dead in a field. Until I met her. I didn't know a woman could be like that. Could be like she was. She had a way with flowers, rebellious. At home, at Bourton, there were these expected little vases down the middle dining table, always, always those boring little vases. And what did she do? She replaced them with bowls full of water; went out and picked hollyhocks and dahlias and roses—all sorts of flowers that had never been paired—cut their heads off and set them afloat. Chaos! In little glass bowls! Like the ones I go on about on Bond Street. A little shop sells them there. Those bowls full of commingled blooms, they were magnificent. No one else could see that, how magnificent they were.

Our sour old housemaid, Ellen Atkins, didn't like her either. She'd caught her running down the passage naked. Not a stitch of clothes on her body. Sally said she'd forgotten her sponge for the bath. That she had to run and get it. I never did believe her, that she'd forgotten her sponge. I think she just wanted to run through the house like that. To see the look on Ellen Atkins's face. To see the look on mine.

She was unfettered, believed she could do anything. She bicycled once round the parapet on the terrace. She smoked cigars. Those little thin ones they have at the tobacco shop on Bond Street. You know the ones. You always complain when I stop. She smoked those! Those very cigars. When we were eighteen. She smoked them.

Unbridled! How unrestrained she was. I remember standing in my bedroom at Bourton when she was visiting. I was holding a hot-water can in my hands. And I said aloud, "She is beneath this roof . . . She is beneath this roof!"

That's how it felt to be a friend of Sally Seton.

It felt like being alive.

The nights were all rooks and setting suns and dressing for dinner. I remember her wearing pink gauze. "If it were now to die, 'twere now to be most happy." That was my feeling. I'd always worn whatever I had, you know. I didn't give it a thought. That a dress could be alive like that. That it could be an expression of something. It changed how I looked at gowns, at fabric. It changed all that for me.

Our friendship, it felt under threat somehow, as if we were both about to face a common foe. We were on the precipice of it, something unknown. No one saw her like I did; if I didn't know better, I would think she was a specter, some spirit who showed herself only to me. Aunt Helena just wandered off after dinner. Your grandpapa Parry read the paper. And it was love, wasn't it? Did I love Sally Seton? Or did I love being who she thought me to be—a writer, a philosopher. That I was someone. Really someone.

And then there was the moon. I remember it. She and I went walking on the terrace, under that moon. We passed a stone urn with flowers in it. She stopped, picked a flower. And kissed me. How she laughed, how that awful Joseph Breitkopf came over and started pestering us about the stars, the constellations. It felt like being in a clock tower, suddenly trapped under clanging bells. All hope of hearing one's thoughts—lost. Listening to Joseph Breitkopf.

But I suppose that's all that happened—I strolled along the terrace with the most wonderful girl I'd ever met and she thought I could write books.

I was with someone who thought I could do something like that.

And your father. He walked in that first night after Sally had arrived, and I got his name all wrong. I called him "Wickham." Introduced him to everyone that way. Finally, he said, "My name is Dalloway!" So all summer long that's what Sally called him—"My name is Dalloway." She couldn't resist. They were cruel to him—Peter and Sally. Your father was as harmless as a fly. He wouldn't even criticize that boor, Joseph, who went around singing Brahms without a voice. At least he wasn't playing Bach's cello suites. They are so melancholy, after all; I'm not sure I could have taken a fugue. No, your father would not criticize, not even Breitkopf's sharp notes.

Your father didn't criticize me either. He quite liked my love of flowers. He even liked my arguments with Peter about the prime minister, the heated speeches Sally and I would make in the wee hours of the night.

Richard was quiet. He was the steady hand that held the canoe so Sally wouldn't end up in the lake; he was the one who rescued my beloved dog, Rob, when he got all caught up in a fox trap. I nearly collapsed with grief. That desperate howl. How I used to love dogs. And horses. The country. I used to love the country. I am certain you'll find that startling. But it's true.

Richard spoke with me on the terrace one evening. He saw my talent for people, he said. That I could read them, like a cat. In seconds I could tell the good from the bad, up my back would go; I could keep them all from tearing each other to shreds. I could handle my own father, the formidable Justin Parry, and Aunt Helena and Peter and Sally and anyone else for that matter. People, he said—like Sally's flowers with their heads cut off and tossed into bowls—I could handle people. Any mixture. He thought I could be the greatest socialite in all of London. A hostess. A kindler of nights. A reader of people. A mother. A wife.

Richard saw that in me.

Richard Dalloway.

He saw Mrs. Richard Dalloway in me.

And I loved him. I think I really loved him. Is there something wrong with that? To want that too? I do like parties, Elizabeth. I like choosing which flowers meet the moment. I suppose it has no value. But sometimes, on a lovely stroll up Bond Street, I allow myself to believe that my parties are offerings. Respite for weary souls. How silly a thought. How silly a woman I am.

The summer ended.

Peter went on to be a reformer, adventuring, abreast of all that needs changing in the world. Richard became what he set out to be—a politician, an MP. Not in the cabinet, but that was never very important to him anyway. He is satisfied. And I became his wife. I became that. And I don't hate it. I really don't. I want you to know that. People assume if you are unhappy, that you want to change everything. I don't.

And Sally. Sally. She did it, she really did it. She pulled it off. She solved the riddle.

She did everything.

She married a wealthy American, and they moved to the country! Can you imagine it! She lives in the country. With gardens for miles. She's still in a garden. Reading books. Watching the rooks rise. The moon. In a house unparalleled, they say. And five sons. She has five sons at Eton.

She did it all.

Is that the right path? The one that leads to happiness? The path that contains all the others? To walk all of them somehow? All at once.

I suppose I'll never know. But my summer. The last season I felt I hadn't made a mistake. The last season my mind was a friendly place.

The thoughts began soon after.

They're so loud, Elizabeth. Like voices shouting.

You weren't ever going to write a book, they say. You aren't smart enough for that. You were just a dull coin shining in Sally's light that summer. You fooled Peter into thinking you had a mind made for facts. For ideas. None of them were ever your own. You needed shelter, Richard's shelter. His support. You get so tired. You're so delicate, they say. Your body couldn't even give Elizabeth a sibling. How she deserved a sibling. And your parties, what charades those are. How sad to like being a hostess. How sad the part of you that loves such a frivolous thing. And flowers. How small! How small a life you've made! That's what they say. That's what the voices say. You had opportunity. Women like Sally have made so much of themselves. Done so much. Why haven't you? It's all over now. Marriage and children and this being Mrs. Richard Dalloway. There's nothing left for you. And you're dreadful for fretting over any of this anyway. You have no right to fret, you frivolous, silly woman. No right.

They're loud, Elizabeth.

So very loud, the voices.

I can't seem to turn them down.

Take this dress. This silver-green dress. It is the one I wore the night it all became clear. The night I heard of a veteran who had thrown himself from a window. A patient of Dr. Bradshaw's. A young man named Septimus Warren Smith, who had survived the war but threw himself to his death.

I understood then as I never had before—

That the battle is in the mind. The greatest war of all. It's in a place no one can see. The longest war.

At first I was buoyed by it, self-knowledge, the battle would not claim me. But that feeling vanished. So quickly. It was not enough to keep the voices at bay. The awful thoughts returned and I knew—I wasn't going to win. I was going to lose just as Septimus had. It felt intimate to me, the loss we were to share. I never met him, but it seemed as though I'd fought beside him somehow. I left him a token. A medal. I used my maiden name on the back—C. P.—Clarissa Parry. It felt as though my message for him came from that woman, that young woman I was, the one who had no idea about the battle she was about to fight. I wanted his family to know he'd fought. Bravely. And fell.

So take this dress. Learn to swim in it, to swim through whatever is ahead. Or burn it if you like. Do not say you are this or you are that. I'm sorry I fretted over gowns so. Fretted over your gowns so. And your hobbies and courtships and all the rest of it. I wanted to steer you down the right path. A path that prevented the voices from arriving. But the truth is—I don't know the path myself. I don't know the way.

Solve the riddle. Of how to do it all. I think that is what a woman is supposed to be.

All.

Do what you must.

To swim. To keep the voices at bay.

And have this summer. Have your summer.

I will be, I am sure, a fog settling among the trees at Bourton. You must think of me there. Like that. A bit of mist hovering over the lake. One droplet a famous novelist. Another a politician. Still another the most joyous hostess in all of London. And know that every droplet of me has only one thing in common with all the others—each one is your mother. Every single drop. The part of me I would never change, the path I would take another thousand times. The path that leads to being Elizabeth Dalloway's mother.

The path to my Elizabeth.

With love,
Your mama

———

Elizabeth

Elizabeth heard a noise behind her then. Steps down the cellar stairs. Theodore.

"How long have you been down here?" He was pale with worry. "I've been calling all over the earth trying to find you. Don't scare me like that, Elizabeth. I was worried you—"

"Theodore." She held the letter close to her chest, rested her head on his shoulder. She called him the name she used only when she felt like a tiny finch in need of a warm nest, in need of shelter. "My William. William Theodore Titcomb." She knew. Of course she knew. "I know where my mother is."

CHAPTER 37

Elizabeth

There was no fog here. No coughing. No burning. They were far enough outside the city. The air was clear. It had taken them ages to get through the snarled traffic, hours to get here; it had taken no time at all.

One dim light was shining on the front porch. It flickered in the dusk. Even as night began to fall, Elizabeth could tell the grand house was in shambles. Several blinds were hanging crooked at the windows. A shutter clung to the bricks with only one hinge. A few glass panes were cracked. It was too dark to tell if there was any garden to speak of. She guessed not.

Elizabeth stepped out of the motorcar, remembered the very few times she'd been here as a child. Mama had told her Uncle Herbert was letting it rot to the ground even then. It was still in the family. Elizabeth didn't even know if Herbert's children ever came here. To the old place. To care for the old place.

Bourton.

"Darling," Theodore said. "They searched this place. We've searched this place. She isn't here."

Elizabeth rang the bell.

No one answered.

Elizabeth peered in one of the windows, into a dark room. The furniture wasn't sheeted; it looked old and tired, but she recognized it from when she had visited as a child. The arms were all curved mahogany, the fabrics rich reds. She stepped back and looked at the second floor, then at the third, at one of the shutters knocking in the breeze, hitting the brick over and over.

Bang. Bang. Bang.

It was hard to imagine that this was the grand place that had haunted Mama's memories. Driven her thoughts and reveries. The place where she had ridden horses and danced and watched Sally Seton run naked down the passage. The place where she had had dinners decorated with wildflowers, rolled in the grass beside the lake, made political speeches, read Plato. Had a mind full of hope, all light and gauze and birds about to take flight from brambles. The place where Clarissa had believed she might write books, march for reform, and still might be a mother. Still might get to be a mother. The last place where she believed in herself.

Now, all that joy had left, had abandoned this house, like it wasn't even bothering to haunt the place.

"I will be a fog among the trees at Bourton."

"Let's sit," Theodore said. "Let's sit here on the porch. We'll listen to the crickets. We'll talk of her all night."

Her William. William Theodore Titcomb. Of course that's what he would suggest. And she knew he meant it. If she needed to sit here all night long, talk of her mother until the sun rose, he would be right there beside her. He would bring the tea.

Elizabeth looked around the side of the house, into the darkness. She thought of Frances. Frances, determined to break into the Marshall pool building, going around the side, climbing up a drainpipe. That American pluck. How shy Elizabeth had felt in the light of it. But not now. "I'm going around to the back."

"Elizabeth—"

She went before Theodore could finish the rest of his sentence. She found herself in what looked like a garden—or what used to be. There were stone urns, cracked and tipped over, dirt spilled around. Did this flowerpot overhear Mama's youthful plans, her childhood hopes? Had it been here all this time, like the wrought-iron chair? Just being. Just being in time. Did it remember her?

She kept going.

She looked at the side of the large brick house, saw a bat swoop through the moonlight.

The moonlight. On the terrace.

There it was—the terrace, the parapet. The railing was broken in a few places, but there it was, still hanging onto the house for dear life. That was it, the place Mama had described in the letter. Was that the place Sally had told Mama she could be a writer? Was this the place Papa said she could be the greatest hostess in all of London? A mother? A wife?

Elizabeth heard something.

A tinkling.

The croak of a frog.

And another and another.

Water.

She followed the sound. Stepped in the dry, tall grasses, tramped farther and farther away from the house. The frogs went quiet. But still, the tinkling. The gentle lapping sound of water.

And there it was, the lake, holding the cold moonlight in its palm. Cattails stood around its banks, dark sentries guarding the shores. Was this the place? The place where Mama had kissed Peter Walsh? Where they had sent the canoe away? Where he'd told her how smart she was? What a future she would have as a reformer?

She went to the edge. It was so cold tonight, the tiniest arms of steam reached for the moon from the surface.

"You must think of me there. Like that. A bit of mist hovering over the lake."

The voice.

It came to Elizabeth then.

The voices Mama heard. The messages in her letter. They were familiar. So familiar.

"You should have written books. You should have been involved in politics. How silly to care about parties! Flowers! How small you are! What a

waste you are. Peter was a success. Richard was a success. Sally did it all. You're nothing. Your little life as a hostess is nothing."

The voice.

Elizabeth knew it well.

It spoke to her too.

You could have done so much! Women of your generation could be anything! Doctors! Veterinarians! Masters of great enterprises! Designers, even. You're just a silly history tutor. Not a real professor. Not anything, really. No children. No accomplishments. You'd die without your husband's money. You can't even host a party anyone wants to come to. But it's too late now. A woman nearing fifty. It's all over now.

The familiar voice.

It had dogged her mother's mind. It had dogged Elizabeth's.

And Septimus's too. She thought of him, of those drawings Octavia had shown her. Those angry faces Septimus had drawn, the ones that looked like they were shouting. The people he said lived in the walls, that yelled at him, sent him messages. The birds whispering to him in Greek in Regent's Park. The voices telling him that he should have died too. That he should have been shot and blown to bits and buried in the mud with all the rest of them. With his friends. Who was he? Who was he to be alive?

The voices.

Loud.

Criticizing.

Drowning.

That was why her mother had left Septimus such a personal message on the medallion. They hadn't met one another, but they each knew the same voice. Intimately. Each of them knew that loud, dreadful voice, the critic embedded within. Mama must have known that's what had driven him out of a window.

The voice.

And Theodore. Even Theodore. Elizabeth remembered that moment from the summer of '23, just outside the barn. She had called him William then. He'd had a saddle tossed over one shoulder, the stirrups hanging down. He had said he didn't measure up. That was the secret a horse would let him keep. That he didn't measure up. That being alive counted against him. A man alive in 1923 was either too young to fight in the war or had fought and survived. A man alive in 1923 would never measure up to his brother's grave.

The voice.

Of course it spoke to Theodore too. Didn't she know that was what he masked with his irreverence, his insistence on gentle humor? Underneath it all, she knew he still felt it. He still heard it.

Elizabeth knew now. She knew her mother's secret. It wasn't Peter Walsh who had hurt her mother. It wasn't a man from her past. It wasn't a woman from her past either. It wasn't a person at all.

It was the voice.

Elizabeth looked down. She saw rocks. All sorts. She knelt, gathered as many as she could hold. Small and large. This one covered with algae, slick. This one jagged. This one smooth as a coin. She picked them all up. She stared at the lake, the still surface. She clutched her rocks and with one great heave—

You should have been more. The path you should have taken, the answer to the riddle. You should have been what a woman should be—

All.

You should have been all.

She threw them all at once. Each stone arced in the moonlight, a granite mist, hovering above the lake. They fell. Like rain. Like grief. Like time—*tick, tick, tick,* they splashed. And disappeared.

You should have saved her.

Your mother.

"Elizabeth," Theodore reached her now, held her. "You're sobbing. What is it?"

Mrs. Richard Dalloway had taken the perfect path, the expected one. Elizabeth Dalloway had taken the opposite, different in every way. Septimus had done the honorable thing. He had enlisted; he had fought. Theodore had been as admirable as any man could ever be.

And the voice was the same.

No path silenced it. No accomplishment satisfied it.

You don't measure up.

It had been handed down. Through generations it lived. Different times and places and expectations. It lived. Unchanged. The same pernicious voice slithering into the stream from one girl to the next. From one boy to the next. From one mother to the next. Poisoning the stream. The stream of consciousness.

You're not enough.

Who did the voice belong to? And who was the one inside listening? Believing it? Believing every whisper.

You're not enough.

It's over for you.

Elizabeth knew the voice now, knew its tenor. It was hers to rebut, hers to battle.

"Elizabeth," Theodore said. "You're trembling."

This lake, a grave. This lake, a gift.

I don't want to listen anymore.

I don't have to listen anymore.

"Tell them to dredge the lake," Elizabeth said. She let him hold her. There wasn't anything wrong with that. To be loved. "They'll find her bones."

CHAPTER 38

Octavia

Octavia Smith trudged up the steep, grassy hill—with a little help.

Her husband was behind her, carrying the satchel she'd given him. And Lucrezia close behind.

The Cotswolds weren't known for their wildflowers this time of year. It was December.

But Octavia had brought orchids and harebells—on the print of her dress, her Liberty dress. This elegant woman who had made a grand journey, a bur that had clutched stockings, taken a ride to a different place on the hill. She'd gone from the countryside of Gloucestershire to the bustle of Bond Street and back again. To this hill. This hill where she first heard Shakespeare. This hill where she last saw her brother.

Her dress brushed against a patch of dried, stiff grasses as they made their way up the limestone hill to her favorite spot—a stand of wych elms and whitebeams. She took them in from roots to tops, let her eyes wander up their sturdy trunks. When she was young, in the heat of summer, she had thought they looked like bossy little girls pushing up green parasols, thinking too highly of themselves. Now, in winter, as a woman nearing fifty, she felt they looked entirely different. The trunks and their bare branches seemed like hands, open to the sun, not afraid to look away from the tiny flowers on the ground, not afraid to reach, to hope, to receive. They looked like their time was far from over. Their time had come.

She thought again about that remarkable visit she'd had from Elizabeth Dalloway. That medal her mother had left for Septimus, for his family. A medal for a soldier who had deserved a proper burial. Because he had died in the war. Because he had fallen in battle.

Octavia turned to her husband. Redvers. To her sister-in-law, Lucrezia. "We're ready?" she asked. "Are we sure?"

They both nodded. "Yes," Lucrezia said. She pulled her hat a little tighter on her head, the lovely one Septimus had made. The felt flowers the brightest on the hill now.

Redvers put his hand in the satchel and pulled out a small wooden urn. Octavia took it in her hands, and Lucrezia removed the top. A gentle wind kicked up and over the hill of Stroud, over the limestone, the golden grasses, the juniper bushes, the places where flowers would bloom again. So many flowers.

Octavia gently tipped the urn, let the wind catch its contents. Septimus's ashes took to the air, rose in the sunlight, burst forth as if thrilling with release. Feathered dandelion seeds riding the wind.

Octavia said aloud the full two verses this time, better than any goodbye:

> *Fear no more the heat o'th'sun,*
> *Nor the furious winter's rages.*
> *Thou thy worldly task hast done,*
> *Home art gone, and ta'en thy wages.*
> *Golden lads and girls all must,*
> *As chimney-sweepers, come to dust . . .*
> *No exorciser harm thee,*
> *Nor no witchcraft charm thee.*
> *Ghost unlaid forbear thee,*
> *Nothing ill come near thee.*
> *Quiet consummation have;*
> *And renownèd be thy grave.*

Septimus's ashes swirled and began to settle, a mist among the trees. But Octavia wasn't done. Not quite. She added several lines. Her first bit of poetry.

"Renownèd be thy grave. Renownèd be all our graves," she whispered. "Each and every one."

CHAPTER 39

Elizabeth

SUFFOLK

The stone wall was high; its stones covered with waxy green vines and wild-flowers. Elizabeth Dalloway wasn't sure her horse could make the jump.

Elizabeth was a bit rusty, having given up riding so long ago.

Her horse's hooves thundered across the field, his muscles tense and taut underneath her, driving them on and on.

Closer and closer to the wall.

Elizabeth narrowed her eyes but couldn't gauge the true height or width of it under all those damned blooms.

Push a horse over a wall like that and it could be maimed for the rest of its life; the rider's might end entirely.

The hounds were far ahead and well out of sight by now, but Elizabeth could still hear their howls, carried back to her on the wind. A call, irresistible, daring Elizabeth to follow, faster and faster to whatever was lurking in the wooded English fields.

Follow us, they seemed to howl. *We've found the path you're looking for.*

Elizabeth dug her heels into her horse's sides.

Together, they could make it. Couldn't they? After all, she was a survivor. A woman of two wars. A flu epidemic. A deadly fog. And she was a soldier in a battle with the deadliest thing of all—the stream. The stream of consciousness.

She was forty-six years old.

On a fifteen-hand borrowed horse.

Surely, she could get over this damned flower-covered wall.

It was time.

She tightened her grip on the horse's reins, leaned forward in the saddle, and gave him a gentle nudge. The horse received the message delivered by Elizabeth's heels:

This way. I'm certain now.

She crouched low on her thoroughbred—a woman who hadn't ridden since she was seventeen years old, a woman in ancient riding boots, the leather dried and cracked. As she felt the strike of horse hooves beneath her—she knew. This was why she used to love to ride. This was why her mother loved it too. This was why those moments of youth—the dance, the swim, the late-night ride in a motorcar—were so delicious. They pinned the mind to the moment. Out of the stream. Above the dark current of criticism, the voices that were waiting in the wings, ready to demand impossible things, ready to drive one under. Elizabeth was separate, in this moment. This moment here. On this horse. She wasn't the voice. She had a bit of distance now. The unnoticed mind—finally seen.

Here. Here. Here.

Her horse seemed to be saying it.

All you have to be—

Is here.

In this field. In this air. In this second.

Here.

You are enough.

Here.

The wall came close. She'd reached it.

This time, Elizabeth knew exactly what to do.

For a few hoof strikes more, there was only the leather saddle beneath her, only the grip of the stirrups. Only the sound of her horse's breath, only the thunder of hooves hitting the earth, only movement.

Only Elizabeth.

And the wall.

Here.

The kick of her horse's hooves against the ground, the push, and then—

They leapt.

Higher and higher she arced into the sky on her horse, daring the wall to be as tall as it wanted to be, tempting the very vines to entangle and trip them both, tip them toward the earth and break their necks as they came to rest.

Leap or die, Elizabeth seemed to say. This woman, this daughter, this wife. This mother. *Leap or die.*

Into the air.

Over the vines, the wildflowers, the stones—the wall a wreathed memorial, an homage to Elizabeth though she yet lived, a marker for all women. For all those who fight. For all those who fought. For all those dead, alive, to all those left somewhere in between.

For the women and their wars.

For men. For men and their wars.

For minds. Minds and their wars.

Elizabeth went over, and for just a moment, she disappeared in the air above those stones.

A mist.

Silent.

Bliss.

ACKNOWLEDGMENTS

While I was editing this book, our beloved house burned down in the historic Colorado Marshall Fire. The wildfire, fueled by one-hundred-mile-per-hour winds, destroyed our entire neighborhood in minutes. The fire moved so quickly, our home was gone before an evacuation order could be issued. My husband, son, and I are extremely lucky to be alive. We watched our home burn on our security camera; we watched the smoke engulf it until the screen went black. My husband looked up at me. "It's gone."

If I could dedicate a book to inanimate objects, I would dedicate this book to the little box of my son's baby things that I lovingly curated for five years. His pacifier, his onesies, his baby blanket. His first real pair of shoes. The bracelet he'd made me in preschool. I ache for those things, for the comfort of knowing they were with me, that I would be able to hold them in my old age and remember when my son was tiny enough to cradle in my arms. I am so grateful to be a mother and grateful that I got to have a box like that even though it was for a short time.

I'd like to thank the people of Boulder County, Colorado, for the unbelievable love and support they gave to fire survivors. Within hours of the fire, clothing donations arrived at our hotel. People brought food. Housing was offered. And the assistance kept coming: businesses donated everything from food processors to backpacks, bikes were promised for every child, free counseling sessions were given to every family. FEMA tents arrived. The Red Cross. A group came to help us sift through the ashes to look for any item that might have survived. Compassion like that changes a person. To everyone who supported us—from our town government, to businesses, to our son's school, to our family and friends, to the thousands of anonymous helpers—you will never know what your kindness meant to us.

When my publisher discovered that our home had burned down, love and kindness began flowing once more. Thank you to Blackstone Editorial Director, Josie Woodbridge, who survived the same type of wildfire we did. Your sincere care and support meant so very much to me. You made me feel less alone. Thank you to Blackstone CEO, Josh Stanton, for his generosity and kindness. This publishing house has supported me from the moment they bought my book, and I am so lucky to be a Blackstone author.

Special thanks to Blackstone Senior Acquisitions Editor, Dan Ehrenhaft. He showed me what a good editor can do for a story, and he always understands my novels and what I am trying to say in them. What a gift. And on top of it all, he is extraordinarily kind.

Thanks to editor Celia Blue Johnson, whose insights and gentle way benefitted my story a great deal. And thanks to the entire team at Blackstone for all you do.

Thanks to my agent, Jennifer Unter, who has guided me in this industry for over ten years now. I am so proud to be your client. Thank you for always being there for me. And your pep talks are invaluable.

Along the way, a very special person read a draft of this novel. Special thanks to Jane Martin, who grew up in Gloucestershire near my character Octavia's home and has memories of being a young child there during WWII. Thank you for reading my book and for sharing turns of phrase and details only someone who grew up there would know. What a privilege to have had you as a reader. And to her daughter, Juliet, and the trail of women who so generously jumped in and helped my draft on its way: Annabel Lukins Stelling, Christina Purdy, Diane Matlick, and Mary Carter Scott. And Diane and Mary, you read like lightning! You would make brilliant book editors. How lucky I am to have found you.

Thanks to Brown University Professor of American History, Howard P. Chudacoff. Because of his brilliant instruction, I came to love history, and he showed me how fulfilling it could be to study it.

Thanks to the supportive community of writers here in Colorado who listened to my ideas, read pitches for the book, and cheered me on.

Thanks to Melanie Crowder, a brilliant writer and friend who comforted me and supported me through the agonizing, beautiful, and exhausting process of writing this book. I will never forget surviving the darkest days of the pandemic with you; I will never forget stealing moments to write at a picnic shelter while our children attended a few hours of preschool.

Mrs. Dalloway has a lifetime of stories and faces she's both hidden and shown to the world—thanks to Lauren Fox for knowing all of mine. And for taking my calls as I panicked about plots and characters and ideas. The best thing I ever did was sign up for French 101 at Brown or I would have missed you completely. I adore you.

Thanks to Megan Smith. This book nearly broke me on multiple occasions, and you always dispersed the timeless wisdom we learned from my father—take it one wave at a time. Thank you for your consultations and for always knowing exactly what to do. You are a treasure to me.

Thanks to Marion for being such a loyal and loving friend. Thanks also to Dave, Alex, Jackie, Renee, and Tara. And thanks to Joanne, who held my hand through the hardest times of my life. I miss you.

Special thanks to my sister, who has selflessly helped our family through our roughest times and has always been there for us. I love you so much; I don't know what I would do without our long talks. I hope you know how much I admire you.

Thanks to my wonderful in-laws, Kevin and Sue, and my sister-in-law, Brittney, who dropped everything and rushed to my aid in Colorado when I desperately needed them. I will never forget your love and support. And thanks to the rest of my wonderful family; I am grateful for you.

I dedicated this novel to my mother, who keeps a tattered copy of *A Room of One's Own* on her shelf. Growing up, I frequently heard Woolf's name at the dinner table; the awe was palpable. My mother's message was clear: when you encounter Woolf, pay attention—you're on sacred ground. How brilliant you are, Mom. Thank you for spending your life loving and caring for me. I can't imagine where I would be without your guidance; you are my first phone call when a fork appears in the road. I want you to know how much I admire and respect you, how much I adore your wit, how lucky I am that you are mine. I will love you forever.

Thanks also to my father, who watched me toil and build a career as an attorney but never once suggested that chucking it all to write novels was anything less than perfectly reasonable. Without you, I would be far too sensible. Thank you for being a model of bravery, a person who helps others, whatever the cost may be. I am so grateful for all that you have done for me; your unwavering support has been one of the greatest gifts of my life. I want you to know that I will always love and adore you.

And thanks to my beloved husband. He has walked with me through many novels now, but none like this one. One evening after writing, I exclaimed that I just couldn't take it anymore, that it felt like Virginia Woolf had moved into our home, that her words were roaming the halls at all hours of the night. I was exhausted. He smiled and said, ever so gently, "I think it will be good for you when she moves out." How we laughed. How I love you. You are a generous, kind, and hilarious husband; thank you for loving me and caring for me in sickness and in health. Sharing this life with you brings me the greatest happiness.

And finally, to the other great love of my life—my son, who has been listening to the clack of my laptop keys since he was in the womb. May you always be kind to yourself, may your mind be a safe and loving place, may you be protected from any voices that whisper negative messages in your ear. You are allowed to make mistakes; you are loved unconditionally. Take root. And bloom. That's what happened to me the day you came into my life. I finally, finally bloomed.

AUTHOR'S NOTE

In 2018, I came across an article about *Mrs. Dalloway* by Virginia Woolf. I had not read the book since college, so I picked it up again. As I read, I noticed a character I had never seen before: Mrs. Dalloway's only child, Elizabeth. I caught a very brief line about her: she had watched her mother nearly die in the 1918 flu pandemic. I quickly did the math: she would have been twelve years old. I already knew a lot about the 1918 pandemic; it killed my great-grandmother and left my grandmother an orphan. The flu pandemic was an important part of our family history, and we discussed it often as I was growing up. I did some research and found pictures of children in masks. I was horrified. Children in masks? I couldn't imagine putting my own child in a mask in hopes that he would survive.

And that was in 2018.

I immediately began writing the book, obsessed with Elizabeth Dalloway, desperate to tell the story of a child who'd lived through a pandemic.

I had no idea that in just two years, I would be putting my own beloved son in a mask during the COVID-19 pandemic, terrified he might not survive.

To create this story, I relied on the original *Mrs. Dalloway* and on actual historical events. In the original *Mrs. Dalloway*, the primary word

Virginia Woolf uses to describe Elizabeth is "inscrutable." And she is. She plays the briefest of parts in the original; we see barely a snapshot of her at age seventeen shopping with her history tutor. But what few facts we have suggest an untold story that runs deep. Not only did she live through WWI and the flu pandemic, she was born in 1906, which made her a contemporary of the Bright Young People—also known as the Bright Young Things—a postwar movement populated by young people who were determined to upend the social order and do things differently than the last generation. As the daughter of a member of Parliament, it is certainly not a stretch to assume Elizabeth would have been invited to join their ranks. 1923 would have been the very early days of the movement—the first London treasure hunt reportedly happened in the summer of 1922 or 1923.

I relied on historical accounts of the group—their treasure hunts, their parties, their disillusionment and angst about their place in a post-war world.

I also relied on the literary news of the day. In the wake of WWI, writers were turning away from the details of outward events to the fragmented movements of the inner ones. Woolf was one of the first to write a novel in this way, to follow the stream of consciousness, to trace nearly every thought in her heroine's mind. It is true, as my character Harold says, that when my story takes place, James Joyce's *Ulysses* had been recently published (1922) and Woolf was writing *Mrs. Dalloway* (published in 1925).

Elizabeth is the heir to her mother's story; she is a member of the next generation of women who will confront new social expectations and face the timeless challenges of consciousness. As I wrote, I came to believe Elizabeth is described as inscrutable because she is a puzzle Woolf invites us to solve.

As for Octavia, she is not in the original at all. Her brother Septimus is one of the novel's main characters yet we know nothing of his past. Woolf tells us he left home because his mother lied—about what we are never told. Who was Septimus's family? His name suggests he is the seventh child; did his mother have an eighth? Elizabeth Dalloway shows us how a mother's tortured mind affected an upper-class daughter from London; how would a brother's tortured mind affect a sister from the rural Cotswolds? I created Octavia Smith to answer these questions.

I relied on historical facts as much as possible, and my swimming party was loosely based on the Marshall Street Baths in London. However, the pool I depict is inspired by a refurbishment that was not completed until 1931.

A special note about mental health:

On March 28, 1941, Virginia Woolf went missing. A search for her began. A headline in the April 3, 1941, issue of the *New York Times* read, "Missing in England. Virginia Woolf Believed Dead."

The truth was that she had died by suicide near her country home in rural Sussex. She had filled the pockets of her coat with heavy stones, stepped into the fast-moving River Ouse, and drowned. Her body wasn't found until several weeks later.

Mental health issues have impacted my family in profound ways. And while I understand Clarissa Dalloway is a character and is not Virginia Woolf—it was in the quick-moving flow of Clarissa's thoughts that I recognized a unique type of suffering, mostly hidden from the world. Sometimes a mental health issue is easy to spot in ourselves and others—and sometimes it isn't.

If you or someone you know is in suicidal crisis or emotional distress, dial 988 to reach the Suicide & Crisis Lifeline.
Free and confidential help is available twenty-four hours a day, seven days a week, across the United States.
For additional resources, visit www.988lifeline.org.